DEATH AT CANDLEMAS

Nicholas Peverell is newly wed to his sweetheart Jane and enjoying married life at his manor house at Dean Peverell. One winter evening they invite the Bishop of Marchester to dinner. Next day, on a hunting party in the salt marshes near Pelham Maris, Nicholas finds the Bishop's murdered corpse lying in a pool of water. His heart has been cut out. Nicholas can't help but remember that their previous night's conversation touched on witchcraft. Has the Bishop fallen foul of it? Nicholas and Jane are determined to discover the truth...

DEATH AT CANDLEMAS

DEATH AT CANDLEMAS

by

Iris Collier

Magna Large Print Books
Long Preston, North Yorkshire,
BD23 4ND, England.

9682709

British Library Cataloguing in Publication Data.

Collier, Iris
    Death at Candlemas.

    A catalogue record of this book is
    available from the British Library

    ISBN   0-7505-2345-X

First published in Great Britain in 2004 by Piatkus Books Ltd.

Copyright © 2004 by Iris Collier

Cover illustration © P. McKenzie by arrangement with
P.W.A. International Ltd.

The moral right of the author has been asserted

Published in Large Print 2005 by arrangement with
Piatkus Books Ltd.

Magna Large Print is an imprint of Library Magna Books Ltd.

Printed and bound in Great Britain by
T.J. (International) Ltd., Cornwall, PL28 8RW

One

'You know what your trouble is, Bishop? You've got no nose for witchcraft.'

Sheriff Richard Landstock paused for dramatic effect and wiped the drips of egg custard off his beard. 'I am always presenting you with the wretches who take part in these evil rituals but all you do is lock them up in your prison. They should be flushed out, got rid of, Bishop, then handed over to me and my men and we'll string them up on Marchester Heath.'

'We see things differently,' said Bishop Thomas mildly. 'You see emissaries of Satan and I see poor misguided wretches led astray by deluded individuals with an inflated idea of their own importance. A little instruction, a little kindness, and we'll have them worshipping with us again in our Christian services.'

'Yet you condemned Martin Pye and his body lit up the countryside for miles around.'

'That was different. Martin Pye was a heretic.'

'What's the difference?' roared the Sheriff, washing down the remains of his apple pie

7

with a gulp of freshly brewed mead.

'All the difference in the world,' said Bishop Thomas in the patient voice of a conciliatory schoolmaster. 'Witches are simply misguided. Heretics, have, by their own arrogance, rejected the truth of the Christian faith.'

Nicholas Peverell pushed his plate away and looked round his dinner table with satisfaction. Life was good – a clear, frosty night; a huge fire burning in his hearth filling the room with the scent of apple wood from his orchards; the candles burning brightly lighting up the faces of his guests and lighting up the face of Jane, his beautiful wife of only four weeks and already a confident hostess presiding over his household and his dinner table. Looking at her now, her beautiful face with those bright blue searching eyes, her copper-coloured hair tucked under the fashionable headdress given to her by her friend, Lady Isabel Hardwicke, when she left Court, her green velvet dress as bright as the leaves of the daffodils which would soon be appearing in his park during Lent, he still could not believe his luck that she had consented to be his wife and had left the Court and come down to live with him here in his manor house of Dean Peverell, the home of his ancestors since Duke William of Normandy had given them the land as a

8

reward for their loyalty.

He had always loved her, but she had promised Queen Jane that she would stay with her as long as the Queen needed her and he, Nicholas, had begun to give up hope that Jane would ever be his wife. But things had changed. The Queen had died giving birth to the King's son and heir in October of the previous year. No longer needed, as the King had no plans as yet to re-marry, she had finally consented to be his wife and they had been married in the King's chapel in Hampton Court on Twelfth Night. Now it was the Feast of Candlemas, the Festival of Light as Jane had called it, and as the number of candles used to illuminate the room symbolised. The Bishop had given the Festival a different, theological meaning, but Jane ignored that and lit her candles to light up the dark days of winter. Tonight they were celebrating the Festival with a good dinner with old friends, the guest of honour being Bishop Thomas, formerly Prior of the priory of Dean Peverell, and now, since King Henry had ordered the expulsion of the monks from their religious foundations, Bishop of the cathedral of Marchester, four miles to the south west of his manor.

The Bishop had taken the transition in his stride and now ruled the cathedral dignitaries as benevolently as he had ruled over his monks. A large man, his girth expanding noticeably as the days went by, his face radiating good humour, the result of a sound digestion and a supreme confidence in his own abilities, he now beamed across at his old adversary, the Sheriff of Marchester, who was always easily aroused by the Bishop's gently provocative manner.

From witchcraft the conversation moved on to the iniquities of the church, and Jane, conscious of Nicholas's rapt gaze, signalled to him that it was time to intervene before the Sheriff started saying things he'd regret later.

Nicholas signalled to his steward, Geoffrey Lowe, to refill the glasses, all except the Sheriff's, who preferred to drink his ale from a pewter tankard in place of the new-fangled glasses which Jane had introduced when she had arrived at the manor. Nicholas stood up.

'Come, let us drink to the King's health and that of his son, Prince Edward. May they both continue to flourish in these troublesome times,' he said, raising his glass.

'And may Almighty God have mercy on the soul of Queen Jane,' added Bishop Thomas.

'Aye, and keep the King from eyeing up another lass soon after the poor lady's death,' muttered the Sheriff.

'And now, another toast to you, Bishop

Thomas,' said Nicholas raising his glass in the Bishop's direction. 'May you grace our cathedral for many years to come. We need the peace and stability which a long period in office will give us under your benign influence.'

'Benign, poof!' muttered the Sheriff into his tankard. 'Idleness I call it. Blindness which can't see trouble coming even when I rub his nose in it.'

'Now, now, Sheriff,' said the Bishop's companion, Lancelot Day, Canon Precentor of the cathedral, a man as lean as the Bishop was well-fleshed, who had said little during the meal but had concentrated on his food, waiting for the moment when the music would begin. 'You should thank God that we have been given a wise and tolerant bishop to rule over our diocese. Not since the blessed St Richard have we had such a just man in the episcopal seat.'

Bishop Thomas threw back his head and gave a roar of laughter. 'Come, come, Canon, anyone would think you were after my office. I don't intend to resign just yet, and I'll certainly keep clear of politics, so I fear you are in for a long wait!'

Time to break the party up, thought Nicholas, exchanging glances with Jane. He could see the Sheriff, his face flushed with good food and a superfluity of mead, becoming increasingly agitated and noticed that Alice, the Sheriff's comfortable, homely wife, was giving her husband anxious looks. Alice knew from bitter experience what happened when her husband's passions were aroused, and it wouldn't do to empty a tankard of mead over the Bishop's bald head.

Much to everyone's relief, the entrance of Balthazar Zampieri, Jane's own lutenist who had come with her from Court, reduced the Sheriff to stunned silence and brought animation to the face of Lancelot Day. Balthazar relished the attention. A native of Venice, he had wandered round the courts of Europe until he landed up at the court of Henry VIII, whose love of music immediately made Balthazar feel at home. Now, in his late thirties, he had managed to keep his youthful, dark looks, but his experiences at Court and in particular, an indiscreet liaison with one of Henry's favourites had made it necessary for him to leave Court for a while until the fuss died down and the lady concerned had returned to her old admirer. Jane had been only too pleased to offer him sanctuary in Sussex and he had well rewarded her. He was a man of many talents, an accomplished lutenist, he could play the virginals and he sang with a pleasant tenor voice. He could also compose music, something which had once endeared him to the King, who also liked to compose

12

music. It had required a great deal of tolerance on Balthazar's part when he recognised that some of the King's acclaimed compositions were really his own. Jane had now become his pupil and was showing an aptitude for composing songs and accompanying herself on the lute and virginals.

That night they sang some of their own compositions and some of the Italian composers, much loved by Balthazar, and then, lest the Sheriff and his wife should feel left out, Jane sang some songs of the people which she'd learned at Court and Balthazar picked up a small hand drum and beat out the strong rhythms in accompaniment. Gradually, Sheriff Landstock relaxed and began to roar out his approval and beat time with his tankard.

Nicholas still couldn't take his eyes off his wife, admiring her slim, elegant body which moved so naturally to the rhythm of the song. When she smiled across at him he felt his heart would burst with the intensity of his feelings. My beautiful Jane, he thought, what children we'll have! What have I done to deserve such happiness? Already his house looked like a great man's house should. She'd done away with the old rushes which had covered the floor and had ordered carpets and tapestries to cover the walls and the stone floors in the modern style. The rooms had all been cleaned, new

13

furniture installed and provided comfort for themselves and their guests. The great hall was no longer used for small dinner parties like the one taking place that evening. Now the great hall would only be used for the great feasts or when the King came to stay. The estates of Lord Montague with which the King had rewarded him last year were bringing in extra income and he had had to hire extra servants to deal with the extra work. Yes, he thought, watching Jane laugh as she sang about a foolish man who'd married two wives, he now asked no more from life – a great estate, good friends, and a perfect wife who had refused the King's offer of a Court post as Mistress of Songs to come and live with him here in rural Sussex.

He noticed, with relief, that Bishop Thomas and the Sheriff were now smiling at one another and Mistress Alice had pushed her chair back and was beating time to the music with her feet. He ought to go over to her and ask her to dance – that's what happened at Court – but that evening he didn't feel like it. Besides, Jane was involved with the music, and there were no other woman present unless he brought in the servants but that would not be appropriate on this occasion. He was glad that Sheriff Landstock had calmed down. He knew he had taken a risk in asking him that night with the Bishop as Richard Landstock too often had a habit of telling the clergy what he thought of them. But he wanted them to be friends. Together with the mayor, they ruled Marchester and kept it the law-abiding place it had always been.

Looking across at Lancelot Day, who seemed fascinated by Balthazar, Nicholas decided it was time to break up the party. It was half past eight, the guests had come at five, and the company was going back to Marchester that night, the Bishop and the Precentor travelling together in the bishop's carriage, Mr and Mrs Landstock riding together on the sheriff's sturdy horse.

Jane, as usual, sensed his wishes and brought the music to a finish. He watched with satisfaction as she supervised their guests' departure; an extra shawl for Alice Landstock, a warm rug for the Bishop and the Precentor. Then, under a star-studded sky, the road lit up by a bright crescent moon, the party left and turned onto the Marchester road, the horses' breath hanging like smoke in the clear, frosty air.

Nicholas turned to his wife when the servants had been dismissed.

'My dearest, you were wonderful tonight, you managed everything so well and you looked like a queen. How did I survive before I met you?'

'You had Mary, Nicholas. You loved her, remember? She was very kind to me when I was a young girl. I admired her. If she hadn't died she would have been by your side tonight.'

'Then I have been indeed fortunate to have had two such wives. But this one I am looking at now will always be with me, even in death we shall be buried together.'

'Don't talk of such things, Nicholas. We don't know what lies ahead. But at this moment I intend to stay just where I am, living in peace with my beloved husband.'

Later that night, Jane dismissed her maid after she had helped her out of her elaborate gown which had so many fastenings that Jane needed help both getting dressed and undressed. Then she brushed out her thick hair, already hanging half way down her back after having had it cut short last summer. She slipped between the sweet-smelling sheets, grateful for the warmth coming from the great log glowing in the fireplace, and waited for Nicholas. How good it was, she thought, to have such a place for her home, and such a man for her husband. No longer was she in awe of the manor house. The Court had trained and refined her. Tonight she felt she had passed her first test as mistress of the house. It had been her first dinner party. She hadn't let Nicholas down. She knew he had been proud of her. It would be a different matter,

16

though, when the King came to stay, as he most certainly would, when the spring came. With the sea so close and the woods full of game, he had already indicated how much he appreciated Lord Nicholas's manor as a hunting lodge. Pray God he'd give them good notice, she thought as she envisaged the preparations she would have to make to accommodate the King and his 'few friends'. It was just as well Nicholas now had Montague's estates to fall back on.

Then Nicholas came in and slipped into the great bed beside her. He took her in his arms and caressed her long hair, kissing her face gently at first and then with increasing passion. Her body never ceased to inflame him and her mind to amaze him. Such physical beauty combined with such intelligence made her his jewel beyond price. And that she loved him too was a constant source of wonder.

At last, their bodies satisfied, they began to give themselves up to sleep. Then he felt Jane stir beside him.

'What is it, my love?' he said, sensing her hesitation.

'Forgive me, Nicholas, from mentioning such a mundane thing at such a moment, but the dinner party emptied our larder. We need to re-stock: birds, game, fish, all those things.'

He raised his head and looked her

quizzically. 'That you should think of these things after we have just shown our love for each other!'

'I know, but forgive me. Remember all this is new to me. I am not only your wife but also in charge of your household and if the weather should change or if the King should come...'

'He'll not come this side of Easter, the roads are too bad. But don't worry yourself about what might or might not happen. If this weather continues, as I think it will, we'll make a hunting trip down to the coast. I have some land down there, mostly salt marsh, but full of wild fowl. You can take that falcon of yours along and see what she brings down. Will that please you?'

'Indeed it will, my lord. But then you always please me.'

'Then tomorrow I'll give the orders to make ready for a hunting expedition. And darling Jane, to sleep now. I shall pray that I continue to please you as you are to me my own special Candlemas – a perpetual celebration of light.'

Two

They left before dawn, the air bitterly cold, their breath condensing in clouds around their heads. On either side of the road the outlines of the hawthorn bushes glittered eerily under their frosting of ice applied with an artist's precision. The road was treacherous, churned up into deep ruts by the carters but frozen solid that morning by the heavy frost. In places the ruts had been smoothed out and some attempt had been made to level off the road using local flint-stones which caused sparks to fly up from the horses' hooves.

Nicholas and Jane rode side by side, urging on their horses, Jane mounted on her white mare, Melissa, and Nicholas on his black stallion, Harry; both horses and riders in high spirits anticipating a good day's sport on a cold winter's day. They rode past cottages crouching by the roadside where no lights shone in the windows, past churches and graveyards which emerged out of the shadows like set pieces in a masque. Soon they turned off the main coastal road and turned onto little roads which were mere tracks leading southwards to the coast. The horses were fresh and sure-footed, effortlessly taking the rutted lanes in their stride. They rode on, the cold air whipping up the blood in Jane's cheeks and freezing her hands beneath the thick gauntlets she wore. But it was not a long journey, not at the pace they were going. Soon they would reach the hamlet of Pelham Maris and the fields and salt marshes where the servants, sent on the day before, would be preparing a hot breakfast in the manor house which Nicholas owned.

With the onset of dawn came the first twittering of the birds in the hedgerows, a sound which made Nicholas and Jane urge their horses on to greater speed. Soon it would be the turn of the ducks to leave their nests to go searching for food; and those ducks were needed to fill the larders.

As the sun rose above the horizon, a big, angry winter's sun, they reached the hamlet of Pelham Maris, just a small collection of cottages straggling along on either side of the road, and the church, the graveyard of which backed onto the marshes. Once Pelham Maris had been surrounded by fields which had provided rich grazing for cattle, but the sea had broken through the sea wall and had flooded the fields, forming a small harbour which was used by the fishermen as a haven in bad weather because their small boats could enter the harbour on the incoming tide. At that time of the year, though, it was seldom used as not many fishermen went out to sea, not wanting to risk being caught out in winter storms; but it had other uses. Surrounding the harbour and extending into what had once been fertile fields were vast expanses of reed beds, the haven of wild birds of every species, a hunter's paradise. And in the fields further back from the sea, hares had established their colonies and flocks of geese retreated there in the winter to graze on the short grass.

The reed beds extended for many miles to the west towards Selsey, the southernmost point of the county of Sussex. Nicholas owned much of the land in this area including the salt marshes. He also owned a small hunting lodge which his father, a keen wildfowler, had built, and installed a bailiff to look after what was in fact his game park; but Nicholas seldom went there. He preferred to hunt the deer in the woods around Dean Peverell. The aged bailiff, Walter, still lived there unperturbed by the isolation and his tranquil life had been rudely shattered by the arrival of Nicholas's servants invading the house and setting up tables for breakfast and dinner.

To reach the lodge, they had to ride along a narrow track, fringed on either side by reeds that were so tall that they met over their heads. Then the reeds thinned out and the track became a wider road leading to the lodge and the fields beyond and then continuing westward towards the island of Selsey. When they arrived, Walter was standing in front of the house, waiting to greet them. He looked nervously first at Nicholas and then at Jane, struck dumb by fear that they might criticise his arrangements.

'My lord, I didn't have time...'

'Don't worry, I know we gave you little warning of our coming, but my men should have brought everything we'll need.'

As Nicholas looked at the old man whom he had neglected for so long and who now looked unbelievably frail, he felt a pang of guilt. Walter had looked after these fields and marshes for so long and yet he hardly knew him. Now, he was standing there looking at them in bewilderment as if they were complete strangers, uncertain of what was expected of him, and Nicholas began to think that the isolation had softened his wits; but Jane realised what was the matter with him – he couldn't hear what they were saying – and jumped down from her horse and led him into the house where the servants had laid up a table with bread and meat and jugs of warm ale. A fire was burning in the hearth and it was bliss to take off her gauntlets and warm her frozen fingers.

The hunters with the dogs and the falconers had all left for the marshes to await their coming, all except Martin, Nicholas's own falconer, whom he had assigned to serve Jane, who had learned how to work falcons at Court and who had come to love the brave birds she handled so expertly. Martin, known simply as Martin the falconer, was a man of indeterminate age, a man of few words who seldom smiled, lean-faced, beardless, whose loyalty to the Peverell family was absolute. Now, with the arrival of Jane, he had adopted her without hesitation and she and Nicholas had become the two most important people in his life.

Jane, a tankard of warm ale in her hand, went over to him.

'Have you eaten, Martin?'

'Thank you, madam, I have, and so have all the men down in the marshes, not that Walter's been much help. The poor devil's as deaf as a post and has lived so long on his own down here that we've driven him witless with our preparations.'

'Then we must see he gets help in the future. It's not right for him to live here on his own, especially if we come here often, which we intend to do from now on.'

'I'm glad to hear it, madam. Your wife, Lord Nicholas, has a way with the hawks and it's good to see them put to good use. But, if you'll excuse me hurrying you, we ought to get going if you've a mind to catch the ducks. There's a number of herons down there too and as we've brought along both the goshawks and the high-flyers we could stock your larder up good and proper. The men have gone ahead with the dogs and carts.'

'And my calivers?' said Nicholas looking severely at Martin whose contemptuous attitude towards the fowling pieces he knew only too well.

'The men have got them, along with all the bits and pieces needed to fire them,' said Martin stiffly. He hated the firearms – noisy, unreliable, slow, messy – whilst a falcon was a creature of delight: intelligent, beautiful to look at, soaring aloft on its powerful wings, descending on its prey like a bolt from heaven, then returning to its master for approval and a small reward.

'Though what the hawks will make of them, I don't know; frighten them to death, I should think.'

'They'll bring the birds down quicker than the hawks, and we can fill the wagons up and get home the sooner.'

'I daresay. The proof's in the pudding, isn't it?'

'And my brave Jenny?' said Jane intervening. She was aware of Martin's prejudices and didn't want a confrontation between him and Nicholas before the day had properly begun.

'She's waiting for you, madam,' said Martin, his manner softening as he looked at her. 'She's as fit as a flea and hungry. The men are only waiting for your orders.'

With Martin running along ahead of them, they rode off along the path leading down to the harbour. Suddenly, the reeds began to thin out and ahead of them the harbour opened up before their eyes. The tide was out, the mud flats, fringed by a frosting of ice, creaked and crackled in the dawn light. All around the edge of the harbour the reed beds teemed with thousands of small birds, starlings and blackbirds and fieldfare. Already, the hunters had coated the branches of the hawthorn bushes with a thick, glutinous substance made by crushing holly berries together with bird droppings which would grip the birds' feet and wings and keep them there until the men scooped them up with their nets. As soon as the spaniels were released, the birds would fly to the hawthorn bushes in terror only to be trapped on the bird lime.

The hunters, with the dogs and carts, had collected in a field near the marsh. When Jane and Nicholas appeared, the dogs became delirious with joy and could only be restrained with difficulty. Jane dismounted and went over to where Martin had taken Jenny from one of the keepers and was stroking her head, calming her eagerness to

25

begin the job she had been trained for. He placed the small goshawk on Jane's gauntleted arm and watched as she stroked the bird's quivering body. Then, at Nicholas's command, the dogs were released and dashed off into the reed beds, barking joyfully in a frenzy of excitement. Immediately, flocks of birds flew up and made for the bushes. With a tremendous flapping of wings hundreds of ducks took off laboriously into the air. With a final caress on the goshawk's head, Jane released Jenny, who flew effortlessly over the flocks of terrified ducks and dived down upon them, plunging her beak and lethal talons into their backs and heads. Again and again she flew after the ducks returning each time to Jane, who released the birds from her hold and rewarded her with a piece of meat. Then the hunters shot arrows into the air from the small crossbows which most of them preferred to use and soon the reed beds were full of the bodies of ducks and geese, which the spaniels retrieved and brought back to the hunters.

Nicholas took up the caliver and brought down a goose with a single shot, but he soon found the firing piece to be too slow to reload and threw it aside in favour of the crossbow, which he used accurately and brought down a pair of herons. Jane's goshawk continued to attack the smaller wildfowl, and the high-flying hawks, with deadly efficiency, brought down the geese that tried to get away across the neighbouring fields. Soon the carts were filling up with the bodies of ducks and geese, pigeons and herons, plovers and bitterns, red shanks and curlews. Soon, there would be enough game to feed the household for weeks.

The sport was exhilarating and the hours went by unnoticed, no one wanting to stop for refreshment. The dogs worked tirelessly until every bird was retrieved. Two swans were added to the pile. They were Nicholas's swans and he alone had the right to shoot them. This was the first time he had made use of his prerogative and he made a mental note to take more interest in his game park in the future. He needed more wardens on the site, Walter's years of usefulness now obviously coming to an end. Then, after he had laid the bodies of the swans on top of the pile of the other birds in the carts, he went over to where a table had been laid up with hot pies and slices of meat for their refreshment. Jane joined him, her goshawk finally needing a rest, and helped herself to the food.

'A good day, Jane? You're satisfied that we shan't starve over the next few weeks?'

'It's been a wonderful day. We could do with some hares, though. I've seen lots of them in the field over there,' she said, pointing to the fields to the west of the marsh. 'We could send the hawks to get them.'

'What's wrong with the firearms?' put in Martin, helping himself to some bread and meat. 'It needs good eyesight and a steady hand to get a hare. They're as cunning as the devil himself when it comes to fooling the hunter.'

'Let's try both then. I'll wager a cask of ale that I bring down a hare quicker than one of your hawks.'

This time they approached the hares stealthily, leaving the horses and dogs behind, and making their way on foot along the path at the marsh's edge. Then they turned inland and took cover behind a hedge of hawthorn trees, gnarled and twisted into fantastic shapes by the prevailing wind. The hares proved no match for the hawks, who dived down on them with incredible speed anticipating their every move. By the time Nicholas had loaded the caliver the hawks had killed three hares and were off after another. Martin looked away to hide his smile of satisfaction.

'It seems you are in for a merry evening, Martin,' said Nicholas flinging aside the caliver. 'The cask of ale's yours.'

'Best keep the guns to fire at men, my lord. With hundreds of you loading and firing at the same time they would wreak havoc against an advancing army.'

'But you can't beat a hawk when it comes to bringing down a hare, eh?'

'It seems so, my lord.'

The short day was coming to an end. With the fading of the light, the cold intensified and Nicholas thought of the ride ahead of them and the weariness of the men and horses. It was time to call the men together, load the carts, check there were no wounded birds left to flounder in the mud or drown in the incoming tide, and set off home.

He sent some of the men to search the reed beds further along the marsh just in case a bird had managed to stagger on further than expected. He couldn't abide cruelty to man or beast. Hunting was necessary, the larders had to be filled, but he liked a clean kill. Suddenly he noticed that the men had all disappeared and he called to them impatiently. Still they seemed not to hear him, and he shouted again with mounting impatience.

'Seems like they've found something,' said Martin, fastening the hoods over the falcons' heads to calm them in readiness for the journey home.

'Then go and tell them to make haste,' Nicholas said, turning to one of the men. 'It will be dark soon and it's cold. Now what the devil? Wait, Jane,' he said as Jane made a move to go towards one of the hunters, who had appeared in the distance waving his arms. 'I'll go.'

The man had now broken into a run and made signs for Nicholas to come. Nicholas, realising the man was serious, ran after him down the path which narrowed once it forked off from the main track and disappeared into the reed beds. Here the reeds formed a tunnel which was eerily quiet as there was no wind to set the reeds rustling. Even the birds were quiet now and the dogs were silent. Suddenly the reeds parted in front of him, revealing a small pool already full of water from the incoming tide. A group of his men were crouching down beside a large object at the edge of the pool. The men stood up when they saw Nicholas.

'We've found a body, sir,' said the leader of the group, 'a priest by the look of him. See here, he's dressed in his priest's robe. The poor soul's drenched with sea water because this pool's tidal and he's just about to be soaked again if we don't get him out of here.'

Nicholas stared down at the body of a man lying face down in the water. Something about him, his size – he was a big man – the back of his tonsured head, the width of his shoulders, seemed strangely familiar. Then the terrible thought came to him.

He'd seen this man only recently. Calling for someone to help him as the body was soggy with water and very heavy, they turned him over and Nicholas stared down into the face of his friend and dining companion of only three days ago, Bishop Thomas Rymes. There was no mistake. He'd know that face anywhere, even though it was now grey and the flesh waterlogged, but the broad forehead and the bushy eyebrows which he'd seen so often raised in quizzical enquiry at something someone had said were unmistakable.

'Look, sir, just look,' said one of the men.

Nicholas, forcing himself to drag his eyes away from that familiar face, looked to where the man was pointing.

'They've cut him open, here. It's no animal's done this. Look how neatly they've cut open his robe and placed the pieces back again.'

Nicholas bent down and pulled open the front of the Bishop's cassock. There he saw a gaping hole, the flesh grey and bloodless around it. He stared down, fighting back the waves of nausea that threatened to engulf him.

'God in heaven,' he whispered, 'they've cut out his heart.'

'Who be the "they" sir?'

Nicholas got to his feet and took a deep breath.

31

'I don't know and you don't know, but we'll find out. He was a friend of mine and a good man. He didn't deserve to die like this. But first we must get him out of this pool and take him back where he belongs, to Marchester, to his cathedral. I'll get the men to bring a hurdle. Poor Bishop, to be murdered here of all places, no one comes to Pelham Maris except a few fishermen and wildfowlers. And what, in God's name, brought Bishop Thomas to Pelham Maris?'

The men brought the Bishop's body to where the hunting party was waiting by the carts, silent now once they'd heard the news. The sun had set, an owl called from one of the nearby trees and then flew over their heads with a great flapping of wings. A wind, bitterly cold, coming from the east, rippled through the reed beds, making them crackle and rustle with a sound like the gentle sighing of ghosts. Jane shuddered.

'Poor Thomas. I sang at his house when he was Prior and I sang for him at Candlemas. And now he returns to his cathedral like this with his body mutilated. And to think, Nicholas, we talked of witchcraft at that last dinner.'

'This is not witchcraft,' said Nicholas. 'See here, these marks were made with human hands.' And he pulled back the collar of the Bishop's robe, showing, by the light of the lanterns which Walter had brought up, the deep purple bruises on the Bishop's neck and the livid indentation where a cord had been knotted tightly around his neck.

'They killed him and removed his heart. Who hated him so much as to do that?' he said.

'Witches would do that,' said Walter peering down at the body. 'And this place is full of the devils. Not that you'd know that, my lord. You'd need to live here to know who they are.'

'And you'll have to tell us, Walter,' said Nicholas. 'I'll be back here tomorrow with the Sheriff, and you're not to leave the house. Go inside and lock the doors as soon as we've gone.'

'Me, tell you and the Sheriff?' said Walter backing away with terror in his eyes. 'Never. Old Walter knows nothing and sees nothing. I'm your bailiff, see. Witches don't come near me. But they'd want to kill the Bishop. The heart's special to witches; it's powerful, see. To eat a bishop's heart is the most powerful of all. Not that I've seen anyone do it, eat a heart, I mean, I've only heard about it. They'd not want my heart – there's no power in it now – I'm too old, of no importance at all.'

What with the cold and the exhaustion brought on by a day's strenuous activity, Jane began to feel faint and would have fallen if

Nicholas had not noticed her stricken face and caught her. The idyll was over. Instead of a brisk ride back to Dean Peverell where a roaring fire and a good dinner awaited them, he would have to take the Bishop's corpse back to Marchester and see the Sheriff immediately. Jane would have to go back with the hunting party, wrapped in a warm blanket. Pray God, she's taken no harm, he thought. But he had underestimated Jane. After a moment's rest against Nicholas's body, she called for Melissa.

'I'm all right,' she said. 'I shall ride back and see that the men are fed and paid for their trouble and see the game is put in store. You go to the Sheriff and alert the cathedral. The Canons will want to receive his body. He should be in his cathedral tonight and lie there tomorrow for everyone to see him. He will be greatly mourned. He was a good man who would have done much for Marchester.'

Watching her mount Melissa and gather up the reins, Nicholas once more marvelled at his wife's stamina. It seemed she would need every bit of it now that she was his wife and mistress of his manor house.

Three

The sun which had shone so brilliantly the day before was now hidden behind clouds as if in sympathy with the crowd of towns-people who filed into the cathedral to gaze at the face of their Bishop, whose body had been placed on a bier in front of the shrine of his great predecessor, St Richard. The shrine, so soon to be demolished by the order of King Henry, was behind the high altar in front of the Lady chapel, and here the cathedral dignitaries had gathered to watch over Bishop Thomas's body.

Lancelot Day, the Canon Precentor, his naturally lugubrious face creased in sorrow, led the prayers which would go on con-tinuously until the funeral.

'Oh God, whose property is always to have mercy and to forgive, we humbly beseech thee on behalf of the soul of thy servant, which thou hast this day commanded to depart out of this world; that thou wouldst not deliver it into the hand of the enemy, nor forget it at the last, but that thou wouldst command it to be received by the holy angels...'

The words were in English as Lancelot

Day was of the new persuasion.

Nicholas and Richard Landstock stood together by the shrine. It was bitterly cold in the cathedral, the air fragrant with incense from a previous mass. Nicholas thought, gazing up at his old friend, dressed in his bishop's vestments, his face in repose, that it seemed impossible he was looking at the same person they had dragged out of the pool the day before. Except for the pallor, his face looked the same as when he had sat at his table receiving Landstock's insults with good-humoured tolerance.

Nicholas glanced at Landstock. He was obviously deeply distressed. He stood with his head bowed and his hands clasped in prayer. Suddenly, aware of Nicholas's scrutiny, he looked up.

'A wicked thing has happened here, in our county, Lord Nicholas,' he whispered. 'And to think that I warned Bishop Thomas only three days ago. There is a darkness amongst us which we must disperse before it infects everyone. These people have lost a good bishop. They must not be allowed to drift away into evil practices because that is just what these infernal followers of Satan intend.'

'It's up to us, Sheriff,' said Nicholas, 'to see that it doesn't happen. The cathedral Canons will keep the services going here to remind the people that Bishop Thomas has indeed died but another will be appointed in due course and the powers of darkness will not triumph.'

They watched the townsfolk file into the shrine area, kneel in prayer before the bier, then turn sorrowfully away. Nicholas knew most of them: Abel Hind, the builder, who kept the townspeople's houses in good repair, Josh Sawbridge, who sold meat to the wealthy citizens and old Agatha Trotter, who made the best cheese. They were all here, coming to pay their last respects before the funeral which was to take place in two days' time.

'Come, Sheriff, we've work to do,' said Nicholas, aware that every hour that passed made their task increasingly difficult.

Landstock jerked himself out of his reverie. 'Yes, we must go. I'll leave two of my men to watch the crowd for any strangers; anyone who looks suspicious, whose grief looks feigned, whose gestures are inappropriate, whose prayers look false.'

Nicholas nodded. 'They will know most of these people and it's the outsider we're looking for at the moment, though I wouldn't expect the murderer to come here.'

'He's no ordinary killer. The man we're looking for would want to come and gloat over his handiwork.'

He signalled to two of his men who were standing by the door to the Lady chapel and they moved into a position nearer the shrine.

'Watch closely now,' Landstock said. 'Take hold of anyone who behaves differently from all the others and bring him to me.'

Nicholas was already walking away from the scene. He'd spent the previous night grieving for his friend together with Jane, who had been inconsolable. Now it was time to put aside that grief and start the investigation. Nicholas was not a particularly religious man, but he approved of the church and supported its fight against the dark forces at work in human nature. He also believed that the Bishop's soul was now with God and His angels and they were on their side and would guide them to the killer, because he must not be allowed to remain hidden in the community infecting everyone, like a rotten apple in a barrel of good ones.

Back in the Sheriff's house they went into a small room, the Sheriff's sanctuary, where ale and bread and cheese was waiting for them. Orders were given that they were not to be disturbed and they sat down at the table. Landstock poured ale for them both. Nicholas waited for him to speak first. This was the Sheriff's investigation.

'Eat up now, we leave for Pelham Maris in a few minutes,' said Landstock decisively. 'The killer's down there in those infernal marshes. I've heard that there is a cult of devil worshippers practising their evil rites in that area, and I should have gone down there before and investigated the rumours. Now's our chance. We'll track these devils down and flush them out. The locals will know who they are, of course, or at least they will have their suspicions, though it will be a devil of a job, figuratively speaking, to get anyone to speak out. We'll make a start with that bailiff of yours; he must have heard something – sounds of cartwheels, horses' hooves and so on. You can't murder a man and dump him in a pool without someone noticing.'

'He's as deaf as a post and the tide will have washed away most marks.'

'Don't be so pessimistic, Lord Nicholas; that will get us nowhere.'

'I'm being realistic, that's all. We don't yet know if the Bishop was murdered in that spot. He could have been murdered elsewhere and his body brought down to the marsh to moulder back into the earth. It would be difficult to bury a man of Bishop Thomas's size without anyone seeing. It would also be difficult to dig a large hole at the moment as the ground is frozen solid; and it would also take a long time. Better to let the sea water speed up the process of corruption.'

'We don't know that he was murdered

elsewhere and we can only find out by asking questions; and we're dealing with a pretty cunning lot of people who live by those marshes. They are used to being left to their own devices. They are a tight-knit community; most of them related to each other. It's a mistake to leave them to themselves for so long.'

'There's a church there, and a vicar, I believe. He'll know who's who.'

'Then we'll talk to him as well. At least he should be a man of God; that's if the Bishop's kept an eye on him.'

Landstock stood up and drained his tankard. He grabbed a hunk of bread and stuffed it into his mouth. Then handing Nicholas a wedge of cheese, he strode out. Nicholas followed him. He wanted more time to think but he was prepared to give the Sheriff his head. After all, they had to start somewhere.

The horses were waiting for them outside the Sheriff's house and a group of people watched them mount.

'Good luck, Sheriff,' someone called out. 'Go and get the devils. Hanging's too good for them. Leave us to rip out their innards and we'll toss them into the flames first, and then toss the devils in after them. Then may God damn them to hell.'

This was received with a roar of approval and suddenly Nicholas was filled with foreboding. He had had to pick up the pieces before as a result of the Sheriff's impetuosity. Now, with the pressure of the townspeople upon him the Sheriff was capable of perpetuating a grave injustice out of a desire to show the townspeople that he could act with speed and determination. The townspeople would egg him on. They wanted an arrest and they wouldn't ask too many questions. The desire for revenge was so strong that it was almost a case of anyone would do. And Nicholas knew only too well that ultimately he would have to try the man and the crowd would be in no mood to tolerate an unpopular verdict. God help him this time if the Sheriff made a mistake.

Once again, they crossed the main coastal road and took the narrow lane leading south to the sea. They rode at speed, both horses taking the rutted surface of the road with surefooted ease. The clouds, like mourning veils, hung low overhead, and the freezing air numbed their faces. Icicles had formed overnight along the banks of the streams which ran along on either side of the road and there was a quality in the air that hinted that snow was coming. Snow, thought Nicholas. That would set back the investigation for weeks. Snow covered tracks. Snow kept people indoors. Snow made roads impassable. In murder cases, speed was of the essence. The procedure was laborious. They would have to rely on interviewing potential witnesses and re-interviewing those whose stories didn't ring true. Then it was a matter of sorting out the suspects, then sorting out the lies from the truth, of checking on alibis and all the time reducing the number of suspects to the one whose guilt had become obvious. And if all this had to take place in bad weather, then the investigation could take months and all the time the culprit or culprits would have time to firm up their alibis and people's memories would fade. Snow would be a nightmare.

They rode through the village of Pelham Maris, where the inhabitants looked at them fearfully from their doorways. Nicholas could only compare this journey with yesterday's when Jane rode beside him on Melissa and the sun had shone and birds twittered their greetings from the hedgerows.

Today there were no bird songs and no sign of the hares that had boxed one another so playfully in the surrounding fields. Today, the smoke from the cottagers' fires covered them in its acrid gloom. Cold, dark, silent as the grave except for the pounding of their horses' hooves on the hard road. It felt as if the powers of darkness had already closed in. Nicholas shivered. What were they up against? In spite of his healthy scepticism concerning witchcraft he began to feel that anything was possible in this place.

They reached the area of the harbour. The tide was out and the thick, black mud smelt of corruption. When they reached the hunting lodge everything looked deserted. A wind was getting up, an icy wind which set the reeds rustling like a chorus of sad ghosts warning them to turn back. Landstock reined in his sturdy horse and jumped down. He strode up to the front door of the lodge and hammered on it. No one came.

'God damn it, Lord Nicholas, where's this fellow of yours?'

'I told you, he can't hear you. Wait, let me go and find him.'

The door wasn't locked. A hefty push and Nicholas walked into the main room, where a fire smouldered in the hearth. Landstock peered impatiently around.

'He's probably asleep. I'll go and wake him.'

'More likely outside with his pigs. Stay here and I'll go and find him.'

He saw Walter across the yard feeding the two pigs with a swill made up of yesterday's leftovers. He loved his pigs better than any man or woman. As Nicholas watched him, he saw Walter stroke one on his head and he felt a wave of pity for the man. The pig seemed to like Walter's caresses. He lifted his snout up from the trough and grunted approvingly and the old man went on murmuring endearments, oblivious to Nicholas's presence. When Nicholas walked over and touched him on the shoulder, he jumped as if someone had struck him, then seeing who it was he cowered away in terror.

'Don't be alarmed, Walter, we only want to ask some questions,' Nicholas shouted.

By this time the sheriff had appeared in the doorway, a scowl on his face as he watched them walk over to the house.

'Is this the fellow?' said Landstock looking Walter up and down with a look of disgust on his face. 'I wonder you keep him on as your bailiff, my lord. He looks half-witted.'

Nicholas, looking at Walter, saw him now through the sheriff's eyes. He looked like a marsh creature: old, dirty; thin, straggly hair; weeping eyes, one of which was closed with pus; bent spindly legs and clothes which had not seen a wash tub in years. He smelled of the marsh too, a sour, rank smell mixed with the smell of stale food, stale beer and wood smoke.

'My God, if this is the man you rely on to manage your property then I strongly advise you to chuck him back into the marsh where he belongs and find yourself a new bailiff. Not that you'd find anyone to take his place. Who'd want to live in this God-forsaken place?' roared Landstock.

'Walter's been a servant to my family for

44

as long as I can remember. He was only a lad when my father hired him. I'll not get rid of him now.'

'Then you are a fool, my lord, a sentimental fool; but then you always were.'

'If by a fool you mean I am responsible for my servants, then I'll happily remain a fool, Sheriff.'

Back in the main room, Nicholas beckoned Walter to a seat by the fire. He kicked up the logs until a flame appeared licking round one of the logs and it spread to the others. Nicholas stood with his back to the flames, making the most of the warmth. He smiled encouragingly at Walter, who was looking at him with eyes that reminded Nicholas of one of his fallow deer just before the kill. The Sheriff had no such sensibilities.

'We're here on a murder enquiry,' he bellowed, 'can you hear me?'

Walter nodded his head.

'Well then, where were you all day yesterday?'

'Here, sir. I had a hunt to see to, see; with Lord Nicholas. And, before you ask me, I was here the day before, and the day before that. I don't go anywhere else these days.'

His voice was low and rasping like the croak of the marsh bitterns.

'You mean to say you don't even go to the village?'

'No sir, why should I? The village comes to

45

me. I have all that I need here.'

'Then did anyone come to see you?'

'Only the usual people, Mother Daltry, who brings me milk for my gruel – it sends me to sleep, see. She sometimes brings me a bit of cheese as well. Oh yes, there's old Edward Bide, who takes a sup of ale with me sometimes. I look after his nets, you see. He gives me an eel of two when he's got any to spare. A real treat, they are.'

'Did either of these people mention that they'd seen a body down there in the pool?'

Walter looked startled and his head began to shake uncontrollably. 'Never, sir. Lord Nicholas, help me. Tell him you found the body, didn't you? You brought him here. I'd never seen him before. I had nothing to do with it.'

'It's all right, Walter, calm down,' said Nicholas annoyed with the Sheriff's rough handling of the interview. He knew it was useless to bully people like Walter. They only became silent or told you what you wanted to hear so that they could get away the sooner. 'We only want to know whether you saw or heard anything unusual before we came and found the body. Think carefully, now. Did you hear or see anyone go past this house? Did you see anyone carrying a burden? They would need lights if they came after dark; did you see any strange lights going along past the house?'

46

'No, my lord. I saw nothing, nothing at all. It's as silent as the grave around here, and at night it's as dark as the grave, too. I don't go out after dark, and I don't look out of doors, either. There's ghosts out there on the marsh. I hear them talking to one another, so I hides myself away, not wanting to draw attention to myself.'

'Oh let's be on our way,' said the Sheriff impatiently. 'We're wasting time. The man's lost his wits. You should get rid of him, my lord. He'd not notice if the house fell down round his ears. But hold on... You talk of ghosts, old man, now what do you know about witches?'

'I know nothing and I don't want to know. I don't have anything to do with the Devil. Look here, I'm safe from all that. I've still got the blessed cross Lord Nicholas's father gave me before he died. Here it is, made from the true cross, he said. Been in the family a long time. Here it is, my lord.'

He rummaged around in the pocket of his old jacket and brought out a cross made from some sort of wood Nicholas hadn't seen before. He kissed it and handed it back to Walter.

'Look after it, Walter; it will keep you safe.'

'But do you see any of these devils?' broke in the Sheriff. 'Do you know who they are? Where they live? Who's their leader?'

'I've never set eyes on them, sir. And I

47

don't want to. Mind you, I've seen their lights out on the marsh and that's enough for me.'

'Then they do exist! I told you so, Lord Nicholas. When do you see these lights? Every night?'

'Oh no, sir. Mostly in winter when the full moon's covered over by the clouds. And it's just before high tide because the devils don't want to drown themselves, do they? I've not seen them recently, mind, but then the sky's been too clear. They need darkness, you see. Darkness to hide their wickedness.'

'Then we'll keep watch and bring these devils back to dry land. You've been a help, old man. I'll see you are rewarded.'

'There's no need, Sheriff. I'll look after Walter. But for now, stay indoors and keep the door locked.'

'But my pigs?'

'Pigs'll look after themselves for a while. We'll be back soon with some news and then everything will be back to normal. You can't kill a bishop and carry his body down to a pool without someone seeing something.'

'Now let's get down to this pool and take a look around. Just to put myself in the picture, so to speak. Most likely the sea will have washed away all traces of men and beasts.'

Nicholas led the way to where the body had been found the day before. The tide had

48

come and gone, and the pool was just a patch of mud now. The Sheriff dismounted and stared around him.

'God, what a desolate place. No one would have found him if you hadn't decided to go wildfowling, my lord.'

'Yes, fortunate for us, but bad luck for the murderer.' Nicholas waited for the Sheriff to look his fill. The daylight seemed to be fading fast although it was only midday. The cold cut through to the bone and he wanted to be off. Finally the Sheriff had seen enough and got back on his horse.

'No signs of horses' hooves. No wheel marks. But the ground's very hard and they could have stopped up there in the fields and carried the body down here. Strange, though, that no one from the village saw them.'

'They could have come from the other direction, Sheriff. Selsey's the other end of this track. They didn't have to come through Pelham Maris.'

'Quickest place from Marchester, though.'

'If the Bishop was murdered in Marchester. We don't know that.'

'And if he wasn't,' said the Sheriff impatiently, 'then what the hell was he doing down here or in Selsey, that God-forsaken hole?'

'Bishops go visiting. Maybe there was some dispute going on in one of the parishes

49

and he had to sort it out.'

'Not at this time of the year and not in this weather, he wouldn't.'

'Well, we can soon find out. His secretary will keep a list of his appointments.'

'Time we've sorted that out the devils will be up and away. No, we'll find the answer here. Your old man said there were witches out on the marshes and we'll go and catch them out. They're the ones who killed our Bishop. They'll not get away with it.'

'Walter mentioned lights. It was only his opinion that they were carried by witches. We don't know. Let's not jump to conclusions at this stage, Sheriff.'

'Oh, get along with you, Lord Nicholas. I didn't think a man like you would be afraid of witches. Let's get over to the church and talk to the Vicar. He ought to know what's going on in his parish, unless he's one of them himself.'

Without waiting for Nicholas's answer, he was off. Nicholas cursed the Sheriff's impetuosity. If he didn't keep his head they'd be returning to Marchester with a brace of wretches in tow accused of diabolical practices and the townsfolk would fall upon them and tear them to pieces. Then the sheriff would talk of justice and suitable revenge, whilst he, Nicholas, Justice of the Peace, would never be able to live with himself if he acquiesced to mob rule.

Four

The man was tall and lean, his weather-beaten face crowned with a shock of yellow hair. He was cutting down the dead grass with effortless strokes of the scythe and when he became aware of them, he stopped work and stared at them with candid blue eyes.

'Good day to you,' he said.

'Your name, fellow?' said Landstock, walking up to him briskly.

'What's that to you?'

'Be careful, fellow, you're talking to the Sheriff of Marchester, you know, and Lord Nicholas Peverell, who owns the land round here.'

'He don't own mine, and he don't own me. My father and me are our own men. We've always owned our own patch, ever since records were kept, that is, and we always shall, if I have any say in the matter.'

'Then good day to you again,' said Nicholas, pleasantly, once again cursing Landstock's inept handling of interviews. 'I'm pleased to meet one of my independent freeholders. Would you mind telling us your name?'

'I'm not one of your yeomen, my lord. If you want to know the name of the lord of the manor round these parts, excluding the marshes which you own, of course, his name's Roger Aylwin and he lives a couple of miles north of here on the Chichester road. His is the big farmhouse on the left as you leave the village. You can't miss it. But since you're strangers here, and you have introduced yourselves, then let me tell you that my name is Luke Pierce, and my father is Matthew Pierce, freeholder and Church-warden of this church of the blessed martyr, St Thomas Becket.'

'Thank you, Master Pierce,' said Nicholas evenly. 'And may I ask what you do? Your occupation, I mean.'

'I do the gravedigging when needed and when I can. We need graves at the moment, I can tell you. The old folk fall like flies in this cold weather, but the ground's too hard to bury them; so they'll have to wait till the ground thaws. In the meantime I clear up the graveyard and get rid of the leaves and the dead grass.'

'And where do you live?' put in Land-stock, annoyed that Nicholas seemed to be taking over.

'Up the north end of the street. The Pierces have lived there in the same house for generations, except for the time of the Great Death, then the Pierces nearly died out, but one survived and the line continued. The Vicar says our records go back to the time of Duke William. We fought for him at the Battle of Hastings, though we weren't called Pierce then, but some French name.'

'This is all very interesting, Master Pierce,' said Landstock, turning to look at the horses, which they had hitched to the gatepost at the entrance to the graveyard. 'But we haven't got all day to listen to your family's history, interesting as it may be to Lord Nicholas. We are, in fact, conducting a murder investigation and we hope you may be able to help us.'

'I suppose it's about the Bishop that brings you here?'

'Then you've heard...?'

'We've all heard. News travels fast round here. Quicker than a burning house in dry weather. We're sorry to lose our Bishop, but then we don't see him much; some of us have never seen him. Only once a year, mostly, when we go to pay our dues in the cathedral at Pentecost. The Vicar'll be a bit upset, though.'

'We're going to see him later, but in the meantime, Master Pierce...'

'As you've shown a bit of respect, sheriff, you can call me Luke, if you want to. Master Pierce takes a bit of getting used to.'

'Thank you, Luke. Now, can you tell us anything that might help us with our enquiries? Can you think of anyone who has a grudge against the Bishop and would be capable of carrying out this foul deed?'

Luke carefully propped his scythe against a yew tree and kicked aside a pile of dead grass.

'If I knew, I'd tell you. But here comes my father and he'd be more use to you.'

Nicholas and Landstock turned and saw a small, slightly-built man of indeterminate age, walking up the church path. He was half the size of his son, and his face and figure showed the effects of a lifetime of hard work. But his eyes were his son's and his manner was cautious but not deferential.

'Matthew Pierce?' said Landstock.

'Yes, sir. And you must be Sheriff Landstock, and Lord Nicholas,' he said, inclining his head towards Nicholas. 'We've all seen you arrive, and we know why you've come here.'

'Then you know what we want to ask you? Have you any ideas as to who could have perpetrated this dreadful crime? After all, it took place in your parish.'

'But on Lord Nicholas's land, sir. No, none of us have any idea who could have done it. Most likely Bishop Thomas was done in somewhere else and his body dumped here because the ground's too hard to bury him in. The sea would dispose of him very quickly. They didn't reckon on

Lord Nicholas coming along to exercise his hunting rights.'

'But did you hear anyone approaching the marsh? Most likely at night. The Bishop would have been brought here in a cart if he had been murdered elsewhere, and carts have wheels and are pulled by horses. These things make a noise. Has anyone mentioned to you that they heard anything suspicious yesterday or the day before?'

'No, Sheriff, no one's said a word. And if you think that anyone from around here was responsible for taking the Bishop's life, then you're barking up the wrong tree. People round here keep themselves to themselves. They don't like trouble and they don't make trouble. Mostly they're poor tenant farmers. Some of us are fishermen, there's a shepherd and those who look after Master Aylwin's cattle. They don't concern themselves with bishops. They don't know who he is or what he does, and as long as he keeps himself to himself up in Marchester we're not likely to bother too much about him.'

'Do you know if anyone has a grudge against him?' said Landstock, feeling the cold and irritated by the lack of progress they were making.

'A grudge against the Bishop?' said Matthew looking up at Landstock in astonishment. 'Why should that be? He's nothing to us, really. Now you could ask the priest,

55

Father Richard we call him, although we've been told that he's no longer to be called "father" now that the King's cut us off from His Holiness the Pope, but old habits die hard and most of us still call him "father".'

'Then let's go into the church and take a look round.'

'By all means, Sheriff. You'll not find him there, though, but you're welcome all the same. The door's unlocked. It always is. There's no thieves around here.'

Landstock stomped off up the path leading to the church porch, Nicholas following. They pushed open the heavy oak door and the smell of damp and decay met them as they went inside. The church was old, built in Norman times with tower and transepts added later, and by the look of it, not well maintained. A poor parish, thought Nicholas. Either that or a lazy churchwarden or a negligent priest. It was gloomy inside, the only light coming through the far east window, which contained some stained glass. The cold was intense.

The floor was covered with straw that looked as if it had been there for years. All around them there were the rustling sounds of tiny creatures disturbed by their entry. Judging by this activity and by the smell which came from the straw when they walked on it, the church had become home to several families of field mice who had come in from the surrounding fields at the onset of winter and would stay there until spring came.

Nicholas looked round at the walls, dripping with damp. Once they had been covered with bright wall paintings depicting biblical scenes – the nativity, the flight into Egypt, the ascent to Calvary and the empty tomb – but the paint had faded to such an extent that the donkey carrying Mary and Christ in the flight into Egypt scene was only recognisable by it ears. It was sad to see such a fine, sturdy building mouldering away through neglect. The church-warden could, at least, clean the place up a bit, he thought.

Landstock was standing next to him, his hands in his pockets, looking round the church in disgust.

'Phew, how the place stinks! This is not fit for any Christian worship. The straw's soaking wet with God knows what filth. I wonder what the state of the vestments is like. Let's take a look. The vestry's back there.'

Nicholas followed him into the small room at the west end of the church where the Priest's vestments hung on a rail. There were very few: an old, black cassock and a chasuble where the colours had faded into a uniform beige, and a couple of surplices which could do with a wash. The choirboys' surplices hung on a separate rail and in the corner there was a pile of albs which the servers had dumped there after the last service. This room was less damp and the floor was covered with an old woollen rug, which made it seem more homely.

'Not much here,' said Landstock, glancing around. 'I wonder if the place has got any bells. Maybe not, as there's probably not enough money to pay for them.'

There was a belfry, next to the vestry, immediately to the right of the main door. This was a dark, windowless area, and they had difficulty making out anything at all. However, they went in, and when their eyes had adjusted to the gloom they could just make out two bell ropes hitched up on two hooks fastened to the wall. An object, covered with rough sacking, hung on one hook beside the bell rope. Landstock went forward to take a closer look.

'My God, Lord Nicholas,' he said jumping back. 'Take a look here. There's blood on the floor and it's dripped out of this bundle. What in God's name is it?'

Gingerly, he parted the sacking, revealing dark brown hair, streaked with blood. 'It's a head, my lord. A human head. What foul things have been going on here? Diabolical rituals in a Christian church! If they can cut off a man's head, then they are capable of cutting out a man's heart. I knew I was right

58

to come here. Now we know what we're up against. There are devil worshippers here and they practise their unspeakable rituals in the parish church, of all places.'

Nicholas parted the sacking and took a long look at the revealed object. 'It's a head all right. Two heads to be exact. But there's no human being on earth, as far as I know, who has ears like these.'

He stepped back, only just suppressing a roar of laughter. Landstock, after looking at him indignantly, took another look.

'Well, thank God they're not human heads after all. But it's still bad. These are two hares strung up here in a Christian church. And you know what hares mean, don't you, my lord?'

'They're very good to eat; especially when they've been hung for just the right amount of time,' said Nicholas, still trying to repress a smile.

'It pays to take these things seriously, my lord. Hares are witches' familiars. As bad as cats. This is the evidence we need that witches have been here.'

'So you've found the hares,' said a voice behind them. Matthew Pierce had come to join them. 'Old Roger Aylwin's warrener's been here. He always gives Father Richard a couple of hares from time to time. He's very partial to them. He'll not get them for much longer, mind you, as the hares will be into

59

breeding soon.'

'Why leave them here?' said Nicholas, immensely relieved by this information. 'Why not give them to the Vicar himself?'

'Because he's not here, that's why. He's been away since Candlemas. Over in Selsey. The priest over there, William Tremayne, invited him over to celebrate the festival in his church, and as Father Richard thinks we're a godless lot and don't come to church enough and don't give him enough money to put the church to rights, he decided to accept the invitation. But he'll be back soon, I daresay. The Bishop's death will upset him and he'll want to be back here where he belongs. He's not a bad priest, just a bit on the short-tempered side, and this parish has got some awkward people in it. But the hares will cheer him up, though.'

They left the church, the churchwarden shutting the door carefully to prevent more wild life from making their homes inside the church, and made their way to the gate where they unhitched their horses from the gatepost.

'Well, that's that, my lord,' said Landstock, mounting his horse. 'No one's seen anything, or heard anything, the Vicar's away visiting another parish, and the daylight's fading, and there'll be a crowd waiting for me in Marchester. I'll send a couple of men

60

down here tomorrow to keep an eye on things and report to me. They can stay at the ale house.'

'And I'll be away to Dean Peverell,' said Nicholas, mounting his horse, Harry, and gathering up the reins. He would be glad to be rid of the Sheriff for the time being. Too many wild goose chases like this and his friendship with Richard Landstock, which was beginning to wear thin at the moment, would come to an abrupt end.

Nicholas parted company with Sheriff Landstock at the main coastal road. Turning north towards his village he urged Harry on to a gallop. Harry was only too pleased to oblige, having been forced to accommodate himself all day to the pace of Landstock's sedate cob. The freezing wind lashed at his face, making it smart with pain. He was angry with Landstock. The first day of the investigation was over and they had got nowhere – only a visit to a dismal place, part of which, to his shame, was his responsibility. Now darkness was setting in and he could do no more.

When he reached his manor house, he handed Harry over to one of the grooms who had come out to meet him, and strode into the main hall of his house where a fire was burning and candles were lit and Jane was there with Balthazar Zampieri sitting by the fire, their two heads together over some book of music. As he stood watching them, he thought how beautiful they looked and how they were sitting too close for his comfort. Jane's hair, the colour of autumn leaves, was unbound and tumbled round her shoulders, almost intermingling with Balthazar's dark curls, and when she sang a wrong note, Balthazar reprimanded her, then, to soften the rebuke, put a hand on her shoulder. Jane was dressed in a rust-coloured dress made of fine wool and she was smiling at Balthazar even as he checked her. It all looked very cosy, Nicholas thought, far too cosy. Could it be possible, that after only a month of married life, Jane was seeking new company? Had the Court so corrupted her that she was no longer content with simple domestic life in a country manor house?

He couldn't bear the sight a moment longer and turned back towards the door, but Jane had seen him. She put aside her book and went up to greet him, calling out, 'Nicholas, don't go. I've been waiting for you all day. Come over to the fire – there's warm ale and I've had Mary make some savoury pasties for you. They're still warm from the oven.'

'I see you already have company,' said Nicholas stiffly, glaring across at Balthazar.

All the same, he hesitated and Jane came up and put her arms round him. The warmth of her body thawed his chilled body and he buried his frozen face in her hair.

'It's only Balthazar, Nicholas. He's teaching me how to compose music. Just think of it – your own wife will be able to write music, the same as Master Cornish. We could send my songs to a printer and maybe the King will like them and have them sung at Court. You'd be proud of me then, wouldn't you?'

Still holding her close, Nicholas raised his head and looked into her eyes. He saw no deceit there, no guile, just love and a trace of anxiety because she knew he'd had a tiresome day.

'I'm sorry, my love, it's been a wasted day. We've got nowhere and Landstock's dashing around like a mad dog on some utterly futile witch hunt, making enough commotion to send the devil himself packing. The way he's going on it will take double the time to find the killer or killers.'

He allowed himself to be led over to the fire. Jane handed him a tankard of warm ale. The pasties were delicious and his body began to relax. Balthazar bowed and made to leave the room.

'I hope my wife is a satisfactory pupil, Master Balthazar?' said Nicholas, mellowing.

'Your wife is a star pupil, my lord. She has an incomparable voice, as you know, and an aptitude for composition. I have no doubt that the King will want to have her music performed at Court.'

Jane laughed and wagged a finger at Balthazar. 'That's enough flattery. Leave us, and we shall resume our lessons later. Lord Nicholas has need of me now.'

Balthazar bowed again and left them. Nicholas felt a pang of remorse for his previous suspicions. The man knew his place, and nothing had taken place between him and Jane except a shared musical enthusiasm. But he'd felt the sharp stab of jealousy and it had hurt.

'Come closer to me, Jane. I want to touch that dear head of yours. You are my own dear wife and I could not bear to think of losing you.'

Jane picked up a cushion and put it at Nicholas's feet. Then she sat down, curling herself up against his legs, which were still clad in riding boots and leather breeches.

'If I were a cat I'd be purring at this moment,' she said as Nicholas stroked her hair.

'Purr away, my love. I've had enough of Landstock's bellowing today.'

'Was he bad?'

'He was at his worst – bullying Walter and making everyone else clam up. He speaks as his belly guides him and goes nowhere.'

'And yet he's got a reputation for finding

64

criminals and speedily bringing them to justice.'

'Common thieves and poachers. Give him something big to investigate, something that requires a subtlety of approach and he starts floundering around like a fish out of water. Finding out who killed Bishop Thomas is not going to be easy. It's no use jumping to conclusions on the flimsiest of evidence. It needs thought and careful handling of possible witnesses and suspects, and we have to move fast. The Bishop's funeral is in two days' time and by then the killer could have left the country or gone to ground.'

'The Bishop was an important man,' said Jane quietly. 'And important men make enemies, as you know only too well. It seems to me that there are two questions here which need answers. The first one is who hated the Bishop enough to murder him – what was the motive? And the second is why was he found in that marsh pool?'

'Landstock seems to think that he was murdered down in Pelham Maris by a bunch of pagan devil worshippers who congregate down there. His method of going about catching the killer is to embark upon a witch hunt.'

'You can't completely rule out witchcraft. After all, the removal of the heart does seem to indicate some sort of evil ritual, but we don't know he was murdered in Pelham

Maris. We only found his body there.'

Nicholas looked at his wife in amazement. 'I've forgotten how wise you are, Jane. You should be working for the Sheriff.'

'Before we were married, you used to consult me on all things, Nicholas. Has becoming your wife changed the way you see me? Have I become a piece of property now – something to admire, something to cherish, but not something to be taken seriously? Why don't you discuss things with me? You say Landstock is a man of passion, someone who doesn't stop and think, then let me be your confidante. At least you can rely on me to look at the evidence dispassionately. The Court taught me more than just music. It taught me about greed and lust and betrayal; all motives for murder, I think. And it's motive you ought to be looking for now. When you've found that, other things will fall into place.

'Don't rule out all possibilities, though, at this stage,' she said, looking up at him very seriously. 'Landstock could be right. A group of pagans could have kidnapped the Bishop and indulged in ritual murder. It's happened before. Come to think of it, it seems to be one of the requirements for canonisation.'

'Jane, you're wonderful! And how fortunate I am to have you as my wife. Yes, I had forgotten we were a good team. Marriage has changed me. I am dazzled by your beauty, your kindness and your many accomplishments. Sometimes I feel just an ignorant churl when I'm with you. But we must work together as we used to. Together we'll solve the Sheriff's cases for him in record time!'

'I doubt it. Most cases need a mixture of brain and instinct for their solution. In the end it's the investigator's instinct that leads him to the culprit. But let me be a wife to you now. I shall remove these wet boots and order Geoffrey to make ready a hot bath and I shall personally add some relaxing herbs to it so that you can soak away all the day's aggravations. Then we can eat dinner together – it's a fine venison stew – and then we'll be off to bed. Tomorrow, you'll feel a different man. Are you going to see Landstock tomorrow?'

'Not if I can help it. He'll be back to Pelham Maris frightening the inhabitants out of their wits and finding witches in every barn and stable. Tell me, Jane, what would you do if you were conducting this investigation?'

'I'd start with the cathedral, of course.'

'What use would that be?'

'That's where the Bishop lived and worked. I'd want to find out what his colleagues thought of him. I'd want to listen to them and find out more about them and form my own opinions because people only tell you what they think you ought to know. This way you might find a motive. But don't despise Landstock's methods too much. He might stumble across something that could be relevant to the case.'

'I put myself in your hands, Jane. How I'm looking forward to my new life! Washed and fed by my wife, my expert adviser in all things!'

'Not all things, Nicholas. I wouldn't dare offer advice on some things.'

'Which are?'

'I'll not tell you now. It would not be fitting for a new wife to offer advice on everything her husband does.'

'Now you're making me worried, Jane. When shall I know what you really think of me?'

'Oh we've years to go yet. But seriously, you will let me know what's going on, won't you? Bishop Thomas was my friend as well as yours. He encouraged me to study when he was Prior here, and persuaded my father to have me educated. I owe him so much. Now I want his murderer or murderers caught as much as you do.'

'I'll consult you on every stage of the investigation, Jane.'

'One warning, my love. Take good care. People don't like being asked questions, and when they see you picking up the scent they'll want you out of the way. I know the ways of the world and I have a feeling that there is more to this case than meets the eye. Now let me take you to your bath. That's what wives are for, you know.'

And smiling sweetly, she led him away to be washed and pampered and restored to his usual equable self.

Five

Nine o'clock on the Friday morning. Barely enough light to see by in the cathedral. The cold was intense. It was as if the place itself was in mourning for the interment of Bishop Thomas which was to take place on the following day. There were no mourners present at that early hour. A light was coming from the sacristy and Nicholas walked towards it along the south aisle, pushing open the door when he arrived. Lancelot Day, Canon Precentor of the cathedral, had just dismissed the choir and was discussing tomorrow's funeral service with the head chorister and pointing out certain places in the liturgy which would be his responsibility. Nicholas had heard of the young man, but had not met him personally. He knew his name, though. Anthony West, one of the vicars choral, Prebendary of Dunston, a small village to the south of Marchester, someone whose good looks and fine voice had made him the talking point of Marchester and the neighbouring villages. When they heard the door open, Anthony West looked up at Nicholas, who was struck by a face that was strikingly beautiful with

70

disturbing overtones of sensuality. The fair hair was smoothed down and cut short, his dark brown eyebrows, unusual with that colour hair, were pronounced and perfectly emphasised, his eyes also of deepest brown. He was beardless and his lips were beautifully shaped with an arching upper lip that was full and sensuous. If his hair had been longer and his cheeks rounder he would have looked like a beautiful woman, Nicholas thought. No wonder he was the talk of the town.

Lancelot Day introduced him to Nicholas as if he were showing off some priceless object. He put an arm affectionately round the young man's shoulders and drew him close to him. Anthony looked Nicholas up and down appraisingly, watched closely by Lancelot Day, who took in every flicker of interest on the young man's face.

'My head chorister, Lord Nicholas. He has the voice of an angel and will sing for us tomorrow, unaccompanied, I might add. No easy feat for a young man with the place packed to capacity.'

'Then I wish you every success, Master West, and I am sorry that tomorrow will be such a sad occasion for your performance. Do you remember, Canon, it was only last Sunday that we met at my house with Bishop Thomas and enjoyed our dinner together?'

71

'Such a short time ago, but such changes have occurred. We are all devastated; the Dean is scarcely able to pull himself together to make the necessary arrangements. We shall take a long time to get over this terrible event; years, I should think. It would have been a tragedy if Bishop Thomas had died of natural causes after such a brief period in office, but to have been cut down like this by the hand of a murderer is beyond belief. Who could have hated him so much, my lord, to do such a thing?'

'And that, Canon, is why I'm here. Could we have a few moments together? There are some questions I would like to ask you. Alone, I think,' he added as Lancelot turned to go out of the room still with his arm round Anthony's shoulders.

'Oh, don't worry about Anthony, my lord, he shares our grief and is just as anxious as we all are to find out who murdered our beloved Bishop.'

Anthony disengaged himself from Lancelot's clutches and turned to give Nicholas another long, searching look, as if he were trying to see into Nicholas's soul. The merest flicker of an eyelash conveyed a hint of flirtation. Nicholas returned his stare until the young man dropped his eyes.

'I would like to talk to the cathedral dignitaries one at a time, if you please, Canon, and alone. I came to see you first because I noticed you had lights burning and also I feel you, of all people, knew the Bishop best because you shared a love of music. I also consider you to be a friend because we have shared many a good dinner together and I am hoping you will be able to point me in the right direction.'

'Of course, Lord Nicholas, I will do anything I can to help you. Leave us now, Anthony, we'll go through the "Like as the hart desireth the water-brooks" later. Tell the others I'll need to have an extra rehearsal this evening; I am not entirely happy with the De Profundis.

'Now shall we go over to the Residentiary, my lord, and take some refreshment?' he continued as Anthony left the room.

'I'd rather stay here, Canon, as I shall have to see the others after we've had our talk and I might meet some of them in the cathedral.'

'The others? Whom do you suspect, may I ask?'

'I suspect no one at this moment. It's simply routine procedure in murder cases to interview anyone who has connections with the victim. In that way we can build up a picture of the victim in his surroundings and can eliminate those who couldn't possibly have anything to do with the murder.'

'In that case your stay here won't be long. Everyone is completely devastated by the foul deed. No member of this cathedral community, its Chapter and its priests, could possibly have had anything to do with the Bishop's murder. The idea is too preposterous to contemplate and I am surprised at you, my lord. Don't you realise that Bishop Thomas is to be laid to rest tomorrow before the shrine of the blessed St Richard? That shows what we think of someone who is at this moment enjoying the company of the saints in heaven.'

'That's as maybe, Canon. I don't dispute that. But the devil stalks abroad, as you well know, even in this cathedral. He is no respecter of persons. The devil is within, I believe; within us and within these hallowed walls.'

Despite his evangelical leanings Lancelot Day crossed himself.

'Hush, don't talk about him. He thrives on attention. And, if I might say so, you seem to be a man of many parts, my lord. First you occupy yourself with the Sheriff's business and now you lecture us on the devil.'

'Sheriff Landstock pursues his enquiries elsewhere. As a Justice of the Peace I am concerned about this gross breach of the peace in my area of jurisdiction. But don't worry, when it comes to making an arrest I shall leave the sheriff to do his business. But come, we are friends, Canon, and we mustn't fall out over procedure. I only want to find out more about Bishop Thomas, what sort of company he kept, what people thought of him, and how he spent the last three days of his life. He ate dinner with me on Sunday night. We found his body on Wednesday evening. Have you any idea how he spent the intervening time?'

Lancelot Day sat down at the table piled high with manuscripts covered with musical notation. He ran his hands through his short, grey hair, still tonsured, because, before the dissolution of his priory, which had happened only two years ago, he was a member of the Order of St Augustine. He was middle-aged, tall and lean; a tense, worried man, a perfectionist in his craft of music making. Now he gave careful consideration to Nicholas's questions.

'Bishop Thomas was loved by everyone. He had no enemies. I saw him at mass on Monday morning – that was at eight o'clock – and on Tuesday morning. The Chancellor presided on Wednesday. On Monday I saw him at ten in the morning to discuss the new penitential rite he wanted to introduce into the Lenten services. He was in good spirits and had very much enjoyed his visit to your house on Sunday evening and was full of ideas for the re-ordering of the cathedral in the spring.'

'He had only held office for eighteen months,' said Nicholas deep in thought.

'Before that, he was Prior of my priory at Dean Peverell. Did anyone resent his preferment? After all, he was brought in from outside, outside the cathedral Chapter and clergy, I mean. Did anyone resent this? Were there any complaints? Any murmurings?'

'Of course not. He was the obvious choice. We all know how well you get on with the King, my lord, and the prior was a friend of yours. Of course you would put in a good word for him when a new bishop had to be appointed. After all, you secured him the post here of Precentor when he lost the priory. We knew it was only a matter of time before he became bishop.'

'I don't think the King would be influenced by anyone else's opinions. He'd met Prior Thomas at my house. He'd thought he'd make a suitable bishop, and he was right, wasn't he? You've just said how much everyone loved Bishop Thomas. The King also prides himself on his powers of discernment when choosing his servants. So my opinions were never asked for. But personally, I think the King chose the right man. And I know the King will be devastated when he hears about his death. But tell me, surely some of the members of the Chapter who have been here for a long time must have felt that they had a better right to the appointment when the previous bishop, Bishop Robert, died?'

'I am not the best person to consult when it comes to cathedral politics, my lord. You forget that I, too, am a relative newcomer here. Two years ago I was priest in a community of Augustinian Canons. I was Precentor there and that is what I am most interested in – music and liturgy. As long as the Bishop and I have the same feelings about music I am happy. I don't listen to gossip.'

'Then who should I speak to, Canon?'

'The other cathedral dignitaries, for a start. The Dean, he's been here for twenty years in one capacity or other. There's the Treasurer, of course; he came over from Salisbury six years ago. And then there's the Chancellor. He's been here a long time. He was a great friend of Bishop Robert but soon settled down under the new bishop.

'Then there's the Archdeacon,' Lancelot Day went on, 'he knows everything. He's in charge of the residentiary canons and supervises the clergy. He is responsible for all the parish clergy. He wasn't all that close to Bishop Thomas, having been appointed by his predecessor, who was a very different type of man, as I'm sure you remember.'

Nicholas did remember. Bishop Robert was an old, reserved man. A bit of a recluse, constantly worried about his health. A Fellow of New College, Oxford, he should have been a university don. He simply hadn't the temperament to be a bishop.

'Did the Archdeacon, the Venerable Jeremy Overton, I believe, resent Bishop Thomas's appointment?'

'Oh no, my lord,' said Lancelot Day, looking at Nicholas reproachfully. 'It would not be right for him to object. Why should he? He knew Bishop Robert was in very poor health and wasn't going to live for much longer. Of course he was bereft when Bishop Robert died but he knew changes would have to be made. But you must talk to him yourself. He should be in his house at this moment so now is a good time to see him. But as to my relationship with Bishop Thomas, why, it could not have been better. You see we both believed that music is the essence of liturgy, an earthly attempt to re-create the music of the heavenly choirs which we shall all, God willing, one day be participators in.'

It seemed pointless to prolong the interview. Lancelot Day would no more have harmed the Bishop, his patron and colleague, than a fly on the wall. But had he overlooked something? Something that had sounded a discordant note in this harmonious picture of cathedral life? The image of Anthony West's face presented itself in his mind as he said goodbye to the Precentor and went in search of the Archdeacon.

The Venerable Jeremy Overton was sitting

behind his desk dictating letters to his clerk, a young man wearing the monk's tonsure but dressed in the breeches and woollen jerkin of the ordinary people. The room was on the first floor of the archdeanery and was spacious with tall windows that let in what light there was on that gloomy day. Candles had been placed on the Archdeacon's desk but even so he looked up at Nicholas with tired, bloodshot eyes that indicated severe eye-strain. He was a man in his fifties, with a lean, intelligent face which, that morning, was creased with lines of irritation at being disturbed in his work. When he spoke, his breath was sour, indicating a poor digestion.

'Lord Nicholas, what brings you here? I was expecting the Sheriff to come and see me, of course, or one of his henchmen, but not someone as exalted as yourself.'

'The Sheriff busies himself elsewhere. As Bishop Thomas was a good friend of mine and my wife is quite devastated by his death I wanted to build up a picture in my mind as to how the Bishop spent his last days on this earth.'

'I understand. We are all deeply upset by this tragedy, my lord. As to his recent movements I am afraid I am of little use. The Bishop, by and large, left me to my own devices. He trusted me completely with diocesan business.'

'Yet you must have seen him at early

79

morning mass on Monday?'

'Of course. We all attend morning mass.'

'Did you see him on Tuesday morning?'

'Let me think. Yes, he was there.'

'On Wednesday?'

'No, the Chancellor presided.'

'And he didn't come and see you at all during those three days? Nothing he needed to know about his parish clergy?'

'Good gracious, what would he want to know about them? They are all a bunch of hard-working, underpaid men, living in peace with their parishioners. Some of them, living in the remoter parts of this diocese, would have benefited from more episcopal visits as sometimes they feel very isolated and begin to lose heart. But that's where I step in.'

'Do you visit the parishes very often, Archdeacon? Not at this time of the year, surely?'

'I have the good fortune to own a carriage, a gift from the late Bishop Robert of blessed memory. I manage to get round to see my clergy as often as I can, but this is a large diocese and my archdeanery covers a considerable part of it. I might say, my lord, that I think I know the clergy rather better than the Bishop did.'

'I'm sure you do, but the Bishop had only been here for eighteen months, I understand.'

'Yes, he was a prior of a Benedictine community before that, as you know; and I think that, as much as I respected Bishop Thomas, it was a mistake to appoint a monk for bishop. A bishop needs to be out and about getting to know his clergy, not shut away in a monastery. How could such a man know about the problems of the poor parish priest?'

'But then he had you to guide him, didn't he?'

'I did my best. I think I know more about the secular clergy than a monk could ever know. My clerk, here, Master Hugh Brotherhood, was a monk from a priory at Hardham and he admits that it took him a long time to adjust to the secular world. Isn't that so, Hugh?'

'Certainly when I came to work first for Bishop Thomas and now for you that was the case. But I think I am learning fast. And I hope to learn more when I accompany you on your visitations.'

'You say you worked for the Bishop, Master Hugh?' said Nicholas mildly. He liked the look of the young man whose fresh face seemed innocent of guile. His wavy dark hair was just beginning to cover his tonsure and he gave the appearance of a young man-about-town of modest means. He looked up at Nicholas without fear.

'I used to take down the Bishop's dictation, yes.'

81

'Did you keep his appointments book?'

The young man smiled. 'Appointments book, my lord? What's that? Bishop Thomas made his own appointments and would never consult me. I never knew from one hour to the next where he went to. Sometimes, with deepest respect, of course, I reproached him for his lack of trust in me, but he always brushed me aside and told me he didn't want to bother me with all the details of his daily life. He always said he'd send for me when he needed me and that's how it was. The Archdeacon, now, consults me on all things.'

'That's because I believe in order and efficiency and the essential element in a smooth running department is good communication between oneself and one's clerks. But now, Hugh, you must leave us and I'll send for you when Lord Nicholas leaves.'

'Just one question before you go, Master Hugh,' said Nicholas as Hugh prepared to leave the room. 'As you worked for Bishop Thomas at the beginning of this week, you might just have an idea where the Bishop went to after mass on Tuesday morning? Did you see him around the cathedral precincts? Did he make any arrangements with you about when he would next need your services?'

The young man paused. Then he looked at

Nicholas. 'No, it was a bit strange really. The Bishop was at mass, very amiable, said he wouldn't be needing me that morning and of course I didn't ask why. I saw him talking to the Archdeacon and then he walked away and that was the last I saw of him. It's just as if he was spirited away.'

'Keep your fanciful imagination under control, Master Hugh,' said the Archdeacon. 'Lord Nicholas isn't interested in the supernatural. He wants facts.'

'I'm sorry. It's just that I feel so upset over what's happened. I loved Bishop Thomas, my lord, even though he never took me into his confidence. It seems terrible that only three days ago we took communion together. Then, nothing.'

'Yet someone must know where he went to. People don't disappear. Surely he would have ordered his carriage if he was going to see someone in the diocese?'

'But he didn't, my lord. I checked. His carriage is still in his coach house and has not been used since Sunday night when he came to see you.'

'Yet he must have left the cathedral premises sometime. He couldn't have flown down to Pelham Maris.'

'Pelham Maris?' said the Archdeacon, looking startled. 'Was that where he was murdered? You're quite sure he was murdered there, my lord?'

'His body was found there, in a tidal pool. Where he was murdered, we don't yet know. And, in case you are thinking of asking, let me assure you his death wasn't accidental. The strangle marks round his neck are quite clear, and his heart was removed with great precision.'

Hugh Brotherhood gasped and gazed at Nicholas in horror. 'Then it seems that evil spirits did carry him off. The powers of darkness are with us everywhere; even in this holy place.'

'Stop this nonsense, Hugh. It was mortal hands which carried Bishop Thomas away and killed him. Now leave us and get on with my letters.'

'But you told me that these powers do exist,' said Hugh, now trembling with fright.

'Yes, as part of the Heavenly order. Lower than the angels, I told you, but part of God's creation. Our God, Hugh. Nothing to do with His enemy.'

'But the enemy has powers, too, you told me.'

'Enough of this,' shouted the Archdeacon, rising to his feet. 'The powers of the evil one cannot harm a bishop. He's been consecrated to God.'

Nicholas, thinking that this theological discussion had gone on long enough, decided to intervene.

'I would be grateful if we could get back to

more mundane matters, Archdeacon. Tell me now, as we can't establish Bishop Thomas's whereabouts at the beginning of this week, may I ask whether you left the cathedral between Monday and Wednesday?'

'I'm sorry, my lord. Master Hugh has a bit of an overheated imagination. It's time he cooled down. As to my movements, I stayed here, of course. I had a lot of work to do, the weather was inclement, and my parlour is very comfortable, as you can see. I had no cause to go out. You can go now,' he said, looking at Hugh. 'Calm your thoughts and I'll send for you when I need you. Be sure your mind is well ordered when I next see you.'

Hugh Brotherhood stayed seated as if he had taken root. He stared at the Archdeacon like someone seeing him for the first time. Then, when the Archdeacon dismissed him again with an impatient wave of his hand, he rose to his feet, glanced at Nicholas, and crept out of the room, clutching the bundle of manuscripts.

'An amiable young man,' said Nicholas, after Hugh had gone. 'You must be pleased to have him working for you. Who did you have as a clerk whilst the Bishop was alive?'

'I had no one. I wasn't considered important enough to have my own clerk. I made do with anyone who happened to be available. It was most inconvenient, I can tell you. With help, I can double the amount of work I can do.'

'And it was agreed you should take on Master Hugh so soon after the Bishop's death?'

'Agreed? By whom? There was no one to consult. Master Hugh wasn't doing anything so I asked him to come and help me. I suppose we shall discuss the arrangement when the Chapter next meets, but I can't see any difficulty as everyone else has his own clerk.'

'And when did he start working for you?'

'Yesterday. I thought it would take his mind off the tragedy, but I fear it has affected him more than I realised. I might have to find someone with a less fanciful mind to help me in the future.'

'I'm sure he will settle down in time. After all, the Bishop died in appalling circumstances. It would take a strong person indeed not to be affected by it in some way or other.'

'But we control ourselves, don't we, my lord. God's work must still go on despite these upsets.'

'The Bishop's death was more than an upset, I think, Archdeacon. But let's move on. We've established that Bishop Thomas vanished into thin air sometime during Tuesday or Wednesday this week. His domestic staff will be able to tell me whether he slept in his bed on Tuesday night. Now what I want to know is whether anyone here in the cathedral had a grudge against the Bishop. Do you know, Archdeacon, whether anyone resented his appointment, for instance? Did he upset anyone? Reprimand anyone? Dismiss anyone hastily? It's gossip I want, Archdeacon. And, if I remember correctly, Archdeacons know everything that goes on. It's part of their job.'

The Archdeacon looked severely at Nicholas. 'Gossip, my lord, is a snare of the devil. Gossip destroys people's reputations; it breaks up communities.'

'And yet sometimes one finds the odd grain of truth in the midst of all the distorted information.'

'A very small grain indeed, I think. No, we are, on the whole, a peaceful community at the moment stunned by a dreadful tragedy. The Bishop was a peace-loving man; tolerant – one could say too tolerant. But I'm sure he would have tightened up in time. Am I the first person you've talked to today, my lord?'

'I've spoken to the Canon Precentor. A very dedicated man.'

'Hm, dedicated he might be, but he's one the Bishop should have checked as soon as he took office.'

'How do you mean?'

'Unnatural vices, that's what I mean. If not in deed, certainly in thought. There's one of the vicars choral who brings nothing but trouble when he's around. I know them all, of course, and mostly they are a quiet, godly set of men, but Anthony West is the bad apple. He has the looks of a licentious woman – some say he's one of the devil's hand-maidens – and he seduces men's thoughts away from their proper channels. Our Canon Precentor makes too much of Anthony West. I advised the late Bishop to intervene but he ignored my advice.'

'Maybe the Bishop thought there was no harm in the Precentor's encouragement of a young man, whose voice, I gather, is very fine.'

'That's as maybe. But it pays to be vigilant in these matters. The devil knows what goes on in men's hearts and minds. He can plant his seeds in our minds and he watches them grow into monstrous weeds ultimately taking possession of our souls and bodies. We must destroy these seeds as soon as they are planted, otherwise they will destroy us.'

'But God is the creator of everything that's beautiful and surely He did this for our benefit?'

'But He did not want us to become obsessed by beauty. Neither did He intend us to make furtive visits to young men's houses late into the night when all righteous people should be asleep.'

'Are you saying that the Canon Precentor visits the house of Anthony West at night, Archdeacon?'

'It's been reported to me.'

'Then ignore it. A Precentor pays a visit to his head of choir? It seems to me to be a perfectly natural thing to do.'

'Not when the chorister in question is Anthony West. He has the looks of the devil's whore.'

'But that doesn't make him Lancelot Day's lover, surely?'

The scowl on the Archdeacon's face deepened. 'Hush, don't use that word, my lord. Not in here, of all places.'

'There's no harm in a word, I think. And I think you should put this whole subject out of your mind, Archdeacon. You should take a wife; then you'll forget all this nonsense about the devil and his whores.'

The Archdeacon leapt to his feet and stared angrily at Nicholas. 'Be careful, my lord, lest you drift into heresy. Remember who I am. The Archdeacon has the power to arrest heretics, whoever they are.'

'Heresy? Because I say a man ought to marry?'

'It's against the church's tradition. We are a celibate priesthood. At least we should be. But already our Dean, our own Dean, second only to the Bishop, head of the Cathedral

Chapter, has produced a wife and a daughter who, he tells us, he's been keeping locked away in one of his manor houses up on the Downs. She lives with him now, in the Deanery, flaunting herself about the cloisters. I'll not tolerate it, my lord. Fornicators, all of them.'

'Come, come, man, you're behind the times. All the clergy are getting themselves wives now. The Archbishop of Canterbury himself allows it since we've broken our ties with Rome.'

'And I say it's monstrous. God's church contaminated by females! With their weak brains and their weak morals they lead men astray. One look, and a man's lost; condemned to eternal torment in the next life.'

A vision of Jane floated across Nicholas's mind, and he smiled. 'I'll certainly agree with part of that statement; one look from the right woman and a man is indeed lost. But not damned. We're meant to be happy, Archdeacon. God loves his creation, remember.'

'Man is happy serving God.'

'I agree with that, too. But let's not fall out over these matters. Bishop Thomas saw no reason to interfere between the Canon Precentor and Anthony West, nor, I take it, did he forbid the Dean from bringing his wife out of hiding?'

'As I said, the Bishop was weak and where

there is weakness the devil slips in.'

'You call it weakness, Archdeacon, I call it tolerance and an appreciation of men's needs. I take it the previous bishop took a different attitude towards the Dean's matrimonial state?'

'Bishop Robert was a man of implacable moral standards. Of course he forbade the Dean to bring his wife into the cathedral.'

'Then Mrs Dean must now be wondering what her fate will be when the next bishop is appointed?'

'Oh you may laugh, Lord Nicholas, but these are serious matters concerning the salvation of men's souls.'

'And I believe in a merciful God, Archdeacon. But I shall leave you now in peace. Don't be too hard on Master Hugh. He seems to be a promising pupil of yours as he seems to believe in the devil. You should get on well together.'

'Don't talk so lightly about the devil, my lord. He doesn't like being mocked.'

'And you seem to know a lot about him.'

'Don't you believe in him, Lord Nicholas?'

'I believe that evil exists in men's minds, Archdeacon. And that's where it would stay if people didn't give in to it.'

Nicholas left the Archdeacon's parlour and made his way down the stairs and out into the cathedral close. Thinking he had opened up a hornet's nest, he decided to walk into the town and find himself some hot food before he went in search of the Dean and the other cathedral dignitaries.

After Nicholas had left, the Venerable Jeremy Overton walked across to one of the tall windows which looked down into the vicars' Close. He saw Lancelot Day walking down the Close and watched him stop in front of one of the houses at the far end of the Close. It was Anthony West's house. He saw Lancelot Day raise the latch and walk in. So, he thought, they were going to eat dinner together. Clenching his fists together he beat against the window frame, cursing the Precentor as a fornicator and the devil's whoremonger.

Six

The Three Bells tavern was packed out with townsfolk wanting to get near the blazing fire and discuss the latest developments in a case which had rocked the county. As Nicholas pushed his way through the throng of customers, he was conscious of their curious stares, and when he reached the landlord, a huge man, whose good-natured face was flushed with his own ale and his wife's meat pies, he asked for his food to be sent to him in a private room. He needed ten minutes' peace to mull over the morning's events before his next move and before the Sheriff involved him in another wild goose chase.

A motive, Jane had said. After just one morning's interviews he had enough motives to make everyone a suspect: a Precentor, infatuated by a young chorister, fearing exposure and the disapproval of the Bishop; an Archdeacon suffering the torments of sexual jealousy, resenting the matrimonial state of the Dean and longing for a return to the strict moral code of the former Bishop Robert. He certainly looked as if he could be the chief suspect. Nicholas had seen his type before. He could be a dangerous man. But was he capable of murder? Especially when the person concerned was his own bishop? The head of the diocese? His own superior in all things spiritual and temporal? It didn't sound probable. And also the Archdeacon had put himself above suspicion. He had said that he had not left the cathedral precincts that week. If that were true, then he'd have to rule out the Archdeacon as a suspect. As he mopped up the last drop of gravy with his bread, a sudden thought came to him. Before he'd left the room, the Archdeacon's clerk, Hugh Brotherhood, had looked startled as if the Archdeacon had just said something ambiguous and he hadn't known how to take it. It had only been a moment's hesitation, but he couldn't ignore it.

Wiping his mouth with the linen napkin and pushing his plate away, Nicholas went back into the room, paid the tavern keeper, and ignoring the greetings of the other customers, he strode back to the cathedral. He made his way round to the back of the Archdeacon's house, where he knew there would be stables and a coach house. The Archdeacon had said he owned a coach and there it was, a handsome four-wheeled vehicle with varnished wooden sides and a leather top. The cathedral's coat-of-arms was painted on the sides of the coach in gold lettering. It was indeed an impressive vehicle, finer than his own, Nicholas thought, and certainly very distinctive. Further back in the stables an old man was grooming a sturdy bay horse, polishing his gleaming coat until it shone as bright as a chestnut. He looked up as Nicholas approached him, his face so wrinkled with age and hard work that he resembled one of the gargoyles which decorated the cathedral roof. He wore a woollen hood well pulled down round his ears, and when he spoke he revealed a jumble of rotting teeth.

'You wanted something, sir?' he said.

'Just making a few enquiries. That's a fine horse you're grooming.'

'It is indeed. It's the Archdeacon's main carriage horse. There's never a better one in the city of Marchester.'

'A fine carriage, too. Does he use it very much?'

'Not much at this time of year. Come March he'll be gadding round the parishes again.'

'He's not ordered it this week, then?'

'Lord, no. It's too cold for making visitations. It's stayed here with Job ever since he went out to Hardham during that soft spell of weather we had in January.'

'Job? That's a miserable name for such a fine horse.'

'I agree with you, sir. But then the

Archdeacon's a bit of a miserable sort of fellow, if I might say so, with respect. And Job here's as sprightly as a spring lamb; especially as he's had little exercise over the past week or so and he's been eating his head off on the Archdeacon's oats. He'd be better off with a name like Joshua or Moses, who had a bit more life in them than Job. I just calls him Boy.'

The horse snorted impatiently and pushed at the old man, who shouted at him to be still. Nicholas, having got the information he wanted, left the stable and walked back to the cathedral, noticing, as he went through the west door into the nave that he wasn't alone. Someone was following him. Stopping to ask a young priest where he might find the Chancellor and being told he was probably in the library, he turned round quickly only to see the skirt of a priest's cassock disappear behind a Norman pillar. He walked over to see if he'd been right, but there was nothing. Perhaps it had just been a trick of the light, a flicker of candlelight coming from one of the side chapels. All the same, it made him feel uneasy.

Fighting back this growing feeling of menace, he climbed up the steep, newel staircase to the cathedral library. Here, Edward Hasledean, Chancellor and cathedral archivist, was sitting at his desk, almost submerged under rolls of parchment. He was a man of middle years, substantially built, with a large face partly concealed by a bushy beard. When he looked up his tired eyes were grey as the February sky outside, but intelligent and wary. He put down his quill pen carefully and sat back in his chair.

'So, you do the Sheriff's work for him, my lord?'

'The Sheriff and I work together, Chancellor. It's urgent that we find the culprit soon. This is too serious a crime not to take seriously. But I'm sorry to disturb you at your work.'

'Oh, don't worry about that. My work goes on for ever. There was a lot to do when I became Chancellor fifteen years ago, and the closing down of the monastic foundations has increased my work enormously. You see, all the contents of the monastic libraries in Sussex came here to the cathedral library. Some, admittedly, went to Oxford colleges if the foundation concerned had a learned patron, but most of the documents came to me. Our King has no use for such impedimenta. He'd rather collect silver chalices and lead from monastic roofs. But I think it important to catalogue these documents properly for the benefit of future generations. They show us how these monastic institutions administered their affairs. Mind you, it's a thankless job sorting them all out, but the Bishop took an interest in what I was doing. Incidentally, we have all the deeds and records from the priory on your estate, my lord.'

'Then one day I would be pleased to take a look at them.'

'And I should be pleased to show them to you. But first let me get them into some order. My plan is to catalogue these records and send them off to be printed into a book which we can store somewhere in our library. It will be much easier that way for people to look at. All these rolls of parchment will have to be put somewhere else. I shall have to get a store room set aside for them, and proper shelves to be built. It's inefficient and not good for the documents to have them piled up here in this small room. It will be a life's work, I can tell you.'

'But necessary work. We shall one day have a record of an event which caused the biggest upheaval in English society this century.'

'I'm glad you think so, my lord. Unfortunately, others regard this work as mere cataloguing, something that could be done by any low-grade clerk. And my salary reflects my status as others see it. Others get given wealthy prebends, but I am expected to live on a pittance. I had hoped for some sort of recognition when the new bishop came, especially as I was cataloguing the records of his own priory, and believe me, they are not inconsiderable; the Priors of Dean Peverell's priory were great collectors of rents and tithes. But he turned down my request for a more appropriate remuneration, saying that cathedral funds would not allow him to pay higher salaries. I found this insulting as others enjoyed his favours immediately he took office.'

'Others, Chancellor? Who, may I ask?'

'The Canon Precentor for instance. He was given the living at Ferring. He never visits it but enjoys the income. And the Archdeacon, of all people, was given a carriage, a very ostentatious carriage, I might add, with a coat of arms decorating the sides. What has the Archdeacon done to deserve that?' he said, raising his voice a fraction. 'He doesn't have to sit here day after day dealing with this mountain of manuscripts, does he? He simply keeps an eye on the cathedral and parochial clergy; and he doesn't exactly put himself out to go and see them very often, if I might say so. Some of those coastal parishes haven't had a visitation for years.'

'But when he does make a visit, then he has to have his own carriage, I suppose. It might not be convenient to borrow the Bishop's.'

'But he seldom uses it and he refuses to share it with me. I have to hire a horse to visit my poor parish of Weatheridge perched up on the flinty soil of the Downs where nothing grows and the parishioners are as poor as church mice. No, I'm afraid Bishop Thomas thought little of archivists. He preferred musicians. But when he wanted to see something, a record of sale, someone's title deed for instance, he expected me to produce it instantly.'

'As you have no carriage, I suppose you've not been outside the cathedral precincts this week?'

'Of course not. Where would I go to? Weatheridge is not congenial in this weather, even if I could afford to hire a horse, which I can't. And the Archdeacon would rather die than lend me his, although it frets for lack of exercise. I can't go gadding off round the countryside enjoying the hospitality of the local gentry like some do, Lord Nicholas. No. I stay here and get on with my work. Mind you, I do take the occasional stroll into the city. I shall be away after morning service on Sunday, for instance. I am visiting the house of Mistress Eleanor Stiles, a very comfortable lady who looks after our vestments. She does the most exquisite embroidery and ever since her husband died, he was a Master Tailor, she appreciates a bit of company.'

'Are you following the Dean's example and taking a wife, Chancellor?'

'I might. I just might. A woman can be very

comfortable around the place especially when she owns a large house in Marchester and has some of the finest embroidered bed linen I have every seen. Don't get me wrong, my lord,' he said, noting the quizzical look Nicholas gave him, 'nothing immoral has ever taken place between us, but she did show me her bed linen stored in a great oak chest just waiting for her next husband to come along and enjoy it with her. A good woman, and a mighty fine cook is Mistress Stiles.'

'Does the Archdeacon know about your plans?'

'That miserable old goat? No, of course not. He's against clergy having wives. But at least I don't go round eyeing up the choristers with lecherous intent. The Archdeacon makes a fine pair with the Precentor. Bishop Thomas, God rest his soul, disapproved of both of them. You couldn't exactly say he wanted us married, but he didn't stop the Dean from bringing his wife Katharine out of hiding and I expect he would have put up with me had he lasted longer.'

'And the next bishop? Who do you think he will be, Chancellor?'

'I have no idea, my lord. It's nothing to do with me. It's up to His Majesty, and I suppose he will consult you as you are a member of his Council and I am sure he consults you frequently on all matters.'

'Then whose name should I put forward, when the time comes?'

'Let us mourn our recent bishop before we consider his replacement, my lord. But I must admit it's an interesting consideration; but, of course, it's merely academic at this moment. The Archdeacon would be a most unsuitable candidate – I can't emphasise that enough – although he'd like to be. And the Dean, of course is out of the running. Deans never become bishops; at least as far as I know. There remains the Precentor and myself and I think His Majesty would prefer a married man, don't you? I'm sure he would not consider anyone tainted with unnatural vices.'

'But how would the King know? Only if you tell him.'

'But you have the King's ear, my lord. You should tell him. Could you not put in a good word for me, by the way, and tell him how long and conscientiously I have laboured to sort out the monastic documents?'

'But there still remains the Treasurer. I haven't had a chance to see him yet. But I hear he's only been here for six years and that's hardly long enough to be chosen bishop. But having said that, I know the King likes financially minded gentlemen and I think the Treasurer's financial expertise would make him a strong candidate as there are so many changes going on in the church.

What do you think of the Treasurer's chances of becoming the next bishop, Chancellor?'

'It will never happen, my lord.'

'What makes you so certain?'

'Because he's disappeared.'

'Disappeared?'

'Yes, my lord. And I think it's safe to say that he's the biggest scoundrel in Sussex. Last week the Bishop called me into his palace to tell me that he'd been going through the accounts with Edwin – that's the Treasurer, my lord, Edwin Stanley – and he'd noticed something was missing. One of the parishes, West Marling, a coastal parish, very wealthy with substantial tithes going back to the blessed St Wilfrid, has not presented its returns. Somehow, it had been left out. Edwin was questioned and an investigation was started. Now Edwin has large manors in Wiltshire and the bishop wanted me to lead an inquiry into how Edwin aquired these manors. He didn't inherit them, we checked on that; he must have bought them. But how, in God's name, could he have bought them when his salary is the same as mine? He's also got a carriage and a brace of swift carriage horses. Bishop Thomas was just going to summon him to the palace to account for these things when he disappeared and his room at the residentiary has been stripped of all his personal possessions. The Bishop was furious, was about to send his officers to go and find Edwin, starting with Salisbury because he used to be Treasurer at Salisbury cathedral and the Bishop wanted to know more about how and why he left that cathedral. But then the Bishop disappeared and we haven't given much thought to Edwin's disappearance. But he's an embezzler, my lord, a wicked appropriator of cathedral money.'

And sounds like a chief suspect, thought Nicholas.

'And how long has Edwin Stanley been away from here?' he asked.

'He was seen at morning service on Sunday, though how he had the cheek to participate in the worship of God when he was just about to run off with cathedral funds, I don't know. That was the last we saw of him. He was never a regular attender at morning service. The Bishop saw me again on Monday to discuss what we ought to do about him – the Bishop was not one to find fault with his servants without a thorough consideration of the facts. The rest you know. I only saw the Bishop again when his poor, lifeless body was brought here last Wednesday evening. What terrible times we live in. What wicked men surround us!'

Nicholas thanked the Chancellor for his time and thoughtfully made his way back down the stairs. It seemed he now had another possible suspect: someone who had done wrong and wanted to stop the Bishop from finding out the extent of his crimes. With the Bishop out of the way, attention would be diverted from him and he could make his departure without anyone noticing he'd gone until it was too late to find him. But where had he gone? thought Nicholas. With such a charge against him he couldn't expect to live peacefully in this country for long. He cursed the fact that the cathedral dignitaries had not reported the Treasurer's absence sooner. But he knew how members of close-knit communities closed ranks when one of their number misbehaved. Now it was probably too late to find him. Communications were slow at this time of the year and it could be a long time before the law caught up with him. Probably he'd left the country by now. The Sheriff would have to check on the south coast ports. Sooner or later, they would find him and bring him back to answer for his crimes. But was murder to be added to the list?

The Precentor was rehearsing the choir as Nicholas descended the stairs into the nave of the cathedral. The music for the service of the burial of a bishop, which was to take place the following day, filled the building with wave after wave of glorious sound. There was someone else with the Precentor, a small, upright man who exuded energy even when pacing out the route of the funeral procession and the movements of the officiating clergy. It seemed churlish to interrupt the rehearsal but the Precentor's companion had seen Nicholas and walked briskly over to him.

'I heard you were here, my lord. You must forgive me if I ask that any proposed conversation with me could be postponed until after tomorrow's sad event. The funeral takes place at ten and we are expecting a lot of people to attend. You will be coming, of course, my lord, and the Lady Jane?'

'I can't answer for my wife, but I shall certainly be here. You are the Dean, I assume.'

'Yes, I'm sorry; we all know you, but I forget you don't of course know us. I'm Humphrey Catchpole, Dean of this cathedral.'

'Of course, I've heard a lot about you, but have never met you. Until two years ago my loyalties were with my priory. It seems unbelievable that I am watching the funeral arrangements of someone who was a good friend of mine and was eating dinner with my wife and I only last Sunday.'

'It is indeed unbelievable. But I trust you will soon arrest the culprit and bring him to the place of execution. But back to the sad present, I hope your wife is in good health?'

'Excellent health, and I'm sure she will

106

want to be with us tomorrow.'

'Then let me invite you to take some refreshment with us after the service is over, Lord Nicholas. My wife and I will be delighted if you would be our guests at the Deanery.'

'You are very kind, Mister Dean, and I appreciate your offer. We shall be delighted to accept, of course. I know that if my wife comes she would appreciate some refreshment after the service.'

'Good, good, that's settled then. Now I must get back to the arrangements. But just to put your mind at rest because I know what you will want to ask me, as I've been told by the other people you've interviewed this morning; I have not left the cathedral nor my house this week. We've had a major upset as one of our number has disappeared leaving a heap of trouble behind which I will tell you about later; although I'm not at all sure it's got anything to do with the Bishop's death. My job has been one of relentless hard work going through the accounts with the Bishop until he, too, disappeared. My wife will confirm that I have been here all the week.'

'Thank you, you have been most helpful. I look forward to seeing you again tomorrow and meeting your wife. I am sorry that the occasion will be such a sad one.'

'The Lord gave and the Lord hath taken

away; blessed be the name of the Lord.'

'Amen to that. But I think that in this case, the Lord did not intend to take the Bishop away from us so soon.'

'Who knows, my lord? Maybe He wanted him for Himself.'

With these words, the Dean resumed the rehearsal of tomorrow's funeral arrangements. With the sound of the choir rehearsing the Gradual, 'Yea, though I walk through the valley of the shadow of death, I will fear no evil, for thou art with me, O Lord,' Nicholas left the cathedral and collected his horse from the Sheriff's stables. Daylight was fading fast even though it was still early in the afternoon but the Sheriff had still not returned. As he urged Harry into a gallop once he was clear of the city, Nicholas thought over the day's events. And as he turned into the drive that led up to the manor of Dean Peverell, he reached the conclusion that any one of the people he'd interviewed that day could have murdered the Bishop. Except the Dean; but he'd find out more about him tomorrow.

Seven

Jane insisted on coming with him to Bishop Thomas's funeral although there had been a heavy frost in the night and the easterly wind was bitterly cold. Nicholas wanted to order his carriage to take them but she'd stamped her foot at him saying that she'd ridden Melissa in all weathers before she was married and she was not going to turn into a sober matron riding in her husband's carriage after only four weeks of matrimony. Anxiety made Nicholas speak to her more sharply than he intended and when he said that she was turning into a scold she'd stamped her foot again and said she'd go to the funeral on her own. Looking at her determined face, Nicholas knew that she would always get her way, but as long as her way was also his way he was content to give her her head.

As it was, they rode together side by side to Marchester. Leaving their horses in the Dean's stables they went into the cathedral where the nave was brightly lit with the light of hundreds of candles and torches fixed to the old Norman walls. The Dean, it seemed, was sparing no expense.

The organ was playing softly as the townsfolk entered the building and discreetly jostled for the best places in front of the high altar where Bishop Thomas's body reposed on its bier. The Dean came forward and conducted Jane and Nicholas to the row of seats which had been put there for the gentry. The Mayor of Marchester was already seated next to his wife, who inclined her head in greeting as they sat down. Behind him sat Sheriff Landstock with his wife. He looked weary and his clothes were dusty as if he'd been up all night. He caught Nicholas's glance and shook his head. So, no arrest, thought Nicholas. He couldn't ask him now, not just as the service was about to begin, but he felt sure that the Sheriff would be at the Dean's dinner where they could talk further. Nicholas tried to compose himself to concentrate on the ancient rituals which would soon be enacted before him, but his mind was too full of thoughts to settle down. He glanced at the organist, an old man, upright and alert, with a severe, intellectual face, his sparse hair smoothed down across a very pink scalp. From time to time the organist glanced at the Precentor, who seemed to ignore him. Then, only when the choir was in place, did he indicate by a slight inclination of his head that he should stop playing. The organist responded with a resigned shrug of his shoulders and ended his introduction on a chord which was rather too loud and discordant for the solemnity of the occasion, causing the Precentor to turn and glare at him. Nicholas made a mental note to ask the Dean about the organist, who was certainly at odds with the Precentor. But then, he thought, organists usually were at odds with most people as they had strong minds of their own.

They used the traditional rite for the Burial of the Dead, and it was Anthony's voice singing, 'Requiem aeternam dona eis Domine; et lux perpetua luceat eis', which immediately hushed the congregation. The purity of his high tenor voice filled the cathedral and, looking round at the people who were crammed into the nave, their heads bared despite the cold, he could see only sorrowful faces, many of them streaked with tears. Yet, he thought, one of them could have been the murderer. He glanced at the Sheriff but he was falling asleep and Alice, his wife, dressed in a splendid dress made of scarlet woollen cloth, was prodding him awake, but without success. Catching Nicholas's eye she resignedly shrugged her shoulders.

The service proceeded with due solemnity. Looking at Jane sitting by his side, he could see that she was fully absorbed in the music, watching the choristers intently, not missing any of the complexities of the music. When the music changed at the Dies Irae and the organ joined in with some complicated chords, he saw her shiver, so great was her involvement with the fearful words of that sequence. Then, when the choir sang in English the words of the Gradual, 'Grant them, O Lord, eternal rest, and let perpetual light shine upon them', Jane gave a great sigh and relaxed back into her chair as if all her terrors had departed and all her doubts gone. The Bishop's soul was at rest.

Through the clouds of incense which enveloped the altar and the corpse on the bier he watched the organist, who was looking more and more disgruntled as the Precentor ignored him, until, finally, when the body was lifted up and carried away for burial in front of the shrine of St Richard, he played the organ with such vigour that he almost drowned the choir. Then, in amazement, Nicholas watched as the Precentor strode across to where the organist was sitting, and hit him on the shoulders. The organist ignored him and the Precentor pushed him so hard that he nearly fell off his stool. If the Dean had not intervened at that point Nicholas could foresee a fight breaking out, and turning to Jane to see if she had noticed the incident, he saw that she, like him, could hardly suppress a smile. Finally, when the Bishop was carried away, the organist broke into a joyful voluntary

112

which relaxed the congregation and sent them away smiling and beating time to the music. Outside, in the space in front of the cathedral, the Dean had set up barrels of ale and dishes of meat and bread and the townsfolk didn't hesitate to drink to the repose of the soul of Bishop Thomas.

The Dean came up to escort Nicholas and Jane to his house, apologising as they walked along for the organist's display of petulance.

'Sometimes I think we have two Precentors,' said the Dean. 'Unfortunately they don't see eye to eye. Adam is a traditionalist, you see. Dislikes the use of English in the services and thinks we give undue prominence to the choir. It was all right when Bishop Robert was here – there was no disagreement then – but Bishop Thomas was always at loggerheads with him, which was surprising, really, when you think about it, as Bishop Thomas used to be a prior, as you know, my lord, and people coming from that background are nearly always traditionalists and against liturgical changes. But then Bishop Thomas was all for things moving on. He hated things to stagnate, as he put it. Certainly the people liked what he was doing. The cathedral was always packed out on Sunday mornings, especially so when he preached. But if this antagonism persists between Adam and Lancelot one or the other will have to go. However, it's not up to me to make the decision. I only have to keep things ticking over until the new bishop is appointed.'

The Dean's wife, Katharine, a plump, cheerful lady in her middle years, as brisk and efficient as her husband, welcomed them as they went into the great hall of the deanery where tables had been set up and a feast prepared. Jane and Nicholas were led to the top table, where the Sheriff was already seated. The food was lavish and very welcome: hot venison pies flavoured with spices and succulent with onions, a stew made with hares which had been well-hung, and fat sausages made with pork and oatmeal and flavoured with herbs. With generous quantities of ale, the guests soon relaxed and the noise increased despite the sadness of the occasion. However, as the Sheriff said with his mouth full of venison pie, 'The Bishop, God bless him, has gone to God, so let us be happy for him.'

As the meal progressed and people settled down in conversation with those people they were comfortable with, Nicholas turned to the Sheriff.

'What news, Sheriff? You look as if you've been up all night. Have you made any arrests, yet?'

'I've got three witches locked up in the bishop's prison. The Archdeacon says he'll look after them until a new bishop's appointed; but whether they're suspects or not remains to be seen. We'll know after the interrogation.'

'What evidence have you got?' said Nicholas impatiently – the Sheriff away all day with only three crones to show for it. He really was a fool.

'The three hags are members of a coven. Everyone says so.'

'Everyone?'

'All the people we spoke to in Pelham Maris. Even the local lord of the manor, Roger Aylwin, said he'd seen one of them putting a curse on his cow which was giving birth at the time and produced a calf so badly deformed that it died after two hours.'

'Newborn calves don't always live, Sheriff; how can you possibly prove that the woman had anything to do with it?'

'Because old Agatha Trimble – she's the one with the wart on her face as big as a crab apple; the devil's mark if ever there was one – walked past the calving barn just as the calf was leaving its mother.'

'What rubbish you do talk, Sheriff; the poor woman's old and ugly, like her two companions, I expect, and the farmer needs a scapegoat. Why is it that every crone in the country is regarded as a witch, just because she's old and poor and unable to defend herself?'

'Because these are the people Satan consorts with. He teaches them his spells and makes them feel powerful. We've got to clean up this county, my lord, and get rid of these people.'

'And soon our jails will be filled with these poor old souls. On top of their struggle to keep alive they have to face charges of consorting with the devil. You should feel sorry for them, Sheriff, not arrest them.'

'And I suppose you, my lord, have been warmly abed and planning a new hunting expedition?'

'Hardly. I've been here in this cathedral talking to the Dean and the Archdeacon and the others. It's my opinion that the murderer is near to home. He could be here, sitting at one of these tables, eating the Dean's food. There's several who wanted rid of him.'

'Not one of these fat cats, surely?' said the Sheriff, contemptuously waving a hand round the flushed faces of the other guests. 'You must be out of your mind if you think that one of these murdered the Bishop. They would never contemplate such a thing. They're too fond of their rich livings and comfortable houses.'

'Yet that doesn't put them above bearing grudges against one another and the Bishop. They're only human, after all.'

'We don't have to waste time looking for a

motive, my lord. Satan is behind this crime. Satan is motive enough.'

The Sheriff was making no effort to keep his voice down. As the word 'Satan' bellowed out across the table, silence fell, and faces turned in their direction. The Dean leaned forward and fixed the Sheriff with a severe look.

'Are you talking about Satan, Sheriff? The Arch-enemy? I don't allow his name to be mentioned in my house.'

'I'm sorry, Mister Dean,' mumbled the Sheriff, aghast at the effect he'd created. 'I was talking to Lord Nicholas about the terrible circumstances of our late Bishop's death. He dismisses sorcery too lightly, I think.'

'I would never underestimate the power of evil; but I think it comes from men's hearts,' said Nicholas. 'All I am saying is we need a motive and we need more than just blaming Satan. Of course he's behind all the dark deeds which we are capable of committing. But let us concentrate on the more mundane possibility that someone could have born a grudge against the Bishop to such an extent that he wanted to kill him. Maybe Satan put the idea into his mind, but he can only work on what is there already. He is not a creator.'

'Yet his heart was cut out, damn you,' said the Sheriff, who, after a long, cold night, with little food, was losing patience. 'Now who do you suppose would want to do that? Do you think that Mister Dean here would stoop to such infamy? Or the Canon Precentor? Or the cathedral Chancellor?'

There were gasps of horror from all around them and some people got up to leave. The Sheriff staggered to his feet and looked across to his wife.

'Come, Alice, we must go. I need sleep and a change of clothes. I should never have come here. But I am grateful for your hospitality, Mister Dean and Mistress Katharine. Don't let me disturb the gathering.'

At that moment, a man entered the hall, pushing aside the servants who tried to stop him. The Dean rose to his feet, sensing trouble.

'I'm sorry, sir,' the man blurted out. 'I must speak with the Sheriff.'

'Your name, my man?'

'I know him,' said the Sheriff. 'He's one of my men. What is it, Dick?'

The man approached the high table and whispered something to the Sheriff.

'I'll come straight away,' said the Sheriff, becoming instantly alert. 'Go and tell them to make ready my grey hunter. Poor Duke is worn out after yesterday's hard riding. So, my lord,' he said, turning to look at Nicholas with a satisfied look on his face, 'it seems I was right. The coven meets after dark. Dick was told this by one of the members of the coven who couldn't resist the reward offered for any information. I must get down there and catch the devils red-handed. If you don't believe me then I suggest you come with me now. Come and see the devil at work, my lord.'

Nicholas glanced at Jane, who had been talking animatedly to the Dean. 'I'm sorry, my love. I shall have to go with the Sheriff.'

'Of course,' she said smiling sweetly, 'don't worry about me, I can make my own way home.'

'I'll not allow that,' said the Dean's wife. 'Tell her she's to stay here with us, Dean,' she said, turning to her husband.

'Of course she should stay here where there's a good fire, and Philippa can learn some of Lady Jane's songs. She could not have a better teacher if you've a mind to it, my lady?'

'I should be delighted,' said Jane. 'I would love to stay here whilst Nicholas rides off hunting witches in those freezing marshes. Take care, Nicholas, and don't take too long about it. I shall be waiting for you here.'

'And I'll get the servants to pack you up some pies,' said Katharine, rising to her feet. 'And you can give me a hand, Philippa,' she said to her daughter, a slender young girl of about twelve whose fair hair was tied back from her face in a thick plait, revealing a young face beaming with the excitement of the occasion.

Nicholas went round to where Jane was sitting and she lifted her face to his kiss. 'I'm glad you're staying here, my love. The marsh is no place for women in this weather.'

'The witches don't appear to mind, though.'

'Witches are not women, according to the Sheriff; and they appear to thrive on bad weather.'

'Then I am thankful that I am not one of their number.'

'I am not so sure about that, Jane. I'll be back as soon as I can, and leave the Sheriff to his business of finding yet more old hags to fill the Bishop's jail.'

Cursing the Sheriff's obsession with the black arts, Nicholas followed him out of the hall and went to the Dean's stables to collect Harry.

After the guests had gone, Jane retired to Katharine's own room, where the curtains, made of thick Flemish tapestries, had been drawn to shut out the gloomy afternoon light. A fire crackled cheerfully in the hearth, candles had been lit and servants busied themselves in making them comfortable.

'Of course, it's not easy when one is newly married, to be left on one's own so much,' said Katharine, settling herself down in one of the comfortable chairs near the fire. 'Mind you, for years I was on my own waiting for the Dean to come and see me. It's a relief to be able to share a house with him now.'

Jane, thinking it odd to hear a husband referred to by his rank and not by his name, looked at Katharine sympathetically.

'Yes, to be kept in the dark must have felt quite insulting. You must be glad times have changed.'

'Certainly I'm glad; and I'm glad that Philippa can now be recognised and given a proper education. But you, my dear, how do you fill your days? Of course, I know it won't be long before you have other things to occupy your time, but these things don't always come as quickly as we would want them to.'

Jane laughed. 'I've only been married five weeks, Katharine, so I have had no time to feel bored. Getting the house turned round from a bachelor's hunting lodge to a civilised home has taken up all my time. Of course, come the spring, I will need to continue my studies. I have been used to reading books in several languages. It would be interesting to read some of the manuscripts connected to our manor house. I've also been curious to know what happened to the priory archives when the monks were turned out.'

'Why then you must meet our Chancellor, Edward, who works in the cathedral library. He'd be only too pleased to show them to you if you ask him. He'll not be used to ladies wanting to read his manuscripts, but I expect he'll be flattered when he knows you are interested in his work.'

'I should love to see them. Perhaps I could ride over one day when the weather is less harsh and he could show them to me.'

'I'll have a word with him. I should think he won't be able to wait to see you. He's always complaining that he's not appreciated. By the way, he's thinking of taking a wife from the town. I'm pleased. Being on my own here can be trying, especially when some people object to my being here at all.'

'Who could possibly object to you, Katharine?' said Jane smiling.

'Oh, the Archdeacon thinks I'm the whore of Satan. The Precentor is also most uncomfortable when he meets me. But at least Hugh Brotherhood is happy to take a cup of hot blackcurrant cordial when he feels in need of company; and so does Anthony, when the Precentor lets him off the lead, that is. But here comes Philippa. Let us ask her to entertain us on the virginals and the time will pass very quickly until Lord Nicholas returns from his witch hunt.'

Daylight faded imperceptibly into dusk as

Sheriff Landstock and Nicholas, accompanied by two of the Sheriff's men, rode down the track leading to Pelham Maris. The full moon was covered by thick clouds and the darkness fell like an all-enveloping cloak around them.

The Dog and Hare, the only ale house in Pelham Maris, was set back from the road to the north of the village. When they went in, the place was deserted except for the landlord and two men, soberly but warmly dressed, who were sitting in the corner of a wooden settle with pots of ale in front of them on a low table. The Sheriff nodded in their direction and ordered ale for them all.

'Seems mighty quiet in here for a cold night,' he said to the landlord.

'Folks stay at home in this weather,' said the landlord grudgingly. 'It'll be blowing a gale soon. An easterly. Not the night to be wandering around.'

'But some prefer the darkness, eh?'

'I can't say, Sheriff. Folks do what they want to do around here.'

They dragged another bench over to where the two men were sitting. A guttering candle placed on the table provided some light.

'Well,' said the Sheriff, 'what's happened, Peter? Dick said you'd got some urgent news for me. It'd better be important. Lord Nicholas and I have ridden hard to get here before nightfall.'

'We've heard it from a reliable source that there's to be meeting of the coven out there on the marsh tonight,' said Peter, a dark-complexioned, burly man, his face almost concealed by a thick beard. 'Tide's on the flood now and high water's around seven. They are going to come in to Cobenham quay and we can catch them there. There's a track leading to the quay; it's not difficult to find, we've checked. There's a landing stage there – boats can get up when the tide's right. It's a small place; just a few houses and a church. I was told that the coven meets on one of the islands out in the marsh. It gets covered at high water, but as soon as the water drops you can land there. They use flat-bottomed boats and come back before low tide. So we ought to be able to pick them up easy as pie.'

'You've got the guns?' asked the Sheriff.

'Aye, sir. And Tom's looking after the powder. Guns is useless if the powder gets wet. We've got swords, too. Some of us prefers them to guns which can go off un-expected like and frighten off the criminals. Swords is quiet; quiet and reliable.'

'But there's no need to use the guns; just producing them makes people surrender. And remember, we want these devils alive,' said the Sheriff. 'Dead men can't answer questions.'

'You said someone gave you this information,' said Nicholas quietly. 'Do you know
his name? I'd like to question him further.'

The large man glanced across at the landlord, who was taking his time over washing
down the counter.

'Later, sir. I'll not give his name here. I
know what happens to informants.'

'I understand. I just wondered what's in it
for him. Did you have to pay him a lot?'

'The usual rates. He could be useful to us
in the future.'

'Good work, Peter,' said the Sheriff,
draining his tankard and getting to his feet.
'Let's be off, now. Mind you hold your
tongue,' he called across to the landlord.

'I'll not say a word. But, let me tell you,
sirs, everyone knows who you are and why
you've come, so don't blame me if events
don't turn out the way you want them to. I
like a peaceful life and I keeps my mouth
shut.'

'Then you're a happy man, landlord. And
let's hope you stay that way. Now, let's get
rid of this nest of vipers.'

Hidden by the tall reeds which grew on
either side of the path, they rode off towards
Cobenham Quay some four miles west of
Pelham Maris.

By six o'clock that evening, the wind had
got up; an easterly wind that penetrated the

125

warmest clothes and whipped at faces and hands with a numbing intensity. Out on the gravel spit at the entrance to the harbour a light shone. The captain of a merchant ship laden with woollen cloth and casks of fine Rhenish wine, destined for the bishops' tables at Salisbury and Marchester, saw the light and ordered the crew of two to alter course. He thanked God that he had reached Marchester harbour safely and would soon be out of the wind and down in the warm comfort of his cabin. It was later than he had anticipated, having run into a bit of trouble off Dover, but now all was well. Once past the entrance, he proceeded up the main channel on the starboard tack with water still deep under his keel.

Then he saw another light to starboard which would take him nearer the wind but hopefully bring him into the landing stage. For a moment he wondered whether he'd made a mistake as the charts for Marchester harbour did not show such a light. Thinking that maybe the channels had shifted slightly since his chart was made, and knowing this was not uncommon in these coastal waters, he gave orders to pull in the main sail and proceed close-hauled on the same tack.

The channel then seemed to turn more to the north so he could bear away a little which made the going easier as the wind was increasing in ferocity. Not far now, he thought, with relief, as he knew the tide had turned and he couldn't risk running aground. With the wind howling through the rigging and the crew peering nervously into the darkness, he noticed, too late, that the lights had gone. They were alone in the darkness, on a falling tide, with the wind increasing all the time. Suddenly, with a jolt that shook the ship from stem to stern, they stopped. Then the ship was at the mercy of the wind that tore into the mainsail, ripping it to shreds. When the sail was gone, the mast took the full force of the wind's fury and tilted the ship dangerously over to one side. The captain and the crew peered out over the other side into the darkness only to be confronted by a horde of creatures who seemed to be scarcely human in their ragged clothes and hooded faces. Totally unarmed, disoriented by the darkness, they were no match for the invaders, who with cudgels and swords quickly beat them senseless and killed them with a swift slash at their throats. Then, stripping them of their clothes and sea boots, they threw them over the side of the ship into the water where the tide, now rushing out towards the entrance, carried them along the channel and out to sea. All except one, who got caught up on a mudbank and was trapped by the fronds of bladderwrack seaweed. As for the ship, it didn't take long for the invaders to go down into the hold and pass up to willing hands the bales of cloth and the casks of wine which were carefully lowered into the shallow-draught boats which were poled ashore to Pelham Maris, where more willing hands received the goods and bore them triumphantly away.

Then, long before dawn broke, the invaders returned to the ship, which was now lying on its side like a beached whale, and ripped out the planking and hauled out the main mast and stripped the cabin of its comforts.

Eight

They were woken up at daylight by Peter, who had been keeping the last watch of the night.

'Wake up, sirs,' he said, shaking Nicholas roughly by the shoulders, 'the tide's been out and come in again and still we've not heard or seen anything out there. Certainly no one's come into the quay; not unless they've made themselves invisible.'

Nicholas opened his eyes and stared blearily up into the black-bearded face of the Sheriff's man. For a moment his mind went blank; he had no idea where he was, nor how he'd got there. Then he moved his head and saw the Sheriff stretched out on the straw beside him with his mouth open snoring energetically. Suddenly he remembered. Dog-tired and stiff with cold, they'd retreated to this barn near Cobenham quay, leaving the others to take their turns at keeping watch.

He pushed aside the straw which he'd pulled over himself for warmth and got up. He moved slowly and stiffly after one of the most uncomfortable nights he'd ever endured, keeping watch over the bleak

129

marshes, seeing nothing, hearing nothing except the howling of the wind across the mud flats. All for nothing. He cursed the Sheriff for bringing him on yet another wild goose chase. Then he thought of Jane and what she must have been thinking as night fell and still he hadn't returned. There was no doubt that the Dean's wife would have made her comfortable, but would not have been able to stop her worrying.

'Well, it appears your informant's misled us, Peter,' he said as he stamped his feet to warm them up and brushed the straw off his clothes. 'Did he intend us to spend the night holed up over here? Or maybe the weather was too inclement for the witches to hold their coven.'

'I don't know what to think, sir, but I do know that when I find Amos Higges, that's his name, by the way, I shall beat his guts out unless he gives me a good reason why we've spent one of the coldest nights of the year gazing out into darkness. Incidentally, the men are famished, sir.'

'And that includes me,' said the Sheriff, waking up suddenly. 'It's a long time ago since we ate the Dean's pies. Get the men together, Peter, and we'll go in search of some warm ale.'

'We'd best get back to Pelham Maris and stop at my hunting lodge on the way. No doubt Walter can rustle up some ale and some strips of bacon. We can't get very far on empty stomachs. Seems we've been hoodwinked, Sheriff. Either that or the coven decided to cancel their meeting; and I can't say I blame them.'

They stood on the wooden jetty staring out at the hull of a substantial barque lying on its side on the mud flat, which the tide had just exposed. The wind had abated and the pale, February sunshine lit up the scene like a tableau on a stage. The eerie call of the curlew echoed across the marsh. A kestrel hovered over the reed beds ready to pounce on an unsuspecting water vole. Two herons flapped overhead on their way to join the rest of their colony out on the mud flats waiting to catch the fish stranded by the receding tide.

'God damn them, Lord Nicholas,' said the Sheriff, staring in horror at the wrecked ship. 'What the devil's been going on here? This certainly wasn't here on Friday.'

'It seems we've been tricked. You're dealing with a pack of wreckers, not a witches' coven.'

'Hell's teeth, you're right. Lights out on the marshes, tide just right, moon obscured by clouds, this is the work of evil men, wreckers, the plague of our coastal waters.'

'And they wanted us out of the way,' said Nicholas, 'whilst they set about their foul business. And there we were four miles away asleep in a barn whilst all hell was breaking out here.'

'Looks like a Dutch ship, sir,' said Peter. 'We get a lot of them around here, mostly going up to Marchester Harbour or Portsmouth. Lot of places they can get into but never in here. Not unless they were deliberately lured in.'

'Which is easily done in the right conditions,' said the Sheriff. 'You'd only need a couple of lights burning for a short time – just long enough to mislead them.'

A shout came from the other side of the jetty where a couple of the Sheriff's men were staring down into the mud and slime beneath the jetty.

'Look here, sir,' said one of the men, 'one of the poor buggers got himself caught up round one of the posts. Looks like he's been done in. I'll get down to him.'

Nicholas and the Sheriff went over to the other side of the jetty just as the man's head disappeared over the side of the wooden platform. They gazed down into the dark water underneath the jetty where the sluice gates were partly open allowing water from the surrounding fields to drain into the marsh. There, caught between the wooden struts of the jetty, was the body of a naked man. As they watched in horror the Sheriff's man released the body and shouted for a rope. The Sheriff picked up the rope, which was tied to a cleat ready to tie up any small boats coming in to the quay at high water, and threw it down to the man. Slowly the body was pulled up and hauled on to the platform. They stood looking down at a youngish, sturdily-built man, his white body covered with dark bruises from the battering he'd received, his shock of yellow hair gleaming incongruously in the pale sunlight. Peter was the first to speak.

'Look here, sir, his throat's been cut. Looks like the devils murdered him and his mates; stole their clothes, too. Where's the rest of them, I wonder?'

'Washed out to sea,' said Nicholas, 'where this one would be had he not got caught up somewhere out there and brought back here on the tide. We're dealing with a ruthless band of wreckers in this God-forsaken spot, Sheriff. And we must not let them get away with this. Search every house, and every barn. Find where they've put the cargo from this ship – it can't be far away as they'll not have had time to hide it properly – and you'll catch the wreckers. They'll not leave their loot for others to find. But let's get this poor devil up onto dry land and give him proper burial in due course. Meanwhile we'll need him for evidence. I wonder who he is. We could, of course ask the port authorities at Marchester whether they were expecting a ship from Flanders. The captain could be someone they knew from a previous visit. They might even be able to identify this man. You'll need extra men, Sheriff, to deal with all this.'

Suddenly a bell rang out from the parish church of Pelham Maris, which was only a few yards from the jetty. It was a mournful sound like the tolling of the bell for a funeral. Suddenly Nicholas remembered. It was Sunday morning. The faithful were being summoned to prayer.

'It appears that someone thinks there are some God-fearing people in this place,' said the Sheriff grimly.

'I wonder that anyone here has the effrontery to attend a Christian service after what happened last night,' said Nicholas. 'There's more than just a couple of people involved in this. Probably the whole village knew about it. Mind you, I expect they've done this before. They're obviously well organised.'

'And I'll make sure they'll not do it again,' said the Sheriff, suddenly taking charge. He was glad to be back on a job which he was familiar with – restore order, round up a horde of flesh-and-blood thieves and murderers motivated by simple greed. Witches – well, he'd leave them to the clergy, who knew all about the supernatural.

'We'll start searching the village now.

Dick, you get back to Marchester and call out the rest of our men. And be quick about it. Use my horse; he's faster than yours. These devils have a knack of disappearing into thin air and taking their ill-gotten gains with them if we give them a chance. Meanwhile, you, Peter, get after Amos Higges, who lied to us. Bring him in. He'll certainly know who the other members of the gang are. Where are you off to, my lord?' he said as Nicholas had left the group on the jetty and was setting off towards the village.

'I'm going to Morning Service, Sheriff. I'll leave the wreckers to you and your men. You might remember we are in the middle of a murder investigation and I want to have a word with the parish priest of this benighted place. Maybe we'll be able to kill two birds with one stone. In the meantime we'll take over the Dog and Hare. Tell the landlord to make himself scarce. We can leave messages for each other so that we know what we're both doing. Good luck, Sheriff. Get this gang of murderers rounded up and I'll be off to talk to the congregation.'

The service had started when Nicholas went into the church. Unexpectedly, the place was full: mostly women and children with a row of men standing at the back, who looked surreptitiously at him as Nicholas took his place next to the churchwarden,

135

Matthew Pierce, whom he recognised. He saw Luke Pierce up in the chancel, holding the incense burner. He was standing next to the priest, a short, stout man, with sparse grey hair and a cherubic face which indicated a love of the good living. Suddenly the feeling of numbness he'd experienced when he saw the wrecked ship and the dead man gave way to a surge of fierce anger. Some of these people standing so quietly next to him must have known what went on last night. Some of them might even have climbed on board that unfortunate ship which they had lured into the harbour, murdered the captain and his crew, fellow seamen, like themselves, stolen the cargo and returned to their beds. And now they had come to this service to say the responses and receive communion. They had not even been put off by the presence of the law which they had so successfully hoodwinked last night.

The priest had started on his sermon, an exhortation to the congregation to turn away from the darkness of evil to the light of God's grace. Nicholas watched him intently, finding not a trace of hesitation in his delivery. He was either a consummate hypocrite or was unaware of what had gone on last night out in the harbour. This he found hard to believe. But whatever he was, the congregation listened to him intently and when the time came to take communion,

136

knelt down respectfully to receive it with no signs of guilt on their weather-beaten faces.

When the priest had given the blessing and people began to shuffle and clear their throats ready to leave, Nicholas strode up the central aisle to the chancel steps, much to the surprise of the priest, who extended his podgy arms as if trying to stop him.

'You must excuse me, sir,' Nicholas began as he turned to face the congregation, 'if I speak to these people. You probably know who I am and why I'm here with the Sheriff of Marchester. Now last night,' he said raising his voice, 'an act of great wickedness was perpetrated out there on the marshes. A ship was lured into a shallow channel and went aground. Instead of offering hospitality to the captain and crew whilst they waited for the ship to float off on the next tide, a group of wicked people invaded the ship, murdered the captain and his crew – we know this because we've found one of the poor souls, stripped naked with his throat cut and showing marks on his body of having been beaten. Then these devils, because that's what they are, stole the cargo. The Sheriff is, at this moment, searching all houses and barns to find it. You heard your priest talk of wickedness. Now what happened last night was wickedness beyond belief. A ship, making its way to safety on a freezing winter's night, deliberately lured into unsafe waters, its crew murdered, its cargo stolen. Now some of you must have known what was going on, some of you, though this is hard to believe, might be here at this moment having taken part in that wicked act. Some of you might be receivers of those stolen goods and have them hidden away in your houses.'

'And what's more,' said a voice from the back of the church, 'none of you is going to leave this place until you've accounted for your whereabouts last night. Every one of you, except the women and children. We'll be speaking to them later to find out if they can confirm what their men tell us.'

The Sheriff had come in to the church, two of his men carrying the body of the dead seaman. They placed him on the floor and one of the men covered him with his cloak. The congregation was horrified. With cries and lamentations they clustered round the dead body. A woman fainted. Some of them fell on their knees by the side of the body and started to mutter prayers. The priest, recovering from the shock of the interruption to his service, marched down to the back of the church, pushed aside the congregation and looked fiercely at the Sheriff.

'Stand back, sirs. This is my church and I'll not tolerate such behaviour. This man died in our waters. We must now pray for him and ask God to receive his soul into heaven with his saints and angels.'

The priest knelt down and soon immersed himself in the prayers for a person overtaken by sudden death. The Sheriff waited, scarcely able to control his impatience. When the priest had finished he asked for permission to bury the dead man in his churchyard.

'He's not to be buried until I say so,' roared the Sheriff, 'and he'll not be taken from here until I and my men have questioned everyone and we've searched all the houses and outbuildings. No one is to leave without my permission.'

Nicholas looked at the priest. 'And you and I, sir, could have a talk over in your house, if you don't mind. There are a lot of questions I want to ask you. We can leave the Sheriff to get on with his work. But first, Master Pierce,' he said turning to the churchwarden, who was vainly trying to restore order amongst the congregation, 'if you would be so good as to tell me whether Amos Higges is here this morning. We've a score to settle with him.'

'Amos Higges?' said Matthew Pierce, his face white from the shock of the disturbance, 'why he's not here, sir. He never comes to church. He's most likely up in his place, a tumbledown sort of place behind the Dog and Hare. It's just a hut, really, with no proper roof on it. You'd better get there quick before he knows you're here.'

'Don't worry, my lord,' shouted the Sheriff, 'Peter'll find him. Now, let's start with you, sir,' he said turning to Matthew Pierce. 'Where were you last night?'

Nicholas and the priest walked across to the priest's home, a small, modest house, with thick, flint-stoned walls buttressed against the force of the wind with a thatched roof and a low front door. The windows were mere slits in the walls. It crouched at the edge of the marsh like some amphibious animal that had been there since time immemorial. The priest opened the door and led the way in to the dim interior, lit only by the glimmer of light coming from the smouldering log in the fireplace. Nicholas stared around the room with interest. The room was warm and comfortable with tapestries on the stone floor. Two wooden chairs with arm rests and cushions on the seats, stood at either side of the fireplace. A sturdy, polished table was laid with one place setting for the priest's dinner. Whilst the priest lit a candle, Nicholas walked over to the fireplace, kicked the log into flames and stood with his back to the heat. The priest, having set the candle on the table, lifted a pewter pot of ale from the edge of the fireplace.

'You'll take refreshment, my lord?' he said.

'Thank you, sir priest. Would you tell me your name, before we go any further.'

'Richard, sir. Richard Rushe. Vicar of this parish for the last fifteen years.'

'Then you must know your parishioners well.'

'Does a priest ever know his parishioners? Yes, I suppose I hear their confessions, but that custom's dying out now. Times change. They used to call me "Father", but now it's "Vicar" or plain "Mister Rushe", or just "Reverend". It's a bit confusing until someone sorts things out. But we're a conservative parish and don't think much of changes and being told what to do or say after we've been saying things one way for years. But I suppose we'll get used to it.'

Richard Rushe handed Nicholas a tankard of ale and settled himself down in one of the chairs by the side of the fire. He was still wearing his cassock and surplice, which hid the outline of his great belly, and Nicholas noted the two impressive gold rings on his plump fingers. He looked like a statue of the amiable pagan god Bacchus and Nicholas found it hard to believe that he had anything to do with the Bishop's murder or the evil events of last night. But he knew only too well that appearances can be deceptive. Nicholas waited for him to speak.

'This is a sad day, my lord, when foreign seamen are murdered in our waters and their ship's cargo stolen.'

'Indeed it is. And I would have thought that you, living so near the harbour–' Nicholas indicated the small window which looked out to the sea wall and the marshes beyond '–would have heard something last night. Something which would have alerted you to what was going on out there.'

'I sleep very soundly, my lord. I heard nothing.'

'Do you sleep upstairs?'

'Yes. There's just one small room above this one. I sleep there. It's no more than a loft. Do you want to see it?'

Nicholas shook his head. 'No. I just wondered if it too overlooked the harbour.'

'The room has no window, sir. I only use it for sleeping and a candle is all I need to guide me to my bed.'

Nicholas drained his tankard and shook his head when the priest offered more. 'Thank you, no. I have to get back to Marchester and I must keep my head clear. I am sorry I didn't meet you at the Bishop's funeral yesterday. It was a sad event. The people were grieving. Bishop Thomas was well-loved, I believe?'

'Oh yes, sir. Much loved. I am sorry that I couldn't be there but I was needed here in my parish. The Bishop would have understood. Several of my parishioners are afflicted with a virulent fever and a congestion of the lungs that prevents them breathing properly. Indeed, two of them died on Friday night and there are others whom I shall have to anoint today. This is a bad time of the year for the elderly and the young. When Lent is past and spring is on its way the sickness dies away; but we always have a full graveyard, my lord.'

'I am sorry to hear it. But you live in some comfort, sir. The tithes from this parish must be very generous?'

'On the contrary, this is a very poor parish and I have a job collecting my tithes. But I was fortunate to come here from a wealthy parish near Oxford and I brought a few comforts with me. My house is comfortable, I admit. It's strongly built. It withstands the gales very well and as you see it's warm even when it's freezing outside.'

'You are fortunate then. Many priests live in far worse conditions. But, if you'll allow me, I would like to ask a few questions about your whereabouts last week.'

'My lord, I would be pleased to answer any questions you put to me. After all, that's why we're here, isn't it?'

Nicholas nodded. 'Then let us start with the first part of last week. On my previous visit here with the Sheriff I was told that you were not in residence. Is that so?'

'Then you were rightly informed. I went to a colleague of mine to celebrate the feast

143

of Candlemas with him. He is the Rector of Selsey, William Tremayne by name, a young man, who sometimes needs a bit of support. He's only been a priest for six years and finds parish work very arduous. Selsey is even more remote than we are and the people quite barbarous, which is strange, really, as the blessed St Wilfrid first landed there to bring the light of the gospel to the pagan people of Sussex. I would have thought that would make the people of Selsey even more holy than the rest of us, but, alas, it is not so. The late Bishop never went to see them and William found that very disappointing. He felt that the Bishop, along with everyone else in this diocese, had given up on him and his parishioners. So I took the service here on Sunday morning, just as I did today, and went over to join him for the evening and he asked me to stay on.'

'When did you return here?'

'On Friday, sir, to attend to the sick people.'

'So you didn't hear about the Bishop's death until you returned?'

'Oh yes, sir. News travels fast, even to places like Selsey. My colleague was devastated by the news and I know he intended to go to the funeral. As I have been so busy here I don't know whether he got there.'

Thinking it would be easy enough to check with the Dean whether the Rector of

Selsey had attended the funeral, Nicholas continued his questioning.

'How well did you know the late Bishop, sir?'

'Oh not well. Of course I went to the cathedral at Pentecost, along with my parishioners, to pay our dues, but I can't expect a bishop to come down here. We live simple and peaceful lives, sir, and don't want to trouble anybody.'

'Yet it appears things were not so peaceful last night.'

'No, indeed, and I hope the wicked men who perpetrated that unspeakable crime will be quickly caught and brought to justice.'

'I'll say, "amen" to that, sir. I'm sure that the Sheriff and his men will be hard at work now tracking down these evildoers. But I will leave you in peace now. I trust there will be no more disturbances to trouble you in the future.'

A succulent smell of stewing meat and onions was coming from the pot hanging over the fire. The priest was looking at it longingly.

'You'll surely stay for some dinner, my lord?'

'Thank you, no. I must away to see if the Sheriff's caught Amos Higges yet. We want to speak to him, sir, as he misled us last night. Is he someone you know well?'

145

'Amos Higges? Oh no, my lord. He is not one of my flock. You see, he doesn't come to church and keeps himself to himself. He owns no land and relies on other people's charity. If anyone is behind last night's evil-doing it would be Amos Higges. I can say nothing good about him, I'm afraid.'

Leaving the Reverend Richard Rushe to his dinner, Nicholas went off to find the Sheriff.

There was no one in the Dog and Hare when Nicholas got there except Peter, the Sheriff's man, standing with his back to the fire, tankard in hand. Nicholas greeted him and asked him where the Sheriff was.

'Outside searching people's houses. Extra men are on their way. Everything's in hand, sir.'

'Has he taken anyone in yet?'

'Not yet because there's no evidence. Nothing's been found.'

'Not even Amos Higges?'

'Seems he's vanished, sir. Not a trace of him. His house, if you can call it a house, has been searched. Nothing. He's got nothing, mind you. Not a stick of furniture. Just a pot over a fire that's gone out and a pile of rags on the floor – for his bed, I suppose.'

'I hope you find him. I'm sure he's a key person in this investigation.'

'Key person he may be, sir, but I'll have difficulty keeping my hands off him having made us spend the night out on that quay.'

'Keep a bit of him for questioning.'

'I'll try to remember, sir. Any message for the Sheriff?'

'Tell him I'm off back to Marchester. I've got to collect my wife and check up on the priest's account of where he was this week past. We can only find the Bishop's murderer by careful checking and cross-checking.'

'I understand that, sir. It's a pity that we didn't catch those devils red-handed last night. I've never seen so many innocent-looking people this morning. Butter wouldn't melt in their mouths. Not a sign of anything out of order in their homes. Everything as it should be – fires lit, children playing. A lot of folk ill, though. Some at death's door. I suppose it's the time of year. Old folk can't stand the cold.'

So one part of the priest's story had been confirmed, he thought. Now to check on the rest of it.

'Tell the Sheriff not to lose heart. He'll soon get a breakthrough; especially if you've offered money for any information which might help the investigation. People are short of money at this time of the year with last year's crops running low in the barns and winter fodder in short supply.'

The short day was almost over when Nicholas arrived at the Dean's house in Marchester. Despite the offer of accommodation Nicholas insisted on returning to Dean Peverell in the hour or so's daylight left to them. Jane wanted to go home, too. Thanking the Dean and his wife for their kindness, they rode back to the manor house, where a fire was burning brightly and supper laid ready. The discomforts of the previous night and the grim finds in Pelham Maris's harbour soon began to recede. Smiling across at Jane, Nicholas felt a surge of happiness that she was there with him. His days of lonely introspection were over.

Nine

After a restless night in which Jane and Nicholas, by tacit agreement, had not discussed the day's events, they drifted off to sleep after a love-making that was both intense and satisfying. Next morning, they awoke in each other's arms, their bodies so tightly entwined that it was as if they had become one person. It was late when they ate breakfast in the small room which Jane had turned into her own boudoir and where it had become their habit to eat breakfast. A fire burned brightly and tapestries covered the stone walls and floor, making the room feel comfortable and feminine. Jane was wearing her morning robe, a long woollen dress, the colour of daffodil leaves in early spring, a gift from the late Queen Jane. Her hair hung loose as it always did in the mornings, unless she was thinking of taking an early ride, and the light from the fire lit up her hair, turning it to the colour of burnished copper.

'It's hard to believe such dreadful events happened in this peaceful county, Nicholas,' she said after she had satisfied her appetite with bread and clover honey from their own hives. 'It must have looked like a scene from a nightmare, the dead man and a wrecked ship. Are you sure it was local people who did it?'

'If you mean by local, people from more than one coastal parish, then yes,' said Nicholas. 'Only local people know those channels and inlets. They also know the tides and what effect the wind has on ships approaching the narrow entrances to these harbours. They also know where the best places are for setting up their lights to guide ships into safe and unsafe waters. It takes a lifetime to know these things. Also strangers would be noticed immediately and driven away by local inhabitants. They are a close-knit bunch. All in it together: Selsey, Cobenham, Pelham Maris, wherever there is an inlet and no port authorities to keep a check on things.'

'Then that narrows down the field for the Sheriff, doesn't it? He should soon find the culprits in a place so small as Pelham Maris.'

'It won't be as straightforward as it seems. They're probably all in it together and by now they'll have closed ranks. It only takes a short time when you are practised at it to hide cargo and get rid of the evidence. They also have special boats for those tidal waters, which means that they are used to shallow water and can get to the ship which

150

has run aground in no time at all. Wrecking has always gone on around our coasts, I am aware of that, but it's the first time I've had first-hand experience of it.'

Nicholas finished his breakfast and stood up, reaching for his cloak. Jane looked at him in surprise.

'You're surely not going back to that awful place so soon?'

'No, I'll leave the Sheriff to deal with the inhabitants of Pelham Maris. I'm away to the next parish along our benighted coast, to Selsey and its rector, to check on the Reverend Richard Rushe's account of his whereabouts last week.'

He paused. 'Last week! My God, we're five days into this investigation and we've got nowhere. Five days since we discovered the Bishop's body and all I've got to show for it is a few vague suspicions. I don't know what motivated the killer and I have no evidence to justify bringing in anyone for questioning. Oh, for the Sheriff's certainty that witchcraft was behind this murder. When he's finished with the wreckers he'll be off to round up more old women to fill the Bishop's prison. He's brought in three crones already. And I shall be left to interview reluctant clerics who all assure me of their loyalty to their former bishop.'

'But someone did it, Nicholas, someone with a devious mind. This was not a

151

spontaneous killing. It was well-planned. The Bishop was lured away just like the wreckers lured that ship into dangerous waters, and he was murdered in what seems like a ritual killing. Or it may well have been that the killer wanted us to believe it was part of a ritual killing to throw us off the scent. We must be careful to keep an open mind until we are certain we have the right suspect. We mustn't follow the example of the foreign ship and follow false lights.'

Nicholas put down his cloak and turned to look admiringly at his wife, who was demurely drinking a beaker of warm milk sweetened with honey.

'Jane, why haven't I got your brains?'

'Because you have other attributes, Nicholas. I am only allowed to observe and think whilst you dash off hither and thither risking freezing to death in inhospitable places. But why don't you tell me what happened when you interviewed the cathedral dignitaries and the Archdeacon? I talked a lot with the Dean's wife and I think you can safely eliminate the Dean from your enquiries. He's a good man and conscientious. He wants to preserve the life of the cathedral in these troublesome times. I also think he would make a very good successor to Bishop Thomas but I am equally sure he has no hopes of obtaining that position at this moment. He is both competent and discreet.

He has taken charge of the cathedral affairs without the others appearing to notice it. Now tell me, who did you talk to when you went to see the Canons? What were your impressions of them?'

Nicholas sat down and re-filled his tankard with the warm spiced ale Jane had ordered for him. 'Where to start? The place is a witches' cauldron of intrigue and jealousy. The Dean, I agree, appears to be a most unlikely person to murder the Bishop. But he's the only one I can say that about with any confidence. Take the Precentor, Lancelot Day, for instance. He dined with us not so long ago, you may remember?'

'What, that old pussy cat?'

'Pussy cat he might be, but he's madly in love with his head chorister, Anthony West...'

'As anyone would be!'

'Jane, be serious. You're supposed to be in love with me.'

'Which I am, my lord, as I proved to you last night.'

'Which was only right and proper, but seriously, love between two men is frowned upon as you know perfectly well and especially within the precincts of a cathedral.'

'Did Bishop Thomas raise any objections?'

'Not that I know of. But then he was always ready to see the best in people. I suppose if it had been brought to his attention that one of

153

his cathedral Canons was performing immoral acts with his head chorister he might not have been able to turn a blind eye any longer and would have felt compelled to dismiss them both.'

'Maybe he wouldn't have wanted to look too closely? Anyway, who says immoral acts are taking place?'

'The Archdeacon, the Venerable Jeremy Overton, who hates the Precentor and is, I'm sure, attracted to Anthony West although he will never admit it, not even to himself. If he had definite proof that his colleague and West were indeed indulging in illegal acts, he would certainly have denounced them to the late Bishop. And if Bishop Thomas had not taken any action then he would have been bitterly resentful.'

'He'd have to hide under the bed to get that proof.'

'Jane, I'm warning you, these are serious matters.'

'I know they are; but they are part of our human nature. Now what really motivates a murderer, Nicholas?'

'Greed, lust, jealousy, resentment, fear, I suppose.'

'Interesting you put greed first. I would put lust and its obverse, jealousy. But tell me more about the Archdeacon. He sounds interesting.'

'I'm glad you find him so. There's too

much bile in the man for my liking. He served under Bishop Robert and admired him. Also I think he had expectations of stepping into his shoes when he died. Of course he didn't admit to it, but that's my impression. He's got a comfortable position, of course; owns his own carriage though doesn't use it very much and stole Bishop Thomas's clerk without asking anyone's permission. However, he didn't leave the cathedral at all last week. I checked.'

'So that rules him out?'

'I suppose so but I don't trust him. There's a darkness around him. Disapproves of the Precentor's obsession with Anthony and thought Bishop Thomas should have put a stop to it, yet lusts after the young man himself.'

'Not a strong enough motive for murder though. It's unlikely he'd murder someone for not doing what he wanted him to do. If that were the case there'd hardly be anyone left alive in the cathedral!'

'I know, Jane, it all sounds highly improbable. If it had been the Precentor we'd found in that pool and not the bishop then we'd have good reason to suspect the Archdeacon. Then it would have been a straightforward case of jealousy. I just don't think he had a strong enough motive to go to the lengths of murdering the Bishop, getting his body down to Pelham Maris and cutting out his heart just for good measure. No, we are looking for a vindictive man who hated the Bishop to such an extent that he wanted his body mutilated. But there is just this feeling I have which I find difficult to put into words. His clerk, Hugh Brotherhood, looked uneasy over something the Archdeacon said, but I can't remember what prompted the look. Anyway, whatever it was, the Archdeacon dismissed him pretty quickly. I think I should talk to that young man on his own very soon.'

'I'm sure it will come back to you, Nicholas. But let's keep an open mind when it comes to the Archdeacon. Tell me about the others.'

'The Chancellor, Edward Hasledean, seems a straightforward sort of man. I talked to him in the cathedral library. He resented the fact that Bishop Thomas didn't seem to appreciate his work and passed him over when it came to rewards. He resents the Archdeacon for owning a carriage, for instance, and resents the Precentor receiving the prebend of Ferring whilst he had not been given any prebends. But these things don't constitute a strong enough motive to kill one's superior. Also he didn't seem to have any real dislike of Bishop Thomas and in fact thought the Bishop would have approved of him taking a wife, which is what he's thinking of doing. I think it was no more

156

than the grumblings of someone who's held a post for a number of years without receiving what he considers adequate reward for his labours.'

'I met the Chancellor when I was at the Deanery. He came to drink a glass of wine with us later in the evening when you were down in Pelham Maris. We got on well. He's going to let me look at some of the cathedral manuscripts. Apparently all the contents of our priory's library were removed to the cathedral library and he's having to catalogue them.'

'Beware of elderly clerics, Jane; they can seduce you with their manuscripts.'

'Now who's being frivolous? Is that the end of the cathedral Canons?'

'No, we've left out the chief suspect and a disgruntled organist.'

'Adam Wright? What on earth's he done?'

'Nothing, I hope. Only he challenges the Precentor and disliked Bishop Thomas's modern views on church music.'

'Seems like a typical musician. They all fall out with one another; but they usually stop at murder. But who's this chief suspect, Nicholas? And why didn't you tell me about him before?'

'Because he's vanished. The Bishop was in the middle of examining the accounts when he was murdered, and Edwin Stanley, that's his name, the cathedral Treasurer, was forgotten in the general confusion. Apparently he embezzled some of the money which should have been paid into the cathedral treasury and he ran off as soon as he realised he was going to be found out. God knows where he's gone. Probably out of the country by now.'

'What good would it have done him to murder the Bishop before he left? Others would know of his crimes sooner or later. He couldn't murder them all.'

'Maybe, he, like the Chancellor, resented the fact that Bishop Thomas hadn't rewarded him sufficiently and, out of revenge, he could have paid others to do his dirty work for him after he left.'

'But would he have instructed them to remove the Bishop's heart? That's the stumbling block in this affair. To murder someone out of resentment, revenge, fear of being discredited, I suppose I can just understand, but not that awful vindictive act of cutting into someone's body and removing his heart.'

Nicholas stared at Jane in horror. 'It seems we have a deadly brew seething away inside the hallowed walls of our cathedral. I'd best get back there straight away and talk to the Dean and take another look at these unholy Canons.'

Suddenly there was a commotion outside in

the courtyard. The noise of horses' hooves on cobblestones, the slithering sound of a horse being reined in sharply, a shout, a banging of doors and finally the entrance of Nicholas's steward, Geoffrey Lowe.

'My lord,' he said, struggling to get his breath. 'The Earl's here and wants to see you urgently.'

'Then don't leave him standing around in the cold; bring him in.'

Geoffrey rushed off. 'It's Southampton,' said Nicholas, turning to Jane. 'He always has this effect on Geoffrey. I wonder what he wants. It's not the sort of weather to pay a social call without prior warning.'

The door opened and Sir Ralph Paget, Earl of Southampton, came in. He and Nicholas were old friends. A bluff, vigorous man in his middle years, he had been created Admiral of the Fleet by King Henry and rewarded with monastic lands in Hampshire through services to the crown. A soldier through and through, he was dressed in clothes suitable for hard riding in cold weather. He strode across to the fire, his wet, short-cropped hair plastered down on his head, his leather riding boots gleaming with rainwater, his jerkin spattered with mud and the sweat of his horse. He shook Nicholas's hand vigorously and bowed to Jane, raising her outstretched hand to his lips.

'Forgive me intruding on you like this, Nicholas, but I've come from the Court, staying last night with Fitzroy at Arundel. The King's heard about the shocking murder of Bishop Thomas and he wants the culprit or culprits caught and brought to justice without delay. He liked the Bishop, whom he met here at your house, I believe, and found the manner of his death very disturbing. Then Fitzroy was brought the news that a foreign ship was deliberately enticed into an unsuitable harbour at the wrong state of the tide and all who sailed on her were murdered and the ship's cargo stolen. Fitzroy's very concerned, Nicholas, and he, too, wants the perpetrators rounded up. I'm to take him a full report of what action is being taken. He wants these coastal waters cleaned up. There have been too many similar incidents lately. We shall get the reputation that our channel ports harbour dens of pirates worse than the infidel corsairs who swarm along the Barbary Coast of Africa, to the detriment of our national wealth. The King, I am sure, will also be incensed when he hears about it. God damn it, Nicholas, foreign ships will be too scared to trade with us and will take their trade elsewhere. Fitzroy threatens to call out the militia if this gang is not rounded up soon. Law and order must be restored as quickly as possible otherwise the county will appear to be sliding into anarchy. And the King will take it upon himself to come down here – to the great inconvenience of us all. Thank you, Master Lowe,' he added as Geoffrey handed him a tankard of mulled wine. 'Just what's needed. It's not the weather to be riding round the countryside and I'm needed back in Portsmouth. The King, it appears, is expecting to find the castle completed when he comes down next month. He's thinking of staying with you, Nicholas. He's taken a liking to "Peverell's hunting lodge" and he wants to hear Mistress Jane, as he calls you, madam, singing her delightful songs. He misses you both,' he said, drinking down the wine and holding out his tankard for more.

'Now let's have it, Nicholas,' he continued, turning round to face the fire having toasted his back sufficiently. 'Tell me what you and Landstock are doing and we can go from there.'

'The Sheriff's down in Pelham Maris, Ralph, tracking down the wreckers. For the moment he's pushed the Bishop's death to the back of his mind, but it's in the forefront of mine. Jane and I were just going through the possible list of suspects when you came in. Yes, don't look so surprised, I've married a clever wife and we need her calm appraisal of the situation. I am just leaving for Marchester to see if the Sheriff's come back yet, and then I must go to Selsey to talk to a

161

rector. It's a God-forsaken place but I have to check on someone's story. You may rest assured that we've not given up on the job, but a murder investigation can be a lengthy business and there are too many people who could have wanted the Bishop out of the way, but none with a strong enough motive to justify an arrest. However, there is one way you can help us if you've a mind to, that is; otherwise it's going to be up to me to be in three places at once.'

'I'm pleased to be of any assistance; that's why I'm here, Nicholas.'

'One of the suspects, the cathedral Treasurer, Edwin Stanley by name, has disappeared. It appears that just before Bishop Thomas was murdered, Stanley was found to have embezzled money destined for the cathedral coffers. He's got his own carriage, and took his household goods with him. We must find him; even if it's only to eliminate him from the list of suspects. Now, he's hardly likely to have gone aground round here. He has manors in Wiltshire and we shall have to alert the Sheriff of Winchester to start a search for him. I think he might have left the country and the obvious port for him to make for would be Portsmouth. And that's your territory, Ralph. Could you make some enquiries for us? Find out if he left the country during last week, and what ship he sailed on. And you could also find out, whilst you're at it, what ships the port authorities of Marchester were expecting last week and whether any didn't arrive. It would help us if you got the names of the ships and asked them to send someone over to see if he can identify the body of one of the seamen who wasn't washed out to sea with the rest of the crew. The Sheriff's holding on to him for the time being, but we'll have to bury the poor devil soon.'

'I'll get started right away,' said Southampton, putting his tankard down. 'What does this fellow, Edwin Stanley, look like? Any distinguishing marks?'

'We'll have to ask the Dean. I've never met the Treasurer.'

'Right, I'll see the Dean. Are you off to Marchester, now, Nicholas? To check up on Landstock?'

'And I could come along with you to Marchester and I could talk to the Dean,' said Jane sweetly.

'You'll do no such thing,' said Nicholas sharply. 'I would prefer it if you stayed here. Anyway, you can't keep staying at the Dean's house and I have no idea when I shall return.'

'I could take Balthazar with me.'

'That Italian fop? A lot of use he'd be if you're attacked by robbers.'

'We'd be riding in daylight over a distance of four miles, Nicholas. What could possibly happen to me? You do exaggerate.'

'And you, madam, must learn to obey your husband,' said Southampton, turning round to face her. 'Didn't you promise that not so long ago in the chapel at Hampton Court? I was there, remember?'

'So you were, my lord, but things are different now. Nicholas needs the subtleties of the female mind to apply to the investigative process.'

'That's not a woman's job,' said Southampton, gruffly.

'Oh yes, my lord. We are as subtle as the serpent, remember?'

'And I'm glad you're not my wife. God damn it, madam, you should take a lesson or two from my wife. I hardly ever see her these days. She keeps to the house and manages it to perfection and is happy as a lark in spring. I go about my business; she does hers. We're a perfect team.'

'And I look forward to making her acquaintance one of these days – if she's allowed out of the house, that is. But won't you take some refreshment before you set off?' said Jane demurely. 'Let it not be said that Lord Nicholas's wife neglects her house-wifely duties in order to gallivant around the countryside with her music master.'

Monday morning in Pelham Maris and every barn and house had been searched and nothing unusual had been found. Everyone, it seemed, had been asleep in his lawful bed on Saturday night, wives accounting for their husbands and grandparents for the others in the household. And now he'd been told to watch the priest's house. Peter silently cursed the Sheriff and his job. Too much waiting and watching in freezing weather; too little action; too much disappointment. One good thing, though, he thought, the weather had turned milder. It wasn't so numbingly cold, but with the warmer weather came a new hazard: fog, which had come rolling in from the sea, across the mudflats, curling round the hovels of the people of Pelham Maris, muffling all sounds as if a veil had been dropped over the countryside.

Crouching behind a thick yew tree which had stood there in the churchyard since before the Christian missionaries landed along the coast at Selsey, Peter decided he might just as well go back to the Dog and Hare and warm himself with a jug of ale, but he knew the Sheriff would be waiting for him and expecting a report. And nothing had happened nor was likely to happen in that fog. He couldn't even confirm that the priest was still in his house, as it was impossible to see anything in those conditions and the priest could quite easily have left by a rear entrance. There was nothing for it, he'd have to stay where he was until the fog had thickened to such an extent that even the Sheriff could see that it was useless to keep watch any longer.

A movement from behind him made him jump. He peered round, trying to make sense of the shapes around him partly obscured by the fog. Then a twig snapped and he knew someone was near.

'Who are you?' he called out. 'Come and show yourself.'

'I'd rather not be seen,' said a voice which Peter recognised even though it was muffled, probably by a cloth over the person's mouth.

'I'll not speak to a voice. Give me your name.'

'No name. I dare not. Is there still a reward?'

'There might be.'

'How much?'

'Three sovereigns if the information is any good to us.'

'It'll take you to the wreckers.'

Despite the clumsy attempt to disguise his voice, Peter knew who was there. He had been trained to watch and listen and file away impressions and information in his head. Especially a person's voice. That never changed, even if the rest of the person's body had been mutilated or broken by torture. This soft, wheedling voice which could turn into a plaintive whine, a strong local accent, a voice full of cunning. Untrustworthy, like

166

the man: Amos Higges.

'Tell me what you know and be gone.'

'Show us the three sovereigns.'

Peter took a leather pouch out of his breeches' pocket and tipped out the three coins on a nearby tree stump. Then he stood up and put one hand over the coins.

'The money's there. You'll have to trust me.'

'I'll trust you. You'd not cheat on me. You're the Sheriff's man, aren't you? The one I saw before?'

'I am and you should be up at the Dog and Hare now with the Sheriff giving him this information and he'll pay you the reward.'

'I can't risk it. You know what they'll do to me if they find out I've informed on them.'

Peter did know. Informants had a short expectation of life. Unless they were lucky and took the money and left the vicinity quickly they would be set upon by the other members of the gang and killed in unspeakable ways as a warning to other would-be informants.

'Tell me what you know first, then take the money. And leave immediately. Where will you go?'

'I'll hole up somewhere until the fog lifts and then make for Portsmouth. I'll be safe there.'

'Right, let's go. Tell me what you know.'

'Have you searched everywhere?'

'We have.'

'Including Aylwin's house?'

'That was searched first.'

'Underground as well?'

'We searched the cellar, yes.'

'Look again. Outside in the yard there's a trapdoor under the straw. It's the entrance to a tunnel. One bit of it goes north to higher ground outside the village, where Aylwin owns a barn. The other bit of the tunnel goes to the priest's house, but that's not used much as it's too wet. There's nothing there now.'

Of course, thought Peter, there was no time to distribute the cargo but plenty of time to shift it out of sight along a tunnel.

'Why are you doing this? You know it's dangerous. These three gold sovereigns could be the death of you.'

'They'll not catch me. This money will set me up fine. Besides, they cheated on me. They didn't pay me enough last time, and this time Aylwin threw me out of his house just because I helped myself to a dram from one of the casks, and he caught me at it. Oh, the taste of the Rhenish wine! I'll dream about it until the end of my days.'

'Pretty poor treatment, I'd say, seeing as how you helped them by sending us off in the wrong direction.'

'They don't think of that. They don't like

me, see, and always give me the dirty jobs. But now I'm rid of them and can set up my own business.'

'Then take your money and go.'

Peter drew back his hand and watched the slight figure of Amos Higges dart forward and seize the money. Peter shivered. In this place and in this fog, Higges looked like one of the dwarfs that country folk still talked about on winter nights round the fire. One of the little people who used to inhabit these marshes; a hobgoblin who tormented humans and stole their cattle and their children. Then he vanished and the place was quiet again with the dead quiet which only fog can induce. Still, he was uneasy. Had someone been watching them? He pulled himself together and ran back up the Street to the Dog and Hare where the Sheriff and his men were waiting to hear his news.

It was soon all over. Roger Aylwin's house was searched again, the tunnel located, and an underground room, capacious and tailor-made for the purpose, was discovered, with bales of cloth stacked up to the ceiling and casks of wine lining the walls. Roger Aylwin, a farmer of moderate wealth, was arrested. The tunnel to the priest's house was located but there were no signs that anyone had recently walked along its marshy floor. The stone-lined walls were dripping with moisture, very unsuitable for storing bales of cloth, and the tunnel stank of marsh vegetation and decay.

Roger Aylwin was taken away to Marchester and despite threats of interrogation, refused to name his accomplices. As darkness fell, the Sheriff began to feel satisfied with the day's work. But it wasn't over yet. Aylwin would soon name names; they always did under his interrogation, and then he'd have to return, with the militia, if necessary, and flush out the wreckers. Only then would these shores be safe to foreign shipping.

With the coming of darkness, Amos Higges set off for Marchester. There was only one road leading north out of the village and Higges took to the ditches and hedges which ran along the side of it. He made good progress. Being small and nimble, and crouching low, he was hardly higher than the hedges which protected him. He wanted to get as close to Marchester as he could that night. Then he could hide in a barn and wait for the first light, when he could cover the last mile quickly and lose himself in the back streets of Marchester.

After two hours of creeping along the hedgerows, he saw the spire of a church ahead of him with a barn standing in the field next to it. He knew the place. Woodhurst. A tiny hamlet with only a handful of inhabitants. With luck, the barn would be full of autumn produce and maybe some cattle would be wintering there. He could feast on apples and hazel nuts and drink fresh milk. Then on to Marchester and the taverns. He slipped his hand in the pocket of his breeches and felt the three sovereigns. They would buy him safety and blissful oblivion for as long as he pleased.

He left the cover of the hawthorn bushes and ran the few yards to the barn. Three men emerged from behind an oak tree and formed a semi-circle in front of Higges. He stopped, tried to run back but the men closed in and one grabbed him.

'Got you, Amos Higges,' said one of the men. 'You didn't think we knew what you've done. But we saw you, you bloody traitor, you and the Sheriff's man. May you rot in hell. You'll not tell on us again – not in this life, anyway, and I shouldn't think God'll want you in the next.'

Terrified, Amos Higges screamed for mercy. 'I've done nothing, I swear it. I helped you, didn't I? You only got the ship through me. I got nothing.'

The man picked up Higges as if he were a sack of corn, and swung him upside down so that his head was only inches from the ground and his short legs kicked helplessly in the air. The three coins fell out of his

171

pocket onto the ground and one of the men pounced on them.

'So, they paid you well for your trouble, I see. Traitor's gold, that's what we call it. And by God we'll show you what we do to traitors. Shut that noise,' he said as Higges was begging for mercy, 'you'll frighten the cows.'

Then they dragged Higges into the barn by his hair and threw him face down on the floor, watched by a row of cows impassively chewing the cud. They began to beat him remorselessly with cudgels which they'd brought along with them for the purpose, until his screams turned to whimpers. Then they threw down their cudgels and began to kick him with their heavy seaboots until all sounds ceased and he lay still. With a final kick to his head, they stopped to pause for breath. Finally, they dragged him outside and tied a rope round his neck. One of the men threw the other end of the rope over a branch of the oak tree and pulled until the tiny, battered body of Amos Higges was hoisted aloft and hung there like a sack of turnips.

'Cut off his balls,' said one of the men drawing a knife from his belt.

'Slice open his belly,' said another.

'Leave him to the crows,' said the ringleader, the one who had seized hold of Higges in the first place. 'He's gone straight to hell and worse things are waiting for him there. Meanwhile, we've got three sovereigns, and no one knows we've got them; and Marchester's only an hour away. There's no hurry. They'll not find him till daylight when they come to milk the cows.'

Ten

By Monday afternoon, the fog which had blanketed the coastal parishes had drifted northwards to the Downs. Southampton, who had enjoyed a hearty dinner at Nicholas's manor, decided against leaving for Portsmouth that day and suggested a musical entertainment and an inspection of Nicholas's stables and cellars. It was late before the household retired to bed but Nicholas couldn't sleep. He fretted about the slowness of the investigation. He knew that, in a case of murder, unless the scent was picked up quickly, the more difficult it was to be certain that the right person had been arrested. And he, as presiding magistrate, could only pronounce judgement if the evidence against the accused was incontrovertible. He knew that the Sheriff, with his impetuous nature, would arrest anyone on the flimsiest evidence, but for him the proof would have to be blindingly obvious before he sentenced a man to death.

Jane stirred uneasily beside him. He knew she shared his anxieties and he wanted the case over with and their peace of mind restored. Why couldn't he just leave it to the

Sheriff and settle back into the life of a country gentleman? Surely he had done all that was expected of him. He'd asked Southampton for his help and in time an arrest would be made. Why didn't he just take the easy way? Give up. Wait for the next Quarter Sessions and deal with the Sheriff's suspect in the appropriate way. That was his job, not this persistent ferreting out of information that might be useful or might be totally irrelevant. Eventually, he came to the conclusion that he might as well give up, and he tried to compose himself for sleep.

But one thought would not go away. Bishop Thomas had been his friend. He had been his Prior when there had been a community of monks not a mile away from his house. The Peverells had always been patrons of that priory ever since the Normans built it four hundred years ago. Patron and prior had always worked together for the benefit of the parish. And more than that, Bishop Thomas had always been intricately involved in his own affairs. He'd been there at his wedding, celebrated with him afterwards, and would no doubt have baptised his first born when that time came. He could not let Bishop Thomas's wicked murder go unavenged. He owed it to him to see that his murderer was brought to justice. And the truth was he didn't trust the Sheriff to arrest the right man. That person

175

could only be found, not by impulsive action, but by a dogged sifting through the facts and following every lead, however improbable it seemed. Like his hounds he had to keep his nose to the scent and never give up.

Just before dawn, he drifted off to sleep but was awake again after a couple of hours. Leaving Jane to finish her rest, he dressed and went downstairs where, to his surprise, he found Southampton eating and drinking a hearty breakfast. He looked refreshed and ready for action and got up to greet Nicholas with a cordial slap on the back.

'I hope you slept well, Nicholas. An excellent evening. A fine musician, your wife, and I quite like that Italian fellow of hers. I hope he's not going to give you any trouble. However, it's time we thought of making a start. The wind's got up in the night – did you hear it? – and the fog's dispersed. Much better that we waited and had a good night's sleep. No point in groping our way round the county. I've ordered the horses to be brought round in an hour. I hope that suits you, Nicholas.'

'It suits me very well. I'm glad you've made yourself at home, Ralph.'

'What did you expect? After all, we're friends, aren't we? Now here comes that steward of yours. Eat heartily as we have a long day ahead of us and little prospect of dinner until nightfall.'

Jane appeared just as they were setting off and seemed put out that no one had woken her. Nicholas kissed her and mounted his horse.

'Rest yourself, my love, and I'll be back as soon as I can. I have a lot of travelling to do and might be late but occupy yourself with writing some more songs and perhaps you would tell Mary to make some more of that apple jelly. We have plenty of apples in store. It will go well with our young spring pork.'

Jane curtseyed. 'I will see that everything is in order when you return, my lord. God go with you both.'

Nicholas looked at her sharply, suspecting sarcasm; but she smiled so demurely that he suppressed the thought and, with a cheerful wave, set off for Marchester.

They parted company on the outskirts of the town, Nicholas turning north into the centre and Southampton continuing westward towards the cathedral where he was to see the Dean. Nicholas made his way to the Sheriff's house, situated near the newly-built market cross and handed his horse over to the Sheriff's ostlers. Then he went into the Sheriff's office and pushed his way through the mob of people.

'Ah, there you are, my lord,' bellowed the Sheriff across the roar of conversation. 'I'm indeed glad to see you. Have you caught the Bishop's murderer yet? No? I thought not. You're barking up the wrong tree, you know. Now come over here and listen to what I've got to report.'

Nicholas made his way over to where the Sheriff was sitting at a table, a map of the coastal region in front of him.

'We've caught the leader of the gang of wreckers. Roger Aylwin. Calls himself lord of the manor of Pelham Maris. A fine tale! He's a thief and a murderer, my lord. God knows how many crimes he's guilty of. I've put him in solitary confinement for the time being. If he doesn't cooperate when we question him again we'll string him up on the irons. But he's bound to talk soon as he knows what's coming to him if he doesn't. No light, no food, no air; he'll soon break. Then we can clean up that area. But give us your news, my lord. Any progress with those fat cathedral cats?'

'Very little. Just suspicions. I'm still keeping an open mind, but I'm on my way to talk to the Dean now and then on to Selsey to speak to the Rector. I'll be back to see you later in the day when I've finished my business. But tell me, how did you get on to Aylwin?'

'Oh, the usual way. Money always works. Peter Ironside met up with his informant who pointed him in the right direction. It

178

cost us three sovereigns. A bit expensive but it was worth it. We've found enough evidence to send Aylwin to the gallows but we want him to give us the names of the other villains. We can't bring in the whole damn parish. I've got my eye on the priest, by the way. We've found a tunnel linking Aylwin's house with the vicarage cellar; nothing in it at the moment unfortunately, but the cellar under Aylwin's barn was stuffed full of the ship's cargo. Now who knows what the vicarage cellar's been used for in the past? I can't trust him so I'd better have him watched. Yes, John, what is it?'

A man had entered the room and was pushing his way through the crowd to get to the Sheriff. He was dishevelled and mud-spattered and judging by the expression on his face, he looked as if he'd just encountered the devil himself.

'We've found Higges, sir. Hanging from a tree, he was, outside a barn in Woodhurst. Beaten black and blue, poor devil.'

Peter, who was warming himself by the fire, looked up. 'I knew it. It happens to most informants. I don't know why they take the risk.'

'Money, Peter,' said the Sheriff briskly, 'that's why they do it. And they always hope to get away with it, but very few do. But don't waste your sympathy on Higges. He tricked us, remember. He was one of the wreckers. There's no blame on us that he turned King's evidence. Now, my lord, you'll take some refreshment?'

'Thanks, then I must be on my way.'

'We shall want you to be here, tomorrow, my lord,' the Sheriff said, nodding to one of the servants to bring Nicholas a tankard of ale. 'I propose to interrogate Aylwin and we might have to use stronger methods of persuasion. That'll break him.'

'If you don't kill him first,' said Nicholas accepting the tankard and drinking deeply.

'I'll see we treat him gently. Good luck with your questioning, my lord. I think our methods produce quicker results.'

'But my way ensures we don't arrest the wrong person. By the way, Southampton's in town, Sheriff. He's going to be useful. He's promised to call on the port authorities in Marchester and see if they can identify that ship and the member of the crew we picked up. You've got his body here, I presume?'

'Yes, we can hold on to him for a day or two as long as this cold weather lasts. Then we'll give him a Christian burial. Soon these troubles will be behind us, my lord.'

'I hope so, but clearing up wreckers is one thing, finding a murderer is an entirely different matter. Southampton's going to start hunting for an Edwin Stanley, former Treasurer of the cathedral, who's absconded with the funds. I doubt if he's the culprit, but we must leave no stone unturned.'

'That's the way, my lord. Bring him in. Keep talking. Someone out there's telling a pack of lies.'

'And I wish you could tell me who that person is, Sheriff.'

Once again Nicholas entered the cathedral and made his way to the sacristy, where a gleam of light was coming from under the door. Once again he was aware that someone was watching him, but he could see no one when he looked round. Then, suddenly, he felt a strange frisson of fear, a feeling of dread that an unknown assailant was watching him and waiting for the opportunity to strike. Maybe, he thought, it was simply the result of a restless night or the eerie atmosphere in the cathedral – the semi-darkness, the cloying smell of incense – which made his heart beat faster and his stomach churn sickeningly. Then the door of the sacristy opened and the brisk figure of the Dean emerged, quickly dispelling his unease.

'Someone there? Oh it's you, Lord Nicholas. You're very welcome. I've just had the Earl here asking questions about Edwin. Thank God he's going to try and find him. He wanted a description – a bit awkward, that; I never took a lot of notice of him. But fortunately I remembered that he's got a wen on the side of his face; he's had it since birth apparently, and he can't disguise that even if he does change his clothes and travels around in an ox cart instead of a carriage. But what can I do for you, Lord Nicholas?'

'With your permission, Dean, I'd like to talk to Hugh Brotherhood. I have to check up on something that bothers me. It shouldn't take long.'

'Then you'd better talk to the Archdeacon. He purloined that young man after the Bishop died. And talk of the devil, here he comes. Archdeacon, come over here a minute. Lord Nicholas wants to speak to you.'

The black-cassocked figure of the Archdeacon emerged out of the shadows as if on cue, and for a moment Nicholas wondered whether he was the one who had been watching him.

'Again?' said Jeremy Overton, coming up to join them. 'You treat us like suspects, my lord. Do you think your murderer resides here in the cathedral amongst us?'

'I keep an open mind, Archdeacon,' said Nicholas looking once again into the blood-shot eyes and breathing in the strange smell of badly-digested food and the personal sharp acidic odour which seemed to characterise the man. He looked like someone who had been so long closeted up in this atmosphere of incense and candle grease that he'd forgotten what fresh air was like.

'Everyone is suspect until we make an arrest,' Nicholas continued, stifling his dislike of the man. 'At the moment I'm simply looking for answers to my questions. I would like to talk to your clerk, if that's convenient, Archdeacon.'

'I'm sure I could answer any questions you might have in mind, my lord.'

'I would prefer to speak to Hugh on his own, if the Dean agrees.'

'Oh go ahead, my lord. Anything we can do to help is fine by me. We all want this devil caught, although I can't quite see what Hugh Brotherhood has got to do with it. Where do you keep that young man, Archdeacon?'

'I'm sorry to have to report that he's gone away for the time being. He received a message from a friend of his family about his mother, who lives in Winchester. Apparently she's seriously ill and not expected to live long. She was asking to see her son before she died. I could scarcely refuse such a request.'

'When did he leave?' said Nicholas suddenly on the alert.

'On Saturday, before the funeral. I lent him one of my horses as he had a long way to travel.'

'Do you have more than one horse, Archdeacon?'

'Certainly. I have an extra horse for just such an occasion as this.'

Was it his imagination, or was the Archdeacon beginning to look uncomfortable?

'And you keep this horse in your stable along with your carriage and your other horse?'

'Certainly, and if you consult my groom as you did on Friday last he would confirm this. So there's no need for you to pay him another visit.'

'That's for me to decide, Archdeacon. But it was good of you to lend the young man one of your own horses.'

'He has no horse of his own, my lord. Our faith expects us to be charitable.'

'You should have consulted me first,' broke in the Dean impatiently. 'Damn it, man, first you purloin the late Bishop's clerk and now you send him away to Winchester without telling me. I must insist, Archdeacon, that in future you take no further actions without consulting me.'

'And I insist that no one leaves these cathedral precincts until the Sheriff and I say so,' said Nicholas. 'Don't you realise what you've done? I needed that young man for questioning. He could be an important witness. You allowed him to leave these precincts without telling anyone. That could make you a suspect, Archdeacon.'

'I'm sorry, my lord. I thought I was showing compassion on an unfortunate young man who is just about to lose his mother.'

'But we are in the middle of a murder enquiry, just in case you've forgotten that, and in future, Christian duty or not, I must insist that none of you – and that includes your servants – leave these precincts. I leave it to you, Dean, to make the necessary arrangements. Now we've got to go to the trouble of finding Brotherhood. You say his mother lives in Winchester? Then we shall have to send someone to Winchester and retrieve that young man. You can see the inconvenience you've caused us, Archdeacon?'

'And I'll not have my authority flouted,' said the Dean, his face flushing in anger. 'I'll not be swept aside like this. Now tell us the address of Hugh's mother so at least Lord Nicholas can send someone straight away to bring him back.'

'I'm afraid I don't know where she lives, Mister Dean. He's only worked for me for less than a week and I didn't enquire into his family details. The late Bishop might have noted his parents' address, but I doubt it. He came from a priory of Canons at Hardham, as you know. That was enough for Bishop Thomas, who always acted on instinct when it came to choosing his servants, and in Hugh's case he liked him well enough without bothering to check on his credentials.'

'It shouldn't be too difficult to trace him,' said Nicholas impatiently. 'There can't be too many people of the name of Brotherhood living in Winchester. But it's going to hold us up. I need to speak to that young man urgently and, until I do, a necessary part of the investigation won't fall into place. Meanwhile, Archdeacon, am I right in thinking that you are responsible for the parish priests in the diocese?'

'That is one of my responsibilities, yes.'

'Then you might tell me what you know about William Tremayne, Rector, I believe, of Selsey.'

The Archdeacon looked at Nicholas in surprise. 'What an extraordinary thing to ask, my lord. Your enquiries take you along some very strange paths.'

'We have to check on every detail.'

'How very conscientious of you, but since you ask, yes, of course I know William Tremayne, a very devout young man, a dedicated parish priest. I cannot say a bad word about him. For someone who lives in the most inaccessible part of the diocese, he does very well. Why should you need to speak to him? Surely you don't think he has anything to do with Bishop Thomas's death? It's a difficult journey down there at the best of times, and now it will be especially unpleasant. That's why William didn't attend the Bishop's funeral, and neither did I expect him to; there are reported to be footpads about. Why don't you tell me what you want to know and I am sure I can help you.'

For a second, Nicholas was tempted to take the Archdeacon into his confidence, but something made him hold back. It wasn't wise to trust anyone at this stage; especially someone who gave leave of absence to a person who might possibly turn out to be a key witness.

'Thank you, but I have to speak to the Rector myself. Meanwhile we must start the search for your clerk. I hope that you have understood what I have just said. No one must leave the cathedral precincts until I, or the Sheriff says so. That must be taken as an order, Dean, in my capacity as Justice of the Peace. If you disobey we shall have to put you under arrest.'

'I understand, my lord, and I'll do my best to see that your orders are complied with. And as for you, Archdeacon,' said the Dean quietly, 'I want you to come with me to the Deanery now. I am not happy at the way you conduct yourself. May I remind you that you are only an Archdeacon and consequently subject to the authority of the cathedral dignitaries.'

As Nicholas walked back to the Sheriff's house to collect his horse, Harry, and give the Sheriff instructions to send someone to search for Brotherhood, he thought bitterly how too many people were disappearing. They would have to tighten the net if they were to make an arrest in the near future.

The road to Selsey took him across flat pasture land intersected by streams, now full to overflowing, and dotted with trees twisted into grotesque shapes by the strong prevailing wind. On either side of the deeply rutted road were ditches full of running water bordered by thick hazel hedges. The fog had disappeared but the temperature had dropped and the keen east wind lashed his face and numbed his fingers even though they were encased in thick leather gauntlets. Above him was the immense grey sky, the sun hidden by lowering clouds full of rain. It was a scene of utter desolation. Not a human being in sight. He felt as if he was riding into unknown territory where what living creatures there were existed in holes dug into the soft, loamy soil, too ugly, too shy to face the light of day. Harry, too, felt his unease and took to shying at every bundle of twigs by the wayside. As they rode south the wind deposited a layer of salt on his lips and Nicholas knew they had not far to go. He thought of the wintry sea dashing against the shingle beach at the tip of the peninsula gradually wearing away the surrounding fields and nibbling at the gardens of the inhabitants. Already the sea had broken through to form the harbour of Pelham Maris which was on the eastern side of Selsey Bill and was doing its best to wear away the western side. Now Selsey was an island at high tide, inaccessible except by a ferry. At low water it could be approached by two fords. But on the whole the people of Selsey seldom travelled far. They preferred to stay close to the sea which gave them their livelihood and the marshes which they knew like the back of their hands. They formed a tightly-knit community, living together, marrying close relations and worshipping together in the Saxon church built by the early missionaries who had been sent by Rome to convert them.

As Nicholas approached the island the fields on either side gave way to marshes and the road became a causeway which the same missionaries had built to open up communications with the outside world. Now he passed several tumble-down houses, mere shacks, offering scant protection from the fierce winds that blew along the coast. Nicholas thought of his own prosperous village of Dean Peverell nestling at the foot of the Downs, where many of the cottages were built of stone with slate roofs and the inhabitants were well-fed and independently minded, and he felt sorry for these unfortunate people trying to wrest a living from the sea and the desolate marsh lands.

He passed the tiny hamlet of Norton where once there had stood a cathedral which served the southern part of the county before the Normans had transferred the site to Marchester. Now all that remained was the dilapidated chancel standing at the edge of the marsh, a forlorn relic of a once much grander building.

He arrived at the channel which separated the island from the mainland, and found the tide was out. He paused before crossing over. Again he experienced that feeling of dread which had come over him in the cathedral. Above him, two seagulls swooped and soared, screeching out what sounded like an awful warning. Harry, too, was showing all the signs of not wanting to go any further. He, too, sensed the desolation around him and could hear the distant pounding of the sea on the gravel banks just off-shore, a sound full of menace, which conjured up images in Nicholas's mind of ships running aground and breaking up under the force of the sea.

Then common sense prevailed. He was only going to check out someone's account of his whereabouts. He could leave as quickly as he came and be back in his own manor before dark. He urged Harry across the ford. Once on the island, though, Harry refused to go any further and reluctantly Nicholas had to use his whip. Then, as if he were being asked to walk across hot coals, Harry pranced his way along the narrow track to the village and the church, whose small, pointed spire was now visible. When he reached the first of the hovels, the rain, which had been threatening to fall all day, came sheeting down, slashing against his face with icy blows. With flattened ears and snorts of disapproval Harry continued and with obvious relief turned into the yard of a small house next to the church.

Nicholas dismounted and banged loudly on the door. It opened and a man dressed in a black cassock stood there. He was not as Nicholas expected. He looked quite young, in his twenties, Nicholas thought, with a round, peasant face, close-cropped hair and pale eyes which looked warily at horse and rider. Nicholas introduced himself and asked for stabling for Harry. The man pointed to a nearby shed.

'You'll find room in there for him and some hay. Help yourself. He'll be all right in there; it's dry.'

Nicholas led Harry away and made him comfortable. He returned to the house, where the priest was still standing in the doorway.

'Come in, sir. A bad day for riding round the countryside. What brings you here?'

'I need some answers to a few questions, that's all. I won't trouble you long.'

'Then come in. Will you take some refreshment? I've bread and cheese and ale.'

'Thank you, Priest, I'm most grateful to you.'

They went in to the main room, which was warm and comfortable. A sturdy, wooden table, laid up for one person with a wooden platter and a pewter mug, stood in the centre of the room. There was a chair on either side of the log fire and a woollen rug covered the floor between them. A large wooden crucifix, reaching up almost to the ceiling, stood on the ledge over the fireplace. A truckle bed was tucked away in the far corner of the room. A candle glowed brightly on a small table by one of the fireside chairs. Outside, the wind lashed against the thick, oak door and the noise of the sea was a reminder that all this comfort could soon be dashed away by the sea only to join the other houses which had been submerged over the centuries. But at that moment all was peaceful. The candlelight caused shadows to dance on the white-washed walls of the cottage and the room was filled with the sweet smell of burning driftwood. Nicholas took off his cloak, shook off the rainwater, and draped it over one of the chairs by the fire. He accepted the mug of ale which the priest handed him.

'You seem very comfortable here, Priest. You are William Tremayne, I take it?'

'That is my name.'

'How long have you been in charge of this parish?'

'Six years, sir.'

'Are you content to be here?'

'It's where I've been called to serve. Someone must look after these poor souls.'

'You sound resigned to it.'

'Then I must ask forgiveness. I have all I want for my needs, as you see. My parishioners look after me. Poor as they are they bring me fish and whatever they can spare. In the summer this place is very different. The boats can go out and the sea provides for all our needs. You see it at its worst today.'

'Do you have many visitors?'

'Very few, sir. The priest from Pelham Maris comes to see me when he can. He's my nearest neighbour and I'm grateful to him. His is a much more prosperous living and his tithes are far more that I could ever contemplate. He was here recently.'

'When was that?'

'He came to join us in evening prayer last Sunday. It was Candlemas, you see. He left on Friday, if I remember rightly.'

'Then you were both here when news came of the Bishop's death?'

'Yes, the carrier from Marchester told us.

193

A terrible day for us all. I understand he was murdered, sir?'

'Yes, there is no doubt about that. His body was found in your neighbour's parish.'

'A dreadful thing to happen. Richard must be deeply shocked.'

'He returned to even more terrible events. A ship ran aground in the harbour and the crew was despatched by a band of thieves. The Sheriff is confident he will find them soon. You knew nothing of this, Priest?'

William Tremayne shook his head. Despite his stolid appearance, Nicholas could see he was not relaxed. There was a tenseness about the set of his shoulders and he gripped the handle of his tankard so tightly that his knuckle bones shone white in the candle-light. He obviously wanted Nicholas to go but was aware of his duty to provide hospitality to a traveller in bad weather. Nicholas finished his ale and accepted a refill.

'Sir, I know nothing of these evil things. In this winter weather I stay inside my house as much as possible and only go out to attend to the church services and visit my parishioners, who are, as is always in February, prone to sickness. Our graveyard fills up in February. I baptised a child on Saturday and he died just a few hours later. That's what it's like round here. We shall gather our strength when the spring comes and we look forward to the May Day celebrations. What happens in the outside world means very little to us. Of course we were all shocked by the Bishop's death and I am sorry that his body was discovered in Richard's parish. As for the ship, I'm sorry for her crew and I shall pray for their souls at evening service today. That's all I can do.'

'I can see you must appreciate a visit from Richard Rushe. You must be very lonely here. How did you pass the time when he came to stay with you?'

'We are good friends, sir, and comfortable with one another. We took the services together and visited the parishioners. We talked together in the evenings. Simple things but they bring us much comfort. You see, Richard knew my parents. They come from over his way and he's my only contact with them. They are both dead now.'

'I'm sorry. How long have they been dead?'

'It must be seven years now; time passes very quickly. I went away to train as a priest in Marchester; it was what my parents wanted me to do and all I could do as I was left in poor circumstances.'

Nicholas could see the priest was distressed and he felt it was churlish to probe into his past life. He began to think that his coming here had been a waste of time. Why did he doubt Richard Rushe's story – an old man who had known William Tremayne's

195

father and mother and wanted to make sure that his friend and colleague was in good health in a difficult time of the year when sickness was abroad and death stalked the hovels of the poor. What reason was there for mistrusting him? However, he'd come a long way to talk to William Tremayne and he decided to ask one more question before he left the priest in peace.

'Did you know the late Bishop very well?'

'Hardly, sir. I live in one of the most remote parishes in the diocese and he hadn't been long in office. I was much looking forward to meeting him at Pentecost.'

'You didn't attend his funeral, then?'

'No, sir. My duty was here with my parishioners.'

'Did you approve of his appointment?'

'It's not my business to approve or disapprove. He was my bishop. I obey his instructions.'

Nicholas finished his ale and accepted a slice of bread and a morsel of cheese and took it over to the fire. He wished the priest would come and join him but the man wouldn't relax but hovered around him like a servant anxious to grant his every whim. This obsequiousness grated on Nicholas, who liked a certain independence of mind in those around him. When he finished his food the priest removed the plate and took it over to the table. Nicholas sensed that he was anxious for him to go, and indeed there seemed little reason to stay longer. He reached for his cloak.

'Well I must be on my way, Priest. Thank you for your hospitality. I wish you well and trust that this sickness amongst your parishioners soon goes away. You must grow weary of funerals.'

'Indeed, this is a time of much sorrow. I have to leave now and get the holy oils from the church and take them to a dying man. I hope I am not too late.'

'Then God go with you. But I see this house is well protected.' Nicholas nodded towards the crucifix over the fire.

'Indeed, He looks after us even unto death. A safe journey, my lord.'

Nicholas followed the priest to the door. The wind was blowing a gale now and the sound of the sea was like a continuous ground base to their activities. Nicholas stood for a moment fastening his cloak.

'A bad night for sailors, Priest.'

'No one will go out tonight. No fish have been caught for several days what with the fog and now this gale. My poor people, how they suffer.'

'But you bring them the consolations of the church.'

'I do my best to try to keep the powers of darkness at bay.'

'A pity you weren't there when the Bishop

departed from this life.'

Leaving the priest to go into the church to collect the holy oils, Nicholas went to find Harry and wrench him away from the comforts of the shed. This time Harry needed no urging. He covered the eight miles back to Dean Peverell in record time.

Eleven

Jane watched Nicholas and the Earl of Southampton disappear through the main gate. She envied them their freedom. She also envied their total absorption in their work. Geoffrey Lowe came up to her.

'Will you take breakfast in your boudoir, madam? There's a good fire of apple wood burning there and it's very cosy. This cold air will do you no good.'

For a moment she felt a surge of rebellion. Why did they all want to cosset her? She wanted to say, Not this morning, Geoffrey. Tell Tom to get Melissa ready for me – Tom being her own personal groom – but she dismissed the thought; her action would only cause consternation amongst the servants. No, she thought, her work was here, making the manor house of Dean Peverell comfortable for its owner, her husband whom she had chosen and promised to honour and obey as long as he lived.

'Thank you, Geoffrey,' she said, 'and after breakfast, tell Mary that I will see her in the kitchen.'

Geoffrey bowed and went into the house, Jane following. She went into her boudoir, which was indeed snug on the February morning, but even after eating newly-baked bread spread with butter from their own cows and honey from their hives she could not settle down. She felt angry with herself. How could she dare to be discontented when she had everything a woman could desire – a beautiful house to organise, servants anxious to please her, a devoted husband whom she loved and wanted to please. She had all the clothes she could desire, jewels, her own musician and complete freedom to order books and furniture from the best merchants in the land. Yet still she was not content. Maybe it was the enforced inactivity due to being confined inside the house in bad weather, she decided, jumping to her feet. The solution was to immerse herself in suitable work.

Putting on a practical linen apron over her morning gown, she went into the kitchen where her cook, Mary, was already at work making brawn and a great pork pie for when Nicholas returned. She glanced up at Jane and suggested she could make the apple jelly.

The morning passed pleasantly enough and the pots of apple jelly stood in a tidy row on the pantry shelves. She ordered soup to be sent to the cowherd's wife who was laid up with a fever and unable to cook for her husband and brood of small children.

She'd only recently been to see her father and daren't fuss over him any more as he was safely ensconced in the clutches of his sister, Jane's aunt. At midday she ate a meal of cold ham and spiced pear chutney with Mary and gave orders to the maids to polish the great oak dining table in the hall. She noticed how they looked at one another with a resigned look on their faces, and she realised that she was getting in everybody's way. They knew what work they had to do. Mary had told them. They wanted her back in her boudoir suitably occupied with her embroidery. That decided her. She removed her apron, much to Mary's relief, and gave orders for Melissa to be saddled and brought round to the front door. Geoffrey's jaw dropped.

'You'll not be thinking of riding out on your own, madam?' he said.

'And why not, may I ask?'

'Because it's not seemly.'

'That's nonsense. Before I was married I rode everywhere on my own. Why should I not do so now? Besides, I only intend to ride to Marchester, a distance, as you know, of only four miles.'

'But Lord Nicholas expressly gave orders that I was to look after you at all times. How can I do that if you leave the house on your own?'

'I shall deal with Lord Nicholas, Geoffrey.

I am not yet an invalid who must be cossetted at all times. Now I am going to change my dress and you must go and get me Melissa.'

Looking distinctly worried, Geoffrey went to do as she asked. Mary looked up from her pastry making.

'You'll take care, madam, won't you? You'll find things change when you marry someone like Lord Nicholas. There's many around in the countryside this moment who would cut your throat for those riding boots of yours, let alone your horse, a beauty if ever there was one.'

'No one could outstrip Melissa when I give her her head. We outride all the others when we hunt the fox.'

'Aye, so I've heard. But footpads are up to all sorts of tricks and have no respect for persons of rank.'

Jane was about to issue a sharp reprimand but could see the anxiety in Mary's face and knew she meant well. 'Don't worry about me, Mary. I'll go carefully and will be back with Lord Nicholas in time to enjoy that pie of yours.'

'You should be resting, madam,' Mary grumbled, giving the ball of pastry a great swipe with her clenched fist. 'Lord Nicholas won't like you riding forth like a maid.'

'Then I'll see he changes his mind. He married a robust country lass, remember, not a delicate lady of quality.'

'Aye, but you're still his wife, madam. Best not forget that.'

Half an hour later, Jane set off for Marchester, riding Melissa fast over the country footpaths and setting her to jump the gates and hedges in their way to make sure she had not lost any of her spirit. But Melissa had not changed and took each obstacle in her stride, flying over the hedgerows as easily as if they were fallen logs. On the outskirts of Marchester, she reined her in and rode sedately through the main streets to the Dean's house where Katharine Catchpole, the Dean's wife, and their daughter, Philippa, welcomed her effusively.

'What a wonderful surprise. You are just what we need on such a bleak afternoon. Tell your servant to take the horses round to our stables. You'll be staying a while, I hope?'

'I haven't got a servant, Katharine. I rode here on my own.'

Katharine's matronly face crumpled into a look of horror.

'You rode all that way on your own? My dear, what will Lord Nicholas say when he hears about this?'

'Why should he be concerned? I've ridden on my own ever since I was a child. The countryside is deserted. I didn't see a single person on my way here, not until I reached Marchester, that is.'

'Even so, it's dangerous to be out on your own. There are too many disorderly people around with nowhere to go now that the monasteries have been closed. How will you get home?'

'The same way I came. Melissa is quite capable of covering eight miles, especially as she will have had a rest in your excellent stables. Don't worry about me, Katharine. Why does everyone worry about me?'

'Because you are disobedient and impulsive, my dear. But that is the way God made you, and we shall just have to keep an eye on you. But the problem is going to be that I can't let you borrow one of my servants to escort you home as your husband has forbidden any of us to leave the cathedral precincts.'

'Nicholas? He's been here today?'

'Not to the Deanery but he spoke to the Dean in the cathedral. But now you're here, let us enjoy one another's company and we can see about getting you home when the time comes. I was just going to take a cordial over to one of the old women whom the Sheriff has deposited in the bishop's jail. She's not well – a terrible cough and fever – and I feel it's my duty to relieve her sufferings if I can. But I can always go later. Come and talk to Philippa.'

'Don't let me stop you from doing your charitable work, Katharine. In fact, let me come with you. I am anxious to see these witches, as the Sheriff calls them. I, too, feel sorry for them being dragged away from their homes and locked away in a prison. Has he got any evidence that they were engaged in the black arts?'

Katharine smiled. 'He's not actually seen them riding around on broomsticks, but rumour has it that the one who's ill, her name is Agatha Trimble, puts curses on people and animals. And that's good enough for Sheriff Landstock. He wants them put under lock and key whilst the investigation is under way, though what connection they could possibly have with the death of our Bishop I fail to see. I don't think you should come with me, Jane. The Bishop's jail, although better than the town jail, is still no place for a lady. And I don't like to think of what might happen to you if you breath in the noxious vapours of the cells. It's a cold and damp place, very unwholesome, and Lord Nicholas would disapprove strongly of your going.'

'There you go again. First, it appears that Lord Nicholas disapproves of me riding on my own, and now it seems that he won't want me to visit some unfortunate woman needing compassion. Also, if I might express an opinion, I think that a cold, damp cell is not a suitable place for a sick, old woman – whether she's a witch or a saint.'

'I've seen to it that she's got a good fire burning in her room. That's one of the things I must see to; the jailer's not much interested in keeping his prisoners comfortable.'

'Then I'll come with you and protect you from their curses. Nicholas can't object to me protecting you from the evil eye.'

'Well then, we'll protect each other. And then we'll come back here and eat cakes and listen to Philippa's musical efforts.'

The Bishop's jail was a small, low building made out of the local flint stone and situated near the Bishop's palace within the confines of the cathedral precincts. The arched doorway encased a solid oak door studded with iron nails. Tiny windows, mere slits in the wall, were placed on either side of the doorway, letting in the minimum light and air which was considered necessary for the survival of the prisoners. Katharine pulled the bell rope and its clanging summoned the jailer, a small wizened figure whose slight body seemed scarcely strong enough to support the bunch of keys hanging from the belt round his waist. He knew Katharine and opened the door wide to let them in. Inside was a small hall where a fire burned at the far end, and a table and two chairs were the only furniture. Standing by the fire was the tallest woman Jane had ever seen, whose head almost reached the low, vaulted ceiling. With massive shoulders and body built like a wrestler's she looked as if she had drained the unfortunate jailer of all his bodily strength. Her moon face was pleasant enough until she opened her mouth to speak, and then an ugly row of protruding, decaying teeth was revealed. Her dark hair was smoothed down beneath a white cap and her dress, made of cream, woollen cloth, was clean and respectable.

'How is Mistress Trimble, Beatrice?' asked Katharine, putting down her basket of provisions.

'Poorly, madam,' said the giantess, bending her body into an ungainly curtsey. 'She's taken to her bed, which is the right thing to do in this weather. If she's any sense she'll stay there till she recovers. She's grateful for the blanket you sent her, Mistress Catchpole.'

'I'm glad of that. I've brought her some quince jelly to ease her cough. How are the other two?'

'Well enough. Old Phoebe's wandering in her mind and can't tell whether it's morning or night. Jenny Dobbs is as cheeky as ever. I can't think why the Sheriff inflicted her on us. Witch or no witch we want her out of here. Come along now, Aldred,' she said looking at the jailer, 'take the ladies to see

Mistress Trimble. Don't get too close to her, madam,' she said, looking at Jane, 'you don't want her to give you the evil eye. She might have taken to her bed but that doesn't mean that her evil powers have lessened. Once a witch fixes you with her stare no good will come your way for many a moon's waxing and waning.'

The jailer, Aldred, led the way through a small door at the far side of the hall and they entered a low passage dimly lit by the light coming in from the far end. There was a row of doors along the passage and from one of these came the sound of someone singing. It was not an unpleasant sound, thought Jane, but there was a wildness about it that showed that the singer had never been near a music teacher.

'Jenny's up to her tricks again,' muttered Beatrice, ushering them along the passage to the end door. 'Mistress Trimble's in here. We keep them separate,' she said by way of explanation to Jane, 'so that they can't contaminate each other. Usually for ordinary prisoners we shove them together down there in the cellar, but these are no ordinary prisoners and who knows what spells they'll hatch up if we put them in together? Enough of that noise,' she called back down the passage, 'we've got two ladies coming to see Mistress Trimble on a charitable mission and they don't want to listen to your bellowing.'

A coarse, cheerful laugh greeted this remark and for a moment, Jane felt a certain curiosity to see the owner of that voice. But Beatrice had arrived at the door of Mistress Trimble's cell and the opportunity was gone.

'Don't keep on at her, Beatrice,' said Aldred, who was trailing along behind them. 'It keeps her spirits up and that'll stop her falling ill and giving us more trouble.'

'Don't you go soft on her, husband,' said Beatrice turning round to glare at him. 'I know how she looks at you with those big, black witch's eyes and you go all weak at the knees. Men,' she said, raising her eyes to heaven, 'they're all the same. Show them a woman with a bit of a shape to her and a lustful gaze and they'll give them anything they ask for. Now, let us in to see Mistress Trimble, husband, and stop thinking about Jenny Dobbs.'

Aldred opened the door of the cell and they went in. In the dim light coming from a slit window way up near the ceiling, Jane saw a figure lying on a narrow bed at one side of the cell. Going closer she could see that the figure was a woman, her hair concealed by a woollen cap, a woollen scarf covering her shoulders, and the rest of her covered by a warm blanket. A small fire burned at the far end of the room and although the room was gloomy and airless, it was at least warm.

'Here's Mistress Catchpole come to see you, Agatha, and another lady of quality's come with her. You're a lucky old witch, aren't you? Look, she's brought you honey and some quince jelly for your cough. Sit up now, and say your thanks.'

The old lady struggled to sit up and Katharine arranged the pillow behind her head. The movement caused her to break out into a paroxysm of coughing which was soothed by the sweet cordial Katharine held to her lips.

'Keep the fire going,' Katharine said to Beatrice. 'I'll give you the money to pay for the wood. Keep warm and drink the cordial and you'll soon be better, Mistress Trimble, and if all goes well, you should soon be out of here.'

'Thank you, madam,' said the old woman sinking back onto the pillow. 'I'm grateful to you.'

'Well, you certainly look better than you did when I came to see you yesterday. You'll need to keep your strength up when it comes to the trial.'

'When will that be, madam?' said the old woman anxiously.

'We don't know yet. If a bishop is not appointed soon, then the Archdeacon will have to preside.' said Katharine.

'Not him, mistress. Not that old goat.'

'Enough of that. Show some respect to your betters,' said Beatrice, aiming a swipe at the old woman's legs.

'If my betters is Mistress Catchpole, then I'll show her all the respect in the world. But that old goat of an Archdeacon stinks of the devil and I don't want him near me.'

'It's not for you to say who'll try you,' said Beatrice, dumping the pot of honey on the table by the bed. 'You spoil her, Mistress Catchpole. See what happens when the sickness begins to go away, they start saying who they'll see or not see.'

'It's good to see you on the way back to health, Mistress Trimble. Now look after her, you two,' Katharine said, looking at them severely. 'Remember no one's guilty until proven. Treat those entrusted to your care properly and God will treat you properly.'

They left the old woman's cell and walked back along the passage to the hall. The singing had started again, a song of the country folk, Jane noted, a lovely, lilting song about a man and a maid in spring time. She asked if she could see the other two prisoners but Beatrice seemed reluctant. Old Phoebe'd like a bit of company, Beatrice admitted, but she was too confused to hold a proper conversation. As for Jenny Dobbs, best to leave her alone. She'd only start ranting and raving and making eyes at Beatrice's husband, Aldred. He grinned and

211

led them back to the hall where they left a jug of ale for the jailer and his wife and walked back to the Deanery.

'So much for our Sheriff's witches,' said Jane. 'One's a sick old woman, one sings lovely old songs and the third doesn't know where she is or who she is. I hope he lets them go home soon. There's no point in keeping them here.'

Cakes made of butter, eggs and honey were waiting for them when they went into Katharine's room in the Deanery. They drank mulled wine laced with spices and Jane began to think it was time she took her leave and made her way back to Dean Peverell. But she was enjoying the company of Katharine and Philippa, who wanted her to go over to the cathedral library to look at a Book of Hours which the Chancellor had shown her the day before.

'It's beautiful, Jane, and the pictures are exciting. It's very old, you know, painted by the monks. Why don't we go across and see if the Chancellor's there.'

'Another time, Philippa,' said Jane, very much wanting to see the book. 'It's too late in the day, now.'

But Philippa was insistent and said they needn't stay long so Jane gave in and together they walked across to the cathedral and up the stairs to the library where Edward Hasledean, the cathedral Chancellor, was sitting at a table, surrounded by rolls of parchments. In one corner of the room sat a young man, a priest, who was obviously Edward's assistant. He was a slightly-built man, absorbed in his work, and didn't even look up when they went in.

Edward Hasledean, on the other hand, was delighted to see them. His large face creased into a smile and his tired eyes twinkled with pleasure.

'Jane – I can call you Jane, can't I? – how good to see you and you, little wench,' he said turning to smile at Philippa, 'have you come to distract us again? What do you want from me now?'

'Jane wants to see the Book of Hours, Edward; that is,' she said, suddenly remembering her manners, 'if you can spare us the time. The pictures were so exciting and the colours so brilliant that I can't get them out of my mind and I do want Jane to see them because I know she'll love them, too.'

Jane smiled ruefully at the Chancellor. 'I'm sorry to interrupt your work, Edward. You seem very busy. Perhaps you could just show us where you keep the book and we can look after ourselves.'

'Nonsense. No trouble at all. Anything's better than going through these accounts of the former monastic foundations in Sussex. Here, let me get the book for you. You must take it over to the light and take as long as you like over it. It's good to see these beautiful things appreciated, though I suspect Philippa really wants to take another look at all those baby devils.'

'They are such fun, Jane. You wait till you see their long, curly tails.'

The Chancellor got up and went over to a cupboard on the other side of the room. He opened the heavy door and took out a slim, beautifully bound book and handed it to Jane.

'Here it is. One of the Priors gave it to us when his priory was closed down. It was written about a hundred years ago. Obviously, as you shall see, one of his monks must have been a very talented artist. Come, sit over here, and you can look at it in peace.'

Jane placed the book carefully on the table and sat down on one of the chairs, indicating to Philippa to bring her chair close to her own. The book was a book of devotions, familiar prayers and psalms, written in Latin in a beautiful cursive script. But it was the illustrations that made her exclaim with pleasure. The initial letter of each piece of text was outlined in gold leaf and decorated with angelic beings wearing gold halos, but it was in decorating the margins of each page that the artist had allowed himself the greatest freedom. Here were little people from all levels of society playing musical instruments, small boys playing on pipes, an old man with a wicked grin on his face beating on a small drum and children dancing everywhere, up and down the margins. In the corners of the page were angels, large and small, playing harps, and cavorting, along with the humans, all round the sacred text. Jane was enchanted. Turning the pages of fine vellum, she came across a chorus of grinning skeletons, their bony mouths open wide as they sang the psalm written on the page. Philippa was beside herself with glee and got up and began to dance round the library playing an imaginary pipe like the children in the book until Jane had to check her as even the clerk had raised his head from his work and was looking severely at them.

At the top of the last page of the book there was a picture of God, surrounded by angels, sitting in judgement. At the bottom of the page, however, the wicked were being hurled down onto a desolate plain where hordes of small devils with long tails and evil faces seized hold of them and carried them off in triumph to the fires of hell, the flames of which could be seen flaring out of several deep pits. The theme was serious, but the artist's interpretation was so cheerful and his devils so entertainingly drawn that Jane could only sit back and laugh in pleasure.

'What a wonderful book, Edward,' she

said, 'what amazing talent this artist had. If only he had painted some large pictures which we could hang on our walls to cheer us up in midwinter.'

'I'm glad you like the book, Jane, and I would love to give it you as a present, but, unfortunately, it's not mine to give. It was meant for a lady, though; a lady like you, for her private devotions. But there are many other books which you would enjoy and you are welcome to come here any time you like. It's not often that we enjoy the company of young ladies, is it, Hubert?' Edward said, looking across at the clerk.

'No, indeed, Chancellor. It's been an unexpected pleasure having them here this afternoon.'

The young man permitted himself a mere ghost of a smile, then, pursing his lips primly, he bowed his head over the manuscript he was reading.

'I'd love to come again,' Jane said. 'Perhaps I can be of some help to you in your work. At least I can read some of these documents,' and she pointed to the piles of parchment rolls heaped around on the floor. 'I could write a brief summary of the contents which might be of some use to you as, at least, you'll know what's in the roll before you start on it.'

'Why, thank you, Jane, that would be immensely useful. I take it you are familiar with Latin texts.'

'Oh yes, my father saw to it that I had a thorough training. He was very indulgent and I had my own tutor.'

'Then come any time you like. Hubert will look after you if I'm not here. This pile might interest you,' he said, pointing to a heap of parchment rolls by the side of his desk. 'I intend to start on them next. These are your own priory's records. Bishop Thomas had them all sent here when the priory was closed down. They are mostly records of rents collected, and benefactions made, by people living in the twenty-six parishes in Sussex who had the Prior of Dean Peverell as overlord. They cover a period of about two hundred years, as far as I can tell, so there is plenty of work to do in sorting them and cataloguing their contents. I think it might make interesting reading for you.'

Suddenly, Jane realised that the room had become very dark. Daylight was fading fast. She thanked the Chancellor for his kindness and hurried back to the Deanery, where Katharine insisted she stayed to dinner. Thinking of the ride home, Jane declined, but her objections were over-ruled by the Dean, who wouldn't hear of her riding back alone in the dark and he wasn't allowed to send one of his servants to accompany her. Lord Nicholas, he said, would never forgive him if anything happened to Jane on her way home.

Feeling distinctly guilty, but enjoying the hospitality all the same, Jane went with the Dean and his family into the great hall where a log fire was burning cheerfully and the smell of the mulled wine and spiced meat made her mouth water. She had only just sat down when there was the sound of angry voices raised at the far end of the room. Looking up, she saw Nicholas standing there, dressed in his riding clothes and dripping water everywhere. He looked furious.

'So, madam,' he shouted, 'you disobey my orders and come running to your cathedral friends the minute my back is turned. Are you aware of the trouble you've caused? I returned home after a hard ride only to find Geoffrey and the servants frantic with worry because you hadn't returned from Marchester. I guessed you were here and had to come looking for you. Now, please go immediately to collect your cloak, order your horse to be made ready, and we'll leave for home straight away. Come, madam, make haste and say your thanks to the Dean and his family for putting up with your whims and fancies. I must apologise, Mistress Catchpole,' he said, striding up to the table, 'for my wayward wife. She has not yet been trained in her housewifely duties. I'll make sure she doesn't trouble you again.'

Katharine got up and came over to Nicholas, whose face was dark with anger. She took him by the arm and led him gently over to the fire.

'My lord, don't be angry. Jane is always a welcome guest here. It was our fault she stayed so late and we couldn't let her travel alone in this bad weather and without a servant. She wanted to go back and was prepared to risk the journey but we insisted she stayed here. Please stay with us and at least dry your clothes. And won't you accept a tankard of this mulled wine? It will warm you up before you make the return journey.'

Reluctantly, Nicholas took the tankard of wine and felt the warmth return to his body. Then, less reluctantly, he allowed himself to be led to a place at the table where he ate heartily of the Dean's excellent fare. And, later that night, he and Jane went up to one of the Dean's guest rooms and settled down comfortably in a great bed with a soft mattress and curtains round it to keep out the cold.

Twelve

On Wednesday morning Nicholas and Jane ate breakfast alone in the Dean's guest room. Although Nicholas's anger at her insubordination had been dissipated by the close proximity of sharing a bed, the atmosphere was frigid. Mentally they were not in harmony even if their bodies were. Ever tactful, Katharine had given orders that they were not to be interrupted until after breakfast. Nicholas was first to break the silence.

'Promise me, Jane that what you did yesterday will not happen again.'

'What do you mean? Am I never to visit my friends in Marchester?'

'You must take a servant with you and always be back by nightfall.'

'Am I a child to be ordered about in this manner?'

'Sometimes I feel I married a child, a wayward one at that.'

'And was I wayward when I put on boy's clothes and came to help you when you were captive in Porchester castle?'

'It was an irresponsible act which fortunately turned out well. You also had Simon to escort you.'

'And who do you suggest should escort me in future? Balthazar?'

'Rubbish. You couldn't let him loose on a donkey, let alone a horse. Besides, you'd not see him for dust once trouble arrived. I shall have to speak to Geoffrey. If necessary, I shall take on another groom to look after you.'

'You never showed this concern when I rode out alone before I married you,' said Jane, helping herself to the compote of stewed figs and apricots steeped in honey.

'You weren't my wife then.'

'And now I suppose I am your treasured possession?'

'Certainly. You are a Peverell and will be, God willing, the mother of my future children.'

'And has it not occurred to you that I am also a person, Jane Warrener, trained to think and have her own interests? It seems to me, Nicholas, that you would prefer me to be like a Moslem woman, enclosed in a harem.'

'I think it's a pity if education leads you into irresponsible behaviour, that's all. Please consult me in future if you wish to pay calls on your friends in the county.'

Inwardly seething with resentment, but realising that assertiveness would get her nowhere, Jane resorted to guile. She had

221

learned at Court how all men were susceptible to flattery.

'It would be a pity, though, to give up my visits here, Nicholas,' she said demurely. 'I have just made the acquaintance of the Chancellor, who showed me not only an exquisite Book of Hours, but also some of the contents of our priory library. It seems that Bishop Thomas deposited all our records in the cathedral library and the Chancellor said he would be glad of my assistance in cataloguing them. Surely you could not object to me doing some research into the archives of our own priory. After all, our family has been patrons of the priory since the coming of the Normans.'

Nicholas looked at her sharply but saw no challenge in her demeanour; just pride in being a member of his family.

'Very well, Jane, I shall be interested to hear what you might discover. The former priors held manors all over the county and it will be interesting to find out what came of them after the priories were closed down. The tithes paid to our priory must have been considerable. I suppose now they are paid to the cathedral. I doubt if the incumbents of the parishes have benefited. I believe that the parishes on the coast were subject to the priors' authority. I must remember to ask William Tremayne about the details of his living when I next pay him a visit.'

'William Tremayne?'

'Yes, he's the Rector of Selsey, poor fellow. A Godforsaken place if ever there was one.'

'Why did you have to see him?'

'Because of Richard Landstock's pre-occupation with witches and wreckers. I don't happen to think that either the Vicar of Pelham Maris or the Rector of Selsey has anything to do with either activity, but we have to go down all roads. Richard Rushe, the Vicar of Pelham Maris, knew Tremayne's family and is still friendly with him. It seems unlikely that they plot together how to lure ships into shallow waters on a falling tide or murder the Bishop of Marchester, but we must make sure of their innocence. Things are not always as they seem. Richard Rushe, for instance, appears a kindly sort of person, a bit fond of the pleasures of the table but no harm in that, yet the Sheriff's men have found a tunnel leading from Rushe's house to the local lord of the manor's house. They found nothing in Rushe's tunnel, but Roger Aylwin, the lord of the manor, has been brought in for questioning as his cellars were full of the wrecked ship's cargo. Maybe, in the past, previous vicars were guilty of aiding and abetting the wreckers; maybe, even, Richard Rushe has been guilty of receiving illicit cargo in the past and this time he was just lucky. We have to keep open minds, Jane. Everyone is suspect until the evidence for a person's guilt stares you in the face. But now I ought to go and see Landstock and find out what he's learned from Aylwin.

'There's a lot going on, Jane,' said Nicholas getting up from the table, 'and I think I'll ask the Dean if we can use his house as a base whilst the investigation proceeds. It would be convenient not to have to return to Dean Peverell every night. That would also please you, Jane, wouldn't it? You could enjoy yourself with the Priory records and I could work more closely with Landstock. We're also expecting Southampton soon. He's finding out more about the ship which the wreckers lured in the harbour of Pelham Maris. He's also sent one of his own men to Portsmouth to check on all people leaving the port last week. He's trying to track down the cathedral Treasurer, Edwin Stanley, who recently absconded with cathedral funds. We need to find him. He could be a suspect in the murder case either directly or indirectly.'

Jane nodded. 'As you say, Nicholas, a lot going on. Maybe I could be of use to you in some way. I know I shall be enjoying myself, as you so pleasantly put it, researching into our archives, but I might be able to investigate anything you haven't got time to check on yourself. By the way, I've already seen one of the Sheriff's witches and I can't think why he brought her and the other two unfortunate women in. I can truthfully say that if he thinks the motive for the Bishop's death is witchcraft, then that poor soul I saw has nothing to do with it. She can barely keep herself alive let alone get involved in killing anyone else. But I am sure there will be other suspects brought in which I could talk to and maybe learn something.'

'If you think I shall agree to your consorting with every aged crone whom the Sheriff has taken a dislike to, Jane, then you have made a mistake. You forget that not only are you my wife, but I also love you and would be desolate if anything happened to you. Besides, it would not be proper for me to allow you to interfere with the Sheriff's investigation. There is also the real risk of you falling sick. Many people are ill at this time of the year and I won't have you exposing yourself to the foul vapours of pestilence.'

'Nicholas, you are now becoming pompous. You forget I helped nurse the sick in our village for years, and I still do. My father has been subject to fevers and rheums ever since I can remember.'

'Nevertheless, I must insist that you stay away from these pestilential villages along our benighted coast. Stay here in Marchester, by all means, if that is your wish, and pursue any enquiries you wish to make from the safety of the Dean's house and the cathedral library. Now, I must talk to the Dean and then visit the Sheriff. I shall expect to find you here when I return. At least I can now contact you should I be delayed. Now promise me, Jane, that you will not leave the cathedral precincts unless I am with you.'

'Yes, my lord; as always, I am your obedient servant.'

'Indeed you are not. You are my rebellious wife, but I love your spirit and would not have you changed.'

'And you are my pompous husband whom I happen to love and always will.'

She stood up and Nicholas took her in his arms and held her close. No, he would not have her any different. She would always be wilful but there would never be another woman like her.

Nicholas knew something was up as soon as he went into the Sheriff's house. The men, who were clustered round the fire, averted their eyes as he came up to join them. No one said good morning; no one offered him a drink; no one pushed forward a chair.

'What's the matter?' he said.

'Best if Sheriff tells you,' muttered one of the men.

At that moment, Sheriff Landstock came in. He seemed to have diminished, Nicholas thought. He'd lost his usual brisk demeanour and he looked dejected, like a man who had just suffered a severe setback.

'What is it?' said Nicholas, suddenly alarmed.

'It's Aylwin. God damn the fellow who was in charge of him.'

'Aylwin? What in heaven's name has he done?'

'Only gone and hanged himself, that's all. It's incredible how he did it. Tore up his shirt and tied it into strips. Used his belt – yes, his good, strong leather belt which my fool of a jailer didn't think of taking from him. Can you believe it? Shoved him into the cell, closed the door, and that was that. I gave orders for him to be left alone in his cell hoping he'd give us more information before we had to resort to the irons. I've no stomach for torture and hoped the cold and the dark and no food or water would persuade him to talk. But no. He makes himself a rope, uses the stool I allow for prisoners out of charity, and he strings himself up on a beam and kicks away the stool. A terrible sight to see first thing in the morning, my lord. We're not used to suicides here. Usually, the suspects are only too pleased to talk long before the irons are mentioned. But this one decided to end it all. This is a great blow, my lord. Now we'll never know the names of his confederates.

First Higges gets silenced, and now Aylwin's silenced himself. I'd not have thought it of him.'

'Nor I, Richard. Why should he want to hasten his own death? I know his guilt was obvious. You said you found the contents of the ship's hold in his cellars, but why should he want to compound his crimes by killing himself? He must have known suicide's a mortal sin. Now he stands condemned to hell. May God have mercy on his soul.'

'Amen,' said the men round the fire, and one or two of them crossed themselves in the old way.

'I'm not too bothered about his immortal soul, my lord; that's God's business. But why did he do it? Who, or what was he afraid of?'

'He was afraid of what he might say under torture; even though it was only the mild torture of the manacles.'

'I agree with you. But for God's sake, he was going to die anyway – not straight away, but as soon as you'd sentenced him at the next Sessions. It would be a clean death up on the Heath with a priest standing by to give him absolution. Why hasten his death and put his soul in jeopardy?'

'Because he didn't want to confess to what he knew.'

'But why? He had nothing to lose. He knew he was going to die anyway. And now he's taken the information we want with him. We are wading into ever-deepening waters, my lord. Soon we shall be out of our depth and drowning unless we clear this mess up quickly.'

The Sheriff sank down onto a chair and accepted a tankard of ale from one of the men.

'We should return to the marshes, Richard,' said Nicholas. 'We must find out who were Aylwin's associates. This time we'll talk to everyone however unlikely he seems. And I must talk to Rushe. If anyone should know what's going on in a place it's the vicar; unless he, himself, is involved in the wickedness.'

Landstock looked up at Nicholas, who saw hope return to the Sheriff's face.

'Indeed we should, my lord. I think you and I are reaching the same conclusion, incredible as it may seem. I think Aylwin killed himself because he feared one or more of his associates in this affair. He was frightened of what they would do to him, not in this world, but in the next. If he told us who they are, they could put a powerful curse on him that would ensure for him a life of eternal torment in the hereafter. The fool didn't realise that God, in any case, would condemn him for taking his own life. My lord, he feared someone in our midst more than he feared God. A terrible thought.

Someone out there wields incredible super-natural power. Mark that, my lads,' he said turning to look at the group of men round the fire, who were staring at him with terror-struck faces. 'I told you this was not a straightforward case, didn't I? Wreckers, witches, murderers, they are all in this together. A hideous brew of wickedness, my lord. This is a case of the Devil going about his business; and someone's going to have to stop him.'

'And that means you and I, Richard, because no one else is going to stand up to him.'

The Sheriff drained his tankard of ale and stood up, his old energy returning at the prospect of action. Suddenly the door opened and a man, cold and mud-spattered, came in and introduced himself as a messenger from the Earl of Southampton.

'The Earl's gone on to Portsmouth,' he said as he made his way over to the fire, the men making room for him. 'He's instructed me to say that the port authorities of Marchester will be here soon to take away the body of the seaman you found in the harbour, Sheriff. They think they may know him. You see, a ship from Antwerp was expected to arrive in Marchester last Saturday but didn't arrive. They thought she might have turned back or gone on to another port, which they thought was a bit

230

odd because the ship, the *Flandria*, was one of their regulars and they knew the captain and his crew. If she had been running late and had been lured into Pelham Maris by false lights, she could be the ship you found. They want you to put a guard on it until they send someone over. They also wanted to know why you didn't find out the name yourselves. It was painted on the stern in gold leaf; very distinctive, they said.'

'And one of the first things to be ripped off,' said the Sheriff.

'And probably hidden in someone's barn or house,' said Nicholas. 'Find the board with the name of the ship on it and we've found another wrecker, Sheriff.'

'You're right. And this time we'll force them to speak before they go and kill themselves. Come, get the man some ale,' he said to one of his men. Then, turning to the messenger, he said, 'You bring good news. The best we've had over the last week.'

It was still bitterly cold but a pale sunshine gave a hint of the spring to come. Arriving at Pelham Maris, Sheriff Landstock and Nicholas rode straight down to the harbour jetty where the hull of the wrecked boat could still be seen resting on a mudbank. By the side of the boat two figures, dressed in dark woollen jackets with the hoods pulled over their faces as protection from the biting wind, were ripping off the planking from the side of the ship. They worked quickly. Already the ribs of the ship were exposed and a pile of planks on the muddy foreshore bore witness to their industry. The Sheriff's face flushed in anger as he turned to look at Nicholas.

'Look at the buggers, my lord. Like vultures picking over the carcass, they are. I hope the harbour master gets his guards down here quickly or else there'll be nothing left to salvage. You two,' he bellowed, 'get back here right now. Don't try to run away; the place is surrounded.'

This wasn't strictly true but two of the Sheriff's men appeared from behind the bushes as if on cue and that was all that was needed. Flinging down the planks of wood they had torn off the ship, the two men waded through the liquid mud to the shore.

'We're not wreckers,' one of them mumbled when they were brought to the Sheriff. He was a small, wiry man, his face weather-worn and twisted into an expression of bitter resignation. 'We're salvaging what's left of the ship and there's no harm in that, is there? If we don't, someone else will. First come, first served is our motto – the poor people round here, that is. Job here and me is short of fuel at this time of the year. You wouldn't want to see our families perish with the cold, would you? Not when good wood is sitting out here on the mud only waiting to be collected. You're Christian men, aren't you?'

'It's against the law, and you know it,' said the Sheriff. 'Now get along with you both. We'll have to search your homes and then talk to you further.'

'Search as much as you like,' said the man called Job. He was older than the other with bent back and short legs twisted by rheumatism. 'You'll find nothing in my house because I have nothing. You can't object to me having a bit of wood to make a cradle for the new babe now, can you?'

'It's not up to me to object,' said the Sheriff. 'It's against the law and my job is to enforce the law. When the ship breaks up, which it will soon in the spring gales, and the wood comes ashore then it becomes driftwood and you can send your families down to the shore to collect it. But meanwhile until that happens, the ship stays out there until the Marchester authorities come and look at it. Take them away,' he said to his men, 'search their houses and yards and don't let them get away. I'll have them brought to Marchester later along with others who disobey the law. I'll interview them there.'

Loudly protesting their innocence, the two were led away. The Sheriff turned to Nicholas.

'At least we've caught two red-handed; a good start, I think. Are you coming with us, my lord?'

'Later. I want to see Walter, my bailiff. I can't believe that he lives in this small place and knows nothing about what goes on here. Besides, I want to get one of my servants over here to keep him company. We need fresh eyes and ears around here, Richard.'

'You're right, my lord. Block up the holes, send down the ferrets, we'll soon flush out the lot – wreckers, witches, murderers. We meet later, then, at the Dog and Hare.'

Nicholas rode swiftly along the path by the edge of the marsh which led to his hunting lodge. It seemed scarcely possible that only last week their peaceful lives had been shattered by the discovery of the Bishop's body in the pool. And still they were no further forward in finding his murderer. He had to admit, he thought ruefully, that the Sheriff had been remarkably active in filling Marchester's jails with possible suspects; but not necessarily for the murder of Bishop Thomas. There were three old women in the Bishop's jail, and no doubt by nightfall the town jail would be filled with suspect wreckers. There was also one suicide to be taken into consideration. And one man hanged by his former confederates. Almost certainly that was an act of revenge. But what, in fact, did all this add up to? That there was a lot of wickedness taking place along the southern coast of the county? That went without saying. But there was nothing new in luring ships into unsafe waters; that had always gone on. Desperate people resorted to desperate measures. And Aylwin's suicide? What did this tell them? That he was a desperate man, who knew that he would have to swing for his crime, yet he preferred to hasten his death by his own means rather than risk confessing under torture to what he knew. Who was he so terrified of? More terrified of this person and what he could do to him than Almighty God? He shivered and urged Harry forward. He suddenly felt helpless, faced by the powers of darkness which threatened to engulf him. He must keep a clear head and an open mind if he was going to discover the source of this evil.

Old Walter, too, seemed terrified when he saw Nicholas ride into the yard of the lodge. He was chopping wood for kindling and stopped when Nicholas rode up and made a futile effort to hide the pile of wood under a bale of straw.

'So you, too, Walter, want to strip the ship bare of its timbers. I wouldn't have thought that anyone employed by me would stoop to robbery.'

'The wood was given to me, my lord. I'd

235

not strip wood from an unfortunate ship grounded out there in the mud. Old Adam Holt brought me a few planks in exchange for a couple of ducks I gave him. I thought it was driftwood. It makes good kindling, you see, and I have to have warmth for my old bones at this time of the year.'

'Yes, yes, I know about your old bones,' said Nicholas not unkindly. He knew how precious wood was in winter, especially in places like Pelham Maris where there were no woods to provide kindling. 'Now finish your work and don't go out there stealing more from the ship. It will soon be under guard and that will put a stop to this pilfering. Now come inside and tell me all you know about this place. I want the truth, mind you. Who do you know? Who's this Adam Holt, for instance? What goes on here at night when all law-abiding people should be in bed and asleep? Come now, bring us some mead and let us talk.'

They toasted themselves by the fire and drank several tankards of mead until Walter's tongue was loosened. Yet he said nothing of importance and soon his head began to droop down on his chest and he closed his eyes. According to him Pelham Maris was a peaceful community. Admittedly when a ship ran aground the inhabitants helped themselves to its wood, but that was only to be expected. Anyone would do that. People were poor in these parts and the roads were impassable in winter and the weather made fishing impossible.

'Don't you hear any gossip when you go to church on Sundays?' said Nicholas, pushing him roughly to make him open his eyes.

'I don't go to church,' Walter muttered, sitting up abruptly. 'Not any more.'

'And what's put you off worshipping God in His house?'

'I don't trust them, the priests, I mean, that's why. Fat pigs looking after their own comforts whilst poor folk starve to death. What do they care about us?'

'I thought Richard Rushe a good man.'

'Aye – that's how he wants us to regard him. But why should he keep running off to that other one over in Selsey? Why doesn't he stay with us here and suffer with us? And who comes to see him at night, may I ask? No one knows who he is because he shuts himself away in a carriage. And he never comes here in daylight. He doesn't stay long, either; just collects the priest and they go off for days. He's gone now.'

'What are you saying? That Richard Rushe's gone away?'

'For sure; but he'll be back. He's probably away seeing that friend of his. That's who you should be keeping an eye on, my lord. Not troubling poor folk like me. I look after the place like you said I should, but I'm not the one you should be talking to if it's information you want. Go and see old Matthew Pierce. He's churchwarden and he ought to know where his vicar goes to. After all, he says he's the ears and eyes of the Bishop and although we haven't got a Bishop at the moment he must have used his eyes and ears when the last one was around.'

Leaving Walter to sleep off the effects of the mead by the fire, Nicholas re-mounted Harry and made his way over to the church, where he'd last seen Matthew Pierce and his son Luke.

The door was open and Nicholas tied Harry to the gatepost and went in to the church. It took a few minutes for his eyes to adjust to the gloom but then he saw the figure of Matthew Pierce standing on a ladder, studying a patch of damp under one of the windows in the north aisle. Matthew looked down when he heard the door creak as Nicholas pushed it open.

'Good day to you, Lord Nicholas,' he said. 'Seems the place is becoming quite popular these days. Sheriff's turning out people's houses, including mine. Roger Aylwin's been carted away and now I hear from one of the Sheriff's men that he's gone and hanged himself. It's time we were left in peace to get on with our own lives. Me and my son Luke lead godly lives. We have to otherwise we'll be in trouble with the Archdeacon when he takes the trouble to come and visit us.'

'Does he come often?'

'Not him. Only once a year when he makes his visitation. Pats us all on the back, tells us to get on with the good work, and off he goes. Now just take a look at this place. Patch of damp here, rain coming in through the windows, field mice everywhere nibbling at the vestments, making their homes in the straw on the floor. They've even had a go at the bell rope.'

'Is your priest at home, Matthew? I need to speak to him again.'

'No, sir. He's away over in Selsey.'

'Again?'

'Oh yes. Father William's a great friend of his. But I'd like to ask you, sir, if I may, why do you think Roger Aylwin went and killed himself? He was a very level-headed man, you see, not one to do anything extreme. We all liked him. He did a lot for us; especially when members of families took sick. Very charitable he was.'

'But the leader of the wreckers, by all accounts.'

'I find that hard to believe, sir. But I suppose the Sheriff's men did find some of the stuff from that ship in his cellar.'

'They did indeed, Matthew, and there's a great deal going on here which we want to know about. We found a dead bishop here last week; we found a ship lured into the harbour last Saturday night; we've caught a local man of good standing with his cellar stuffed full of stolen goods; a man's been found hanged at Woodhurst, and I've now heard a rumour of a nocturnal visitor who comes to visit your priest in a windowless carriage at night. Now have you seen such a carriage, Matthew? Do you know who could be inside it?'

The change in Matthew was startling. It was as if shutters had come down over his face, which froze into an inscrutable mask. He turned away and stared up at the damp patch on the wall.

'I've not seen any carriage around these parts, my lord. But then I'm a law-abiding man and sleep in my bed at night.'

'But you must have heard rumours?'

'I don't listen to rumours, sir. I mind my own business. Now, if you'll be so good as to excuse me, there's work to be done.'

Nicholas cursed his own clumsiness. He'd been foolish to put pressure on Matthew. But the interview had not been a waste of time. There was indeed a lot going on in Pelham Maris, but no one was going to enlighten him. Someone, somewhere, had put the fear of God into this community. Not God; most likely the Devil.

He heard the Sheriff's voice calling him

from outside.

'You there, my lord? We've got a piece of good news, at last.'

The Sheriff walked into the church and strode over to Nicholas. 'We've found the stern board. It was in Job's barn under some hay. The ship was the *Flandria* right enough. Name was painted in gold letters. Job said he wanted it for his baby's cradle. Now, I know it's no proof that he was one of the wreckers, but he must have known where the board came from and was party to the crime. He and some others are on their way to Marchester where we'll start questioning them straight away. They'll be in irons by nightfall.'

'Then make sure you don't kill them before they have a chance to speak. Go slowly with them, Richard.'

'You don't have to tell me, my lord. I'm too merciful, that's my trouble. But have you discovered anything significant?'

'Only that the whole village lives in a state of terror and no one's going to say a word. Someone's got them dancing to his tune, and it's a pretty evil tune he plays. He's the man we want, Richard. I also heard that Richard Rushe receives nocturnal visits from someone who drives around in a windowless carriage, though no one's going to admit to seeing it. But I'm sure everyone knows about it and knows who's the person inside that carriage. And they are never going to tell us, Richard, however hard you apply the irons.'

Thirteen

After Nicholas had left that Wednesday morning, Jane offered to help the Dean's wife in her domestic duties, but Katharine would have none of it.

'You now have the opportunity to help Edward in the library,' she said. 'You ought to make use of the hours of daylight and do something you would enjoy. Maybe Philippa would like to come with you. She's told me that she wants to make her own devotional Book of Hours.'

Jane glanced at Philippa and her heart melted. She looked so young and enthusiastic and reminded her of the time when, at about the same age, her father had arranged lessons for her in Marchester with an elderly priest and how, day after day, over the winter months, she had mastered the language of the ancients and had studied the Classics and the works of the Church Fathers and everything else she could lay her hands on. Blessed with an excellent memory, she had learned by heart huge chunks of scripture and the main liturgical prayers. Was Philippa going to travel along the same road which she, Jane, had travelled along? It would be a pity to deny her the pleasure of that journey.

Philippa's interests, it appeared later, as they settled down to work in the library, turned more towards the artistic. She began to copy out the prayers of the main services and to decorate the capital letters and the margins of her book with colourful, naturalistic pictures in the manner of the old scribes. The Chancellor, having seen that they were happily occupied, left them to their own devices as he had work to do elsewhere. In one corner of the room sat his clerk, Hubert, who studiously lowered his eyes to the roll of parchment in front of him.

Jane sat down at the Chancellor's desk and soon immersed herself in the deeds and financial transactions of the former Priors of Dean Peverell's priory, puzzling over the scripts of the monks from the thirteenth and fourteenth centuries, which were written in a mixture of French and Latin. Some words were abbreviated and she had to ask Hubert to help her, which he was able to do without hesitation. Soon she, too, was able to decipher the words and they worked away in silence.

Suddenly she was conscious that Hubert's attention had wandered. Looking up, she saw that he was gazing at Philippa with an intensity which she found disturbing. Philippa, she noticed, was unaware of his scrutiny. She was sitting at the table under the window and the pale sunlight shone down on her, lighting up her golden hair which hung in two plaits down the front of her green dress. She looked enchanting, like a painting by one of the Flemish artists – a young girl absorbed in her work. She deserved to be looked at; nevertheless Hubert's scrutiny made Jane uneasy. The young man was too intense, too serious. There was no lightness about him. His pale, intellectual face, his fine, light brown hair not quite concealing a monk's tonsure, a slim body clothed in clerical black blended in well with the cathedral setting, but was not the type to appeal to a young girl. But obviously, Philippa was making an impression on him and Jane began to feel increasingly uneasy. She felt responsible for her. There was no harm in looking, she thought, but just let him take one step away from his desk and across to the window, and she would have to intervene. Maybe it hadn't been such a good idea to bring Philippa with her to the library. But the young man seemed content just to look and after a while he settled down to his work again, and Jane relaxed. Of course it was unsettling for him to have women around in the library and Philippa, on the threshold of womanhood, was a sight to melt most men's hearts.

They stopped work at midday and Jane and Philippa returned to the Dean's house, where there was no sign of Katharine. One of the servants said she had been summoned over to the Bishop's jail where one of the inmates was taken poorly. Leaving Philippa in the parlour, she went out across the yard to the prison, where the jailer let her in.

'It's Mistress Trimble, madam. She's been taken real poorly. Mistress Catchpole's with her now.'

'Then I must go to her. Open the door and let me through,' she said to him.

Grumbling that this was no place for a young lady, the jailer took her along the passage, silent now, to Agatha Trimble's room. The door was open and Jane looked in to see the jailer's huge wife closing the old woman's eyes. Then, gently, she folded the old woman's arms across her chest and made the sign of the cross. Katharine, who was standing by the bed, glanced at Jane.

'It would be better if you kept away, Jane,' she said. 'I don't know why Agatha died so suddenly, but I'm sure Nicholas would not want you to come too close.'

Jane ignored her and approached the bed, where the old woman appeared to be asleep. She looked so peaceful as if death had crept up to her and carried her away without any struggle or resistance.

'This is indeed very unexpected,' Jane said, looking at the jailer's wife. 'When I saw her yesterday she looked as if she was well on the way to recovering from her fever.'

She glanced round the room. The fire still burned brightly and the room was warm. A jug of water and a goblet stood on the table by the bed and everything looked clean and tidy. There was no indication that the jailer and his wife had neglected their duties.

'I don't know, madam,' said Beatrice, the jailer's wife, obviously puzzled. 'She was fine last night. Said she'd get up today. She took a cordial last night – the goblet's still there – and I gave her a little more this morning when I came in to do the necessary cleaning. She was drowsy, but not uncomfortable. Then I came back later to see if she wanted me to help her get up and found her like this. At first I thought she was asleep but then I realised she'd gone. It must have been her heart. She was old and she'd had a high fever and a terrible cough and it had all been too much for her. Poor soul, at least she didn't suffer. The angel of death was merciful to her.'

Jane stared down into the old woman's face. What was wrong? Why was she feeling so uneasy? It was the same feeling she had experienced before, not so long ago; but the face she had looked at before was that of a young girl who happened to be in the wrong place at the wrong time. Then she forced her mind back to the present. Of course the two deaths were entirely different. The young girl had been a witness to a conspiracy. Who would want to get rid of a sick, old woman locked away out of harm's way in a prison? Then her eye fell on the goblet on the table by the bed. She picked it up and looked inside. Every drop had been drunk. She sniffed but could smell only the pleasant scent of blackcurrants preserved in mead.

'Did you give her this cordial, Mistress Beatrice?' said Jane.

'I did indeed,' she replied, her voice sharp at the prospect of criticism. 'It's from my own store. I make it myself in the summer months and no one's allowed to sample it without my permission. I have a few jars left and keep it for the serious cases, mostly those with bad throats and coughs.'

'And when did you say you gave her this?'

'As I said, madam, last thing at night and a drop more this morning.'

'And no one else came to see her?'

'Lord, no, madam, who'd want to see old Agatha? She had few friends, by all accounts, and those she had lived a good way away down on the coast. No, she was a nasty old witch, and it seems she cast one spell too many and God wanted rid of her, but being merciful, he treated her gently. Had she lived, she would have suffered a lot more up on Marchester Heath before she died.'

'Then between giving her the cordial last night and you giving her another dose this morning, no one else came near her?'

'No, madam, as I told you, no one came.'

'What's bothering you, Jane,' said Katharine, looking at her with concern. 'Why should you worry about an old woman for whom death has come as a merciful release?'

'Only that death was unexpected. Yesterday she seemed to be on the road to recovery and looking forward to getting up today.'

'These things happen, madam, when you're old,' said Beatrice. 'The body just gives up the struggle of trying to stay alive. Come now, let me lay her out, and, as God was merciful to her, we'll see she gets a Christian burial.'

Still uneasy, Jane followed the others back to the hall of the prison where Aldred, the jailer, was standing with his back to the fire.

'Lady Jane is not happy about old Agatha's death, husband,' said Beatrice to the diminutive jailer.

'She mustn't worry about her,' he said, 'it's only to be expected at her age. Her old body's been racked by coughing and wheezing for days now. It just couldn't take any more.'

'But she was getting better,' said Jane. 'Did you go and see her after your wife settled her down for the night?'

Aldred looked at her in surprise. 'Me? Good Lord, no. Why should I take a look at her late at night? My wife sees to all that?'

'She didn't ask for anything in the night?'

'If she did, we didn't hear her. My wife and I don't listen out during the night. We sleep soundly as we should, being good Christian souls. The prisoners have to look after themselves.'

'And you didn't go and see her this morning?'

'No, of course not. That's my wife's job. I did let the priest in, though. He insisted she should have communion. I tried to stop him saying that as she was a witch she didn't want communion, but he said she should as she'd been ill and this might be her last chance to receive the sacrament. So I let him in. He didn't go and see the others as they hadn't been ill and they had plenty of time to change their ways and return to the church. But Agatha might not have much time left to her. She must have been alive and taken the sacrament because he didn't say anything when he left.'

Jane's heart missed a beat. Yes, this was all too familiar. She couldn't ignore the old woman's death.

'Who was the priest, Master Aldred? And when did he come to see her?'

'What time? I don't remember. After my

wife had been to see her and given her the cordial. It was early because Beatrice always checks on the inmates early. As for his name, I don't know. I've never seen him before. Mind you, there's a lot of priests around at the moment looking for jobs. They come and go when they are needed to help out.'

'Could we find out who sent him? Surely he'd know his name.'

'Well we could ask the Archdeacon and if he doesn't know then the Dean would know. He's head of the cathedral and his job is to know everything that's going on. Isn't that so, madam?' he said, looking at Katharine, who nodded in agreement.

'Then would you find out his name, Master Aldred, and let me know as soon as possible. We ought to speak to him.'

Aldred looked at her severely. 'It seems to me, madam, that you're doing the Sheriff's job for him, and it's not your place to ask all these questions. If I were your husband, and you must pardon me for saying so, you should be kept away from these unpleasant matters. Dirty old witches should be nothing to you. If anything untoward has taken place then it's his job to investigate. Not yours. Meanwhile I could try to find out the priest's name, if that'll please you, and who sent him. He was one of the young ones so it shouldn't be too difficult. But I suggest you now go back to the Deanery and occupy yourself with activities suitable to your position.'

'Thank you, Master Aldred. I will see you are well rewarded,' said Jane meekly.

Katharine and Jane returned to the Deanery in silence. Once inside, Katharine dismissed the servants and closed the door.

'What's behind all this, Jane? What's troubling you?'

'Only that there is something here that's not quite right. We have had two sudden deaths: one was Roger Aylwin, who killed himself just when he was about to be interrogated; and now we have the death of an old woman just as she was about to recover from her sickness. Can it be possible that these two people were witnesses?'

'Witnesses, Jane? Witnesses to what?' said Katharine, looking bewildered.

'To something that could be connected to Bishop Thomas's death. I only pray that there will not be any more deaths. There is evil in our midst, Katharine. The people of two of our coastal villages are in a state of terror and are too frightened to tell us anything about what is going on down there. Agatha Trimble's death looks to me as if someone wanted her silenced before she said anything that could incriminate him. And Nicholas and Sheriff Landstock are still a long way away from finding out who that person is. I pray to God that they will soon find him and people can live in peace once again.'

The death of Agatha Trimble weighed heavily on Jane's mind as she waited impatiently for Nicholas's return. Philippa did her best to amuse her but the hours dragged by until the sun set in a vivid slash of scarlet across the sky. Then Nicholas rode into the Dean's yard. He came in to where she was sitting and after greeting her in a perfunctory manner accepted a tankard of ale and sank into a chair by the fire without speaking.

'What is it, Nicholas,' she asked. 'What's happened?'

'The Devil rides out, that's what I've heard, and now I am beginning to believe the rumours. He's terrorising the people living along our coast. People haven't seen him – or, at least, they say they haven't – but they say he rides around at night in a carriage which either has no windows, or the curtains are always drawn, so they have no idea who is inside. If they do know who he is, or suspect who he is, nothing is going to make them tell us. Jane, we are in the midst of a wicked conspiracy of evil that permeates the people of this county. We know only one thing about the person behind this conspiracy – and a person it is, Jane, because you and I do not believe in an independent Devil – and that is that he must be a powerful figure of authority who knows how to control people's minds through fear; and we have to track this person down and end his reign of terror. But Jane,' he said, as if seeing her for the first time, 'what's happened here? You look very solemn; not like my usual, carefree wife. Come now, tell me what's on your mind?'

She came over to him and sat down on a stool at his feet. The fire was hot and the steam rose from Nicholas's doublet and he stretched out his legs for the fire to dry them as well.

'Agatha Trimble has died.'

'So? She was old and ill, I heard, so it's to be expected.'

'She was getting better yesterday, well on the way to recovery. The fever had gone and her cough much improved. She died this morning after the jailer's wife brought her a cordial and before she went to check that she was all right later on in the morning. To her surprise, she found her dead.'

'Did anyone else see her during that interval?'

'The jailer, Aldred, said a priest brought her communion, Nicholas, after the jailer's wife gave her the cordial first thing in the morning. Don't you think this sounds familiar, Nicholas? Do you remember that young girl, Bess, who had the misfortune to be in the wrong place at the wrong time and had to be silenced? Could we be witnessing the same thing here in the case of Agatha Trimble?'

'But who would want to silence an old woman who was probably going to die soon in any case? Even if she didn't die of the fever, she would almost certainly be hanged on Marchester Heath for witchcraft.'

'But in the meantime she could still talk. And that's what your Satanic figure doesn't want.'

'But she was an old woman, and, by all accounts, an unpopular witch.'

'So? She still had ears and eyes and probably noticed a lot.'

'And would probably talk when subjected to interrogation.'

'Most likely. It takes extreme fortitude to remain silent under torture, however mild, and she might well think there was much to gain by giving away information which could be important to this case.'

'But where, in God's name, could she have gained this information?'

'Nicholas, witches meet in covens, and one of their major festivals occurs at this time of the year at Candlemas. This was when Bishop Thomas was murdered. Not on the actual feast day, but shortly afterwards. Now, could it have been possible that he was killed during those fearful ceremonies which take place during the meetings of the covens?

Nicholas, Agatha Trimble might have been present at the Candlemas festival!'

Nicholas stared at her in horror. 'Jane, how do you know these things? Surely you haven't made a study of the evil rituals of the Satanic powers?'

'Don't worry, I'm not a witch, but I have studied their beliefs and most of them are harmless old women, living on their own, and well-versed in the healing arts. There are others, I agree, who have chosen the powers of darkness rather than the Christian God of Light, and I am sorry for them, because Satan exerts a terrible power over his followers.'

'If Agatha Trimble was one of these "others" as you call them, and she was present at the Candlemas meeting of the coven, then she might well know who was the President of the rituals.'

'Yes indeed. And that President would want her silenced, wouldn't he? Someone tampered with that cordial, I'm sure, and ensured her death. And the only person who could have done that, was the priest who gave her communion.'

'Do we know who he was?'

'No. The jailer said he was a young priest but he'd never seen him before.'

'But someone must know. I'll ask the Dean who was the priest on duty this morning. Is it not strange, too, that communion should be brought to someone who was not Christian and who, by all accounts, was not in imminent danger of death?'

'I mentioned that and the jailer said he was hoping she might change her beliefs before she died. Nicholas, I must talk to the other women in the prison. There are two women there, one is senile and her mind has gone, but the other is very much alive and well. She might be able to tell us more about Agatha's activities. Also I must tell the jailer to keep a close eye on her because she could be the next person to be silenced.'

'No, Jane, I forbid it.'

'Then I must disobey you, Nicholas. Remember we are partners and I want to help you in your fight against the Powers of Evil. Besides, I can come to no harm. The jailer and his wife will be with me, and I am sure Jenny Dobbs and I will have a lot in common.'

'What you, and an old witch?'

'She's not old and has a beautiful singing voice. Untrained, but with great potential.'

'And of course you want to rush in and save her and get the Precentor to train her voice? Jane, will you stop interfering in other people's lives.'

'No, my lord. I won't. I agreed to be your partner. This woman, Jenny Dobbs, might be able to help us. I might be able to help her in return. As for taking risks, all our lives are at risk, yours and the Sheriff's and his men. Are we then to do nothing? Shall we just stand by and watch this evil spread throughout the county so that no one is safe and people live in fear? Risks must be taken.'

'But not by you, my darling wife.'

'I shall always take care. I do not court disaster. Besides, no one will take any notice of me. I shall simply say that I am making a charitable visit. Everyone will understand that. It's what ladies like me do, isn't it? Though some call it interfering! Katharine will come with me and the jailer will be within call. And who knows, we might learn something.'

At that moment, they were interrupted by the Dean, who entered the room and looked at them in surprise.

'So serious? What's happened now?'

'Do you happen to know who took communion to Agatha Trimble this morning, Dean?'

'I leave these matters to the Archdeacon, Nicholas. I can soon find out for you. He ought to know what his clergy are doing.'

'Tread carefully, I pray you,' said Jane. 'Just refer to the matter casually.'

'Why, Jane, my dear, what's going on in that head of yours? Why should it be a matter of importance to you which priest took communion to an old woman who could be coming to the end of her life?'

'Because I saw the old woman yesterday and would like to thank the priest for his kindness, that's all.'

'I admire your Christian charity but the priest was only doing what was expected of him. But I am sure the Archdeacon will pass on your thanks to the appropriate person.'

'And I would like to know his name, if that's not too much trouble, because I should like to speak to him about the other women in the prison. Maybe they, too, should be offered communion.'

'How kind you are, my dear. Why do you bother yourself with two old crones reported to consort with the Devil?'

'Because I believe no one is beyond redemption. Who knows, I might be able to persuade them to turn away from their evil master and join us in Christian worship.'

The Dean threw back his head and laughed heartily. 'My lord Nicholas, you must keep an eye on this wife of yours otherwise she'll be coming to see me about organising an evangelical mission.'

'And what's wrong with that?' said Jane provocatively.

'Because it's none of your business. I've got a fistful of priests hanging round the cathedral wanting occupation. I don't know most of them because the numbers have increased markedly since they were turned out of their monasteries. I'm not at all sure the Archdeacon knows all of them, either. But by all means go and see the old women if you must. You can't do any harm.'

Then he beamed across at Nicholas. 'Time your wife had a nursery full of bouncing babies. They would keep her busy.'

'After only nearly six weeks of marriage, that would indeed be a miracle,' said Jane.

He laughed and reached out for the flagon of ale which the servant had left on the table. Just then, a servant came in and whispered something to the Dean. Nicholas saw his manner change. The servant left the room and the Dean stood there, lost in thought.

'Bad news, Dean?' asked Nicholas getting to his feet.

'I'm afraid so. The Sheriff's men have just found the body of Hugh Brotherhood, the late Bishop's clerk. He'd been given leave, if you remember, Nicholas, to visit his ailing mother in Winchester. Well, he's been found in a ditch just off the Winchester road. His body has been badly mutilated by foxes and wild dogs and his face and shoulders have been beaten black and blue. It appears that he was set upon by thieves and thrown in a ditch. His purse was stolen and there is no sign of his horse. If it had been an accident, then his horse would have not wandered far and people would have noticed it. The poor man would have stood no chance if a band of robbers attacked him. This is terrible news and shows how law and order is breaking down in our shires. The Archdeacon will be very upset. Hugh was an excellent clerk and was destined to go far.'

'I am shocked at the news, Dean. Let me come with you when you tell the Archdeacon. It is not good to break bad news on your own.'

'Thank you, Nicholas, I would welcome your support.'

They found the Archdeacon eating an early supper in his house. Nicholas was surprised at the austerity of the meal. There was a loaf of coarse bread, a tankard of ale and a handful of dried plums. He was reading a devotional book and looked up in surprise when they were ushered in.

'Mister Dean, my lord, what can I do for you? Please sit down. I'm afraid I have little to offer you by way of refreshment as this is one of my fast days, but I can send for more ale.'

'Please don't trouble yourself. You fast too much, Archdeacon,' said the Dean impatiently, 'a man's not at his best when he starves himself. Tell your cook to roast a good capon and I shall send you over a couple of ducks. There's good fat on a duck and fat is what you can do with.'

'Thank you for your generous offer but I seldom eat meat and I find my body works best when not over-indulged.'

'As you wish. Now, we bring sad news, I'm afraid.'

Nicholas watched the Archdeacon closely as the Dean broke the news of Hugh Brotherhood's death. Of course the Archdeacon looked surprised, then horrified. Why should he do otherwise? His clerk had been set upon by thieves and his body devoured by wild beasts. But at the back of his mind was the look on Hugh Brotherhood's face just before he was dismissed by the Archdeacon at a previous interview. It was just a look; but one that Nicholas could not ignore, if only because it lingered at the back of his mind. Had Hugh been murdered because of that look? He pushed the thought to the back of his mind and asked the Archdeacon which of the many priests under his authority had been on duty that morning and had taken communion to Agatha Trimble.

The Archdeacon looked at Nicholas in surprise. 'My lord, I have no idea. I have been thoroughly upset by the news of the death of my clerk and cannot turn so quickly to another matter. Allow me time to collect my thoughts.'

'I'm sorry, Archdeacon, but the matter is

important. Please take your time.'

'It must have been one of the vicars choral – they take the sacraments to the sick,' the Archdeacon said after a moment's silence. 'It could have been Father Oswald; he's one of the older priests and it is a suitable job for him. He likes to be useful. I'll go and check after I've seen the body of poor Hugh.'

It was dark now but instead of going back with the Dean to his house, Nicholas went to the back of the Archdeacon's house where the old ostler was shutting the stable doors for the night. He seemed older and sadder than when Nicholas had last seen him and as far as he could tell, there was no sign or sound of a horse in the stable. But the carriage was there. He could see it just as the doors were about to be closed. It still looked in pristine condition as if it had never been used. The varnished sides of the coach gleamed with polish and the coat of arms stood out distinctly in the fading light. But it wasn't quite dark enough to conceal the two windows, one on either side of the coach, large enough to let everyone have a good look at who was inside.

The ostler looked up at Nicholas and paused in shutting the doors.

'Good evening to you, master,' said Nicholas evenly. 'You seem to have little work to occupy you these days as, obviously, your master has not ventured out lately in this fine coach of his.'

'No, my lord. It'll not be used much until the spring. And my poor Boy has been lent to Master Brotherhood, the Archdeacon's clerk, and he's not been returned to me yet. I miss my Boy. He and I were friends, like.'

'Then you've not heard the news?'

'No, my lord. No one tells me anything. Nothing's happened to Boy, I hope?'

Nicholas told the ostler about the death of Hugh Brotherhood. When he said that the horse, Boy, has not been found, the ostler broke into a loud wailing which was dreadful to hear.

'Not my Boy! Oh no, they didn't steal Boy?'

'It looks like it, but the Sheriff will do his utmost to find the thieves and bring the horse back here. No one would harm a valuable horse like Boy. It's a wonder that the Archdeacon lent such a valuable horse to his clerk.'

'I told him not to. I can't bear having Boy out of my sight. Dear God, I hope the thieves treat him well.'

'Have no fear. No one would ill-treat such a valuable horse. But it's Hugh Brotherhood you should be grieving over. A horse is only a horse.'

'Not that one. He was special. I told the Archdeacon to let him use one of the other old nags, but no, it's Boy he lent him.'

'Does the Archdeacon have more than one horse?' said Nicholas, suddenly aware that he was on to something of importance. Hadn't the Archdeacon said something recently about another horse – that time when he'd told Nicholas and the Dean that Hugh Brotherhood had been given permission to visit his mother in Winchester? Something like, 'I lent him one of my horses.' If so, where were the others?

'Does the Archdeacon stable all his horses here, ostler?'

'Lord no, I'd not have room here to stable another horse.'

'Then where does he keep them?'

'How should I know, sir? I only do as I'm told. I look after Boy; or, at least, I did until now; and I polish my master's carriage; and that's all I'm paid to do.'

'Then he must have other stables in the district.'

'I dare say he does, but I don't have anything to do with them. Mind you, I've only seen him on one other horse; nothing like Boy, but serviceable enough, I admit. But he wasn't stabled here. You'll have to go and find him yourself, my lord.'

And so I shall, thought Nicholas grimly as he walked back to the Dean's house. The Venerable Jeremy Overton, Archdeacon of Marchester, had lied to him. He'd said that he'd kept his 'other horse' in his stables along with his carriage and his first horse. And now, it appeared, this was not always the case. He cursed the fact that the Archdeacon had not been brought in for questioning so that one of the Sheriff's clerks could have written down his statements. And it had been a pity that a record had not been kept of that conversation they'd had with the Dean in the cathedral where he'd talked about his horses. Now everything could be denied. Even the Dean, who had been present on that occasion, could not be relied upon to remember exactly what had been said. It would not have seemed important at the time. The Dean was much more interested in the giving leave of absence to Hugh Brotherhood without first consulting him.

Maybe he was attaching too much importance to a casual remark, he thought as he entered the Dean's yard. The trouble was he was dealing with intangibles – just looks and bits of conversation – not real evidence. Certainly not enough to bring the Archdeacon in for questioning under oath. They could not risk making a mistake with such a senior churchman as the Archdeacon. And there still remained the question of the carriage. He'd just seen the Archdeacon's carriage with its two large windows. And it had not been used over the last week or two. Nothing fitted. No clear picture was emerging. And, meanwhile, people were dying and there seemed to be no connection between the deaths. Every one of them had a reasonable explanation. Yet, and yet... He paused and stood in the Dean's yard, shivering in the frosty air. A thought then came to him which set his heart racing and cleared the mist in his brain. He suddenly felt alert with all his senses sharpened. He recognised this feeling. It was how he felt in the hunting field when the hounds scented their quarry. But he must go carefully and trust his instincts. One false move and the quarry would go to earth. And when that happened he knew from long experience that it took a long time to flush it out and restart the chase.

Fourteen

Jane watched Nicholas and the Dean walk across the courtyard of the Dean's house and out into the cathedral Close in search of the Archdeacon. It was getting late and in normal circumstances they would be sitting down to supper very shortly, but that Wednesday night everything was thrown into confusion by the news of Hugh Brotherhood's death. Telling Philippa she would be back shortly, she put on her cloak and went to the Bishop's prison, where Beatrice, the jailer's wife, looked at her severely.

'You shouldn't come here on your own, madam,' she said.

'There was no one to escort me,' Jane said, 'and I would like to see Mistress Dobbs please, if it's convenient.'

'What's the reason for your visit, madam, if you'll excuse my asking? I have to keep a record of all visitors, Sheriff said.'

'A good precaution,' said Jane, glad that someone was taking security seriously. 'I only want to see if I can be of any help to Mistress Dobbs. Anyone, with a voice like hers, should not waste it in a prison cell.'

'She's accused of witchcraft, madam.

She's used her voice most likely at the meetings of the covens. It'll be of no use to her when she comes to trial, as she will, very shortly.'

'She might not be found guilty. We can't prejudge anyone, Beatrice. But in the meantime I'd like to hear her sing and maybe I could suggest how she could improve her voice and how she could employ herself should she be acquitted.'

'She'll love the attention, that's for sure. She's a bold, bad lass and deserves what's coming to her. She's fortunate that someone like you takes an interest in her. Well, you'd better come with me but leave the door open and call out if she gets a bit uppity.'

Jane was surprised to see Jenny Dobbs sitting quietly by her fire – a brazier filled with glowing charcoal – reading a book. A single candle provided just enough light for her to read by. When Jane came into the cell, she jumped up, dropping the book on the floor, and glared at Jane like an angry bear facing its tormentors.

'Well, well, if it isn't my lady Jane! What brings you here? You're not going to try to convert me, are you? Now that poor old Agatha's gone, I suppose you're looking for someone else to preach to. Well, you're wasting your time on me. I'm not of your kind.'

'Hush your voice,' said Beatrice angrily.

'Lady Jane Peverell's come to see if there's anything she can do to help you. Don't turn on her before you know what she's come for. Good luck, madam,' she said, turning to go. 'I wouldn't waste your time on this trollop if I were you. I'll stand here, just outside the door; not to listen, of course, just in case she lets fly at you.'

'There's no need for that, Beatrice,' said Jane quietly bending down to pick up the book Jenny had dropped. 'Mistress Dobbs and I are only going to talk about pleasant things like music and books. I want to know how she learned to sing as well as she does.'

'Singing's a natural thing,' said Jenny, tossing back her tangled mane of bright red hair. 'At least, for those of us who are born to sing, that is. Most of us can sing if we try. The secret is to start when you're a youngster.'

'And you like poetry, too?' said Jane handing her the book, in which she could see poetry written in English.

'Poems, singing, they go together, don't they? A friend gave this book to me. Set these poems to music, he says, so I'm trying. The problem is I can hear the tunes, feel the rhythm, but can't write them down. No one's taught me how to write the notes, see. Besides, that old misery out there won't let me have pen nor paper and charcoal's a bit clumsy.'

'I could help you there,' said Jane easily. 'You see, I, too, like singing, and was shown how to write down songs. Why don't you sing one of your poems now, and I can join in? The music's there, in your head, as you said.'

Jenny looked at Jane in astonishment. Her face was beautiful, pale, through being confined in a prison cell, but her skin was smooth and her lips full and sensuous and her eyes were a deep blue, the colour of cornflowers. She was still young, though older than Jane, her body fuller, as if she had born children. Dressed in clean clothes, with her hair washed and combed, she would grace any nobleman's household, Jane thought.

Beatrice, deciding that the conversation had moved on to safer ground, gave a sniff of disapproval and left them together. Both stood there in silence whilst Jenny made up her mind. Then, suddenly, Jenny started to sing, without affectation and with a clear, bright tone which reverberated round the prison. The words of the song came from the book of poems and told of the coming of spring. The tune was simple with a strong rhythm and after listening to one verse, Jane joined in, adding her clear treble to Jenny's alto. At the end of the poem, Jenny clapped her hands and beamed at Jane.

'My Lord, mistress, you certainly know how to sing. Who taught you?'

'It's a long story, Mistress Dobbs, but, more to the point, how did you learn to sing like that?'

'Mine's a long story, too, but let's say that I wasn't always dressed in rags but was once befriended by a wealthy man – gentry, but married. I should have given him up long ago, but, foolishly, I loved him. I had his child, a girl, but she died, and after a while, he told me to go. But he gave me some books, because he said I had a brain in my head, and I deserved to get on, and he provided me with a cottage and a bit of money so I wouldn't starve. But he's lost interest in me now, more's the pity, but I still have his books and I saved most of his money.'

'Where is your cottage, Mistress Dobbs, if you don't mind me asking?'

'No, I don't mind. Why should I? Also, you'd better call me Jenny because they all do. I live down on the coast, near enough to Pelham Maris, but not too near. The cottage is tucked away near the seashore so I can hear the waves pounding on the shingle banks off the Point. It suits me and I can gather driftwood along the shore for my fire, and pick up all sorts of bits and pieces for my comfort.'

'Then why should the Sheriff pick on you and bring you in here?'

'Oh, he listened to gossip, I suppose. I was friends of a sort with old Agatha. Not too friendly because I didn't always go along with her ways. But I've picked up a lot about how to cure people and Agatha had her own potions and sometimes she'd suggest remedies when I came across someone with a disease new to me. People came to see me for cures and some of 'em, mostly the husbands, I should say, stayed a bit too long. But they paid for their pleasures and their wives didn't like it. It's their own fault, of course. They should hang onto their menfolk a bit harder. Mind you, some of them came to me when they wanted to get their husbands interested again. It's amazing how men's interest wanes when the babies come too often. But then I knew how to help the women deal with that problem, too. But I always saw that these unwanted babes got a decent burial. Everyone knows me down there along the coast. Most tolerate me because I have my uses, but there's lots want to get rid of me and would say the word to the Sheriff. But I've done no harm. I wasn't like Agatha.'

'What do you mean?' said Jane, studying the book of poems intently.

'Well, she's dead now, so no harm can come to her from my gossiping to you. It's common knowledge that she was someone who knew about and practised what I call the black arts. She made no secret of the fact that she had made a pact with the

273

Devil. She called him her master, silly old fool; it's a wonder she wasn't brought in before but somehow she got away with it. We live a bit too far away from the authorities down there in Pelham Maris, I suppose. Nobody comes poking his nose into our affairs unless something big happens, like when they found the Bishop's body down there in that pool. Then they all come asking questions. Anyway, old Agatha was always flitting off to meetings with this master of hers, along with some other old biddies. She called it her coven and I suppose they all met up and talked about spells and who was going to be treated to their next curse. I think they are all mad, but harmless, because I don't think curses work unless you believe in them, and I don't. Lord, I should know. I've been cursed enough in my time. I don't believe in any of it, mistress. I don't believe in a Devil or God, for that matter.'

'What do you believe in, Jenny?'

'I believe in a creator, of course. Not the God of the Christians. But you've only got to see a newborn lamb or the first shoots of the grass in the springtime or listen to the sound of the sea. There's a force in everything, and that's what I believe in. I can feel this force and pass it on to others, when asked, and they feel better, too. I suppose I am a heathen, but I know you'll

274

not tell any of the powers-that-be. I honour the old gods which were here long before the Christians came along and drove them away. They were gods I could understand, gods of the trees and water, the sun and the moon and the stars. Old Agatha was not like me. She was what I would call a black witch. She worshipped a fallen angel, an angel who brings evil and distress, and I'll have none of him. But you, mistress? You worship the new God, I suppose like all your kind.'

'New, in your terms, yes. But His spirit seems very like the spirit, or force as you call it, which you worship. I also believe in goodness and healing, and the triumph of good over evil. You and I are not so far apart. But tell me, Jenny, did Agatha go to any of her meetings recently? And if so, where did she go?'

Jenny's expression suddenly became more guarded and she turned away and sat down on the chair by the fire. 'Lord, mistress, you sound like one of the Sheriff's men. I was not Agatha's keeper and I didn't go round asking questions. She couldn't have gone far away because I've never seen her ride on a broomstick and she was certainly too old to ride a horse. We only talked about healing remedies. I never liked prying into her affairs.'

'Do you know if old Phoebe went along to these meetings?'

'Phoebe? She'd not remember if she'd met the Devil in person. Maybe she did, once upon a time, and that's what someone's told the Sheriff. Because she's old and ugly and has got a wicked tongue in her head, people want to get rid of her. She frightens the children, too. No, she was no friend to Agatha. Not lately, anyway. Maybe when she was younger. I felt sorry for her and gave her the odd potion when her body ached something terrible in the damp weather. She's better off in here in this prison at this time of the year. At least she's got a fire and the food's regular. But here comes Hecate, Queen of the witches. Seems you're wanted, my lady Jane.'

Whilst they had been talking, Beatrice had returned and was standing in the doorway to the cell, scowling at Jenny.

'Watch your tongue, Mistress Dobbs,' she said, 'or we shall have to stop visitors coming to see you. Madam,' she said, looking at Jane, 'I am sent to tell you that supper is ready and Lord Nicholas is getting anxious.'

'Seems you're in a spot of trouble,' said Jenny, grinning. 'Better run along now and do as you're told. But thank you for coming to see me and showing an interest in my singing. I should welcome another visit if you are so minded.'

'Don't count on it,' said Beatrice standing aside to let Jane leave the cell. 'Madam will soon grow tired of your ruderies.'

Jane smiled across at Jenny and returned to the Dean's house, where the evening meal was being served. Katharine looked relieved to see her and Jane went over to Nicholas and put her arms round his shoulders and kissed him lightly on the top of his head. 'I'm sorry, everyone,' she said 'but I have not been wasting time.'

'Talking to witches is not a commendable occupation,' said Chancellor Hasledean who, with the sheriff, was a guest at the Dean's table.

'There was only one witch in that prison and she's dead,' said Jane, taking her place next to Nicholas. 'The other two are quite harmless. Indeed, one of them is as skilled in healing as she is in music.'

'That's not what I heard,' said the Sheriff, tackling his game soup with gusto. 'The locals call her the beautiful witch and say their husbands can't be trusted to go near her. She consorts with the Evil One, they say, and learned her tricks from him.'

Jane laughed. 'We all say that when our husbands start to stray. You don't want to listen to that nonsense, Richard.'

Nicholas turned to look severely at Jane.

'Remember your manners, Jane. Your tongue can be as sharp as a knife. The sheriff knows what he's doing and by all accounts has done well today. Had you been here earlier you would have heard how he has been tracking down the wreckers and has filled up the town jail with a batch of suspects.'

The Sheriff looked suitably mollified and the rest of the meal passed peaceably. By the time they were eating the sweetmeats, he was prepared to listen to Jane's account of her visit to Jenny Dobbs.

'A pity she didn't tell us where these witches meet,' he grumbled.

'She'll not tell; not yet, anyway. As you know, Richard, people are too terrified to speak out. Soon, someone will let something slip. We have to keep listening, that's all.'

'We have to, Lady Jane? Since when were you part of this investigation?' said the Sheriff, looking disapprovingly at Jane.

'Ever since I married Lord Nicholas,' said Jane sweetly. 'We are a team, you see.'

'A team, you say? Nothing good will come of it, mark my words. Wives should obey their husbands in all things, isn't that so, Lord Nicholas?'

Nicholas reached for a handful of the dried figs and grinned across at the Sheriff.

'I think you should ask your wife, Richard. I am sure she is an expert on the subject of wifely duties.'

It was just after midnight when the four hooded figures took their seats in the sanc-

278

tuary of the church. One of them, wearing a goat-skin cloak, his face masked by a goat's face with huge yellow eyes painted on it, out of which his own eyes stared balefully, took his seat on the wooden armchair placed in front of the bare stone altar. The other three, wearing dark cloaks, their hoods drawn down over their faces, which were covered by masks representing wild beasts, took their places on chairs at the bottom of the three steps leading up to the altar. This east end of the church still had a roof. Solid, Norman pillars supported the vaulting overhead, and the beginnings of the north and south aisles. From the top of the pillars grotesque faces, carved in stone, creatures of those old stonemasons' imagination, leered down on the proceedings. The long nave stretched away in front of them. Once, it had been the nave of a cathedral before the sea encroached and it was decided to build a cathedral in Marchester where it would be more central for the diocese and less in danger from the sea. The roof of the nave had collapsed long ago and on that clear, frosty night, the stars shone like lanterns above them, and the moon shed its pale, ghostly light on the stone floor, which was filthy with old straw and the droppings from the jackdaws' nests in the holes and crevices in the ruined walls. In the distance the sea surged restlessly against the shingle banks – an ominous sound like the rumble of an advancing army.

Bats flitted around overhead, drawn to the light of the single taper which had been fixed to one of the pillars, squeaking out their warning signals to one another. An owl, in the grove of yew trees outside in the neglected churchyard, hooted, and another returned its call. The four figures ignored the bats and remained motionless. Then suddenly, the goat-man stood up and stretched out his arms over the other three.

'*Dominus vobiscum,*' he intoned, to which the three replied, '*Et cum spiritu tuo.*'

Then the goat-man made the sign of the cross over them, starting with his head but going from right to left across his chest. The three figures did the same.

Then he intoned the first part of the 'Credo'.

'*Credo in unum Deum, Patrem omnipotentem, factorem coeli et terrae, visibilium omnium et invisibilium.*'

After this he sat down and the others raised their heads to gaze at him.

'Welcome brothers: Baphomat, Calconix and my beloved Grésil,' he said, turning his head towards one of the figures, who, because of his slighter build, appeared to be younger than the others. 'We meet in difficult times. The accursed Lord of Dean Peverell is asking too many questions and our arch enemy, the Sheriff of Marchester, in his blundering and incompetent fashion, is stirring up the people, our people, unnecessarily. The Lord of Darkness grows angry with us. We must not become careless. We were nearly exposed when the fool of a Sheriff arrested our beloved Mistress Trimble. Fortunately we were able to make sure she could not pass on any of our secrets. Yes, what is it, Baphomat?' he said, turning his head towards the tallest of the masked figures.

'We have suffered a very great loss in the death of Mistress Trimble, master. Who now will supply us with those miserable children we need for our Sabbats? She knew who was going to give birth to an unwanted baby and was only too pleased to sell the brat to her for a few pence. Now we shall have to rob the graves. Fortunately the graveyards fill up at this time of the year.'

'Don't worry, faithful Baphomat; I am working on another supplier. From your district, Calconix,' he said, inclining his head towards the shorter and the stouter of the three. 'He is not yet one of us, but I think, for a fee, he will provide us with what we want.'

'Who is this person?' they whispered.

'I will introduce him later at the next Sabbat. But, in the meantime, I am more concerned about those meddling fools in Marchester. Especially the Lord of Dean

Peverell's wife. She is sharp, too sharp; and asks too many questions.'

'She is very beautiful,' said Grésil.

'She is indeed and our master would welcome her to our ceremonies.'

'We all would,' said Calconix with a short laugh.

'Save your mirth until later,' said the goatman. 'But I agree with you. She would please our master. She is too pure, too proud, too arrogant. We must debase her, humiliate her.'

'Yes, yes,' said the others. 'We must teach her a lesson.'

'Give her to the congregation,' said Baphomat, his voice shaking with excitement. 'Let's see whether her poor old God will come to her rescue.'

'There is another whom our master would welcome to our next gathering,' said Grésil quietly. 'I know we are not short of women. Many come to celebrate here with us, but mostly they are ugly and old, worn out with childbearing but still lascivious because that's what our master wants. But above all, he would delight in a young virgin offered up to him in this place on this altar. Master, a virgin is the most powerful offering there is; more powerful than the Bishop. Give her to our master, who will order us to deflower her in his name and in his presence. It would be a fitting climax to our ceremony.'

There was silence as all turned to look at Grésil. Then the goat-man spoke in a soft voice which barely concealed his excitement. 'Oh my beloved Grésil, what a brilliant mind you have. Yes, seize her and bring her here. And bring the other bitch, Peverell's whore. She's not a virgin, but she will please our worshippers. Then they will all leave us in peace. We shall talk further on these matters, Grésil, and meanwhile, you two, think about the next Sabbat. Make it soon. I shall communicate with you in the usual manner. Now come, pay homage to our master, whose servant I am, before you return to your homes.'

He stood up and lifted up his goat-skin cloak high above his waist, exposing his lean buttocks, which shone white in the torchlight as if they had been daubed with white paint. Then he leaned forward, placing his hands on the edge of the altar, and presented his withered posterior to the three men, who approached reverently and kissed him on that place. Grésil came last and lingered longest.

They returned to their seats and waited for the goat-man to adjust his cloak and take up the torch. Then they filed out down the nave, making the bats, alarmed by the light from the torch, twitter frantically to one another.

Fifteen

The next morning – it was Thursday – one of
his grooms arrived at the Dean's house and
told Nicholas he was wanted urgently back
at his manor. He said that the King's messenger, Sir Percival Darlington, wanted to
see Nicholas immediately. Nicholas knew
Darlington; he had seen him around at
Court. He was one of the King's favourites,
a rising star. Nicholas could not ignore the
summons. Could Darlington not come to
the Dean's house? he asked the groom, who
shook his head. No, he said, Darlington
would not come to Marchester. What's
more, he intended to stay in Dean Peverell
until the King's business was completed to
his satisfaction. Nicholas, who intended to
speak to the Sheriff that morning, cursed
silently. He was not ready to make a report
on the investigations. Neither could he leave
the Sheriff to his own devices at this stage of
the enquiry. But he knew the King only too
well. He loathed being kept waiting and if his
temper was aroused he could make things
very awkward for Nicholas by summoning
him to Court and keeping him there whilst
blaming him for procrastinating. Ordering

284

Harry to be made ready, he explained the reason for his sudden departure to Jane and promised to be back as soon as possible to bring her home. Meanwhile, she said, she would be quite happy occupying herself in the library. Satisfied that the Dean and his household were quite happy with the situation, he mounted Harry and rode off to his own house.

Jane seized her chance. Philippa was having her French lesson with her tutor, Katharine was occupied in the kitchen giving orders for the day's menus and checking on stocks in the store cupboards; no one would notice her absence. She put on her cloak and slipped out to visit Jenny Dobbs in the bishop's prison. Beatrice reluctantly took her to Jenny's cell and opened the door. This time she returned to the hall of the prison, leaving them together.

Jenny was pleased to see her. She had acquired a piece of old parchment from the jailer and was using a scrap of charcoal to write down her version of musical notation. Jenny had brought a recorder with her and a quill pen with ink and a sheet of clean parchment which she had cajoled out of the Chancellor. Looking at Jenny's efforts, she saw that it would not be too difficult to teach her the more orthodox system.

They were happily occupied in playing, singing and writing down the music to their songs when the irate figure of the Dean appeared in the doorway of the cell.

'Lady Jane, what, in God's name, are you doing here? May I remind you that this is a prison cell and that this woman is accused of witchcraft. I must insist that you leave immediately.'

They were taken by surprise and all Jane could do was stare at the Dean with the recorder still at her lips. Then she collected herself.

'I'm sorry to have caused you any inconvenience, Mister Dean. I was allowed to see Mistress Dobbs yesterday and thought I could continue with my lessons today. Lord Nicholas has had to leave on urgent business and I thought this would be a useful way to occupy myself.'

'It might please you to play the music teacher to inmates of prison cells but please confine your activities to more law-abiding citizens. Come now, I insist you accompany me.'

Jane had no choice but to obey. Once out in the courtyard of the prison, however, she decided to take the Dean into her confidence. It was worth a try, she thought.

'I'm sorry to have acted hastily, Dean, but I thought no harm would come of it. In fact, the reason for my visit to Mistress Dobbs was not only to develop her musical talents but to find out how much she knows about the goings-on in Pelham Maris. You see, she and Agatha Trimble were friends of a sort. She knew all about Mistress Trimble's activities. She told me about the meeting of the covens and how Mistress Trimble attended them along with others. She, too, is surprised as I am by Mistress Trimble's death. Now I know she could tell me a lot more but first I must gain her confidence. Do you now see what I am doing? I am not just a bored lady looking for a protégée.'

The Dean paused and turned to look at her. He was still annoyed but he knew Jane was not stupid. If she were a man he'd recommend her to the Sheriff as one of his officers. She could be on to something. Maybe there was a place for a woman in an investigation, he thought, his anger diminishing a little. After all, women were quite capable of committing crimes; so why shouldn't women be involved in unmasking them? All this went through his head as he stared at Jane's serious face. The Dean was also decisive.

'Jane, what's going on in that head of yours?'

'Sir, the Bishop was murdered in a particularly loathsome way. Probably he was abducted and subjected to a ritual murder. To find out who committed this act we have to look at what sort of people would engage in these sort of rituals. The Sheriff would probably say, "witches", and, if he's right, and I think he is, then we must know where the covens take place and when. Then, somehow we shall have to infiltrate these covens and find out who attends them. In that way, we might have some idea who would choose a Bishop as one of their victims. Usually, these evil people choose babies and young children who have died suddenly. Now I think Jenny Dobbs knows who attends these meetings of the covens, although I'm sure she doesn't attend them herself. And, what's more, I think she might tell me when I have gained her confidence. Music is the way.'

'Jane, I have underestimated you. You are ahead of us all. But I don't approve of your getting involved in this enquiry. It's too dangerous. Who knows what you might stumble upon? But now I understand your reasons for wanting to befriend Mistress Dobbs. Let us make some sort of compromise. I agree to let you continue with the music lessons, but no one must ever guess the real reason for your doing so. Jane, you must learn discretion. No, don't say anything,' he said raising his hand. 'I know what you are thinking. If Mistress Dobbs were an ordinary criminal, we could let her out on bail. But she isn't and we can't. But we could make her promise not to try to escape, upon pain of death, and then I could give you permission to bring her over to my house, under guard, of course, and continue with her lessons in my music room. There now, what more can I do? Go and tell her to tidy herself up a bit. The jailer's wife will fetch her some water and something to smooth down her hair; then bring her over. Only for one hour, mind. Let's see if kindness will make her talk. God forgive me, I talk like the Sheriff!'

Jane was quite overwhelmed by the Dean's generosity. She treated him to a deep curtsey and rushed back to talk to Beatrice, who would need a lot of persuading to let Jenny Dobbs out of her cell.

Sir Percival Darlington was in the small, retiring room leading off the great hall which Jane and Nicholas used after dinner when they would talk over the day's events in preparation for bed. It was a very special room and Nicholas felt a ripple of irritation that Sir Percival had taken upon himself to go in there and make himself at home. A tray of broken meats stood on a table and he was standing in front of the fire, tankard in hand, as if he owned the place. However, Nicholas forced down his resentment and called for more ale.

'I'm glad my servants are looking after you,' he said. 'I trust His Majesty is well.'

'Oh yes – in robust health,' said Darlington, inclining his head graciously as if he were personally responsible for the King's well-being.

They talked of inconsequential things whilst they sized each other up and the servants cleared away the broken meats and brought in fresh ale and refreshments for Nicholas. Darlington was the King's tennis partner and was also an expert falconer. A young man, in his twenties, with a slim figure not yet showing signs of over-indulgence at the King's table, he had a lean, intelligent face framed by soft fair hair which merged neatly into a curly, blond beard. It was not long before Nicholas warmed to him and the conversation turned to more important matters.

'What does the King want of me?' asked Nicholas, refilling both their tankards.

'A report,' said Darlington. 'A full report on the sad death of the Bishop. The King regarded him as a friend, you see; I believe they met here in your house. He was shocked by his murder and between you and me, he doesn't have much confidence in Sheriff Landstock. Says he's too impetuous and liable to rush off on a wild goose chase. But he does trust you to get on with the business of finding the person or persons responsible for the murder. The Bishop was your Prior, I understand, and the King knows you would personally want to see his murderer captured. The King also said he wants the perpetrators of the crime caught and brought for trial in London.

'He also has views himself about this case,' said Darlington, pausing to take a mouthful of ale. 'He appears to think the manner of the Bishop's death smacks of witchcraft; this he will not tolerate. He is orthodox in his beliefs, as you know, Lord Nicholas, despite his rejection of the Pope's authority, and cannot abide heresy. If the Bishop's murderer is a member of a witches' coven, then he can expect no mercy from the King and will face a terrible death at Tyburn. I hope this report will not be too arduous a task. I am not to return to Court without it, and he wants me back soon as I am to partner him in a tennis tournament against the French Ambassador, who has enthusiastically taken to the game. I should be most grateful, Lord Nicholas, if I might make use of your home for the time it takes for you to make your report.'

Nicholas bowed. 'Be my guest. I will give orders for the falcons to be at your disposal, and please choose any horse in my stable should you wish to hunt the deer or chase the hares up on the downland. I am sure you understand that I shall have to return to Marchester to exchange information with the Sheriff. It will take time as we are in the middle of the investigation and not ready to make a report. But one good piece of news is that the Sheriff's jail is full up with wreckers – those wicked people who lure ships into unsuitable inlets along our coast. I am not sure if there is any connection between the wreckers and the witches' covens which we think take place in this area; that has not yet been ascertained. But it will please His Majesty that we are not being entirely slothful. Things can change by the hour at this stage of an investigation and I should get back to liaise with Sheriff Landstock.'

'I trust Lady Jane is well. I was surprised she was not here when I arrived but I was told she is in Marchester.'

'For the time being, whilst I rush round the county, she is staying with the Dean and his wife. It's better if one of us stays put and Marchester is more central to the enquiry than here. In the meantime, please be at liberty to make full use of my house as long as it takes me to write a report. It appears that I have changed houses.'

'Not for long, I trust,' said Darlington cheerfully. 'But, rest assured, I shall look after your manor for you and see that the servants don't take too many liberties in your absence. Now, perhaps I could be taken to my room.'

Already beginning to feel like a visitor in his own house, Nicholas summoned his steward to look after Sir Percival whilst he made ready for his return to Marchester.

The music room was one of the finest rooms in the Dean's house. Big windows let in a lot of light, a cheerful fire radiated heat, lutes and viols were resting against one of the walls and Jane was playing the virginals, watched by Jenny Dobbs. Standing by the door, her plain face stiff with disapproval, stood the jailer's wife, ready to pounce on Jenny should she make one move towards the door. But escape was the last thing on Jenny's mind as Jane got up from the seat in front of the set of virginals and invited Jenny to take her place. Then she began to show her how to place her hands on the keys and teach her the notes.

They were so involved in what they were doing, that they didn't hear the door open and the murmur of voices. A man came into the room and stood there watching the two women. After several minutes, the jailer's wife jiggled her keys to draw attention to the newcomer. Jane turned round, saw who it was, and smiled a greeting.

'Why, Sir Ralph, how good to see you.' She went over to him and offered her hand. 'I'm afraid Nicholas has had to return to Dean Peverell to see the King's messenger. He shouldn't be long, however. Meanwhile, can I be of any help?'

'Jane, you are as beautiful as ever,' Sir Ralph Paget, the Earl of Southampton said, bowing low to kiss her outstretched hand. 'Marriage appears to agree with you. But Mistress Dobbs,' he said, staring across at Jenny, who had turned round to see who Jane was talking to. 'I didn't expect to see you here, in the Dean's music room.'

'Do you know one another?' said Jane, looking in surprise from one to the other. Jenny, she noticed, had turned quite pale and looked as if she was on the verge of fainting. Southampton also seemed lost for words.

'Jenny has a fine voice and a musical talent,' said Jane, conscious of the need to smooth over an awkward moment. 'I am teaching her to make use of that talent.'

'And she's to go back to where she came from in a few minutes,' said Beatrice angrily advancing on Jenny. 'She's supposed to be outside in the jail, my lord. She's been accused of witchcraft and is awaiting trial. She shouldn't be in here talking to the likes of you and Lady Jane, but the Dean's got a soft heart, too soft, I say. Come on now, Mistress Dobbs, let's away. No fuss now. Your time's up. One hour the Dean said.'

Jenny, still gazing at the Earl of Southampton, slowly crossed over to the door.

'Wait, Jenny,' said Jane. 'Beatrice, leave her for a second. It appears Sir Ralph knows you, Jenny. Have you nothing to say to him?'

'We said all we had to say years ago,' said Jenny, collecting herself. 'It's good to see you again, sir, looking so well,' she said to Southampton, who still couldn't take his eyes off Jenny.

'And you, Jenny, are as beautiful as I remember you. What made the Sheriff bring you in? You were never interested in the black arts. You were a creature of the woods and hills. There was not a bad thought in your head. There must be a mistake.'

'I hope the Sheriff will come to the same conclusion. But at the moment his mind is set on witches and he brings in anyone who has been denounced. But I hope your wife is well, sir?'

'My wife? Oh yes, she's in good health, God be thanked. But Jenny, do you want for anything? Have you enough money?'

'Thank you, sir, yes. I am well provided for. But I would very much like to be free from my prison cell.'

'I will see what I can do. As Lord Nicholas is not here, I will be on my way to see Sheriff Landstock and have a talk to him. I can vouchsafe for your innocence,' said Southampton.

'Thank you for taking an interest in me. Yes, Beatrice, take me back to my cell. I am ready to go.'

'But you shall not be there for much

longer,' said Southampton with more emotion in his voice than Jane had ever heard before. 'I will do my best to get you freed.'

'And I will see you soon, Jenny,' Jane said, sorry to see Jenny looking so crestfallen as the jailer's wife led her away. 'We shall not stop our lessons.'

Jenny stopped and looked round. Already tears were running down her face. 'Oh I hope not, my lady. I hope not.'

Jane looked at Southampton, whose face was also showing signs of emotion. 'She is a talented musician, Sir Ralph,' she said.

'She always delighted me with her singing,' he said. 'But we mustn't dwell on the past. She gave me great pleasure once upon a time and I hope she will spend the rest of her life in comfort. I will see that the Sheriff releases her, Jane.'

Leaving Sir Percival Darlington in charge of his manor house, Nicholas rode back to Marchester, stabled his horse in the Dean's stables and walked round to the front of the house as the back door was fastened. From the front door there was a clear view to the cathedral cloisters and, as Nicholas glanced in that direction, he saw two figures standing in the gateway to the cloisters. He recognised Jeremy Overton, the Archdeacon, and it took him a little longer to see that the other person was Anthony West, the head chorister.

They were talking animatedly together and as he continued to watch, they moved away from the doorway and into the cloisters. Nicholas decided to follow them. Keeping close to the wall that marked the edge of the path leading down to the cloister gateway, Nicholas went in to the cloisters and ducked behind one of the solid Norman pillars. From there he had a clear view of the proceedings. The conversation between the two men now appeared to have become acrimonious. Nicholas couldn't hear what the Archdeacon was saying because he spoke quietly, but whatever it was seemed to annoy Anthony West, whose fair face was flushed with a mixture of anger and embarrassment. When the Archdeacon put a hand on Anthony's arm, he brushed it off impatiently and said something which seemed to incite the Archdeacon even more. Wondering whether he should intervene before things got worse, he was about to step out from behind the pillar when another man came rushing down the cloisters from the far end and confronted the Archdeacon. Nicholas recognised Lancelot Day, Canon Precentor, who had been his guest at his table with Bishop Thomas on that last dinner before the Bishop disappeared. Nicholas would recognise that tall, lean figure anywhere. He began to talk urgently to Anthony and the Archdeacon and then grabbed hold of

Anthony's arm. To Nicholas's astonishment an unseemly tug-of-war followed between the Archdeacon and the Precentor with Anthony in the middle. Suddenly, Lancelot Day, furious with rage, raised an arm and hit the Archdeacon full in the face. The Archdeacon reeled back but released his hold on Anthony's arm. Quick as a flash, Lancelot Day gathered up Anthony like a mother hen rounding up a wayward chick and urged him along the cloister. But the Archdeacon, wiping the blood off his face with the corner of his cassock, went after them. This time, Lancelot Day turned and waited for the onslaught. They were both about the same age but there was no doubt who was the fitter. Stepping aside like a prize fighter in the ring, he checked the Archdeacon's onrush with another blow to the side of his head. This time he caught the Archdeacon off balance and he fell onto the stone floor. Lancelot Day aimed a vicious kick at his backside and rushed off with Anthony West. Nicholas decided it was time to put in an appearance. He stepped out from behind the pillar and went to help the Archdeacon, who was struggling to his feet.

'Good morning, Archdeacon, can I help you?' he said.

'Thank you, Lord Nicholas, but it's nothing. I tripped, that's all. These flagstones are very dangerous. I must have a word with the

Dean about them. Don't put yourself out. I can manage. Some cold water to my face and in ten minutes I shall be fully restored. Thank you, though, for your kind offer.'

Helping him to his feet, Nicholas watched as the Archdeacon limped away. But someone else had witnessed the scene. A young man dressed in a clerical cassock emerged from the doorway to the cloister and walked quickly after the Archdeacon, who greeted him warmly and allowed the young man to put an arm round his shoulder and lead him away.

Nicholas was shaken by the scene not only because it was incongruous to see two senior clerics argue over one of the choristers, but also the emergence of the slim youth reminded him of the time when he was conscious of being watched in the cathedral. Then he'd only seen a dim shape and a flick of a cassock, but it was possible the young man could have been that person. Did the Archdeacon employ spies? If he did, what was the reason? Was it simply to keep an eye on the security of the cathedral because, with the tomb of St Richard attracting scores of pilgrims, anything could happen? Thieves were rife. But that was the Dean's job, not the Archdeacon's.

Deep in thought, Nicholas returned to the Dean's house, where Katharine Catchpole greeted him warmly and informed him that the Earl of Southampton had just left to see the Sheriff and would Nicholas join them as soon as possible. He thanked her for the message and said he would leave as soon as he had seen Jane, who, Katharine said, had gone to the library to do some work for the Chancellor.

She was alone in the library, seated at the Chancellor's desk, her head bowed over a parchment roll which was spread out in front of her. So deep was her concentration that she didn't hear Nicholas come into the room and only looked up when he stood in front of the desk patiently waiting for her to become aware of his presence. At length she reached the bottom of the roll and looked up, her face lighting up with pleasure when she saw him. She jumped to her feet, ran round the desk and threw her arms round his neck as if he'd been away for months.

'Nicholas, you're back. It's wonderful to see you.'

He laughed and held her to him. 'What makes you think I would abandon you to the Chancellor? Where is he, by the way?'

'He's gone off somewhere; he didn't tell me. Hubert's not here this morning, either, so I've got the place to myself and can pretend I'm the Chancellor.'

'Thank God you don't look like Edward. But come, show me what keeps you so enthralled; unless it's highly secret and I'm not allowed to see it.'

'You're the one person who should see this particular document. It's a record of all our priory's leases and financial transactions over the last century or so. I've skipped most of the early stuff but I'm up to the years when Prior Thomas held office. I didn't realise how business-minded these heads of religious houses were, Nicholas. Most of the entries are about money paid in from the prior's tenants working the farms and mills belonging to the priory. Sometimes these tenants did a particularly useful service to the prior and were given some land for themselves; it was something every tenant wanted. Here's one for example,' she said, going back to the desk and finding the entry in the document. 'Stanley Knighton, merchant of Marchester, for making a special trip to Bordeaux on behalf of Prior Thomas to buy one hundred casks of wine for the prior's cellars. He made the trip at his own expense – I'm sure he bought some casks for his own use – and, of course, the prior paid for his own wine. He did this as you can see, in return for the prior's blessing and the hope of leniency from "God, Our Father, in the hour of my death." Prior Thomas seemed to think Stanley Knighton should be recompensed in this life as well and gave him a manor house and thirty acres of pasture just outside Marchester.'

'He was a cunning old fox, Prior Thomas, but, give him his due, he shared the wine with everyone and didn't take favours for granted. I must say, I envy you, Jane, sitting here in this cloistered calm whilst I dash from one place to another obeying the King's orders.'

'What does he want from you, Nicholas?'

Nicholas told her briefly about Darlington's visit and how he now had to see the Sheriff and liaise with him and Southampton.

'He's been here – Southampton, I mean, not the sheriff. Did you know that he and Jenny Dobbs know one another? I think they were lovers at one time or another.'

'Jenny Dobbs? Oh, you mean the musical witch. Have you been seeing her again?'

'The Dean very kindly let her come to the music room, under guard, of course. She's an interesting woman and could give us a lot of the information we need. Unfortunately Ralph interrupted us before I could begin to ask her questions. I think she knows a lot about Agatha Trimble's activities.'

Nicholas kissed her fondly on the top of her white-capped head. 'Jane, you've lost me. Here I am ordered to report to the King on the murder of a bishop and you talk of daft old women.'

'Don't talk to me as if I am a child,

Nicholas. These daft old women could just give us the lead we need.'

'If you say so, my love. But what did Ralph Paget say he wanted to see me about?'

'He didn't say because he was so startled at seeing Jenny Dobbs. But I'm sure if you go to the Sheriff's house, you'll find them together and you can get all the information you need to keep the King happy. In the meantime, I shall concentrate on these old leases and deeds and talk to my daft old women.'

'Don't get involved with any of Jenny Dobbs's activities, my dear, otherwise I'll be in trouble with Richard Landstock. You'll be safe here, Jane, working on your own.'

'Hubert will take good care of me, when he returns.'

'Hubert?'

'Edward's clerk. He doesn't say much, I'm glad to say. It's quite companionable, really.'

'Good. Then we meet again at dinner. Don't spoil those beautiful eyes of yours with all this reading. You really should wait until the sun returns and brightens up this room.'

A young man came in just as Nicholas was leaving the room. He glanced at Nicholas, who, for a moment, wondered where he had seen him before. He saw him go over to the other desk in the room and open a roll of parchment. So that is Hubert, he thought.

Then he nodded to the young man, smiled at Jane, and walked away. Then he remembered where he'd seen him. He was the young man who had gone to the aid of the Archdeacon, with whom he seemed to be on familiar terms. He was Edward Hasledean's clerk and a friend of the Archdeacon. Was he also one of the Archdeacon's spies? That young man needed watching, Nicholas thought, as he left the cathedral and went into the town.

Sixteen

'The King, Lord Nicholas, will have to wait for his report,' said the Earl of Southampton, warming his backside in front of the fire in the Sheriff's office in his house in Marchester. 'We're nowhere near ready, it seems, to come to any conclusions about this case. In God's name, the Bishop has only been dead for just over a week and we can't expect to perform miracles. In fact, this investigation seems to be extraordinarily complicated with the absence of any witnesses willing to testify. Most people appear to have lost the use of their tongues.'

Nicholas joined him by the fire, took off his cloak and accepted a tankard of ale from a servant, who bowed and left the room after a perfunctory gesture of dismissal from the Sheriff.

'It's not for me to tell the King that he's being unreasonable, Ralph,' he said to the Earl. 'You know him as well as I do and reasonable is not part of his vocabulary. We've not exactly been idle, but that's beside the point. We'll have to collate our investigations and concoct some sort of report to keep him quiet. I'll not have Darlington eat-

305

ing me out of house and home and wearing out my horses for much longer.'

Southampton laughed heartily and slapped Nicholas on the back. 'I can't say I feel sorry for you, Nicholas, my friend. You did very well out of the King last year when he gave you several more manors to add to your estate. This, I fear, is the price you have to pay: your house becomes a hunting lodge for the King and his friends and you are expected to jump to his tune however awkward the timing.'

'Don't look so smug, Ralph. Your turn will come soon.'

'Too soon, I expect. His Majesty likes to visit his fortifications along the south coast of his kingdom and he likes to make sure he's getting value for money. He'll be knocking at my door, come Easter, and then I shall be facing bankruptcy.'

'Thank God His Majesty steers clear of Marchester,' said Sheriff Landstock, seated at his table, watching the two lords with an amused smile on his face. 'It's quite a relief to know that I have only two bedrooms in this house and a barn to stable my horses. It pays one to own little, my lords.'

'Don't look so cheerful, Richard,' said Nicholas, 'the writing of this report will fall on your shoulders. You have the clerks; you are officially in charge of the investigation. The King will expect the report to be signed by you with me and the Earl as witnesses. However, I'll gladly read it over when you're ready.'

The Sheriff jumped to his feet, an appalled look on his face. 'Lord Nicholas, he's asked you for a report. I have not been approached.'

'Don't get excited, Richard; both of us will have to compile it, but it will have to come from you officially. However, let's not waste too much time deciding on who's going to write the report; let's see what we've got to put in it so far. You led us to the arrest of the wreckers, Ralph,' Nicholas said, 'and we are grateful for your assistance. Let's hope we have no more trouble from that quarter again. But what news of the Treasurer, Edwin Stanley's whereabouts? Have you found him yet?'

'I'm afraid the news is not good, Nicholas; not in the sense, that is, of retrieving the money. But at least we can eliminate him from the murder enquiry. He's fled the country. I got a description of Stanley from the Dean and he told me what his carriage looked like. He didn't go to Salisbury where, as you know, he has, or rather had, estates, but to Portsmouth, where the port authorities remember seeing him and his small retinue of servants embark on a French ship called *Cormoran*. It sailed on the Tuesday of last week – the day before the body of the Bishop was found. It means that, by now, he is somewhere on the Continent with a great deal of money in his coffers. Apparently, there were some shady financial dealings in the past when he was Treasurer of Salisbury cathedral, but such being the foolishness, or naivety, of the clergy, he was dismissed but allowed to be Treasurer of Marchester cathedral where the same thing happened again; but this time he got away with it. But I am sure that he had nothing to do with the Bishop's murder. Unless he arranged the Bishop's death before he left, which is unlikely because he was only interested in making off with the money, I can't see he had anything to gain by his death. It was entirely fortuitous that the other cathedral dignitaries were so knocked back by the Bishop's death that they forgot all about their Treasurer. It was unfortunate for us because he had several days to get out of the country before we heard about it. However, I can see that finding that one's bishop had been done to death in a most dreadful fashion would take precedence in people's minds over a defaulting Treasurer.

'Besides,' Southampton went on, 'by all accounts, the manner of the Bishop's death does seem to indicate that he was killed as part of a ritual, and I doubt whether Edwin Stanley, hell-bent on getting out of the country with a large part of the cathedral's money, would stop to take part in a Satanic ritual before he set off. We know he was an embezzler; we don't know he was a Satanist.'

'Which brings us back to my original contention,' said the Sheriff, 'that this murder is linked to the activities of witches who bedevil our countryside and, in their practice of the black arts, resort to every sort of wickedness. To please their Satanic master they offer up children, even babies, as sacrifices, and drink the blood of the victims and grind up their bones for their foul potions. What a feather in their caps to capture a bishop and offer up his heart to their bestial gods of darkness! I would not put it past them to have eaten the bishop's heart as part of their hellish rituals.'

Nicholas stared at the Sheriff in horror, but realised that, even allowing for the Sheriff's love of melodrama, he could be right. But could these evil things really take place in Sussex? One of the most civilised counties in the country? And even if these things did go on, how could they possibly prove it? They would have to find out where the witches' covens met. They would have to find out the means to infiltrate them. And they were running out of time. The King wanted his report soon. To infiltrate a coven would take months, possibly years and in that time other people might suffer the same fate as Bishop Thomas.

Southampton scowled across at the Sheriff. 'You take this witchcraft theory of yours too far, Sheriff. I suggest you take a good rest and keep that lurid imagination of yours in check. You are wasting time with your witch hunts. What have you done so far? You bring in two old crones, one on the point of death, the other out of her mind. But the other one I can personally vouch for. She has absolutely no interest whatever in the black arts. She should be released immediately.'

The Sheriff stared at him angrily. 'Release Mistress Dobbs? Never. She has a reputation for putting spells on people, causing any amount of mischief in Pelham Maris.'

'Jealousy, that's what it is, Sheriff, jealousy. She knows how to cure illnesses, she's beautiful and men are attracted to her. She has never harmed anyone.'

'I'm surprised you know her so well, my lord,' said the Sheriff, controlling his anger with difficulty.

'Let us just say that once I knew her well. She entertained me with her voice and her beauty. She would not harm a fly. She is one of nature's miracles.'

Nicholas decided it was time to intervene before the Sheriff lashed out at Southampton.

'Nevertheless, Ralph, Sheriff Landstock

did well to take reports of witchcraft seriously. This is one aspect of the case which particularly interests the King. He abhors witchcraft and wants it stamped out throughout the country. We cannot say it doesn't exist here in Sussex. Down there in those coastal marshes and the creeks and waterways of Marchester harbour all sorts of things could go on which no one in Marchester would ever hear about until something happens to draw attention to them. We know witchcraft exists. We know the covens meet. Candlemas is the time when the witches' major festivals take place. The Bishop was murdered at this time. It was not a usual murder where robbery was the motive. This was a ritual killing. The Bishop could have been murdered at a Candlemas Sabbat.

'Now, it's not enough to bring in any poor old soul who is suspected of witchcraft. We need to know who presides over these meetings of the Sabbats. And I believe there is someone behind all this who is the incarnation of evil. He uses the covens for his own reasons. He wanted Bishop Thomas dead; he used the witches' Sabbat as the means. We have to find this person, Richard. That's where we should next turn our attention to. The problem is no one is going to help us; no one is going to inform against him. He so terrorises the people in those coastal villages that no one is going to come forward and give us any information. Remember Roger Aylwin? He killed himself rather than be compelled under torture to reveal the name of this person.'

'He was a wrecker, not a witch,' shouted the Sheriff impatiently.

'I think there is a link between the two. It needs a clever man to mastermind a wrecking. It needs a clever man to entice a Bishop away from his cathedral. It needs a manipulative person to use the covens to satisfy his evil desires. Remember Agatha Trimble? She died suddenly, just as everyone thought she was getting better.'

'She was old. Old people die suddenly,' said the Sheriff.

'But someone brought her communion just before she died.'

'So? That's quite normal. At least she died in a place where there is no shortage of priests.'

'Indeed. But if that communion wine had been tampered with Agatha Trimble would not be able to tell us who presided over the meetings of her coven.'

Nicholas paused. Something was stirring in the back of his mind. Something he must pursue straight away.

'This is all supposition, Nicholas,' said Southampton evenly.

'I know and that's the trouble with this

case. I have my suspicions – I am sure we all have – but we have no evidence. Another man dies; very convenient if he, too, knew too much.'

'You mean Master Brotherhood?' said the Sheriff. 'He was set upon by thieves, my lord; not unusual in these unsettled times.'

'That's what we were led to think. But he could have possessed some knowledge which could jeopardise our man. Witnesses have to be got rid of, Richard, as you know only too well.'

'We don't know he was a witness. For God's sake he was the Bishop's clerk before he started work for the Archdeacon. He happened to be unlucky, that's all. My men are searching the horse fairs to try and find his horse. When it's found it could lead us to the thieves who robbed him.'

'I hope you do find it, Richard. It would relieve my mind to find that he was indeed murdered only for his possessions.'

'What's on your mind, Nicholas?' said Southampton quietly. 'Whom do you suspect?'

'I still keep an open mind, Ralph, but there are several things going on here in Marchester that I am not happy about. I am not satisfied that Agatha Trimble died a natural death and I must go straight away and check up on something. No, I can't tell you now,' he said, holding up his hand to check the Sheriff's questions. 'I am also not satisfied that Hugh Brotherhood's death was a simple case of robbery with violence. My wife is also of the opinion that the solution to this case is to be found in the covens. She has been trying to get Jenny Dobbs to reveal anything she might know about these gatherings.'

'I told you Jenny Dobbs is not and never has been involved in witchcraft,' said Southampton impatiently.

'No, but she was friendly with Agatha Trimble who might have told her about what went on at the meetings of the covens. She might even have attended the Candlemas Sabbat and would know who presided.'

'Your wife, Lord Nicholas, should steer away from these matters. It is too dangerous for her to talk to prisoners. If Jenny Dobbs tells her anything of importance, then, she too, will be a witness.'

'She is aware of that. And what's more I have ordered her to keep away from now on.'

'And you think she'll obey?' said Southampton with a hint of a smile.

'I am sure she will. She knows how much I worry about her safety. Besides, she spends much time in the library working with the Chancellor.'

'A good thing too,' said the Sheriff. 'That will keep her out of mischief.'

'But you haven't yet told us whom you suspect, Nicholas,' said Southampton.

'I cannot say at this moment. As I've said, I think there is a clever, manipulative person behind this case. And I think he drives round at night in a distinctive carriage. Now I know this because my steward down in my hunting lodge at Pelham Maris, which I have sorely neglected to visit for a long time, told me that a visitor drove up to the vicarage at night to take Richard Rushe, Vicar of Pelham Maris, to see his friend, William Tremayne, Rector of Selsey. I think only wealthy men can afford a carriage, however modest it might be. Someone like this, clever, owning a carriage, on friendly terms with parochial clergy, could originate from the cathedral, unlikely as it seems. So, over the last few days, I have been talking to the cathedral dignitaries and have got nowhere. None of them, it appears, has left the cathedral precincts over the last ten days, except the Chancellor to visit a lady friend in Marchester. He resented Bishop Thomas, whom, he said, underestimated his work and did not reward him as much as he rewarded his colleagues; but that's hardly a motive for murder. For all he knows the next Bishop might underestimate even more than Bishop Thomas. Also, more important, he does not possess a carriage. Nor does he own a horse. And I'm certain that the person we're looking for rides out quite frequently around the countryside.

'The Treasurer,' Nicholas continued, glancing at Southampton, 'we have eliminated. The Dean is the last person in the world to murder anyone, let alone his Bishop, although he does own a carriage. But I am staying in his house as guest and he is kindness itself to my wife and I, and is deeply immersed in this enquiry. He wants the Bishop's murderer found as much as we do. The Canon Precentor was a good friend of the Bishop. He dined at my house only three days before the Bishop's body was found. He says he never left the cathedral last week, and he owns no carriage.

'That leaves us with the Archdeacon. I think he is someone who is capable of murder because he is a man of deeply repressed passions. He was also fiercely loyal to Bishop Robert who was the bishop before Bishop Thomas and he was critical of Bishop Thomas's tolerant attitude to married clergy. But he swears he did not leave the cathedral last week and his groom confirms this. He does own a carriage – a fine one, given to him by the previous bishop, but it has not been taken out since Christmas, so the groom says. He will not use it again until the roads improve in March when he begins his spring visits around the parishes. Certainly his carriage looks in pristine condition but it does not in any way resemble my steward's description of the carriage that visits Pelham Maris at night. I simply cannot think why any of these people should want to kill the person set above them by God and to whom they owe unquestioning obedience. I cannot find a motive, Ralph,' said Nicholas despairingly, 'and, until I do, I cannot see an end to this case. And certainly I am in no position to write a report on it to the King.'

Silence fell. Southampton picked up his cloak. 'Then the King must wait until we have more evidence. Get on with your work, Sheriff, and find out more about these covens. I shall be away to Marchester harbour to see my friend the Harbour Master. I must tell him that many of the wreckers have been arrested, but he must not relax his vigilance. He must see to his harbour lights. And you, Nicholas my friend, look after that wife of yours. She should confine herself to her embroidery and not go around asking too many questions. Good luck to you both. We must meet again soon.'

He left the room and Nicholas made ready to leave.

'So, it's back to those infernal marshes for me, and the Dog and Hare, Lord Nicholas. I shall have to speak again with Richard Rushe and try to find out who his nocturnal visitor is. I also ought to have another talk with that old steward of yours.'

'And I must see if I can find the Arch-deacon. Let us meet again very soon, Richard. You know where I am staying. You can always leave messages there for me. This case drags on too long and we must try to bring it to an end.'

'It'll soon be over,' said the Sheriff opti-mistically. 'At least we now know what we are looking for.'

Nicholas looked at the Sheriff in astonish-ment. 'Do we, Richard? Please enlighten me.'

'Why, the leader of the covens, my lord. Satan himself.'

The Dean was only half the size of Lancelot Day, Canon Precentor of Marchester cathedral, but he made up for his lack of physical height with an abundance of energy. When annoyed, as he was at that moment, he had a habit of bouncing up and down on the balls of his feet as if he were trying to add inches to his height. It gave him the appearance of a bantam cockerel about to pounce on one of his hens and it had the effect of reducing his opponent, in this case the Precentor, to a nervous silence.

'I won't have this unseemly squabbling in my cathedral, Precentor,' he said, springing up on his toes.

'It's not the first time you and the Archdeacon have come to blows. And it will not happen again. If you can't control yourself, I shall have to see about having you transferred to another place where your musical talent will be appreciated without you having to live and work in a cathedral chapter. An organist in a parish church would suit you well, I think. One of the isolated Downland churches far removed from the centres of population. The shepherds won't bother you at all.'

The Precentor watched the Dean's gyrations in an appalled silence. Then he broke out into a great wail of protest like the lamentations of an Old Testament prophet.

'No, no, Dean. Spare me that. Please, please let me stay here. I have done nothing to deserve such a punishment.'

'Done nothing,' roared the Dean, his face turning a dangerous shade of red. 'You've only punched the Archdeacon on the nose and pushed him so hard that he fell down onto the stone floor. It's a wonder he didn't break any bones.'

'But he wouldn't let go of Anthony. He hung onto him like a limpet clinging to a rock. Mister Dean, it was not right, not right at all.'

'Hung on to Anthony West? Don't be such a fool, Precentor; you sound like a doting old woman. The Archdeacon says he was simply having a chat with Anthony; surely there's no harm in that? It's unseemly for you to behave as you have done and I won't have it. For God's sake, man, pull yourself together and go and find yourself a wife. Anthony West can talk to whoever he wants to. You are not his keeper.'

'I am responsible for the moral welfare of the choir. It is my duty to protect him.'

'And what makes you think that the Archdeacon is going to harm Anthony? He has every right to speak to anyone he pleases without asking for your permission.'

'Anthony didn't want to talk to the Archdeacon. He didn't want to go over to his house and drink wine with him. He didn't want to be a special friend. He loathes the man. The Archdeacon's too intense, Dean, too personal. He can't take his eyes off Anthony when he's in choir. I've seen his lecherous gaze; it's not healthy and I can't ignore it. I have a duty to the people entrusted to my care.'

'That doesn't mean that you have the right to assault one of your colleagues whom you happen not to like.'

'I'll hit him again if he lays a finger on Anthony. He's a wicked man, the Archdeacon; not to be trusted with any of our youths.'

He stared defiantly at the Dean, who stopped his agitated springing in the air and gave a sigh of despair. 'Very well, I'll have to talk to the Archdeacon and tell him to stop paying Anthony any special attention. As for you, Precentor, just curb your jealous passions and get on with your work, which I can't fault. You are an excellent musician and the choir respects you. For God's sake keep away from the Archdeacon and I'll order him not to talk to Anthony West.'

The Precentor bowed to the Dean and rushed out of the room, nearly knocking over Nicholas who was coming up the stairs to the Dean's private room. Nicholas greeted him only to receive a blank stare in return as if the Precentor didn't recognise him. Nicholas knocked on the door and received permission to enter. He went in and saw the Dean standing by the window, looking down into the Close.

'You seem to be having a bit of trouble,' said Nicholas mildly. The Dean turned round and his face relaxed into a smile when he saw Nicholas.

'Just an aggravation, that's all. There was an incident in the cloisters this morning involving Lancelot Day and Jeremy Overton – my Archdeacon, of all people. I can't have this squabbling and wrangling in the cathedral premises. It does the church no good.'

'I think I saw this incident you talk of,' said Nicholas, joining the Dean at the window. 'It seemed that your Precentor resented the Archdeacon's familiarity with the Head Chorister. There was a bit of a tug-of-war and the Precentor hit the Archdeacon, who fell over. Fortunately someone else came to his aid as he seemed reluctant to make use of my services.'

'Well, thank God I have an independent witness. Thank you for clearing up the matter. Now I shall have to speak to the Archdeacon and order him away from Anthony West who, between you and me, is too good-looking for his own safety. We must not have any more scandal, Lord Nicholas. It's bad for the church in these unsettled times. I trust you will not mention this matter to anyone else. Let us just keep it between ourselves.'

'Of course, it will go no further than these walls. But I want to ask your permission, Humphrey, to speak to the Archdeacon on a certain matter connected to the murder investigation. I was told he would be here with you.'

'He'll be along shortly. In the meantime you might catch him before he leaves his house. I hope to see you at dinner with us shortly, Nicholas. This investigation takes up much of your time and I should hate to see you neglecting your food. I know you and Sheriff Landstock are doing your best, but it worries me to have the matter unsolved. Everyone is so on edge. We have all become suspicious of each other and attribute sinister motives to everyone's actions. God grant that you find the guilty person soon so that we can all sleep peacefully in our beds at night.'

'I shall say "Amen" to that, Humphrey, then you will be relieved of the presence of myself and Jane from your house.'

'Nicholas, this is the one aspect of the case that I enjoy. It's good to have you and Jane here. She works wonders with Philippa and the Chancellor can't praise her highly enough.'

'I am glad of that. Sometimes I fear that her impetuosity will lead her into trouble.'

'Don't worry. We shall guard her well and see she comes to no harm. When you've spoken to the Archdeacon, Nicholas, tell him to come and see me straight away. There is much that concerns me about that man's behaviour.'

Nicholas saw the Archdeacon coming across the Cathedral Close on his way to see the Dean. He seemed preoccupied and would have hurried past Nicholas without seeing him. Nicholas, however, stopped him and was horrified to see the livid bruise on his face where the Precentor had punched him. One eye was partly closed and the other bloodshot.

'Good day, Lord Nicholas, you must forgive me for not recognising you but there is much on my mind at the moment and now, it seems, the Dean wants to see me.'

'I shan't detain you long,' said Nicholas, 'I only want you to clear up a tiny point. But I am sorry to see that bruise on your face. I hope no bones were broken as a result of your fall this morning.'

'It's of no consequence,' said the Arch-deacon impatiently. 'I should take more care. Now I am afraid I have no time to exchange pleasantries; I must not keep the Dean waiting.'

'No indeed, he asked me to tell you that he was waiting for you. But perhaps you would put my mind at rest on one matter concerning Agatha Trimble.'

'Agatha Trimble? She's with God, my lord; or should be, if God has forgiven her her sins. Why should you be remotely interested in her now?'

'My wife wants me to find out the name of the priest who took her communion in the last hours before her death. She would like to thank him for taking the trouble to bring the consolation of the sacrament to an old woman whom most people think too wicked to bother with. I know you did tell me before, but perhaps you would remind me.'

'I admire your wife's concern but the priest was only doing his duty. But as you ask, the priest was Father Oswald, one of the older, retired priests who likes to help out now and again. Now if I might get on my way…'

'Thank you Archdeacon. You have put my mind at rest. I am sorry to have troubled you.'

The Archdeacon hurried over to the Dean's house. Nicholas stood there lost in thought. He remembered the conversation he had had only yesterday with Jane when she had told him that the jailer had said that the priest who came to administer to Agatha Trimble was a young man. Now why should the Archdeacon lie to him? Could it be that the jailer was mistaken? Could it be that the Archdeacon had given him the first name to come into his head in order to keep him quiet? Or could there be a more sinister reason – that the Archdeacon wanted the identity of the priest kept secret? If so, why? There was only one thing for it – he would have to find Father Oswald and ask him in person. But first, he wanted to see Jane and take up the Dean's offer of dinner.

Seventeen

The corpse had hung there a long time in its iron cage but the weather had been so cold that the body was frozen solid and decomposition was minimal. The cage, hanging from the beam of the gibbet, swayed gently in the light breeze, squeaking mournfully as the iron chain rubbed against the shackle which fastened it to the beam. The dead man had murdered his wife and the child he had been convinced was not his and no one had had any sympathy for him or appealed for a mitigation of his sentence. His head, fixed in position by the freezing cold, slumped forward on his chest; his hair, dark and matted; his empty eye-sockets – the crows had long since feasted on his eyes – stared down on to the frozen earth. Above him the sky was clear. A waning moon lit up the scene with its ghostly light, and the stars sparkled in the cloudless night sky. A solitary fir tree stood near the gibbet and one or two dead trees were scattered over the Heath, their rotting branches like the fingers on a dead man's hands.

Marchester Heath was just outside the north gate of the city. It was a bleak, bare place. No tree flourished there. No birds made their nests there. No owl called out from its nest in the hole in the dead tree's trunk. A single stake indicated the place of execution for those poor wretches dragged there on hurdles to face death by fire: witches, heretics, those found guilty in the Archdeacon's court of sexual perversions.

No one came here in the daytime except when an execution was to take place. Then they stood there drinking their tankards of ale, calling out encouragement to the condemned if he was popular or hurling obscenities at him if he wasn't. Then, when it was all over, they crept away in silence. No children ever played here despite its proximity to the city. No one ever came here after dark. But that Thursday night was an exception. Two figures dressed in black cloaks with the hoods pulled well down over their faces emerged from the shadow of the wall that marked the boundary of the Heath and went over to the gibbet and stared up at the doleful occupant of the cage. Then they turned to face each other and held hands.

'*Je te renonce, Jésu,*' they whispered to each other by way of a greeting. Then, 'Welcome, Grésil,' said the taller of the two men.

'We can talk freely here,' he went on, 'away from that infernal place where even the walls have ears. At least he can't hear us,' he said, pointing up at the corpse.

Grésil nodded his head in agreement and, gathering his cloak around him, he sat down on a mound of hard earth under the cage. His tall companion did the same. They crouched there looking like two monstrous toads let out of hell in order to wreak havoc on the people of Marchester.

'We need to decide on when to hold the next meeting of the covens,' said the tall one, who seemed to be the leader. 'This is a good time of the year – too cold, too dark for any interfering fool to disturb us. Same place, of course. We are never disturbed there.'

'When shall we meet, Master?'

'Call me Lucifer, Grésil, as I taught you. I am Satan incarnate, am I not? You all agreed on that. Why should that old, powerless God of the Christians appear on earth in the person of Jesus whom they call the Son of God, and our mighty Satan not have the same? Let me hear you say it now. Lucifer, I worship you.'

'Lucifer, I worship you,' said Grésil quietly, his face turned away.

'I sense a lack of commitment here, Grésil. Look at me when you say it.'

This time Grésil looked at his companion and said the words louder and clearer.

'That's better. There's no turning back now, Grésil. You are either for us or against us. Forget those vows you made to that other God; Satan rules our lives now.'

'I'm sorry, Lucifer. Forgive me.'

The man called Lucifer inclined his head. 'I grant you forgiveness. I shall give you your penance when we next meet. Sunday, I think. Our master likes the Christians' holy days. Sunday is the most powerful day of the week.'

'There is not much time to get ready.'

'There is enough. We have three days to prepare. Send Vérin to alert the covens. Tell him to use one of my horses. The word will get round quickly. Vérin rides hard. He's young and tireless.'

Grésil nodded. 'I will do so straight away, Lucifer. What else do you want me to do?'

'We have no babies now that the old hag has gone. Behemoth approached the stupid wretch of a churchwarden to see about getting some of the unbaptised babies who are buried in unconsecrated ground outside the churchyard but he refused to co-operate. Said they had as much right to lie in the earth as their more holy counterparts. We shall have to look elsewhere in the future. Meanwhile we can use the women, especially the virgin.'

'Lucifer, it is going to be difficult to capture them. They are well guarded,' said Grésil, his voice rising in panic.

'Be quiet, Grésil. Of course it's not going to be easy. Our master knows this and will reward your efforts. You will have to use your initiative. It is not so difficult to seize hold of an unsuspecting person after daylight has faded. You captured a bishop, remember.'

'That was easy. He simply walked out of the cathedral to the spot you suggested. The two women will have to be lured away. But how?'

'Grésil, Grésil, your brain seems to have frozen up inside your skull tonight, like that fool up there. The woman is married and appears to love her husband. Make use of that.'

'And the virgin?'

'She admires the woman. Make use of that.'

'Where do I take them?'

'Usual place. I'll arrange for you to have the carriage. Keep them at my place until Sunday and have them brought to the church on Sunday night. But these are details. The weather, you see, is going to change.'

Grésil looked up at the starry sky. 'It seems very settled, Lucifer.'

'Tonight it is. Tomorrow, Friday, it will turn warmer. That will put paid to our friend up there,' he said, looking up at the corpse. 'With the warm air the wind will get up. By Sunday there will be a storm, wind and rain. With any luck, a violent storm. Satan has told me this, Grésil, because he

330

knows what he wants.'

'What does it matter what the weather's like? We shall be inside the church.'

'Because a ship is on its way from a Spanish port, bound for the port of Marchester. It carries wine and bales of fine velvet cloth. And also, this is the most important bit, Grésil, a great crucifix, made of the gold brought back from the Americas by the Spanish soldiers. The craftsmen of Seville have turned it into a magnificent work of art and the Chapter of Salisbury cathedral have commissioned it for their own use. Some benefactors left money for that purpose. Just think of it, Grésil. A solid gold crucifix. With just a few modifications, we can use it in our own services!'

'We can trample on it, defile it, tear off the figure of Christ, pour over it the blood of our sacrifices!'

Lucifer put an arm affectionately around the young man's shoulders. 'How well I have taught you, Grésil. When I leave this earth and go to meet our master you will most certainly step into my shoes. There never will be a more suitable candidate. Now, you must see Behemoth and tell him to make ready to see his friend in the port of Marchester. We must have the lights extinguished on Sunday night, as the ship approaches the harbour entrance. Remember, she will be running before the wind and

331

going fast. When she misses the entrance, which she certainly will if there are no navigation lights, she will end up on our shingle banks. When our Sabbat finishes, we can go down to the shore and join our friends there to receive our reward. We shall give them the wine and the cloth and we take only the crucifix. This will give us immense power, Grésil. People will flock to join us and that stupid chorister will regret he refused to speak to me.'

'We shall deal with him later, Lucifer. At the next Sabbat.'

'We think alike, you and I, Grésil. We shall make Anthony West regret the day he ever rejected me.'

'I look forward to planning what we shall do to him when we get him.'

'Calm yourself, Grésil. We need clear heads at this stage and much careful planning. Go and see Vérin and Behemoth now. I've told them to be ready for you. Explain what they have to do. Now, one more thing, wake up Sonnillon. We shall need his strength.'

'What shall I ask him to do, Lucifer?'

'Come closer, Grésil. This must be kept secret. Tell Sonnillon that the greatest delicacy must be employed. It will be a real test of his skill. There must not be the slightest indication that anything is untoward. Now listen closely...'

They sat huddled together until Grésil nodded his head by way of agreement and got to his feet. Lucifer followed suit. Then pulling their hoods down over their faces, they walked swiftly back to Marchester.

On Friday morning, Father Oswald woke up as usual at a quarter to six. He'd lived in the cathedral for forty of his sixty years, living an almost monastic existence, saying the morning, midday and evening offices and attending the eight o'clock mass in the cathedral each morning. As one of the vicars choral, although his voice had long since deteriorated, he still lived in the tiny house which stood, along with other such houses, around the cathedral Close. He lived on his own, having never considered matrimony, and preferring his own company. But his front door was always unlocked in case anyone needed his services or wanted company. In summer he sat on a bench in front of his house like a beadsman, talking to passers-by and soaking up the sun's warmth. Almost deaf, he heard little of what people told him so he said little and thus acquired a reputation for wisdom. In actual fact, he thought little and was content to exist quietly and gave thanks to God daily for giving him this house and his food so that he could end his days in comfort.

Lately, however, he hadn't been feeling

well. The icy cold had seemed to penetrate his body right through to the bones and he was reluctant to get up in the dark each morning and had begun to leave saying the morning office until later, just before he went over to mass. This morning he noticed it was warmer, which pleased him, but the rain which accompanied the change in the weather caused his joints to ache most painfully. All things considered, he thought, it was wiser to stay where he was that Friday morning, cocooned in the warmth and comfort of his bed in the little front bedroom in his own home.

He didn't hear the front door open. He didn't hear the footsteps on the wooden stairs. It wasn't until he turned over and opened his eyes that he saw the black shape of someone standing by his bed. For a moment he couldn't make out who it was. There was only a faint glimmer of light, the precursor of the dawn, coming in through the uncurtained window. He struggled to sit up and light the candle by his bed but his body was stiff and uncooperative. And then the man spoke and Father Oswald knew who it was and relaxed back on his pillow.

'How are you today, Father?' the man said.

'How good of you to come so early. You must have known I was not feeling too good.'

'Then you must stay in bed and rest. I shall go and get you some warm milk and bread.'

'You are so kind. It's not often I take to my bed.'

The man looked down into Father Oswald's face. He had closed his eyes and his breathing was regular. In a few seconds he would be sleeping. The man held behind his back a pillow which he now produced and placed over Father Oswald's peaceful face. Then he pressed down. Father Oswald could not fight back. One tiny cry like an animal in pain, a faint struggle, and then silence and stillness. After a while the man removed the pillow and looked down at the frail body. Then, quietly, he left the room.

On Friday morning, Jane and Nicholas breakfasted early. The Sheriff had sent a messenger to say that he wanted an early start as the weather had turned warmer and this meant that, if rain came, the roads would be impassable. Nicholas bolted down the bread and cold meat and kissed Jane.

'Not long now and we shall be back home. Does that please you, my love?'

'Very much. The Dean has been very kind but I miss my own kitchen and our own bed.'

Nicholas laughed. 'You promised "To be bonny and buxom in bed and at board," and

335

how well you have fulfilled that promise. Make ready to leave when I call for you. I'll tell the groom to have Melissa ready for when I get back from Pelham Maris. We'll be home tonight even if we ride back in the dark. How will you occupy yourself whilst I'm gone, Jane?'

'I'll go to the library. I am enjoying reading about all the financial transactions which took up so much of Bishop Thomas's time when he was Prior of our priory. He appeared to be financially astute and increased the priory's wealth. He used his charm to get people to do him favours and he also had a shrewd sense of when to sell property. He had a good legal sense, too, and never went contrary to the law. But he was also a hard man and lacked charity.'

'I shall look forward to hearing more when this case is closed. Stay out of harm's way, Jane. Don't go wandering off to see your witches.'

Jane stood up and went to Nicholas, who held her close for a long time. He loved feeling her slim body pressed against his and he delighted in the warmth of her embrace. The memory of it would be with him through the day and all its aggravations. Then they drew apart and she watched him go.

Just as she sat down the Dean bustled into the room and joined her at the breakfast table, where he helped himself to ale and cold meat. He smiled abstractedly across at Jane and she remained silent as she didn't want to disturb his thoughts. Finally he became more aware of her presence and collected himself.

'I'm sorry, Jane. I am poor company this morning. What with all the comings and goings of the Sheriff's men and the bad behaviour of two of my colleagues I can't get on with any work. And now my Precentor has shut himself away in a sulk in his house and won't speak to anyone and there's no one else to rehearse the choir. I shall just have to order him out and if he won't comply then we shall have to drag him out for this afternoon's evening service. The townspeople come to that and I can't have them disappointed. On top of all this, one of the old priests has died – in his bed, I am glad to say, at peace with the world.'

Jane looked up. 'I'm sorry to hear that. Who was he?'

'Father Oswald. You don't know him, Jane, my dear. He's been with us for over forty years or more and his time had come. He was one of the vicars choral and lived in the same house he'd lived in all these years. He's been getting a bit slow lately and more abstracted, so his death has come as no great surprise. However, it's always sad to lose a colleague.'

Jane wished Nicholas had waited just a little while longer. This news would interest him. So she made her excuses to the Dean and went over to the stables to see whether Nicholas was still there. But she was too late. He'd just left, said the groom; with one of the Sheriff's men. Slowly she walked back to the house. Maybe the news was of no importance, she thought. The death of an old man in February was nothing unusual. It was a cruel time of the year but coming now after all the other deaths it could not be dismissed lightly. However, there was nothing she could do. But why did she feel so uneasy? What was wrong? Why should anyone want to harm an old priest? It was a natural death; of course it was. Pray God we all die in such a way, she thought, as she opened the door and went into the Dean's house.

The jailer's wife woke at her usual hour on Friday morning and prodded her husband awake. He had drunk more than he should the previous night and greeted her interference with snorts of disapproval.

'All right, then,' she said irritably, 'stay where you are. Pigs like to wallow in their own filth.'

She dressed, fastened on her bonnet, and went to fetch water and see to the fires. She noticed it was warmer and the wind had got up and for once she felt pleased. Not long now before spring burst upon them and she could open doors and windows for gusts of fresh air.

She saw to old Phoebe first. Despite her rambling mind and dishevelled appearance she kept herself scrupulously clean. Her bed was already straightened up ready for the following night; blanket shaken out and folded neatly on the mattress, the straw pillow in its rough linen case plumped up and put at the head of the bed. Beatrice took the bucket away and emptied it and brought fresh water. Then she left the regulatory jug of ale and hunk of bread on the table. She glanced at Phoebe, happy in her own world. She was mumbling away to all the imaginary people who inhabited her head: people she'd known in the past, and people she knew in the present in her village. Beatrice watched her reach for the bread and bite into it with her broken teeth, laughing and talking to these people, and she envied her. If only everyone's lives could be as simple as Phoebe's.

Her visit to Jenny Dobbs was not so straightforward. Admittedly she was up and dressed but her hair was dishevelled and her face was streaked with tears as if she had been crying all night. When Beatrice came in she jumped up from where she had been sitting on the edge of the bed and faced her defiantly.

'I was told that I would be released from here.'

'Well, I've been given no such instructions, Mistress Dobbs, so you will have to stay put.'

'He said he'd see the Sheriff and get me out of here.'

'What my Lord of Southampton says and what he does are two different things.'

'Ralph Paget is a man of honour, I'll have you know.'

'Oh ho, so it's Ralph Paget now, is it! He's the Earl of Southampton, Mistress Dobbs, and don't you forget it. What he told you to call him in the past is all over and done with. You're lucky he recognised you yesterday; but don't go hoping for anything to come of it. The past is the past, never to be repeated. He used you once, by all accounts, and that's it. He's finished with you, finished and forgotten. You're nothing to him now.'

'How dare you say that, ignorant, stupid peasant, like all your kind. You know nothing about us, nothing.'

'And you, my lady, can mind your tongue. There's your water. Go fetch your own bread. I'm not waiting on the likes of you.'

Beatrice turned to go. Suddenly, Jenny's manner changed. She ran to Beatrice and held onto the sleeve of her blouse.

'I'm sorry, I'm sorry. I shouldn't have

spoken to you like that, but Ralph has been good to me and I treasure my memories. But as you say, the past is the past and it's over and done with. The present's what matters now and I must concentrate on that. I must speak to Jane Peverell. I can help them – the Sheriff, I mean, and Lord Nicholas. Please let me speak to her.'

'You help the Sheriff? That'll be the day. Lady Jane's been good to you, but that's over and done with now. She's off after new things and won't be thinking of you. I know how it is with the gentry. You give them a few hours' amusement; you make them feel good; and then they're off. Anyway, I expect they'll be leaving for home today before the rain sets in and the roads become fouled up. So you'll have to get used to your own company until the Sheriff gets round to dealing with you. And shut your mouth, if you please. We've had enough of your caterwauling.'

She jerked her arm free from Jenny's grasp and stalked out of the cell, slamming the door behind her. Jenny sat down on the edge of the bed again, and stared across at the wall. She had to speak to Jane. There was something they ought to know.

Gilbert Judd, Assistant Keeper of the lights for the Port of Marchester, stopped work at midday as he always did, and went off to the

Harbour Tavern down on the quay to eat bread and cheese and drink the freshly-brewed ale. His was not a particularly arduous job, although vitally important for shipping venturing into the port after dark. There was no comparison between Marchester and its big neighbour, Portsmouth, where most of the King's ships were stationed. Marchester harbour was tidal with only a narrow channel open all the time, whereas Portsmouth was accessible at all states of the tide. But Marchester made up for it by being handy for small ships with more select cargoes. In particular, the cathedral chapters of Winchester, Salisbury and Marchester used it when they were expecting cargoes for their own particular purposes. It was cheaper than Portsmouth and safer, as the thieves were more active around the larger port.

Gilbert Judd had been Keeper of the Lights at the harbour entrance for ten years now, stepping into his father's shoes when he died, just as his father had stepped into his father's shoes. There was nothing the Judd family did not know about the waters along the South Coast. He was much respected and he ate heartily, safe in the knowledge that he would never find himself out of work. He liked his food and he liked his house, newly built in bricks and flint with a proper slate roof and windows which his wife had insisted on. They were proper windows, he thought with satisfaction, with glass like the gentry had. And, like the gentry, he owned two horses and a carriage in which his wife liked to ride around the town, envied by everyone. He would like a second carriage for his daughter who was quite the young lady now and she had set her cap at Sir Graham Northbrook's son, and he would like to see her wed into that family. Then there would be real wealth in his family and he would be someone of importance and his wife could hold her head up high like the gentry did, and then there would be no more meetings with Mark and he could lie in bed at night with an easy conscience.

He didn't like to think too much about this part of his life, so when the door opened and the man he knew only as Mark came in and sat down opposite him, he tried to ignore him and buried his head in his tankard. Mark beckoned the serving boy over and ordered cold meat and ale. Then he leaned forward, putting his strong arms on the table in front of him, and stared at Gilbert who, at length, was forced to look at him. Mark saw uncertainty in Gilbert's eyes and didn't like it.

'Hallo, Gilbert,' he said softly. 'How are you? How's that fine house of yours? Finished yet? How's that lovely Arabella?

Betrothed to Northbrook's son? Not yet? I thought not. Not a big enough dowry, I expect. You need more money, don't you? And you know I can give it to you, don't you? Just one small service, that's all I require.'

'A small service but with dreadful consequences,' Gilbert said, staring miserably into Mark's florid face. How he hated the man! Hated his thick, coarse hair that curled round his ears, hated his stout body and protruding belly that showed an overfondness for food and wine.

'The consequences are no concern of yours,' said Mark, taking the tankard of ale from the serving boy and indicating where he was to put the plate of cheese and cold meats.

'You just do what you've done before,' he went on, speaking softly. 'With that one small action the ship will keep sailing past the harbour entrance. What's difficult about that?'

'It's not the action I'm worried about. I can arrange what you want very easily but there's a storm approaching, the ship concerned is a small barque by all accounts and she will be running before the wind with bare poles. If she tries to make the harbour entrance and doesn't see the lights she'll run straight past too close to the shore and end up on the shingle banks off Selsey point. I'll not be responsible for that. It will be the death of all hands and the breakup of the ship.'

'Nonsense, the captain would not alter course until he sees the lights. He'll keep to his offing and run along the coast.'

'Then why stop him entering the harbour?'

'We want him along at Shoreham. The King's officers are there and want to see the captain and search the ship. We think someone's on board who shouldn't be there; one of the King of Spain's spies.'

Gilbert still looked uncertainly at his companion. He didn't believe a word of what Mark was saying. The last time he'd done this service, the ship approaching the harbour from Flanders had ended up on Old Harry's spit a couple of miles along the coast. That time very few questions were asked. Everyone believed the captain had made a mistake. But he couldn't chance his luck again.

'I'll not do it,' he said finally, and resumed eating his food, glad to have made the decision.

'Oh yes you will, Gilbert. You're in this up to your neck now. One word from me and you lose your job and swing on Marchester Heath. But cheer up, man,' Mark went on, 'there's real money for you this time. One hundred gold sovereigns! How does that strike you?'

Gilbert swallowed the mouthful of bread whole.

'One hundred?'

'That's what I said.'

'One hundred and fifty.'

'Don't be greedy. One hundred will set you up fine and your daughter's marriage prospects will be ensured. You'll be a man of importance, Gilbert. You can retire from looking after the lights. No more going out to sea in cold open boats on freezing nights. A warm bed, as much bread and beef as you can stuff yourself with and a grateful family.'

'And you'll not ask me again?'

'That's right. And your fortune will be made.'

'Can I have some of it now, in advance?'

Mark unfastened a leather purse fastened to the belt round his waist. He put it on the table and pushed it over to Gilbert.

'Here's ten to keep you going. You can plan what to do with the rest. Remember, now, Sunday night, whatever the weather. The rougher the better. No one will take any notice of what you are doing. They will all be safe in their beds.'

They finished their meal and got up to go. Gilbert patted the bag of coins in the pocket of his jerkin. Suddenly they began to feel as heavy as lead – as heavy as the guilt he would feel for the rest of his life.

Eighteen

It was afternoon before Jane was able to extricate herself from the Dean's household and go to the library. Philippa, who had a Latin lesson, said she would join her later.

There was no one in the library when she got there: Hubert was not at his desk; the Chancellor, she knew, was in a meeting with the Dean and the Precentor. It was good to have the place to herself, she thought, as she settled herself at the Chancellor's desk. She loved the smell of the old parchment rolls and relished the sight of the rows of leather-bound books on the shelves, all waiting to be read. With a sigh of satisfaction she unrolled the parchment which contained the details of the expenditure on Dean Peverell's priory for the year 1530.

Bishop Thomas, when he had been the prior, had certainly loved luxury, she thought. He also had had a gift for getting people to give him money, money which he spent on furnishings for his priory church. There had been many benefactions in that year: two new altar frontals given by the Northbrooks family in October, 'for the high altar of the priory church of Dean Peverell, to be used at the feast of All Souls'; six hides of land at nearby Halnaker to provide 'fine candles for the church'. Nicholas's father, it seemed, had left money for a new set of vestments for the celebrating priests and a second silver chalice had been purchased from the silversmiths at Winchester in December 1530.

The expenditure, however, was not always confined to the church. The Prior's house seemed to be constantly in need of repair; a solarium added in 1531 had cost the community more than the Prior's colleagues approved of and they had been forced to sell some land. Also, 'There was dispute over the payments to the workmen who demanded more than their due.' Altogether, the solarium seemed to have been more trouble than it was worth.

Prior Thomas had been astute in property matters, she thought, as she read further. What he wanted, he got, even if it made him unpopular. Hubert came in at this point and Jane glanced up and smiled across at him. He acknowledged her greeting with a polite inclination of his head and started work straight away. He seemed even more tense and pale that afternoon and she began to worry about him. Then, when she noticed he kept glancing across at the table by the window where Philippa worked on her Book of Hours, she thought he must have fallen in love with her and it was a blessing that she was occupied with her studies that afternoon.

Jane resumed her reading and, as she read on, an item appeared which made her pause. Then she reached for one of the Chancellor's quill pens and a piece of old parchment which the Chancellor kept for making his own notes on, and copied the item out as she thought it would be of interest to Nicholas.

The item referred to a repossession of some land, which included a water mill, in the hamlet of Lower Rife some two miles north of the village of Pelham Maris. These fields had been in the possession of one John Tremayne and his wife, Elisabeth. They had not owned the land, she noted, but had leased it from the Prior of Dean Peverell as the Tremayne family had done since *1452*. But in May 1531, John Tremayne had defaulted on his payments to the Prior, who had, with the consent of his colleagues, meeting in Chapter, repossessed the land and put in new tenants, turning the Tremaynes out of their family house.

The mill, she read, did well under new management, but what, she wondered, had happened to the Tremayne family? She remembered Nicholas telling her that he was visiting a William Tremayne who was the Rector of Selsey, and she wondered whether there was any connection. If there were a connection, then William Tremayne would have deeply resented Prior Thomas's ruthless eviction of his family. She would have to ask the Dean if he knew anything about the Tremayne family.

She glanced up as Philippa came in, carrying her Book of Hours. Hubert looked up and stared at her and Jane was glad that she had got there first before Philippa. Philippa, unaware of the effect she was having on Hubert, came over to look at what Jane was reading.

'Why do you spend so much time on all those dull accounts, Jane?' she said. 'Come and help me with my book. It's much more fun to draw pictures and use colours.'

'I haven't your gift for painting, Philippa. Besides, what I'm reading isn't a bit dull. Look what our extravagant Prior spent money on: a new altar in his church, some new benches for the priests to sit on, a good quality oak table, big enough to seat forty guests, for use in his own dining room. Look how much he spent on the oxen to pull it all the way from the Weald of Kent.'

Philippa came round the table and tried to read the accounts but the monk's handwriting was difficult to decipher.

'Why, you've copied out a bit,' she said, picking up the scrap of parchment. 'Something about some fields and a mill belong to someone called John Tremayne.'

Her voice was clear and carried well in that vaulted room and Jane saw Hubert raise his head when she spoke. She felt uneasy as if Philippa had said something untoward, and she told her to get on with some work before the daylight faded. Philippa went over to her table and began to paint the outline of a capital letter 'O' at the start of a prayer whilst Jane copied out the item on the Tremayne family and then read on, engrossed in Prior Thomas's financial affairs.

As the afternoon wore on, she remembered she had promised Katharine that she would send Philippa back before the light faded so that she could start her lessons in Greek with the Dean's chaplain. She told her to pack up her things and she would take her back to her parents' house. Reluctantly, Philippa complied and they left the room together.

Once they had gone, Hubert got up and walked over to the Chancellor's desk, where he read what Jane had been copying out. Then he memorised the item and went back to his own desk and resumed his work. Jane came back to make the most of the hours of daylight and she carried on reading the accounts for the year 1531, determined to finish that year before she, too, had to go back to the Dean's house for dinner.

As daylight faded, and it was necessary to light a candle if she were to carry on studying, she glanced up and saw that Hubert had already gone. She, too, ought to go. Nicholas would soon be back and dinner would be announced. She made a mark with her quill pen by the side of the Tremayne entry which she had copied out, and put the roll of the priory's accounts to one side in case the Chancellor came back and wanted to get on with his own work.

Suddenly she was aware that someone had come into the room – one of the priests, she assumed, as he was dressed in the customary black cassock. She had not seen him before, but there were several priests attached to the cathedral who came and went when they were no longer needed and it was impossible to keep track of them all.

He was young, pleasant-faced, with unruly, straw-coloured hair and when he smiled, which he did then, he revealed a row of very white teeth. It was an open face. A face to be trusted, Jane thought. When he spoke, his voice was gentle and well-modulated. Jane recognised the voice of a singer.

'A message for you, my lady,' he said.

'What is it?' Jane answered, thinking Katharine or Philippa wanted to see her.

'He didn't give his name. He wanted to see your husband urgently about something concerning Bishop Thomas's death, but it appears Lord Nicholas hasn't yet returned.'

'Why didn't you direct him to the Sheriff's house?'

'The Sheriff, too, is away and taken several of his men with him. The man said he couldn't give the information to the Sheriff's assistants; it is too important.'

'Then the Dean would be the best person for your man to talk to. I know nothing about the case.'

'But this man knows of you and trusts your discretion. He also knows you will be the first person Lord Nicholas talks to when he returns. The man is trustworthy, my lady; I believe he is one of the Earl of Southampton's men.'

Jane relaxed. Of course, Ralph Paget knew that she could be relied on and would pass on the message accurately.

'Very well. Where does he want to see me?'

'In the Bishop's garden, by the south gate. He doesn't want either you or himself to be seen. It would be too dangerous.'

Jane paused, just for a second. The word, 'dangerous' alerted her to Nicholas's words of caution about her safety. But the bishop's garden was within the cathedral's precincts and very few people outside the cathedral community knew of its existence.

'Very well. But won't you tell me your name?'

'I'm Father David, my lady. One of the vicars choral. I must go now because the evening service starts in a few minutes.'

Jane picked up her cloak and wrapped it around her. Then she walked with him out of the library and down the spiral staircase which led to the south aisle of the cathedral. She could see the choristers assemble for the evening service and watched as Father David took his place amongst the tenors. Then she left the cathedral by the door in the south transept which took her into the cloisters. At the far end there was a door which led to the Bishop's palace and into his garden. The door was unlocked and it was only a short walk to the secluded area which, in summer time, was full of flowers and where exotic trees which a previous bishop had imported from the Levant grew in profusion. Birds loved this area and in the summer butterflies perched on the heads of the flowers, spreading their brightly-coloured wings to soak up the sun's warmth. It was always peaceful here, whatever the time of the year and it was where the Bishop used to pray and meditate during his busy days. Now, all was quiet. The birds had gone to their nests. The stark outlines of the trees, bare of leaves, stood out like gibbets against the darkening sky.

Jane stood there uncertainly in the drizzling rain. She saw the clumps of snowdrops under the trees and noticed there were buds on the winter aconites. Nature was already beginning to stir. It was good to think of spring. She thought of the gardens which she and Nicholas had tended together and she was filled with homesickness to see for herself their own snowdrops and hear the jackdaws squabbling over the best nesting sites in the ruins of the Prior's house.

This garden marked the edge of the cathedral precincts on the south side. Beyond the south gate were the water meadows and the river fringed with willow trees. A path ran by the side of the cathedral walls and in the summer these meadows were a popular meeting place for lovers and townsfolk in need of exercise. The gate was shut and a tall figure stood on the path in front of it. His cloak was wrapped around him as protection from the rain, and the hood was pulled low over his face. When he saw her, he came forward to greet her.

'Lady Jane?' he said.

She nodded. 'What do you want with me?' she said, glancing round to see whether they were alone.

'A message from the Earl,' he said as she approached. 'For Lord Nicholas. He wants...'

Then he seized hold of her, putting his hand over her face to muffle her scream. Two men came out of the bushes on either side of the path and tied a cloth tightly over her head. Then her hands were tied behind her back and she felt herself lifted up and flung over someone's shoulder. She kicked out with her legs and felt the blows sink into the man's body. She fought wildly, using her legs as a flail until they were seized and tied together. Still she wriggled and fought, trying to get the man to drop her but suddenly she felt a heavy blow on the back of her head. Then another and another until she passed out.

The track leading south from the main coastal road was rapidly deteriorating into a morass as the frozen ruts of the past month collapsed with the onset of the warmer weather. The ditches on either side of the track were full of water, in places over-flowing their banks and spilling out across the track, making progress even more difficult. Soon, Nicholas and the Sheriff's men were covered from head to foot with the mud flung up from the horses' hooves. Two carts, brought along by the Sheriff, repeatedly hindered their progress, so much so that they eventually left them behind to make their way as best they could whilst the Sheriff and Nicholas rode ahead. Even so, a lot of time had been wasted trying to heave the carts out of the mud and it was with a sigh of relief that they arrived around midday at the Dog and Hare.

There was a great fire burning in the main room of the tavern, a fire that burned throughout the year as most of the cooking was done on it or in front of it. The smell of roasting pork and freshly-brewed ale was irresistible after that journey. Nicholas threw off his wet cloak and accepted a tankard of ale from the landlord, who did not seem at all pleased to see them. Two of the Sheriff's men had taken up permanent residence in the Dog and Hare until the investigation was concluded and the landlord was full of complaints.

'The regulars don't like it, sirs. What with your men and the port of Marchester sending over their men the place is crawling with officials and it is not the same as it was.'

'Then it's up to the regulars to help us clean the place up,' said the Sheriff brusquely. 'You don't think we chose to come here, do you? That road's a death trap for horse and rider and it'll be like that until the summer comes. Now get us some food and we'll soon be out of your way. What's the news, Peter?' he said, turning to one of his men, who got up from the place where he was sitting by the side of the fire and offered it to the Sheriff.

'Nothing new, sir,' said Peter taking up a new position with his back to the fire and the pieces of roasting pig turning on the spit. 'What with all the deaths and up-

357

heavals the locals have gone to earth. Aylwin's arrest upset them because he was popular, and they didn't like the way Amos Higges was dealt with outside the law, as it were. But you've got some of the wreckers and that'll teach them a lesson, and no one mourns the arrest of those three witches and the death of the old one. They want the Bishop's murderers caught, of course. Bad as this lot is down here, they don't like to see murderers getting away with it. But, all the same, they'll be glad to see us leave here.'

'Well, we shall soon oblige them,' said the sheriff, stretching out his legs towards the fire. 'So that's all, is it, Peter? Seems to me you'd be more use back in Marchester.'

'That's fine by us, sir. Only one bit of gossip; nothing to do with the investigation, but sad, really. One of the village wenches has gone off her head. Much to everyone's surprise, she produced a baby last week. She's not wed and no one knows who the father is. Well, the gossips were all out – tongues wagging as they do. Then the baby dies, poor creature, and the wench went wild with grief. And then if that's not enough, she won't have the child buried. It's not baptised, see, so it won't lie in the church-yard along with all the other Christians. There's a place for the unbaptised outside the churchyard walls but she won't let them put it there. So she's wrapped it up in a woollen shroud and there it remains. Now there won't be much left of it if this warm weather continues and there won't be much to bury, but we can't get it away from her because she starts screeching like a demon and hangs on to it as if it were the family fortune. Says she won't let "them" have it. We've tried to get her to say more but she refuses. And we can't force her to tell us what she means because she hasn't done anything illegal.'

Nicholas listened to Peter's account with growing interest. At the back of his mind was a conversation he had had recently with Jane, who had hinted at the diabolical practices of the covens. He knew they did evil things to children brought to their meetings, often by parents who had too many mouths to feed. Could it be possible they used dead babies as part of their infernal rituals?

He ate the food quickly and put on his cloak. The others looked at him in surprise.

'Are you leaving us so soon, Lord Nicholas? The weather's foul outside and the horses are hardly rested.'

'Harry'll take me where I'm going. He'll have plenty of time to rest back in Marchester. I shan't be long.'

He went outside and collected Harry, who showed reluctance at being dragged away from his oats. Then he rode down the street to the churchyard where, as he anticipated,

Luke Pierce the gravedigger was at work.

At the church gate, he dismounted and tied Harry to the post. Luke glanced up as Nicholas approached, then looked away again and went on with his work.

'Ground's a bit softer now,' said Nicholas evenly.

'You could say that, sir,' said Luke, throwing a pile of earth to one side. 'It gets harder the further you go down.'

'Is there much call for your services?'

'Aye. February's a sad month. A lot of sickness and a lot of death and a lot waiting around for me to bury them.'

'I hear a child's died up in the village.'

'A child? God help us, sir, children die all the time. Especially at this time of the year. They stand no chance when the fever strikes.'

'Do you bury them here, with the others, I mean,' said Nicholas pointing at the mounds of freshly-dug earth which marked the new graves.

Luke straightened his back and propped himself up on his spade. Then he stared at Nicholas for some time as if making up his mind whether to trust him or not. All was peaceful. Harry had found a patch of grass which wasn't frozen. Above their heads the rooks wheeled and soared around their nesting sites, cawing out their greetings to one another. Snowdrops grew in profusion

360

under the yew tree. Nicholas waited, knowing that you couldn't hurry a countryman.

'That depends, sir,' said Luke eventually.

'On what?'

'Whether they've been baptised or not?'

'Does that matter?'

'Not to me it doesn't, and not to you, obviously. But it does to them interested in canon law. Now it's a funny thing, sir, you're the second person lately who's shown an interest in dead babies. You work along with the Sheriff, I know. Now who does this other man work for, I wonder?'

'Who was he, Luke?'

'I don't know, sir. He's not someone I've seen before. Certainly doesn't come from round here.'

'Can you describe him?'

'Well, I'll try, though he'd wrapped himself up in a cloak so I couldn't see much of him. He was middling in height – not tall, not short. Stout. Oh yes, he was stout all right, what I could see of him. Largish face, red with the cold; most likely with the ale he'd been drinking. Black hair. Had the look about him of a priest. I could see him sitting in the old confessional, hands crossed on his big belly. Wouldn't give me his name. Asked me where I buried the children. I showed him, of course; here they are, I said, along with their parents. They're all here where the Bishop blessed the soil. He asked me about the other poor babes who hadn't been baptised. I said I buried them elsewhere. Not that I approve, mind you. A babe is one of God's creatures and deserves proper burial. It's not his fault he hasn't been baptised. But the priests say otherwise. So we started a bit of an argument, sir, because I got a bit heated and told him he knew nothing of God's mercy. Well, he carried on a bit and I dug my heels in and wouldn't tell him where we buried the unbaptised. But then he can come along here at any time and if he takes a look round he'll see the tiny graves outside the churchyard wall and he'll know what's inside them. I didn't like him, sir, and was glad when he left.'

'Did he have a horse with him?'

'No, sir. At least, not that I saw. No carriage either. But of course he could have one waiting for him up on the road. It's a bit marshy around here for carriages.'

'Tell me if he comes again, Luke. There's a gold sovereign waiting for you up at the Dog and Hare if you can give us any inform-ation.'

'Why's this man important? He seemed very ordinary to me. Just curious like.'

'Anyone interested in the graves of child-ren, baptised or unbaptised, sounds a bit suspicious, don't you think?'

Luke dropped his spade and stared aghast at Nicholas.

'You mean?'

'I don't mean anything, yet. Just tell us if he comes again. Even if you don't see him to speak to. Now I must speak to the vicar. Is he at home, do you know?'

'No, he's away with his friend in Selsey again. He's not been here much at all lately. Seems he doesn't think much of this parish. However, we're pleased to get rid of him. My father and I can run this place much better when he's away. But he needs reporting to the Bishop, when we get one, because he's not doing his job properly. The funerals are beginning to pile up.'

Nicholas walked back to Harry and slowly mounted him. Things were still amiss in Pelham Maris, he thought, as he rode away. Death, disease, these were all natural things; but asking where unbaptised babies were buried was not. And what had the girl said when the Sheriff's men tried to persuade her to let them bury the child? She didn't want 'them' to have it. Who were these people she was so frightened of?

He knew by the slight feeling of excitement that he was on to something, but he was not yet ready to face the Sheriff and report on his conversation with Luke. Besides, he was not sure if the Sheriff would understand the full implication of what Luke had told him. Strangers did come to Pelham Maris and had every right to talk to local people. But they didn't often brave the roads in winter and weren't usually reluctant to reveal their names. Neither did they talk about the burial of babies. He needed to know more before he went back to the Dog and Hare; and there was one person he should see – someone who'd lived here for a long time and would surely know most things that went on in the village.

Instead of taking the road which went back up the street towards the Dog and Hare, Nicholas took the track which ran along by the side of the reed bed to his hunting lodge; the place where, only ten days ago, they had stumbled across Bishop Thomas's body. He needed to talk to Walter again.

Walter was in the barn chopping wood for kindling. He looked up when Nicholas went in and his face broke into a beam of welcome. Nicholas realised that Walter had come to trust him. No longer was he the frightened servant of an unknown master. Nicholas sat down on one of the fallen logs and refused Walter's offer of refreshment. The daylight was fading perceptibly and there was much he had to do.

'There's been a stranger in these parts recently, Walter. Talked to Luke Pierce. Did you see him? He was well built, youngish with dark hair. Luke couldn't give a better description because he wore a cloak pulled well down over his face. Did he come down here at all?'

Walter shook his head. 'No one comes along here, my lord. The path doesn't lead anywhere, you see. Selsey's way over there, as you know, but you have to come inland at Norton Creek before you can cross over to the island. You could manage it at low water, I suppose, but then a visitor would be a bit particular about his clothes, wouldn't he, not being a countryman.'

'Yet Richard Rushe, the vicar, goes there frequently to see Tremayne. How does he get there if it's too difficult to go on foot?'

'Someone comes and fetches him, they say. And brings him back. Usually after dark. I've not seen him leave his house but the churchwarden says he's seen a coach stop outside.'

'A coach? What is it like?'

'Oh, a mean sort of thing, by all accounts. Black as night. No windows. Folk call it the Devil's box and run like mad when they hear it coming.'

'Who drives the coach?'

'No one sees him. He's dressed in black. Face is covered.' Nicholas began to feel the excitement which the hunter feels when the hounds pick up the scent.

'Walter,' he said, raising his voice and pronouncing every word clearly. 'Why does Richard Rushe visit William Tremayne so often?'

Walter put down his axe and came to sit on the log next to Nicholas's.

'I don't rightly know, sir. But let's say they was once thick as thieves. I've been here a good while, as you know, and I remember when Rushe befriended Tremayne when his father killed himself.'

'Killed himself? When was this?'

'About seven years ago, I think. John Tremayne – he was William's father – had some farms near here, up at Lower Rife. He worked the water mill there, too. Then he got into debt – I don't know why – and he lost the farm. He lost everything. It was a sad affair. He couldn't stand the shame of becoming a beggar so he hung himself from one of the beams in his barn. His wife, poor soul, gave birth to a child before its time in a field and she bled to death there, where she lay down, and no one knew about it.

'That left young William. Rushe took him in and gave him a roof over his head. Then he sent him to Marchester to learn how to become a priest. At the right time he was made rector at Selsey and that should have been an end to their friendship. But suddenly he and Rushe start seeing each other again...'

'Walter,' said Nicholas trying to control the urgency in his voice, 'who was Tremayne's landlord?'

'One of those churchmen. Most of the

land around here belongs either to you, my lord, begging your pardon, or the church in one way or another. Tremayne's farm was owned by one of the priors. Yes, that's it; I remember now. It was your Prior, sir. Prior of Dean Peverell. He lost his priory, didn't he, two years ago when the King closed them down, and he became Bishop of Marchester. But he re-claimed Tremayne's land when he was prior. There was a fair old outcry and we all felt sorry for young William. A bit un-Christian I call it to throw a man off his land even though he'd fallen behind with his rent. But the Prior lived a long way away and never met the Tremaynes so it was just a bit of business for him. Are you all right, my lord?' he exclaimed. 'You look a bit fazed. Come inside and I'll get us some warm ale.'

Nicholas pulled himself together. Could this be the motive he had been looking for? Tremayne, having lost both father and mother and the unborn sibling, would surely hate the Prior who had done this to his family. A Prior who, to add insult to injury, had become Bishop of Marchester. Surely he would have wanted revenge. And then the opportunity came along. But how could he have done it? Tremayne had neither horse nor carriage. Unless...

The thoughts came swirling into his head. He looked up at the darkening sky and the mass of storm clouds building up from the west. He heard the wind crashing around in the reed beds outside. Soon heavy rain would fall and the track would become impassable.

He thanked Walter for his help and rode back to the Dog and Hare, where the two carts which the Sheriff had brought with them from Marchester were just arriving, horses and riders dropping with exhaustion.

'We stay here tonight,' said the Sheriff, stomping into the tavern. 'There's straw in the barn for the men and you and I can share a room.'

'I have to get back to Marchester, Sheriff. There's much to see to. Unfortunately we're going to need those carts on the other side of this marsh tomorrow. I've got to get across to Selsey.'

'The carts stay here with me, Peverell,' said the Sheriff impatiently. 'We've just heard that there's to be a meeting of the covens sometime soon. We don't know where they'll meet. Probably out in the marsh on one of the islands.'

'With a storm brewing it's most unlikely. Use your brain, Sheriff. If there's to be a meeting then it will be under cover.'

'Then we'll find it. But we can't leave our posts tonight, however attractive the prospect is of a soft mattress and a warm bed.'

'There's little time to think of that, Sheriff.

Tomorrow I must go and see Tremayne. He could be the man we're looking for. He's got a motive.'

'Tremayne? And what makes you think he could have killed the Bishop, stuck on that island of his? It's your brain that needs looking after, my lord. Well, you go your way and I'll go mine. We'll meet sometime, I suppose. Remember the rain will make the roads impassable. It won't be an easy ride to Selsey.'

'Don't worry about me. God go with you, Sheriff. Fill those carts of yours with more witches and we'll lock them up with the other two.'

He mounted Harry and turned his head towards Marchester. This time Harry needed no urging. Home was home whatever the state of the roads.

Nineteen

Jane opened her eyes and saw nothing. The pain in her head felt like two tiny hammers beating out a rhythm and she felt sick and dizzy from the swaying and jolting of the vehicle she was enclosed in. She could hear the sound of rain drumming on the roof above her and recognised the creaking of leather harness and the crack of a whip urging horses to go faster. She tried to move her feet but found that they were tied together. Her hands, too, were fastened behind her back. She struggled to bring her mind under control and remember what had happened to her. Bit by bit images floated across her brain: the priest with the smiling face; the Bishop's garden at dusk; the figure standing by the gate. She remembered but didn't understand. Who would want to abduct her? What had she done? And where were 'they' taking her?

The carriage was small, the seat she was lying on hard, and the jolting around very painful. Then she became aware that she was not alone. Someone was seated opposite her, but she couldn't call out because a gag had been tied tightly across her mouth. She

370

uttered a low, moaning sound from the back of her throat but there was no response from the other person.

The coach lurched and jolted on its way, sometimes swaying dangerously as the wind whipped against its side. Once it stopped altogether and the person opposite cursed and got out. As the door opened, she felt the wind rush into the confined space of the carriage and she breathed in great gulps of the damp fresh air. She felt someone pushing and shaking the carriage from behind her, heard the coachman shout at the horses and heard the crack of the whip as they tried to free the coach from the deep mud. She was glad of the delay. When people noticed her absence they would surely come looking for her, with any luck on horses which could go faster if the riders took to the fields and kept clear of the roads. Then the thought came to her that she had no idea where they were going and if her rescuers had to ride round the countryside in the dark looking for her it would take days before they found her.

At last the jolting and swaying became less violent and she realised that they were now driving along a smoother, firmer track. Then she felt the carriage swing round as if coming up to the front of a building and the horses stopped. Someone opened the carriage door. Someone shone a light in her direction because she could see the change in the quality of the darkness. Then she was seized and dragged out of the carriage, slung over someone's back and carried away. Dazed and feeling sick, her body aching through the battering it had received on the journey, she felt herself carried into a building, down some steps and into a room which felt cold and damp as if it were a cellar of some sorts. Then she was dumped down on a hard bed and the bandage removed from her eyes. She could still not see anything as the room was in darkness; the only light a faint glimmer from a torch fastened to the wall somewhere outside. A woollen rug was thrown over her and a voice said: 'Lie still and no harm will come to you. We'll remove the gag when we bring you some food.'

Then the door banged shut. She heard a heavy bolt drawn into place and then she was alone in the cold and the darkness. Mercifully, the pain in her head having become so severe during the journey, she slipped into unconsciousness.

It wasn't until late afternoon when preparations for dinner were well under way, that Philippa returned from her lesson and asked if she could go and summon Jane from the library. Katharine Catchpole, the Dean's wife, told her that it was too dark for her to go across to the cathedral on her own and she summoned a servant to go instead. He returned shortly and said that there was no one in the library. Everything looked in order as if the work had been put away for the night.

The Dean came in, accompanied by the Chancellor, who was to dine with them that night. He said he hadn't been over to the library that afternoon because he had been in conference with the Dean. Hubert, he said, might know where Jane had gone.

The servant went to find Hubert and got no reply from his knock on the door. Surely, said the Dean angrily, Jane hadn't slipped over to the prison and given Mistress Dobbs a singing lesson. That would be irresponsible of her, if not downright disobedient, as her husband had expressly forbidden her to go.

'Lady Jane needs a stiff curb,' he grumbled as he sent a servant over to the jail to see if she was there. The servant returned. No, Lady Jane had not visited the prison that afternoon. Then consternation set in and rooms were searched in case she had fallen over and was unable to get up. Or maybe she had fallen and banged her head against a stone pillar or wall and had passed out. Thoughts of dinner were abandoned and the Dean gave orders to search the cathedral because she might have fallen there and not been seen in the gloom. This was all because she was headstrong, the Dean grumbled. Most women would have been content to sit by the fire in a warm room and get on with their embroidery. But not Jane. He began to feel immensely sorry for Nicholas.

He felt even more sorry for him when he saw Nicholas after he had returned from Pelham Maris, cold, soaked to the skin and exhausted. He handed his cloak to the servant, who looked at him fearfully and rushed away as soon as he could. Nicholas felt a twinge of unease. What was wrong with the servant? he thought. Usually he was greeted with cheerful solicitude; not like this, as if the man had seen a ghost.

He decided to go first to the parlour, where he knew the family gathered for a glass of wine before meals. He could change his clothes later. But the parlour was empty and the log on the fire almost burned away. Wondering where everyone had got to, he kicked up the embers of the log and put on more wood until a warm blaze caused his clothes to send up clouds of steam and he felt the numbness in his body ease. He looked round for a servant to bring him some wine, but none came.

'God dammit,' he muttered; 'is this a house of the dead?'

It was at that moment that the Dean came in and looked at Nicholas half fearfully and half apologetically, and Nicholas's feeling of unease began to grow into panic.

'Lord Nicholas...' the Dean stammered, unable to go any further.

'What is it, Dean? In God's name, don't stand there looking at me as if I were an apparition.'

'It's Jane,' said the Dean, coming closer to Nicholas in case he was going to need support.

'Jane? Is she ill? Has she caught a fever from those accursed witches of hers? Come on now, out with it, man!'

'She's gone, Nicholas. We're searching for her, all of us, but she's not yet been found. We're doing all we can; she could have fallen somewhere and I expect we'll soon find her. Take some nourishment and dry your clothes and wait here for any news.'

Then the waves of panic threatened to engulf Nicholas. Jane gone. Why take Jane? Because someone knew she was dear to him and wanted to punish him? Or was she to be held to ransom? Or was there another reason? He began to grapple desperately with his thoughts. He'd left her about to go to the library. Had anything happened there? Waving aside the food which one of the servants had brought in, he turned to the Dean, 'I must go to the library. That's where she was going to spend the afternoon. That's where we might find a clue to where she's gone. Tell your servants to bring lights, Dean, and get someone to bring that young man, Hubert, over here.'

'We can't find him, Nicholas,' said the Dean. And Nicholas felt his fear increase. 'He's not in his house.'

'And I'm coming with you,' said a quiet voice behind them. Nicholas turned and saw Philippa, who had come into the room unnoticed. 'I was with Jane for most of the afternoon. She brought me home for my Greek lesson and went back to finish off some work she was doing. She thought she just had time before the daylight faded.'

'What time was that, Philippa?' said her father.

'My lesson began at four. Jane brought me over here about ten minutes to the hour so that I had time to get my books together. Then she went back to the library. And that's the last I saw of her.'

Then she began to cry and the Dean called Katharine to take her away for comforting, but she refused to go with her mother.

'Was Hubert there all the afternoon?' said Nicholas after her mother had calmed her a little.

'Not all the time. He was there when I got there but I don't know how long he stayed. He'd have to go for the evening service wouldn't he, father?' she said.

'He wasn't there,' said the Dean. 'And I

should know because I took the service. Now where the devil is he?'

Nicholas took a rush light from one of the servants and went across to the cathedral, not waiting for the others. Philippa broke away from her mother and rushed after him. 'Wait, Nicholas. I might be able to help. You see I know the last piece of work Jane was studying before she brought me back home. She thought it might interest you. It could still be there on the desk.'

Together they raced over to the cathedral and climbed the spiral staircase up to the library. Philippa ran to the desk where Jane had been working.

'Look, it's still here,' she said. 'She copied it out for you to see.'

She picked up the piece of parchment which Jane had used for making notes on about the Tremayne entry. Nicholas read it and felt the room begin to swim before his eyes.

'Look at this, Dean,' he said, handing it to the Dean, who had just come into the room, puffing slightly after the unaccustomed exercise. 'This is what I've been talking about this afternoon with my bailiff down in Pelham Maris. It's about the Tremayne family, who were evicted from their land by order of Bishop Thomas, then Prior of Dean Peverell. Now what do you know about William Tremayne, Dean?'

'You ought to ask the Archdeacon about him, Nicholas. The parish clergy are his concern. But let's go back to the house and I'll tell you what I know over a bite to eat.'

Taking the piece of parchment with Jane's handwriting on it, Nicholas followed the Dean back to his house, where a simple supper was waiting for them in the Dean's library. Philippa, protesting loudly, was whisked away by her mother. The Dean shut the door.

'What has William Tremayne got to do with Jane's disappearance, Nicholas?'

'It could be everything, or nothing. If Jane has stumbled upon a piece of family history that might provide Tremayne with a motive for killing Bishop Thomas, then he might well want her out of the way. Pray God he's not contemplating killing her as it now seems likely that he killed the old crone Agatha Trimble, who knew too much. What do you know about William Tremayne, Dean? I know about his family history, but what happened to him after his family died?'

'He trained here in Marchester for the priesthood.'

'Who befriended him?'

'Why, the Archdeacon, of course. Tremayne would have been put with the vicars choral and the Archdeacon would have supervised his training until he became ordained and was given a living.'

Nicholas pushed aside his plateful of food and stared across at the Dean as if making up his mind about something.

'I wonder if I could have a word with Philippa, Dean. She was in the library this afternoon with Jane. I wonder if she could answer a few more questions for us.'

The Dean called a servant to ask his wife to send Philippa to his library, where Nicholas wanted to speak with her. She came quickly, looking anxious.

'What is it, my lord?'

'Philippa, think carefully back to this afternoon. When you were in the library with Jane did she show you this piece of parchment and explain what was written on it?'

'She showed it to me, yes, and I remember it concerned someone called Tremayne. I remember mentioning his name and she sent me back to my place by the window as if I had said something I shouldn't.'

'Was there anyone else in the library beside you and Jane, Philippa?'

'Yes, Hubert was there. He watched me talking to Jane. I suppose he could have been listening.'

'He probably heard every word,' said Nicholas grimly. 'And when you both left the library he probably went across to the desk and read what was written on this parchment. Then he knew that Jane had inadvertently come across the motive for

William Tremayne's murder of the Bishop.'

'Nicholas, Nicholas, don't let your fancy run away with you. William Tremayne might well have borne a grudge against the late Bishop; he had every reason to; but he could not have murdered him by himself. He certainly has no carriage and I suspect he doesn't even own a horse, so how could he have left the island on his own, lured the Bishop out of his cathedral and killed him in such a terrible way? And he certainly could not have dumped him in that pool without help. Tremayne is a poor man in a poor parish. The Archdeacon leaves those coastal parishes well alone for good reason.'

'The Archdeacon,' said Nicholas quietly. 'That name again. Was he at evening service today, Dean?'

'No, but he seldom comes. Unfortunately, he and the Precentor do not see eye to eye. He should be in his house as we have all been told not to leave the cathedral precincts, remember? Also we have Father Oswald's funeral to arrange.'

'Father Oswald?' said Nicholas looking startled. 'I didn't know he died.'

'How should you? He was one of our old priests and wasn't expected to survive the winter. He died in his bed, lucky man. I pray that we all go like that when we're called.'

Nicholas, suddenly sick with dread, stared at the Dean. He cursed himself for being so blind, so stupid. The Archdeacon had mentioned Father Oswald. He'd told him that Father Oswald was the priest who had given Agatha Trimble her last communion. The jailer had said it was a young priest and he'd dashed off with the Sheriff without checking on who was right. And now Father Oswald was dead and could never tell the truth. Had the Archdeacon deliberately lied? And if so, why? There was only one answer and that didn't bear thinking about. Yet the evidence was mounting. Had the Archdeacon arranged the death of Father Oswald because he could disprove his lie? And had he arranged Agnes Trimble's death because she knew too much? And Hugh Brotherhood? And now Jane? Was she to be the next victim?

Nicholas leapt to his feet, horrified by the implications of his line of reasoning. 'We must go and talk to the Archdeacon, Dean. And quickly. But I fear we are already too late.'

Calling for the servants to bring lights, the Dean and Nicholas dashed across the Close to the Archdeacon's house. All was quiet. No one answered the door when they knocked. And no one was in the house when Nicholas ordered the door to be broken down. The Archdeacon had vanished along with Hubert – and Jane.

Twenty

There was no sleep for anyone in the Dean's house that Friday night. Nicholas, waiting for the dawn, listened to the wind howling down the chimney and heard the rain dashing against the windows. This day, he thought, would be a testing time for Harry; roads would be seas of mud, the fields waterlogged and the ditches turning into rivers.

At first light, he ordered Harry to be made ready. The Dean was waiting for him in the hall, his face grey with fatigue and worry.

'Wait, Nicholas my friend. Wait for the Sheriff to return. You can do nothing on your own and you are not in a fit state to make decisions.'

'To wait for Landstock is to wait for ever. Do you know how long it took to get his carts down to Pelham Maris? All the hours of daylight. They'll not be back until tomorrow, I warrant, and by then it could be too late. God knows what the devils will do to Jane by then!'

'But what do you intend to do?'

'Go and see Tremayne.'

'But what makes you think he's got anything to do with Jane's disappearance?'

'I don't yet know. But I do know he's friendly with the Archdeacon, who has also disappeared. I'm beginning to think that those two, Tremayne and the Archdeacon, are part of a conspiracy. Rushe, too, I think is part of it. I know this is all supposition, but today I am going to put an end to these uncertainties and find some proper evidence; and I'm going to find Jane. Can't you see that I cannot rest until I've found her even if I have to search every hamlet and dwelling in the county?'

'I must urge you to be cautious, Nicholas. The Sheriff will send his men to do the job for you. You cannot push your horse too hard. You don't want to risk getting stranded in this weather. This is not like you to act so impetuously.'

'There's no choice. I cannot sit here waiting for things to happen. I can think of only one thing – my wife Jane; my wife, of only six weeks, Dean, let me remind you. It will drive me mad to stay here thinking of all the things that could be happening to her whilst there might be a chance of finding her.'

'You stand a better chance if you wait for the Sheriff and his men. How are you going to bring back any suspects?' the Dean shouted after Nicholas, who had picked up his cloak and was striding off towards the stables.

'They can run behind me.'

'They'll not stand the pace. The roads are too bad.'

'Then I'll drag them along.'

'You're out of your wits, Nicholas. This is going to end in disaster.'

'If Jane has suffered the same fate as Bishop Thomas then disaster has already struck.'

'Then God go with you, Nicholas,' called out the Dean to the empty air.

Nicholas went across to the stables where Harry was waiting for him. He mounted him and turned his head towards the south. The sun had not yet put in an appearance from behind a lowering black cloud and it was difficult to see the potholes and patches of deep mud. But Harry was used to rough going and almost danced along the road, avoiding obstacles which only he could sense.

Back in his house, the Dean stood there lost in thought. He grieved for his friend, whom he could see was heading for disaster. He had to have back-up. Damn the Sheriff for dashing-off on another wild goose chase and leaving insufficient men behind for just such an emergency. There was only one person of any sense he could call on. Summoning one of his servants, he told him to ride quickly to Portsmouth and fetch the Earl of Southampton. He dashed off a letter and handed it to the servant.

'This is urgent, Tom. Tell the Earl to come quickly and bring some soldiers. I've got a feeling we might need them. Take one of my horses – the bay cob will be the strongest as the going will be rough.'

It was noon before Nicholas reached Tremayne's house. Harry was flagging as the going had been rough both along the tracks and in the fields where the mud had come halfway up his legs, slowing him down and tiring him out. The house appeared deserted. No one came to the door when Nicholas banged on it. He seized hold of an axe which someone had left wedged in the top of a log of wood – the kindling lay strewn around it – and broke down the door. Inside, the room was as he remembered it: the bed made up, the fire smouldering in the hearth. But something was missing. For a moment he stood there listening to the wind and the sound of the sea battering away at the shingle bank off the Point. Then it came to him. The crucifix, which had rested against the wall over the fireplace, had gone.

Then terror overwhelmed him and he fell on his knees. 'Oh no, Lord,' he prayed. 'Not that. Not Jane. Tell me where she is. Don't let it happen.'

But there was no reply. Just a gust of wind which blew down the chimney and blew the ashes into the room.

'There she goes again, carrying on like a screech owl who's lost her chicks. Go and shut her up, husband,' said Beatrice, looking across at her husband, the jailer Aldred, who was slumped in a chair the other side of the fireplace with a pot of ale in his hand.

'I'm not going near the witch. That's your job, wife. Care of prisoners, that's what you agreed to. I only lock 'em up and fetch the firewood.'

Beatrice resumed stirring the pot over the fire but after another yell from the direction of Jenny Dobbs's cell, she threw down her wooden spoon, straightened her apron with a decisive tug at the material and stalked off to the cells.

The shouting stopped when she unlocked the cell door and when she went in, Jenny was sitting on the edge of her bed, her clothes in disarray and her hair tumbling around her face.

'Why didn't you come when I called?' she said.

'Because I'm not your slave ready to obey your every whim. You have to wait until I come and no amount of shouting and yelling's going to get me here any sooner. What's the matter with you? You've got a warm cell; you're well fed and you're left in peace. What more can you want?'

'I keep telling you; I have to see Lord

Nicholas or Jane; anyone will do; the Dean, the Sheriff, the Earl.'

'So that's it, is it? You've still got your eye on him. Well, let me tell you again, my girl, that he's not interested in you. A man of his position! It's ridiculous to even imagine he wants to speak to you. He's away in his manor house and he's not likely to come here to listen to your jabbering.'

Jenny slid off the bed and stood in front of Beatrice, face flaming with anger, fists clenched.

'So that's it. How stupid you are! You and all your kind. You think I want to seduce Ralph Paget back into my bed. I've done all that. We had a great time. It's over. But that doesn't mean that I can't still have a word with him, especially when I know I can help him and the Sheriff.'

'What do you know that can be of the slightest importance to anyone? Now stop your yelling and leave me in peace. Lord Nicholas is away somewhere, the Dean's far too busy to see the likes of you and my Lady Jane has disappeared into thin air. So there; you'll have to put up with your own company a bit more.'

Jenny stared at Beatrice in horror. 'Jane gone? Dear God, when did this happen?'

'Last night, if you must know. Seems she's taken off somewhere on her own – foolish, headstrong woman that she is.'

'That doesn't sound like Jane. Most likely she's been abducted. For the love of God, mistress, take me to see the Sheriff; or any of his men would do. Jane could be in serious trouble.'

'You're staying here, Mistress Dobbs, and don't you go pushing your way past me. Get back, you silly wench.'

Beatrice gave Jenny a push which sent her reeling back towards the bed, but Jenny, her face wild with fury, sprang towards her again, hands outstretched to scratch and tear at Beatrice's face. But Beatrice had a long experience of dealing with excitable women. She lifted her arm as strong as a wheat flail and punched Jenny on the face. It was the blow to fell an ox and Jenny fell back on the bed, gasping with pain and with blood beginning to trickle from her nose. As she lay there gasping for breath she heard Beatrice leave the cell, slamming the door behind her.

The hours passed slowly for Philippa, that Saturday. The Dean was preoccupied with interviewing all the cathedral staff and Katharine did her best to keep her daughter occupied so that she wouldn't brood too much on Jane's disappearance. She took her into the kitchens and showed her how to make pastries and sweetmeats; but Philippa wouldn't be consoled. She felt that somehow she had been partly responsible for Jane's disappearance; that it was her indiscretion in blurting out Tremayne's name in the library that had caused it. Whatever it was, she felt frightened and guilty as she waited for news, looking hopefully at every messenger. But the day wore on, and still Jane had not been found. At last the time came when she could bear it no more. When everyone was occupied with their own tasks and she was no longer the centre of attention, she decided to go over to the cathedral, to the Lady chapel where she could pray for Jane's safety before the verger locked the place up.

Looking round, she saw that she was alone in the kitchen except for the cook, who was busy preparing the evening meal. She didn't even raise her head when Philippa sauntered out of the kitchen. The house seemed deserted. She went casually out of the door into the Close and across to the cathedral, passing a young priest whom she didn't recognise. She walked past him and went into the cathedral. Inside, the silence and the darkness, punctuated here and there by a few rush tapers and the candles on the high altar which were still alight, engulfed her. She walked round behind the altar, where Bishop Thomas's body lay in its tomb next to St Richard's, and went into the Lady chapel, where a candle always burned in front of the statue of the Virgin. Overhead, the newly-painted ceiling, which Bishop Thomas had commissioned as soon as he took office, glowed richly in the gathering darkness.

Philippa knelt down in front of the statue and began to say her prayers. She wished she still had her rosary but her father had removed it from her prie-dieu and told her she no longer needed those relics of a superstitious past. As she prayed, she began to feel calmer and felt that Jane was still alive and not far away. She didn't hear the man come into the chapel and stand behind her. Too late she realised that someone was there and she turned her head to see who it was. It was too late to scream, too late to struggle. A woollen rug was thrown over her head. A rope was fastened tightly around her neck to keep the rug in place and she was picked up and tipped over one shoulder. Then, silently, keeping to the shadows in the side aisle, the man left the cathedral by the north door. A carriage was waiting in one of the side streets near the cathedral and he opened the door and threw Philippa onto one of the seats. Then the man got in and sat down opposite her. She tried to kick out with her legs but the man seized hold of them and tied them together. Then he pushed her roughly back on her seat. As she continued to struggle, he leaned forward and punched her on the head. Philippa, terrified and in pain, sank into unconsciousness.

It was dark by the time Nicholas got back to Marchester. He was soaking wet, exhausted, and Harry was limping badly. The Dean's groom rushed forward to see to him, exclaiming over his condition. Ignoring Nicholas's obvious fatigue, he glared at him and told him that no horse should be punished like this; especially a horse like Harry, who was made for speed and not for ploughing through mud like a cart horse.

Nicholas was too tired to rebuke him but told him to be sure to give Harry a good rub down and a feed of oats and see that he was comfortable. Then he went into the Dean's house, into the warmth of the hall. As soon as he went in, however, he sensed something was wrong. Then Katharine came rushing into the hall and, ignoring his soaking clothes, threw her arms round him.

'Lord Nicholas, thank God you've come. Can you tell us what's happening. Philippa's gone! Oh I can't bear it. Philippa, my darling child, not yet a woman. What can anyone want with her?'

As Nicholas held her closely, trying to calm her, the Dean joined them. He looked at the Dean over Katharine's head and shook his head.

'Something terrible is happening to our

community, Dean. People are disappearing. Tremayne has gone; likewise Rushe. Has the Archdeacon returned?'

'No; and two of the vicars choral have vanished along with Hubert.'

'Then they are all coming together for some infernal purpose. The powers of darkness, Dean, are closing in around us.'

Nicholas heard Katharine cry out and felt her body go slack in his arms as she fainted.

'The powers of darkness, Nicholas, will never triumph,' said the Dean with certainty. 'Let us go now to my chapel and pray for God's help. He won't let his ancient adversary get his own way.'

They carried Katharine to the small chapel which the Dean used for his own private prayers and they laid her down on one of the seats. A servant came in and whispered something in the Dean's ear. He turned to look at Nicholas.

'Maybe He's heard us already. Anthony West wants to speak to me. Ask him to wait for me in the library,' he said to the servant, 'and tell him I shall be along as soon as I have summoned my wife's women to tend to her. Nicholas, take care to dry your clothes and take some refreshment before you, too, come and join us after we have said our prayers.'

'I've hated the Archdeacon for a long time,

Dean, I am sorry to have to tell you. He wanted to be friends and I have nothing against that. Our faith is all about friendship, but not his sort. He was too possessive, too intense, and besides, Lancelot and I are quite happy as we are and don't want anyone else to come along and spoil things. But there are things you should know about your Archdeacon, Dean, and I am surprised you didn't know about them already.'

Nicholas looked at the young man in surprise. He had not expected Anthony West to speak with such authority. He had thought him to be no more than a spoilt and beautiful child wanting and encouraging attention. But it appeared he had been wrong about him.

'Why didn't you come forward before, Anthony?' he said. 'Why now?'

'Because things are whirling out of control and I am sure Jeremy Overton is involved in this and he's gone too far. I know he's an ambitious man. He was upset when Bishop Thomas was appointed bishop here. He thought he should have been preferred over him.'

'But that's preposterous,' shouted the Dean. 'Archdeacons are never asked to become bishops. Besides the man's too old, too...' he paused, looking for the right word.

'Too sour,' said Anthony. 'Too sour because he's a disappointed man; disappointed because he thinks his talents have not been recognised; disappointed in his relationships with others. And he wants power, Dean.'

'And such men are dangerous,' said the Dean quietly.

'Are you trying to tell us,' said Nicholas, 'that the Archdeacon was involved in the Bishop's murder?'

'I don't know,' said Anthony, 'and that's the truth. I have no proof. But I do know he wanted Bishop Thomas removed, though I think he'd try other ways to get rid of him. He has a calculating mind. He manipulates people and would use others' weaknesses to get them to do his dirty work for him.'

'You still haven't told us why you chose to come and see us now,' persisted Nicholas.

'Because I've heard Philippa's disappeared and we all love your bonny daughter, Dean, and we don't want her to come to any harm. And your wife, too, has disappeared, Lord Nicholas, and we all admire her. And I think, no, I fear, that the Archdeacon could be behind this.'

'But what, in God's name, could the Archdeacon want with my daughter?' shouted the Dean.

'He has his own infernal reasons, I'm sure, which I can't go into because I have no proof and don't want to alarm you more than you are already. But I think you should try and find him and bring him in for questioning.'

'He's not here, Anthony, and we haven't the slightest idea where to find him,' said the Dean, looking appealingly at Anthony.

'We know he can't have gone far,' said Nicholas. 'He only has the one carriage and I am sure the Dean has checked that it is still there.'

'Of course I have. It is there and the coachman says it hasn't been taken out for weeks. Neither has that horse been found, the one he lent to Hugh Brotherhood. So he has no horse either.'

'Then it was right for me to come and see you because you know nothing. The Archdeacon has more than one residence. Yes, you may look surprised, Dean, but I did say that he liked power. He's probably got more than one carriage and one horse. People who want power have to have an empire, one that is kept a secret from those who might take it away from them. Jeremy has what he calls a manor down in the hamlet of South Several, some five miles away from here, to the west. It's a strange, secret place, just a few fields and the hovels where the fishermen live. His place is set back from the track in the swampy fields bordering Marchester harbour.'

'How do you know this, Anthony?' said the Dean quietly.

'Because I was invited to go there when I had just arrived here. I was just a boy, then, and I trusted him. He had two friends with him, and when I realised what they wanted me for, I ran away and spent the night wandering around in the water meadows until it got light and I found my way back here. It was then that Lancelot befriended me.'

'Did you know these friends of his?' said Nicholas.

'No, they weren't from here, from this cathedral, I mean.'

'Thank God for that,' said the Dean fervently.

'If Jeremy has taken Philippa and your wife, Lord Nicholas, then his manor at South Several is the obvious place to hide them until he is ready for them,' said Anthony.

'Ready for them? What the devil do you mean by that?' said Nicholas, dreading the answer.

'He used to talk of some "ceremonies" he thought I might be interested in and I never knew what he meant. But I begin now to fear the worst. The Archdeacon is the incarnation of evil.'

'Then I must go to this manor straight away,' said Nicholas, who was almost dropping with weariness. He would have dashed off had not the Dean forcibly restrained him.

'No, Nicholas, I forbid it. You aren't fit to walk into Marchester let alone ride round

Marchester harbour in the dark when there's a mighty storm brewing. We need help and fresh horses.'

Nicholas thought of Harry. No, he was in no fit state to undertake another journey like today's.

The Dean went on, his hand still on Nicholas's shoulder. 'I've sent for Southampton and he'll bring reinforcements. We shall have to make use of the Sheriff's stables if he's not back soon. We'll need his carts, too, if we are going to make any arrests.'

'It would give me the greatest pleasure to see Archdeacon Jeremy Overton brought back to this cathedral in the carts used for common criminals,' said Anthony, his face flushed with excitement at the thought. 'And what's more I am coming with you. I want to be in on the kill.'

'Then I shall leave at first light – if I may borrow one of your horses, Dean?'

'I shall give instructions to my groom. I pray now that the Earl comes soon.'

Twenty-one

It was impossible to calculate the passing of time. For Jane, alone, in pain and in total darkness, the hours passed interminably slowly. Twice the door opened and a platter of bread and cheese and a jug of water were pushed along the floor towards the bed she was lying on. The empty plate was not taken away. She reckoned that perhaps six hours might have passed between the meals, the usual interval between meal times under normal circumstances, so two meals could mean that a day had passed; but she had no means of telling whether it was morning or night time. She tried to think back to the time when she was abducted but the event was blurred and the blow on her head had left her confused. She knew there would be consternation when the Dean and his household realised she was missing and no doubt search parties were out looking for her, but where would they start looking? She also knew that, as much of the county was difficult, if not impossible, to reach in winter conditions, it might be a long time before she was rescued.

She also grieved for Nicholas, who would

be out of his mind with worry for her. Now she could see how foolish she had been to leave the library with an unknown person and go into the garden as daylight was fading without telling anyone where she was going. She should have run back into the cathedral as soon as she saw the tall figure standing by the south gate of the garden. But then, she thought, she had no reason not to trust the young priest who had escorted her there. She was used to taking messages for Nicholas in his absence. However, she had promised not to leave the cathedral precincts. But the bishop's garden was still within those precincts. Perhaps she was being too hard on herself in the knowledge of hindsight.

She ate the food and drank the water, knowing that she would soon need all her strength. She used the bucket which someone had provided and tried to collect her thoughts and focus on what might happen next because she felt sure that she was only in a transitional stage. Soon, 'they' would come and take her to another place where the reason for her abduction would be made clear to her.

But she certainly wasn't prepared for the door opening and another person being dumped on her bed. With no word of explanation, the dark figure who had carried the person to her cell left, and she heard the door slam and the bolt drawn into place. With shaking hands and fearing what she might uncover, Jane removed the blanket which covered the other person and one word revealed her identity.

'Jane,' a familiar voice said. 'Is it you?'

'Philippa! Dear God, what happened? Are you hurt? Tell me what day it is? Have you any idea where we are?'

'I don't know, Jane. I'm sorry, I really have no idea. I was brought here in a carriage, about a two hours' journey, I should think. But I'm not sure because I was unconscious for part of the time. Jane, have they hurt you? What are they going to do to us?'

'I'm all right, Philippa. But I have no idea what they want us for. I expect they will soon demand a ransom for our release. Lord Nicholas and your father will pay it straight away so we shouldn't be here long. Come, let's sit close together and we'll try to be brave.'

Jane drew the girl close to her and began to sing quietly. At first Philippa simply listened, then she joined in, and Jane pulled the blankets around her to stop the child shuddering with cold. Although they sang of happy things, Jane was filled with dread at what could be in store for them.

Then Philippa stopped singing and began to sob quietly and Jane held her close and stroked the top of her head to calm her.

'Hush, Philippa, try not to think too much of what has been done. Let's think about your parents and my beloved husband, who will be distraught with worry about us. We could say a prayer for them and some for ourselves asking God to help our rescuers who will be looking for us.'

'Do you really think we shall be released, Jane?'

'Yes I do. Why else would two women be abducted? We are no threat to anyone. Come, drink some of this water and there's a piece of bread here, too. Our captors don't intend us to starve, obviously, and it's good to keep our strength up.'

Gradually Philippa calmed down under Jane's ministrations and they were singing songs when the door opened and two men came in, threw more blankets over their heads, and carried them off to the coach, where, in the darkness of early Sunday morning, with the wind buffeting against the side of the coach and the rain pounding on the coach roof, they jolted on to their final destination.

On Sunday morning, despite the Dean's protest that they should wait for the Earl of Southampton, Nicholas sent for two of the Sheriff's men to accompany him, and, when they arrived, he set off on one of the Dean's sturdy cobs, as Harry was unfit for another gruelling ride over treacherous roads. Anthony West insisted on coming with them to show them the way because the Archdeacon's manor was difficult to find. Never had travelling conditions been so difficult. A storm was building up rapidly now and high winds, racing in from the west, slowed their progress. Dark clouds hung low overhead, obscuring what light there was from the sun, so it felt as if day had not really started and they were riding out into the night.

The Sheriff's men knew the roads and tracks around Marchester, but once out in the marshes that surrounded the harbour, they slowed down and picked their way carefully along the track, conscious that the pools of liquid mud on either side of the track could drag them down into a bottomless pit should they stray from the path. All around them the marshes stretched away towards the sea. It was a sombre landscape: grey sky, grey-green marsh grass, brown mud and driving rain. Not even the sea birds had left their hideouts that morning.

All this time, Anthony had not spoken except to give directions to the Sheriff's men. He seemed withdrawn, wrapped in his own thoughts, and Nicholas was reluctant to disturb him. He remembered how he'd told them that he had spent the night out on these marshes when he had escaped from the Archdeacon's house and he saw that

Anthony was reliving those moments.

Suddenly, Anthony reined in his horse and pointed ahead.

'There it is. See that spit of land out there – local people call it the causeway – leading to what amounts to an island in the marsh, that's where we want to go. You can see the house, now. Satan's country retreat! We take this track.'

He led them over the causeway towards a long, low, sturdily-built stone house which looked more like a fortification than a gentleman's country house. The windows were mere slits in the walls, the main door was made of solid oak and it only needed a drawbridge and a portcullis to turn it into a small castle. There was a stone chimney at one side of the house and the roof was tiled, unusual in that area where rushes were so abundant. They rode up to the door and dismounted. No one answered their knocking.

'This place,' said Anthony, 'was where I was held captive. This was where the Archdeacon planned his infernal ceremonies. I thank God that I escaped and I thank God for these marshes which protected me that night I made my escape.'

'Come, then,' said Nicholas, 'let's go in. Break down the door,' he said to the Sheriff's men, who had brought stout, metal-tipped battering rams with them for just such a purpose. Even so it took a long time before the great door weakened, but, finally, the lock gave way, and they burst into the house and into the Archdeacon's fantasy world.

There seemed to be only one main room in the house, with a door at one end opening in to what was the stable and, judging by the evidence of fresh dung on the straw, horses had been stabled there recently. The great hall was warm from the fire that smouldered away in the huge, stone fireplace decorated with carvings of astrological symbols and other weird shapes. But whereas in most houses of this kind, Nicholas would have expected to find the floor covered with rushes and simple wooden furniture, here the floor was thickly covered with oriental rugs with intricate patterns woven in glowing colours of red and green and lapis lazuli. The carpets were so thickly laid that there was not an inch of the natural floor showing.

A massive, long table took up the centre of the room. It was made of some exotic, foreign wood and round it were eight intri-cately-carved wooden chairs with a crimson velvet cushion on each seat. At the head of the table was a huge, stone chair, like an archbishop's throne, draped with tapestries depicting strange beasts with bodies of men and heads of the wild animals of the forest, some of them mythological, like unicorns and phoenix.

'That was his chair,' whispered Anthony,

pointing to the stone throne. 'He liked us to pay homage before we sat down. There were only two others seated here when I came, but sometimes, I was told, great feasts were held here and much wine was consumed and strange, hallucinatory drugs were taken, like the crushed-up seeds of the oriental poppies. Come away, my lord. This is a truly evil place.'

Nicholas could still smell the remains of some sweet, cloying fragrance, and looking across at the huge sideboard he saw the remains of what looked like a simple meal, hastily eaten and not cleared away.

'Whoever has been here they have not long gone,' he said. 'Come, let's see what's on the other side of that door.'

There was a door at the end of the hall opposite to the stable end. When they opened it, it revealed a series of small rooms filled with provisions. One room was a huge larder stocked with dead hares hanging dolefully from hooks in the wall. There were sides of what looked like venison hanging up and an entire wild boar. In the far end there was a wooden crate, crammed full of dying fowls, a sight which sickened Nicholas, who hated to see needless suffering in animals.

Next to this room was another store cupboard filled with barrels of dried apricots and plums and two barrels of nuts. Another door revealed a well-stocked wine cellar with barrels of ale and mead.

'We are too late,' said Nicholas bitterly. 'The birds have flown.'

'This is an impossible place to find in the dark, my lord,' said Anthony, 'and I would have been an unreliable guide as my memory of it has faded. But wait, there's another door here. Let me light one of the tapers from the fire and we can take a closer look.'

By the light of a taper they pushed open the door of this room and went into a bare room with no windows, a small bed and a mud floor. There was a straw mattress on the bed and suddenly Nicholas felt that Jane had been here, that she had eaten from these two trays of food and he felt anger well up inside him that she should have endured such indignity and hardship.

'I think the devils brought my wife here,' he said to Anthony, who nodded his head in agreement. 'And not so long ago. This bread is still fresh.'

Nicholas sat on the bed and closed his eyes, seeing Jane here, in this very place, alone and terrified. But had she been alone?

'Look, my lord,' said Anthony suddenly. 'A woman's shoe. Do you recognise this as one of your wife's?'

Nicholas opened his eyes and saw Anthony holding in his hand a small, brown shoe, made of soft leather with a gold rosette on the front. It was an unbearably poignant object in such a place and Nicholas's heart raced. But it didn't belong to Jane.

'Philippa,' he whispered. 'Could it be Philippa's? Had she been here with Jane? Dear God, could it have dropped off as they carried her away?'

One of the Sheriff's men had come to find them. 'My lord, the tide's coming in rapidly with this wind behind it and it's likely to flood the causeway in places. We don't want to be trapped here. We ought to go now.'

Nicholas put the shoe in his pocket and followed the man outside. Sure enough, the sea was beginning to surge around them in an angry way, and was almost up to the top of the causeway. The house, built on higher ground, was safe, but it would be easy to be cut off and then there would be a long wait before they could leave the place. They had no choice but to go. They would have to go back to Marchester, find out if the shoe really did belong to Philippa and then conduct a major search party with the Earl's help and the Sheriff's, if he had returned from Pelham Maris.

Night was closing in by the time they got back to Marchester and they arrived at the Dean's house just as the Earl rode into the courtyard. He jumped from his horse when he saw Nicholas, and clasped him round the shoulder.

'This is terrible news, Nicholas. I've got here as quickly as I could and my men are following but the roads are bad and getting worse. Now tell me the news, and where do we start looking?'

It was late on Sunday afternoon that Jenny Dobbs decided the moment had come to take action. After she had heard from Aldred the jailer that Philippa had also disappeared she knew the situation was desperate. She had carefully worked on her strategy all day. She knew Beatrice went to Marchester on Sunday evenings to see her mother, who was becoming increasingly infirm. That meant Aldred was in charge of her and old Phoebe. Aldred, Jenny knew, was much taken with her, and she had been at pains lately to cultivate his interest and had persuaded him, that Sunday, to bring her a stool so that she could sit at his feet and unlace his boots whilst whispering to him all the other things she could do when his wife had gone to Marchester.

As soon as his wife had left with her basket of provisions, Aldred scurried along to Jenny's cell. He brought with him a flask of mead and a platter of bread with some slices of pheasant breasts on it, and when he went in Jenny was sprawled on the bed, her dress dishevelled, revealing her slim legs and much of her creamy breasts. She smiled at him provocatively and sat up, patting the place next to her on the bed. Aldred sat down with alacrity and offered her the flagon of mead. Jenny drank deeply and stretched out her hand for the plateful of meat.

'Come,' she said, 'there's plenty here for both of us and we have all the time in the world as in this weather, your wife won't be returning in a hurry.'

They ate the food together and all the time Aldred could not take his eyes off her breasts. When they had finished, Jenny fetched the stool and sat at Aldred's feet. Then, humming a sweet, popular song, she began to unfasten the laces on Aldred's boots. Aldred, who had been drinking mead most of the afternoon, soon succumbed to Jenny's charms. When she allowed her hands to stroke his skinny legs, he grew bolder and let his hands stroke the top of her head and the base of her neck. She didn't draw away, so he leaned down further so that he could get a better view of the top of her dress. Feasting his eyes on her creamy skin which glowed in the firelight, he could clearly see the top of her unbound breasts as soft as velvet.

'Aye, lass, if you're going to untie my boots, then I'll return the compliment and untie your laces,' he said as he leaned forward a bit further to touch her bodice.

As quick as a flash, Jenny jumped up, picked up the stool and brought it down with all her strength on Aldred's head. Without a sound, he toppled forward, falling off the bed onto the stone floor of the cell, where he lay, out like a light.

Jenny then walked out of the cell, along the passageway, up into the hall of the jail and out of the front door. Then regardless of the rain and the wind, she dashed over to the Dean's house where a servant refused to let her in. But Jenny, having got so far, would not be stopped, and pushing him out of the way she darted into the hall of the Dean's house, where she was brought up short by the tall figure of the Earl of Southampton, who had come to see what all the noise was about. He stared at her in astonishment as she pushed her hair impatiently out of her eyes and demanded to see Lord Nicholas.

She didn't have long to wait, because Nicholas, thinking the Earl might need some help, came to join him in the hall. Jenny ran to him.

'Thank God you're here. I think I can tell you where they've taken Jane. I've been trying to get a message to you for two days now but that hag, Beatrice, wouldn't let me bother you.'

'Jenny, what do you know? Come tell us quickly,' said Nicholas, cursing the jailer's wife's scruples.

'I know where the covens meet. Agatha Trimble used to go to them and she told me what went on there. She said they would meet, if possible, on a Sunday, Sunday being the most powerful day for Christians. She used to go with others, not me, because I would have nothing to do with those terrible rituals, to Norton Priory, the old ruined cathedral church which locals call the Priory. It's this side of Selsey island, a remote place, near the sea. The church is a ruin, but it's large and open to the sky in places. The high altar is still there, just as it was centuries ago, and there are side chapels and a crypt. The witches hold their Sabbats there. Everyone knows this, but are far too terrified to tell outsiders. Agatha gave up going recently as she said it was becoming too much for her, too evil, she said. The rituals were frightening and everyone seemed to be in some sort of drugged, trance-like state, which frightened her. They were given some sort of potion to drink, which drove them into a frenzy of shouting and dancing during which terrible things were done, my lords. She spoke of the babies being sacrificed on the altar and being forced to drink the blood of the poor little unwanted creatures. I am sure that this is where the Bishop was murdered. A bishop would be the greatest possible gift to their infernal master. There is only one more powerful gift and that is...' and here she looked in terror at the Dean, who had come to join them and was listening to her in horror. 'The blood and heart of a virgin.'

A dreadful silence followed these words, then a terrible wail went up from Katharine, who had followed her husband into the hall.

'Philippa, my darling,' she screamed, rushing forward to beat her hands against Nicholas's chest. 'You must get down to this place, my lord, you and the Earl. It's Sunday today. Today could be Philippa's last day on earth. Tell me, Mistress Dobbs, do you know when these rituals start?'

'At nightfall. Then they go on all night until cock crow.'

Then Nicholas knew what he had to find out. He produced the little shoe from his pocket and showed it to Katharine.

'Do you recognise this?'

She snatched the shoe from him and clasped it to her.

'It's my child's. Oh where did you find it, my lord? Does it mean that she's still alive?'

'I cannot say, Katharine, but with God's help, we'll find her and my wife. Are your men ready for a long and difficult ride to the coast, Ralph?'

'They are ready. Pray God we'll get there in time. And you, my dear,' he said to Jenny, 'must stay here with the Dean and his wife, and when I return I shall see that you never have to go back to that cell again, whatever Mistress Beatrice says.'

It was time to leave the warmth and safety of the Harbour Tavern and entrust himself to an open wooden boat. Gilbert Judd, Assistant Keeper of the lights for the port of Marchester, reluctantly drank up the last of his ale, nodded across to the tavern owner and wrapped his thick cloak round him. The time had come to relieve the Master of the lights. Leaving now, there would be plenty of time to get to the harbour entrance before the flood tide became too strong for the rowers to make any headway.

An hour and a half later, he stepped out onto the spit of land at the harbour entrance where a bright fire of coal and driftwood burned in the brazier at the top of the wooden tower. The boatmen shipped oars and waited for the Master to appear.

'There's a ship approaching,' said the Master as he came out to meet Gilbert. 'The *Hermione*, a clumsy old tub if ever there was one, but she's running before the wind and should get here at high water and provided she sees the light in time she should be able to run into the sheltered waters of the harbour. Keep the light going. Don't stint the coals and she'll be safe and sound. See you tomorrow. Let's hope the wind abates soon.'

Then the Master stepped into the boat and the oarsmen bore him away into the darkness. Two hours to high water. Two hours in which Gilbert Judd took stock of his life and wished he were dead. In fact, he seriously considered throwing himself into the foaming cauldron of the sea at the bottom of the tower but a picture of his daughter, Arabella, kept coming into his mind. Arabella, happily trying on the new dress she was to wear when she married Northbrook's son at Easter. With the money he'd get from Mark tomorrow, she would be married in great style. Just two hours and it would all be over.

In fact, the fire needed attention now, and he climbed up the wooden steps to the top of the tower and stood there watching the flames die down. It was so easy. Even if he did nothing, the light would be almost too faint to be picked up by an approaching vessel. He stared down into the surging water and then looked out to where the Isle of Wight should be, but could see nothing. He listened to the howling of the wind and the roar of the incoming tide, and despite knowing that he would be responsible for sending a ship and its trusting crew to a dreadful death, he prayed for the souls of those men destined never to see dry land again. Then he picked up his heavy cloak, sodden with sea water, and dowsed the fire.

The sturdy carrack, out from Corunna, its capacious hold full of cloth and wine and a great gold cross destined for Salisbury cathedral, soared eastwards along the comparatively sheltered water of the Solent towards the entrance to Marchester harbour. The Captain knew these waters well as they were the main shipping route between his native Spain and the Netherlands so he had little fear when he left the shelter of the Isle of Wight and ordered the helmsman to edge towards the shore. But he could not see the light, usually a great, flaming beacon marking the entrance to the harbour.

Puzzled, the Captain ordered the helmsman to stand off again and to continue eastwards. Still there was no light. He cursed the Keeper of the light, who had probably fallen asleep and allowed the light to burn too low. Peering into the darkness all he could see was the white tops of the waves foaming around the ship. There was no sign of a moon and the stars were hidden from him behind the dark storm clouds.

Then he began to feel fear – the fear that comes when things are not as they should be. He knew he should be making the turn into the harbour; the tide was at its height; the main channel would have plenty of water in it; but there was no light. He was dashing along with the full force of the wind behind him and soon it would be too late to alter course and hope to make the entrance. But to bear towards an unseen shore would be disastrous and he had no means of knowing where he was. Where, in God's name, was the light?

Then, above the sound of the wind and the waves, he heard another sound, a sound which fills every seaman with dread. It was the terrible grinding noise of pebble against pebble; thousands of them crunching together on a vast shingle spit which was marked on the chart but which he thought was still a long way off. And the sound was very near. Desperately, he ordered the helmsman to turn closer to the shore. The entrance had to be there. The helmsman protested vociferously but his protests soon dissolved into a shriek of despair, as, with a resounding crash, the keel hit the western end of the giant shingle spit lying off Selsey Bill.

'My God, we're lost!' shouted the Captain as the vessel shuddered to a halt, the mast cracking under the weight of its canvas, out of control and dragging the boat to one side. Then, with the sickening sound of splintering timbers, the mast collapsed, dragging the carrack, not a well-balanced boat at the best of times, over on to its port side, where the waves poured into the boat, flooding down into its hold.

Rousing themselves from the shock-induced torpor, the Captain and his crew of six began to get ready to jump from the ship. But they never made the shore. Out of the howling darkness dim figures, armed with staves and knives, cut down the desperate Spaniards as they jumped over the side of the ship. Then the dark figures climbed into the ship, whose timbers were already breaking up under the strain of the repeated pummelling of the waves and the grinding of the shingle against its hull.

Twenty-two

The coach lurched to a halt. Someone opened the door and the cold, wet air streamed in to the interior where Jane and Philippa were bound together on the back seat. Jane felt rough hands unfasten the rope which tied her to Philippa and she was dragged out of the coach and into the wild night where, through the muffling blanket, she could smell the sea and hear the crash of waves on shingle. The sound seemed very near.

She tried to twist round to shout encouragement to Philippa, but someone hit her roughly on the head and told her to be still. Of course the girl was coming, the man said with a coarse laugh that sent shivers of terror down her spine, they weren't going to leave her behind.

She felt herself carried into what seemed to be a large building and she could still smell the sea and hear the sound of the waves on the shingle, so she guessed that part of the roof was open to the sky. Then she was carried along a smooth path where, on either side of her she felt the presence of a crowd of creatures, whether human or bestial she could not tell. Then the crowd closed round her, hissing like snakes and she could smell the stench of their breath through the blanket. They began poking her and pinching and laughing excitedly. Then she knew they were human. She felt herself being carried down some steps into a room where the air smelt musty and she could no longer hear the sea. She was propped against a stone pillar with Philippa next to her; the blankets, which covered them, were removed and they were tied together again and fastened to the pillar. At last Jane could see where they were; but the sight that met her eyes was so fearful that she quickly closed her eyes like someone awakening from a nightmare.

They were in an underground room; a crypt of some sort as the roof was vaulted and the walls were windowless and made of thick stone. A rush light was fastened to a wall and the flickering light lit up the faces of her tormentors who were jostling one another on the stairs in order to get a better view of them. Jane saw that they were mostly women, but scarcely recognisable as such with their wild, unkempt hair and dishevelled clothes – in many cases just rags barely concealing their nakedness. Bold, mocking eyes stared at her curiously and they chattered together with sounds like the twittering of birds. They seemed to be waiting for someone to come, and Jane turned her head to look at Philippa, who was staring at the women with terrified eyes. Two of the hags came down the stairs and approached Philippa and began to unbind her hair, stroking it gently, almost lovingly.

But this treatment was not for her. Suddenly, two women pushed through the group of hags on the stairs and came over to her. These women were taller and dressed in respectable grey dresses with white aprons, their hair covered by grey bonnets and they seemed to be held in respect by the others. They beckoned some of the hags to come and hold Jane down whilst they set about untying her hair and ripping off her clothes. They became excited over the richness of the material and held her dress up to be admired by the audience on the stairs. Two of them began to squabble over her cloak and the tallest of the two women told them to stop and pile up the clothes in the corner of the crypt and they would divide them up between them later. She had to speak sharply, but they reluctantly obeyed her.

When all her clothes had been removed, two of the hags came forward carrying a white tunic which they dropped over Jane's head and let it fall to the ground. Then she was tied once more to the pillar and they turned their attention to Philippa, who had also been dressed in a white shift.

'Who are you?' Jane said to the tall woman. 'What are you going to do to us?'

'We are the creatures of darkness,' the woman replied. 'We are the servants of the Prince of Darkness and he demands sacrifices. If we please him, he pleases us. Last time we met, he sent us a bishop and we offered him up and consumed his heart. As a reward we were sent a ship with wine and cloth in its hold to be divided amongst us. Tonight we have a virgin and you, a high-ranking lady, and a ship is already on the shingle bank. Come, sisters of the night,' she said to the others, 'let's away to enjoy the celebrations. We will come for you when Lucifer commands us.'

With screams of delight, the women scampered up the stairs and into the room above, where Jane could hear the stamping of feet and the discordant squeals of fiddles and the sinister beat of a drum. She turned to look at Philippa in her white shift, with her golden hair tumbling around her face, and her heart turned over at the thought of what was in store for her. The girl appeared to have fainted, because she hung forward against the rope which tied her to the pillar.

'Philippa,' she whispered, 'don't give up. I'm with you. I'll not let them harm you. Whatever they want to do to you they can do to me instead. We mustn't give up hope. I feel sure that rescue will come soon.

Nicholas and the Earl and the Sheriff's men will all be searching for us. Come, let us say some prayers for us and for our rescuers.'

Philippa opened her eyes and looked at Jane in terror.

'Those awful old hags. Who are they, Jane?'

'Sad, stupid women pretending to be clever and powerful. But they are nothing, nothing at all. They have been led by someone very wicked and made to feel important. Let's say the Lord's prayer for protection against evil and why don't you say it to me in Latin and I will say it to you in French.'

Anything to distract her mind, Jane thought, until rescue comes. But as time passed and they had translated all the prayers they knew into Latin and French, Jane felt her optimism gradually drain away. How could Nicholas or the Sheriff know about this place? It seemed to be some sort of a ruined church and judging by the sound of the waves on the shingle, they were very near the sea. She knew there was a shingle bank just off Selsey Point and she remembered hearing people speak about a ruined church at a place called Norton which had once been the cathedral for Sussex. But not many people knew about it or thought of it as any more than a ruin. How could Nicholas guess they were here?

They were just beginning to tell stories to

each other, stories of their childhood, of fairies and hobgoblins, and the exploits of the little people who lived up on the top of the Downs who loved playing pranks on the people of the low lands, when the door opened and a gaggle of hags came surging down the stairs. Their faces seemed to be more flushed, their eyes glittering more brightly than previously and Jane realised that they had been drinking and, judging by the wild, uncontrolled look in their eyes, had also been partaking of some sort of powerful drug which had reduced them to demons.

'Dear God,' she prayed, 'let them take me first. Spare Philippa.'

But with squeals of glee, the hags pounced on them both, and, half carrying, half dragging them, hauled them up into the room above, which Jane now saw was the nave of a huge church. There, before the high altar of what was once the old cathedral, stood a stone throne. On it sat a monstrous figure, human from the neck down, because she could see his sandalled feet and he was wearing a priestly cassock, but instead of a face there was a huge goat's head with giant horns curving away from the top of the head. Round his neck was a necklace of dead bats. She heard Philippa scream in terror and she gathered up all her strength and called loudly to her, 'Don't be afraid. It's only someone dressed up. Look at those feet. Did you ever see a goat wearing sandals?'

On each side of the goat-man sat two men. On his right, was a man with a wolf's head on his shoulders, the other, a heavily-built man, had the head of a wild boar. On his left, sat a fox-headed man and next to him was a man wearing the head of a monstrous fish. The women dragged Jane and Philippa up to the altar and flung them down on the steps in front of the stone throne. Then everyone fell silent, waiting for the goat-man to speak.

He rose to his feet and the mob stared at him in rapture, waiting for his commands.

'Brothers and sisters,' he began, his voice muffled by the mask. But Jane knew that voice. It had the nasal twang of someone she had met only fleetingly but, even so, she would recognise that voice anywhere. It was the Archdeacon's voice. Jeremy Overton.

'We have been shown great favour by our master, Satan,' he said. 'At this very moment, a ship has run aground on the shingle bank, thanks to the endeavours of our friend here, Behemoth,' he said, indicating the fish-headed man. 'He arranged for the Captain of the ship to be tricked. There will be much wealth for us all to share out later tonight. But first, we must thank our master and offer him the sacrifices. Only twelve days ago, in this very place, we offered up the so-called Bishop of Marchester, our enemy, someone

Satan has waited for for a long time. We gave him to Satan, didn't we, my friends, and consumed his heart?'

The crowd roared their approval and the fiddlers struck up discordant chords on their instruments. The goat-man raised his hands for silence.

'Now we have two sacrifices, a beautiful and powerful woman, the whore of our enemy, Nicholas Peverell, and an untouched girl, the daughter of that stupid fool who calls himself the Dean of Marchester. Come, lay the whore out on the altar and tie the virgin to a pillar so that she can enjoy the sight of the whore's humiliation. Now, strike up the music and pass round the jars of wine, and charge up the incense burners.'

Jane was seized and dragged past the five monstrous figures and lifted up on to the altar. Behind the altar, she saw a large wooden crucifix. The body of Christ had been covered with a goat skin, and on it had been hung the body of a dead lamb. Then she knew there would be no rescue. Evil had triumphed. Christ, the lamb of God, was dead. She prayed now for a swift death for herself and Philippa.

The noise from the worshippers was increasing steadily. Incense, not the incense she was familiar with, but some sickening, sweet substance was waved over her until she felt giddy and gradually her senses began to fade and she passed into a strange, hazy world where she became indifferent to what they were doing to her. They tied her spreadeagled across the altar, all the time poking and pinching her and pulling her hair.

Then the goat-man approached the altar and stood over her, a knife in his hand.

'So,' he said, 'your ladyship now finds herself in a different place from the soft boudoirs of Lord Nicholas's manor house. I give you two minutes to renounce that pathetic prophet of Nazareth and embrace our master. Just say the words, *"Je te renonce, Jésu,"* and I promise that your death will be quick, with this knife. Refuse, and I shall let this mob loose on you after I have had the satisfaction of cuckolding Lord Nicholas. Only then shall I despatch you with the knife.'

Despite the mist which clouded her mind, and despite the sharp pain of the tight ropes which bound her to the altar, Jane was able to say with a clear voice which everyone could hear, 'I spit upon your master, Jeremy Overton; you who call yourself Archdeacon of Marchester. I ask Jesus Christ to have mercy on me and Philippa and forgive all these poor, deluded people who don't know what they are doing.'

At this, the mob howled in rage, and were held back only with difficulty by the four monster-headed figures. The Archdeacon

426

put the knife back in his belt and, as Jane sank into unconsciousness, he leaned over her.

She didn't hear the soldiers rush into the church. She didn't see Nicholas, with drawn sword, hacking his way through the crowd to get to the altar. She didn't see the Earl untie Philippa and carry her away to a safe place. But the Archdeacon did see them. Quick as lightning, he grasped one of the lighted tapers fixed to a pillar by the altar, and threw it down into the thick, dry straw which covered the floor. In seconds, the straw burst into flames, creating a barrier between him and the approaching soldiers. Amidst the screams and the confusion no one saw him rip off his mask and slip away through the south door and out into the wild night. He ran down to the shore where dark figures were staggering around dragging wooden crates and bales of cloth up onto the beach. As he ran over the shingle, he saw the golden cross, destined for Salisbury cathedral, lying on the beach where someone had thrown it, preferring a crate of wine to an ornament. Seizing hold of it, the Archdeacon staggered into the sea, where the tide, now on the ebb, caught hold of him and dragged him out towards the shingle bank and the outline of the stricken ship. He immediately sank beneath the weight of the cross. He let go of it but could not save himself. He was caught up in the strong undertow and dragged out into deep water where his heavy cassock held him under the water.

The Sheriff arrived in time to give orders that the pathetic collection of human beings who had been so bold under the influence of drugs and alcohol should be locked into the crypt until the carts arrived to carry them to Marchester. The Earl's soldiers had been despatched to arrest the wreckers. Nicholas looked at the four priests now stripped of their headdresses and tied together waiting for the carts to come.

'You are a disgrace to your calling and beyond redemption. I don't feel sorry for you, but, even so, I shall ask God to have mercy on your souls when the hour of execution comes.'

A soldier entered and went up to the Earl and whispered something in his ear. Nicholas looked at the priests.

'Your leader has just drowned himself. You see now how much he cared for any of you. Take them down to the crypt with the others,' he said to the guards.

William Tremayne, who had worn the wolf's head, stared angrily at Nicholas. 'If you had experienced what happened to me and my family at the hands of the former Bishop Thomas, you would understand more and judge less. My friend here, Richard

428

Rushe,' he said indicating the priest who had worn the head of the wild boar, 'understands, and we would rather serve our master than be a servant of a hypocritical Christian bishop.'

Nicholas carried Jane tenderly to the coach that had brought her and Philippa to the church. He laid her with Philippa on the back seat and covered them with his cloak. He would ride back to Marchester with them. Just before he got in, the Sheriff came up to him, looking pleased with himself.

'A good night's work, Lord Nicholas. And no harm done. You got here just in time, as usual. Southampton says he'll billet some of his soldiers down here until law and order has been restored. It's time this place was cleaned up and made safe for shipping again. Now we can get down to writing that report for the King and you can get rid of that fellow who's eating you out of house and home in that manor of yours. It's time you went home, Lord Nicholas.'

This Large Print Book, for people
who cannot read normal print,
is published under the auspices of

THE ULVERSCROFT FOUNDATION

5
C